If She Only Had a Machine Gun crime stories by Richard Credicott

Introduction by Dave Credicott

Edited by John Locke & Rob Preston

Off-Trail Publications
Elkhorn, California

CONTENTS

— THE END —

Richard James Credicott
1906-91

EXPLANATIONS AND ACKNOWLEDGEMENTS

AS FANS OF THE PULPS, we naturally have an affection for the creators of that past world we love, the publishers, the editors, and especially the authors. The vast majority of these people never wrote about their careers, were never interviewed by the papers, and, outside of their publications, didn't leave a paper trail that could be followed sixty, seventy, eighty years later. Thus any desire to know them better usually goes unrewarded.

This is particularly the case with the gang pulps of the early '30s. They had a brief flurry of success that coincided with the dying years of Prohibition, then faded into obscurity. Surviving copies of the magazines are quite scarce, and, with few exceptions, the authors have proven extremely difficult to profile. Most of them didn't adapt their writing to other genres. Many of them seemingly disappeared without a trace.

Therefore, when Rob discovered the terrific gang stories of Richard Credicott, and convinced John of the necessity of getting them back into print, the reasonable expectation was that there would be little to say about the author. Richard published a mere eighteen stories within a four-year span, and then, at the height of his success, did the disappearing act. His output left him an obscure author in a long-forgotten genre. How startling was it, then, to discover that he, of the gang-pulp specialists, may turn out to be the most findable of all? Very.

We had found and read most of the eighteen stories, were fretting about the likelihood of rounding up the remaining magazines—especially the February 1930 *Young's*, which is the least collectible but among the scarcest of Richard's eighteen appearances—and it was time to start piecing together Richard's biography from the accumulated research materials. Since the material was analyzed chronologically, the next startling discovery came rather late in the game: the realization that Richard had a son who was born relatively late in his life, and thus was probably out and about in the world. Thanks to the poor man's private eye—Google—contact was made with Dave Credicott. Who was more surprised? We'll call it a draw. Long odds had been trumped once again.

Some weeks later, Dave and John met at the home of pulp collector and publisher, John Gunnison, otherwise known as Adventure House world headquarters (adventurehouse.com). Many stories were swapped about Richard Credicott's life and writing career, many mysteries mulled over. Dave received a crash course in the history of the pulps and where his father fit into the grand scheme of things. He also saw samples of the gang pulps which contain, in the editors' opinion, Richard's best work. At the end of

*Dave Credicott, John Locke, and John Gunnison holding
pulps with Richard Credicott cover appearances.*

this—to us, historic—meeting, Dave graciously agreed to contribute the reminiscence that appears in this volume. Thus, there are two introductions to follow. Dave's essay, "Dad," gives a personal view of growing up with a father of varied intellectual gifts; it cover Richard's later years. John's historical piece, "Fictioneering in the Golden Age of Gangsters," tells the story of Richard's early years, as the paper trail reveals it. The two complementary parts can be read in any order, depending on whether flashback or strict chronology is preferred.

If Richard had been as undiscoverable as most of his peers in the gang pulps, this book would have simply included his stories and an analysis of his brief career. Following our biases, we might have viewed his pulp career as a major chapter in his life. We might have theorized that he was, like so many other pulp writers, a newspaperman who had "wandered off the reservation." We might have supposed that "Richard Credicott" was a penname. Instead, with so much background information available, our introductory materials expanded to draw in Credicott family history, Freeport history, and Richard's wide experiences, allowing us to see his pulp career as a single colorful tile in the larger mosaic of his life, and understand that he probably looked back on his foray into the pulps as a minor chapter, a youthful indulgence, perhaps. Which still leaves two major reasons to be interested in his writing career. First, his stories are first-rate examples of the gang genre, and extremely entertaining. Second, the pattern of his career—which genres he wrote in, which publishers he sold to, and the timing of his publications—puts in stark relief the challenges to turning pro during the Depression.

Richard Credicott's eighteen known stories were all published in pulps which are now extremely scarce. No one library, collector, or source contains more than a subset of them. Therefore, we owe a debt of gratitude to Dave Credicott, John Gunnison, Mark Leonard, and Jim Steranko for filling in the missing pieces. This collection would have been impossible without their generosity. The Twelfth Labor of Hercules Trophy is hereby awarded Mark for supplying the elusive eighteenth story of the hunt.

Robert Bike

Thank you to Dave for supplying family photos.

Thank you to long-time pulp enthusiast Robert Weinberg, and representative of Argosy Communications Inc., for permission to reprint the two stories from *Dime Detective*.

Thanks also to Joe Palcich of 45thstreeteditions.com for supplying a scan of our haunted *Gangster Stories* cover moll.

And a special thanks goes to Robert Bike, a 1966 graduate of Freeport High School and its unofficial historian, and, coincidentally, a classmate of fellow '66 FHS grad Dave Credicott. The editors spent an entertaining afternoon with Robert poring over 1920's editions of the school yearbook, the *Polaris*, for material on Richard Credicott, brother Edward, Richard's friend Henry Raepple, and associated figures. Robert provided the scans of *Polaris* artwork found herein, and helped with valuable insights into Freeport history. Robert's web pages on Freeport and FHS can be found at robertbike.com.

John Locke & Rob Preston

DAD
by Dave Credicott

"DAD, WOULD YOU READ THIS *Superman* comic to me?"

"Sure, son. Bring it over and hop up in my lap."

Thus began a frequent and happy memory of my childhood. Dad was never too busy for this simple litany. I had no idea that my father himself was an author for pulp fiction magazines, a predecessor to comic books. It was years later that I found two old magazines in grandma's attic, one with gruesome cover art for the story "The Three Horrible Heads," with my father's name as the author! A man of few words, Dad had little to say about the stories at the time. It wasn't until decades later, through editor John Locke, that I learned the extent of my father's story writing career. But more about that later. . . .

I was fortunate to grow up in a loving family. My half-sister, Jeanne, was much older than I. She was a difficult sibling to follow, because she took the lead in all the high school musicals, was extremely popular, and eventually married a Notre Dame football player. We were typical middle-class, living in a rented duplex house in Freeport, Illinois. Situated a ninety-minute drive west of Chicago, the city is a medium-sized community among the Midwest farmlands. Largely of German descent, the city boasts one public and one parochial high school. It has several beautiful parks, intertwined with streams and rivers. Taylor Park was the scene of three recurring activities in my youth. First, I learned to ice skate on the pond. Second, our family would lie on blankets every year to watch the 4th of July fireworks. Third, and perhaps most memorable, Dad taught me to drive on the winding roads in this sprawling park, far from pedestrians and other traffic. Good thing, too. The vehicle he used for my training was an old, beat-up Chevy panel truck with a stick shift. To boost my confidence, Dad would crouch behind the front seats, while my best friend sat in the passenger seat. During one rather abrupt left turn, the right door flew open and the passenger seat, with Tommy still sitting on it, went out the door. Nobody was hurt, other than my pride, and we laughed for a long

Richard & Dave,
October 1950

time. Obviously, Dad was a very patient man. On the other side of town, we had many family picnics, often climbing the steps by the waterfalls at Krape Park. The park had a dam with a fish climb, and Dad and I frequently walked along the water's edge. I recall falling in the water next to the dam at a very young age, and Dad pulled me out. He told me that if there ever was water around, I would invariably fall in and he'd have to "fish me out." The park also has a band shell facing a hillside. When I was in high school, I played trombone in the city orchestra, and my parents always went to listen to the weekly summer night concerts at the band shell in that beautiful park.

I was the envy of other kids in elementary school, because my family owned an ice cream factory. We always had ice cream sandwiches or other treats around the house for friends, and Dad always brought something for school functions. When I was five years old, Dad and Uncle Ed built a red soapbox derby fire engine at the plant and gave it to my kindergarten class. It remained there for many years. In my teens, Dad gave me jobs at the plant. He promised me the worst possible jobs, and he made good on the promise. For many years, I did weekend janitorial work in the offices, including stripping and waxing the floors. That is, until one time when a fuse blew out. Eventually finding the electrical box, I reset the circuit breaker. At that moment, I heard the floor polisher start up in the other room, followed by a crash. When the power went out, I had forgotten to turn off the polisher. When I reset the circuit, the fifty-pound monster flew across the room and through one of the walls. Oops. On another job, I had the pleasure of removing rust accumulation from an ammonia refrigeration system. This took several weeks and was one of the most distasteful tasks I've ever done. It was at this moment that I affirmed my intent to graduate from college and get a professional job. Gee, I wonder if that was Dad's intent all along?

Mom bought an old upright piano from a neighbor for $5 (really!) when I was very young. It was already a relic, with intricately carved rich brown wood. I studied piano on this instrument for years and years; Miss Griswold came to our house every week to give me a lesson. I remember Mom not allowing me to go outside and play until I had practiced a half-hour each day. I wasn't very happy about this at the time, but now I thank her. However, I never forgave her when she painted the piano a mint green color to match the dining room. We took this behemoth with us when we finally got a house of our own, and I lovingly lugged it along later when I moved to Champaign and later to Chicago. Thanks to Mom and Dad, music became a key part of my life. Mom and Dad had a huge collection of classical LP records. In high school, I was the accompanist for the school musicals. I also played trombone, but honestly, wasn't very good. I studied pipe organ in college, and to this day, play piano and organ at church. My parents gave me the opportunity, as well as the motivation, for music.

Dad took me on my very first fishing trip. Frankly, he didn't seem to be very skilled at it. My grandfather was allegedly an excellent fisherman, but apparently the genes weren't passed along to my father. I didn't get them, either. I always felt sorry for the worms . . . first you dig them out of their home, then impale them on a hook, followed up by drowning. If they survived, they'd become dinner for some lucky fish. Dad did the perfunctory fishing trips with me, and I did about the same when I had kids later in life. However, after four camping trips per year with my kids over the course of ten years, we actually got pretty good at fishing!

Uncle Ed was my father's brother and he lived with my grandmother Clara. She was of German descent and her job in life was to spoil me. She did an exceptional job at it, and I was pleased to give her every opportunity to practice. Her cinnamon rolls were beyond comparison, and Thanksgiving and Christmas meals always ended with everybody napping. In addition to working at the dairy, Uncle Ed had several passions in life, which he shared with me. He taught me how to water ski, at which I wasn't particularly talented. Together we built a Lionel train set in the basement. He loved electronics, and with his help, I built many Heath Kit instruments. I built an oscilloscope, frequency generator, DC/AC meter, and an amateur radio. He helped me earn my amateur radio license (WD9IRG). We did photography together, including the dark room processing. He introduced me to astronomy, and helped me grind an 8" telescope mirror. However, by far the greatest gift he gave me was a love of aviation. When I was young, we'd go out to the Freeport airport and watch the airplanes. Uncle Ed was in the Civil Air Patrol, and that gave us many opportunities to engage in events at the airport. He also helped me build U-control-line model planes, although spinning around in circles has some unpleasant side effects. Later in life, when I could afford them, I progressed to radio-controlled models. Since then, aviation has been a passion in my life. Dad cemented this in place by occasionally taking me to O'Hare airport in Chicago, in the days when you could still go up on the open roof and watch the planes take off and land. I loved those trips! In college, I earned my private pilot's license and advanced to an instrument rating during graduate school. To this day, I absolutely love flying and try to do so every weekend. My best friend owns an airplane and we fly it at every opportunity. Appropriately, my auto license plate is "SkyGuy," which reflects my passions for flying and astronomy.

Talking about passions, Dad had some very unique talents. Playing bridge was one of his favorites. From my very early days, I remember Mom and Dad often having folks over to play bridge. They both took the game very seriously, and participated in many tournaments. I believe both eventually earned the rank of "Life Master." After a night of bridge, they'd often come home and talk about the hands that were dealt, how the bidding progressed, and how the tricks were played. Dad could remember every hand, every bid, and how each was played. This was incredible to me. I asked him about it, and, talking about his memory power, he said that in college he had taught himself the value of pi to 108 decimal points—"just for fun." I did almost as well, and learned it to 5 points.

While bridge engaged my parents on a weekly basis, my father's real obsession was with history—Nostradamus, to be specific. I'm sure that you're all aware of Nostradamus, the 16th century French mathematician, apothecary, astronomer, astrologer, and presumably psychic prophesier.

Richard, Best Man at Dave's wedding, 1989

Nostradamus is perhaps most famous for writing 1,000 quatrains in French, published under the title *Les Propheties* (*The Prophecies*). Each four-line poem supposedly predicts a significant event yet to unfold. Nostradamus himself encouraged that belief. His writings were intentionally made obscure, by mixing multiple languages, using word games, and well-placed misspellings. Even today, many people subscribe to his occult powers to predict the future. My father, however, had a completely different perspective. He spent unknown hours in his study each day, for well over thirty years, translating and researching the quatrains. He engaged book dealers in Europe to acquire rare editions of both Nostradamus and his contemporaries. Over the course of three decades, he established a unique theory about Nostradamus and his works, and dedicated thousands of hours to prove his hypothesis. His personal library was probably one of the most extensive and valuable at the time. I won't attempt to explain Dad's theories about Nostradamus. However, I can say that Nostradamus was also a puzzle author, and my father's theory was that his *Prophecies* was, in fact, one of the world's most complex puzzles. My father developed a solution, as well as the proof. He attempted to get his work published a few times, but the publishers were far more interested in the glamour of occultism than in his scholarly interpretation.

When I was about six years old, I made a small contribution to Dad's research. My intent—to be a little businessman. So, one day while he was at work, I went into his study. Opening one of the lower drawers of his desk, I removed a fragile book wrapped in brown paper. The pages were also very brown, dried out, and quite brittle. I couldn't read any of it . . . it didn't even look like English (it wasn't). I carefully selected a page from the middle of the book and ripped it out. Folding it, I placed the page in an empty white envelope, licked the glue, and sealed it. Stealthily, I proceeded to walk to the mailbox on the far corner of our block, and deposited the envelope. I actually remember feeling quite proud of myself at the time. However, that feeling would not last very long. Fortunately (or unfortunately, depending on your point of view), the mailman noticed the unaddressed and unstamped envelope. Upon opening it, he recognized the foreign page as something belonging to Dad. This was back in the era when you might actually know the mailman. He brought the envelope to our home and gave it to Mom. That's the moment when my little businessman career came to a rather abrupt end, so to speak. Of course I did not know at the time that this was an extremely rare book from Europe, which at one time had belonged to some princely character.

As many kids do, I somehow survived adolescence. Dad convinced me to take four years of Latin, which also threatened my existence. I continued to play piano and studied pipe organ in college. My father discouraged me from any attempt to enter the family business . . . it was already in decline because of competition from large dairies willing to undercut prices. He almost forbade me from considering that option. Instead, he told me that I should go to college, discern my own calling, and pursue a worthwhile career. In hindsight, I have great respect for his advice; it would have been far easier for him to simply accept my help at the dairy. With encouragement from my parents, I went to the University of Illinois, where my father had studied several decades earlier. Not having sufficient eyesight for an aviation career, I earned degrees in mathematics and computer science. My father's love and consideration for his son enabled me to find a career that I could enjoy and be successful at.

Moving away from my hometown was symbolic of life transitions to follow. The family business was eventually liquidated and my parents retired. After a number of years, my mother succumbed to cancer. Dad had many good years, continuing his Nostradamus work, playing recreational bridge with friends in Freeport, and visiting my sister's family in Cedar Rapids. Dad was eventually diagnosed with prostate cancer. He followed the appropriate medical treatments, both traditional and holistic, which gave him additional time. He served as Best Man for my marriage to Barb in Richmond, Virginia. On a subsequent trip to our home, he held his granddaughter Abby Marie in his arms. I remember him saying he was afraid he might "break her," but we insisted. Seeing him hold his granddaughter was one of the most important moments of my life.

A couple years later, Barb became pregnant again. Dad was in and out of the Freeport hospital now, and we traveled to Freeport to share the good news. At his bedside, I knew his time was growing short. I told him that

Richard & Abby Marie, 1989

our family was expanding and that it was going to be a boy. I asked him if he would like us to name our son after him. I fully expected Dad to say no, that we should choose whatever name we wanted. That is the kind of person he had always been— thinking of others first. However, he turned to me, and with the most heartfelt and gentle look in his eyes, said, "yes, I would like that." Months later, Richard James Credicott, whom we call RJ, was born. Unfortunately, my father didn't live long enough to meet him in person. But I have every confidence that Mom and Dad look lovingly at Abby and RJ from whatever part of eternity is theirs.

I am extremely lucky to have had such a loving family. My elders have passed away, and I didn't expect that I'd be learning anything "new" about my family. Then one evening, I got a call from a John Locke in California. It's not often that a total stranger calls up to say, "I've been researching your family history and your father's writing career." My father had a writing *career*? Until then, I'd only ever seen the two magazines. I must admit that my first reaction was that it was a scam, and I was waiting for the tell line: "Dave, just send along $20,000 and we'll get the publication started right away." However, John never asked for money, only for more insight into Dad and the family. He filled me in on the background, told me that he and fellow editor, Rob Preston, had been reading my father's pulp fiction, found them to be very good, and intended to republish them. John had already done quite a bit of research and traced the family back into the 1800s; I was astounded at the knowledge that he had already amassed. He told me stories about my father dating back to his high school and college years. There were elements of my father's life which I had never imagined, which John addresses in his introduction. To say that a few were surprising would be an understatement. At that point, John had acquired 16 of the 18 known stories that Dad had published. One of my two magazines, *Young's*, had the

17th story, "A Strange Wife," and John located the final story from a fellow pulp collector. Naturally, I was thrilled that my father's stories would be republished. I was even more honored when John invited me to write this introduction. He said it was very unusual to find a surviving relative of a pulp fiction author, much less as close a relative as a son. A few weeks later, John and I met for dinner in Maryland with pulp collector John Gunnison, who supplied story #16. We shared dinner and many great stories, not only about my dad's work, but also about the pulp fiction phenomenon itself. John gathered an incredible amount of information about my father's life, including high school and college art work. He offered evidence that my grandmother had probably ignited his love of bridge. All in all, this was a very pleasant evening with many new family stories. I later described our encounter as being "a family reunion, but without the family."

Shortly after meeting with John, he sent me his collection of Dad's stories. Our family and best friends happened to be staying the weekend in cabins at Abby's summer research job in the mountains. That night, we lit a fire in the fireplace, opened a bottle of wine, and turned out all the lights. I read, for the first time, the story "Clue" to a captivated audience. It was a special moment for me, and probably for Abby and RJ, too. Without John, I never would have known the extent of my father's writings. I enjoyed the stories immensely, and hope you do as well.

Oh, and Dad, sorry about damaging your book.

RJ & Abby visiting the grave marker of
Richard & Frances, Freeport, 2001

FICTIONEERING IN THE GOLDEN AGE OF GANGSTERS
by John Locke

RICHARD CREDICOTT MADE HIS FIRST VISIT to New York City in May of 1929. Younger brother, Edward, was just finishing the school year at Columbia, a year away from earning a bachelor's from the School of Business. That was Edward, obediently following the plan, obtaining the education that would enable him to take a leadership position in his father's rapidly-expanding dairy.

Richard came out for a three-week visit. Together, the brothers would return to Freeport, the modest city in northern Illinois that had been their home since they were small boys. In the meantime, Richard would take in the sights. A marvel, the city must have been to an imaginative young man from a small town. He looked up and the skyscrapers appeared to evaporate into the clouds. He looked ahead and, right before his eyes, walking in every direction, there were more people, perhaps, than in all of Freeport.

But what really caught his eye were the sidewalk newsstands displaying dozens of pulp magazines with garish, multicolored covers. He'd seen the pulps before, read them; Garrity's Drugs in Freeport carried them. But it wasn't the same. There were so many more titles here, and so many of them that seemed intimately connected to the life of this dazzling, yet dirty, and sometimes threatening city. The crime magazines, in particular. It felt like an act of belonging to actually be in New York while reading the June issue of, say, *The Dragnet Magazine*. "Detective and Crook Stories" read the banner over the title. Inside were sleazy pleasures like "The Murder of Fat Joe" by Arden X. Pangborn. And "The Ruby of Blood" by E. Parke Levy: "It looked as though Darlington was gangland's latest victim, taken for a ride because he knew too much. . . ."

If truth be told, though, there were an awful lot of these magazines, and many of the stories, frankly, that did not live up to their promise. A person might think—a person, that is, who had always fancied himself an artist more than a dairyman—that here were opportunities, here was a veritable gold rush for writers on the sidewalk newsstands of New York City. It wouldn't take a genius to write better stories than were already appearing in the pulps; it might only take an imaginative young man from Freeport.

Once home, Richard took on the challenge without delay. The result was "Clues," a 2,300-word slip of a story. It adheres to a standard formula, describing cocksure criminals in their execution of a perfect crime, and the fatal flaw that trips them up. If unremarkable, it's decently written, better than the first drafts some of the pros were getting into print. It also has a strength that most beginners lack: setups, suspense, a payoff; in short, a firm

*A typical drugstore newsstand of the era (*American News Trade Journal, *July 1930)*

sense of story construction. If the payoff stretched credulity, well, for the novelty-seeking readers of the pulps that might even have been an asset.

Richard sent the story to *The Underworld Magazine*, part of famed pulp editor Harold Hersey's new company, Magazine Publishers, Inc. *The Underworld* ran a variety of crime fiction, but they were increasingly specializing in gangland stories, promising to put the reader on "speaking terms" with racketeers, gangsters, and their ruthless girlfriends, the molls. The choice of magazine was a tacit admission that Richard felt he would have to break in at the bottom of the field. *The Underworld* offered a maximum of a cent-a-word, as opposed to most of the other pulps which offered a cent, and sometimes two, as a *minimum*. Also, *The Underworld* paid on publication rather than acceptance, another bottom-feeder feature, which meant that the treasured check might take a torturously long time to arrive. Amazingly, *The Underworld* took the story. By the time it appeared, in the October 1929 issue, Magazine Publishers was under new management; Hersey had left, to form another new company. It's doubtful that Richard received the top rate of a penny. A half-cent, for the unknown writer, was more likely, which would have yielded him a whopping $11.50. If not a great sum, it had proven the point. If he applied himself, he was good enough to get his name in print.

We don't know that Richard hadn't tried to sell to the pulps before New York. The motivations sketched out above are speculation sculpted from a small handful of facts; the timing of the visit and his first professional appearance are too closely related to be ignored. But if the visit had been the catalyst to write a saleable story, it was not the origin of his writing instincts. As he told *Dime Detective* (December 1932): "I started to write poetry and fairy tales at the age of ten. The poetry is terrible (and still is). Nothing was more natural than to turn from fairy tales to detective stories." Indeed. We know that he had been exposed to the pulps as early as 1924. He wrote a letter to *Weird Tales* expressing his approval for "The Transparent Ghost," a three-part serial that had started in the February issue. The following May he graduated from Freeport High School.

Why does a person write? Because he wants to, because he can, because its what he's best suited for, because he has something to say. To some degree, however, the desire to make art, music, painting, writing, is an act of rebellion against the workaday world, an attempt to escape one's fate. We wouldn't leap to this observation in regards to any writer, but Richard's early life exhibits a clear rebellious streak, a sharp contrast to the life his father had made for himself. H.J. Credicott was a highly successful entrepreneur, one of Freeport's leading businessmen, a pillar of the community. And he had made his name before either of his sons had been born. The success of H.J., and the dairy, exerted an inexorable pull on his sons' destiny; in Richard's case, it seemed to be the tide he was swimming against.

The son of a carpenter, Harley James Credicott was born on June 3, 1879, in Mapleton, Minnesota, a small town about eighty miles south of the Twin Cities. He apparently grew up in nearby Winnebago. He graduated from the Minnesota Dairy School, a branch of the University of Minnesota, Minneapolis, educated in the art and science of butter making. He worked at some of the finest creameries in the state. He soon became an inspector for the Minnesota Dairy and Food Commission, St. Paul, serving for about four years. He did double duty at the Dairy School, as an assistant instructor. Considered an expert in his field, in June 1906, H.J. joined the U.S. Department of Agriculture as a dairy inspector on the Chicago market. He was prominent in dairy industry advocacy, both on technical and economic matters; and often addressed professional organizations.

On August 28, 1905, H.J. married Clara B. Scheid (1885-1985). Clara was born in Easton, Minnesota, about ten miles south of Mapleton, and an even smaller town. Her father, Adam Scheid (*b.* 1816), immigrated to the United States from Germany in 1847, the year her mother, the former Sophia Schneider, was born. Both Adam and Sophia had been married before, and outlived their spouses. In 1900, Sophia was the head of the household; Adam was 84. H.J. was a boarder at the Scheid family farm in Faribault County, in the vicinity of Mapleton and Easton, where he remained until the marriage. The newlyweds moved to St. Paul, where Richard James (May 23, 1906) was born. The Agriculture job necessitated a move to Chicago, where Edward William (February 14, 1908) arrived.

In 1912, Robert Abel Moren, a local butter maker who had learned his trade in his native Sweden, started a creamery in Freeport, a city located a few miles south of the Wisconsin border and about a hundred miles west of Chicago. Freeport offered obvious advantages. It was a growing manufacturing city set amidst beautiful farmland, and a railroad hub. The population exploded from 10,189 in 1890 to 17,587 in 1910, a 73% increase; from 1910 to 1930, it grew another 25% to 22,045. In the same period, neighboring areas experienced similar rapid growth, creating ample opportunities for new business. After several months, H.J. joined Moren's creamery as partner and co-owner; he became the general manager and central figure. We assume that Credicott met Moren through professional contact, but the circumstances are not available. The two men had much in common. Apart from being butter makers, they were born a year apart, and were married less than a year apart. The Morens had a son, Robert William, born approximately 1907, in between Richard and Edward. Both men would be active in local organizations, Credicott in the Chamber of Commerce and the Rotary Club, Moren in the Shriners.

At first, Credicott and Moren were the sole employees of the Freeport Dairy & Produce Company. Their product—no surprise—was butter. They made 300,000 pounds in the first year. The business expanded quickly, adding real estate and taking on numerous employees. They eventually serviced a broad area from Iowa, on the west, to Chicago, and well into Wisconsin. In 1915, they began making ice cream, which was marketed under the Oak Brand label. Over time, the dairy came to be known as the Oak Brand Creamery. The ice cream led to the purchase of the Freeport

Freeport Journal-Standard, May 6, 1918

Artificial Ice and Cold Storage plant in 1917. By 1917, Freeport Dairy was deemed the fourth largest butter maker in Illinois. By 1924, butter production was up to a million-and-a-half pounds a year; ice cream was manufactured at 125,000 gallons a year; and ice, 8,000 tons a year. One hundred people were employed in warm months, seventy-five when cool.

The trajectory of the business was mostly up. There were an interesting pair of setbacks, though. In August 1917, a fire did $15,000 in damage to the plant. The repairs weren't completed until July 13, 1918. Twelve hours after the last nail had been driven, another fire broke out, doing $8,000 damage to the milk bottling department, destroying many supplies. The peculiar timing made Moren suspicious. With the war draft underway in 1917, and local boys fighting in France in 1918, and with Freeport Dairy furnishing large quantities of butter and cheese to the government, he blamed the fires on German agents. However, there were no follow-up reports in the *Freeport Journal-Standard* for either fire, which suggests that they were classified as ordinary accidents or malfunctions; and, as Freeport historian Robert Bike notes, Freeporters of German descent were loyal supporters of the American war effort. In any event, company operations continued throughout the ordeal.

Sparse information is available on the boys' upbringing. They graduated from St. Mary's parochial school in 1918. No doubt, they held some special status in the world of children as the sons of the local ice cream maker.

The Credicott and Moren families were close. They co-owned a cottage next to Lake Kegonsa, Wisconsin. They vacationed together. Fishing was the star attraction. In July 1922, for instance, the *Journal-Standard* reported that H.J. had reeled in a 14½-pound pickerel.

In June 1921, Richard, just turned fifteen, spent two weeks in Boy Scout camp at nearby Apple River Canyon. The *Journal-Standard* quoted a number of boys in a story on the event. Richard said:

> "We were out this afternoon on a Museum hike looking for snakes, birds, bugs, fossils, flowers, frogs, and anything else that might be interesting to put in our Museum Tent, which we were fixing up for visitors. This morning I worked in the kitchen and after making up the bed and after inspection I helped to put up the tents. I am having a fine time and enjoying myself. Now excuse me," he said, as he started away toward a gang of boys, "I think they have a snake up here and I want to see it."

Richard and Edward attended Freeport High, which made them proud Pretzels. Yes, that was and is the school mascot. Freeport is known as The

Pretzel City, owing to the twisty biscuits favored by the county's German immigrants. The annual football classic is called the Pretzel Bowl.

Information on the Credicotts' high school experience comes primarily from editions of the *Polaris*, the school yearbook. Photos show a serious, cerebral pair; wearing glasses, unlike most of their classmates. Both were heavily involved in school activities. Freeport High had a highly successful football program at the time, but neither brother participated in athletics.

Edward Credicott
1926 Polaris

Richard belonged to several clubs: the Latin Club; the Spanish Club, which he served as President his senior year; the Booster Club, an adjunct to football games and pep rallies; the Radio Club, which took an interest in the "new science"; the Senior Hi-Y, whose mission was "To Create, Maintain and Extend throughout School and Community the high standards of Christian Character." He also served on a committee to sponsor a series of mixer dances.

His creative impulses are on display in the *Polaris*. He supplied many illustrations to the 1922 (his sophomore year) and '23 editions, and served as Art Editor for the latter. His illustrations range from not particularly distinguished cartoony line-art in the '22 book, to more elegant full-page pieces in the '23 book, some in color. The 1922 cartoons tend to show Richard's sense of humor, a counterpoint to the demeanor shown in photos of him. One full-page illustration, for the Junior Immigration Party, depicts the party as a circus sideshow. A sign on the ticket booth reads "Drink Credicott Beer," a doubly mischievous gag for a teenager during Prohibition. The bottom two-thirds of the page consists of a ridiculously long hand-lettered party ticket full of quips and malaprops.

He also served on the staff of the school newspaper, the *Weekly Polaris*, as "Inquiring Reporter." And, because it shows an early stab at literature, we

1923 Polaris

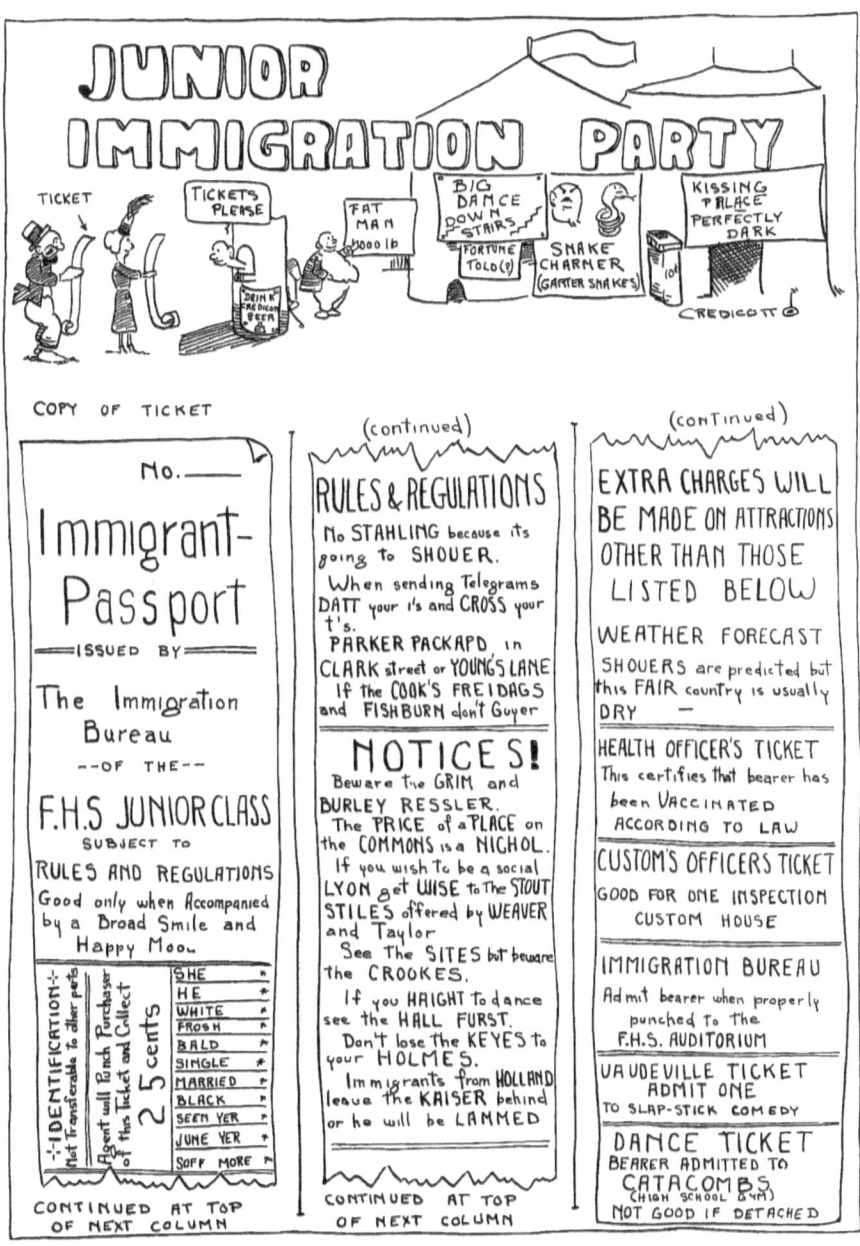

1922 *Polaris*

Artwork by Richard Credicott unless otherwise noted.

ATHLETICS

1922 *Polaris*

ORGANIZATIONS

1922 *Polaris*

1922 *Polaris*

1923 *Polaris*

must cite his "terrible" untitled poem in the '24 *Polaris*: How useless it is to be angry!/How futile it is to be sad!/Why not simply change about,/And just be "glad"?

Richard was known for his intelligence and academic achievements. In May 1923, the *Journal-Standard* cited Richard for making the honor roll. As a senior, he made the Honor Society. Two items in the '24 *Polaris* hint at how his fellow students viewed him. Under his senior photo is added, "Will you name one thing Richard couldn't discuss?" and the Senior Telescope, the humorous predictions feature, notes that while he Wants To Be a philosopher, he Probably Will Be an anthropologist. In 1927, when he made a little news at college, the paper noted that in high school and college, "he has been distinguished as a brilliant and accomplished student." He graduated in May 1924, in a class of 150.

Edward was two years behind Richard. He too worked on the *Polaris*. In his senior year, he served as business manager for the yearbook. He attended a prep journalism convention at the University of Illinois, Urbana-Champaign, where Richard was enrolled. He was President of Freeport High's branch of the Quill and Scroll, The National Journalism Honor Society. The *Journal-Standard* noted: "Edward Credicott, a senior, has managed the finances of the Annual very well this year, and it is just this sort of work should be recognized together with the literary work of others." He also belonged to the Radio Club and the Senior Hi-Y, both with Robert W. Moren. The '26 *Polaris*, Edward's senior edition, noted under his senior photo: "Capable— What 1926 class affair didn't go over big? And he helped with all of them. The jovial—"Eddie" had many responsibilities, but he never let them rob him of his sense of humor."

With this small array of facts, it's clear that the brothers were already steering toward different destinies. Richard was exercising his creative powers; Edward was practicing to be a leader and businessman.

Richard distinguished himself immediately at the University of Illinois. He was recommended for the "star rhetoric section," classified with other "superior freshmen." Most likely, he earned this honor by performing well on a written exam. He was appointed to the staff of *The Daily Illini*; however, it may not have been an assignment he relished. Whereas there were numerous jobs for reporters on the campus—sports, society-church, and city staffs— Richard got stuck in the Classified Advertising Department, probably not the foot-in-the-door he thought he deserved.

In June of his freshman year, his artwork turns up in the campus humor magazine, *The Siren*, whose monthly theme rendered it "The Censor's Issue." Signed "Dick Credicott," his three pieces are similar in quality and style to his work for the *Polaris*, but with an added touch of refinement.

The main piece is a two-page spread titled "With the Censors," and displays his rebellious streak in full bloom. On one side, an old-fashioned couple, delicately caricatured, is juxtaposed with a smiling Satan; in between are the objects of censorship, alcohol, naughty postcards, a kissing couple, books by James Branch Cabell and Ben Hecht, a burlesque show, the campus itself. A second piece is simply a single-panel cartoon in an expressionistic style of a man and woman standing in front of a row of leaning skyscrapers. The third piece is a comic-strip lampoon called "Our Campus Romance, or, Virtue Rewarded." It tells the story of a student romance surviving the intrusions of a conniving professor; the professor ends up dead, the students end up married. Whether the premise may have been drawn from actual experience, we'll leave an open question.

The July 9, 1925 issue of *The Daily Illini* contains the first known published piece of serious writing by Richard. It's a review of a new H.G. Wells book, *A Year of Prophesying*, a compendium of articles from 1923-24. The review is smartly written, though brief. Richard hints at his familiarity with Wells' fiction. He astutely points out his contradictions: "[Wells] is very enthusiastic over the future of the human race though he likes to make dire predictions." If we were to criticize Richard's criticism, it would be that he didn't state a strong enough opinion in either direction to make the piece memorable.

We have no record of Richard's activities during his sophomore year. His brief remarks to *Dime Detective* contain his only published reflections on college: "In the course of time I spent two years each at both the Illinois and Wisconsin universities. The education didn't take; there were so many interesting books to read I had no time for study. Since then I've been writing."

For his junior year (1926-27), he transferred to the University of Wisconsin, Madison. This reunited him with Edward who started there as a freshman for the same term; also, with Robert W. Moren, another Madison student. We don't know the reason for the change. From a purely practical standpoint, Madison is about a sixty mile drive from Freeport, whereas Urbana-Champaign is closer to two hundred. Though it's hard to believe he would have made the change if completely happy in Urbana-Champaign.

We now come to the most memorable episode of Richard's college years, the little bit of news alluded to earlier. In March 1927, Richard, freshman John C. Powers, and eight other charter members formed the Circle of the Godless, a campus organization of atheists. Their goals were to recruit new members, invite speakers to their meetings, and to obtain a charter from the American Association for the Advancement of Atheism (AAAA). The group's initial announcement was made in *The Triad*, a weekly student publication in the

The Siren, June 1925

men's dormitories; and was accompanied by derision from the editors of *The Triad*:

> The thinking person will not become alarmed over the atheists nor any of their actions. He will not fear for the future of civilization because a small group of young boys brazenly announce they are atheists and proud of it. The fireworks can be set off at any time, and when the last spark dies the world will be found to be pretty much the same.

The university took a low-key response, Scott H. Goodnight, dean of men, saying that there would be no official intervention. However, the colorful story was reported by the *Milwaukee Journal* on March 25, the same date of publication as *The Triad*. The following day, it was picked up by the news syndicates and reported in newspapers as far away as Los Angeles, with Credicott and Powers named as the ringleaders. It also went out as a radio news story on the day after—which is how the news reached Freeport. The *Journal-Standard* quickly contacted Richard's father for a reaction. Though the family were staunch Catholics, H.J. was touchingly tolerant in his remarks. He labeled Richard's activities as "merely a youthful indiscretion," elaborating:

> While it is scarcely a pastime that I would recommend to any young man, I cannot understand why the metropolitan press should give so much publicity and prominence to a matter of minor importance. College students are seething with ideas and opinions, some of which do not last very long, and hardly need to be put on record.

Whether H.J.'s private communications with his son took on a different tone, we'll never know.

If nothing else, the incident is a further example of Richard's rebellious, independent nature. The Circle of the Godless, however, was part of a broader movement, analyzed by Homer Croy in "Atheism Rampant in Our Schools" (*World's Work*, June 1927). Croy fingered the AAAA for infiltrating both high schools and colleges to promote the formation of atheist groups. The AAAA was happy to accept the credit. In addition to Richard's Circle, among some twenty "infiltrated" institutions were groups with names like The Devil's Angels, The Damned Souls, God's Black Sheep, The Legion of the Damned, His Satanic Majesty, and, juiciest of all, the Hedonic Host of Hell-Bent Heathen. Today, that would be the line-up at a heavy metal festival, and they would have to pay for their publicity.

Richard's prominence in the controversy lasted no more than a couple of days, though the Circle was the match that set off "fireworks." The controversy itself managed to ruffle feathers for several months. It reached a peak, of sorts, in a *New York Times* editorial of June 5, "Irrepressible Youth," which managed to echo H.J.'s public comments in about twenty times as many words. The *Times* linked school atheism with comments on the healthy rebelliousness of youth made by appellate judge Learned Hand in a commencement address at Bryn Mawr. "Let a few years elapse," concluded the *Times*, "and you will find these ostentatious young atheists pillars of the Church."

Why would an atheist movement gain traction in 1927? We need retreat no farther than 1925 for the answer. From July 10 to 21 of that year, a *really* big story commanded the nation's attention. It was the Scopes Monkey Trial in Tennessee, which put school teacher John Scopes in the crosshairs for teaching Evolution in violation of a new state law. The trial, dramatized in the play and film *Inherit the Wind*, managed to pit Faith against Reason in a court of law. Former Presidential candidate and fundamentalist Christian, William Jennings Bryan, represented Faith in aiding the local prosecutors, while famed civil rights attorney—and atheist—Clarence Darrow took the side of Scopes and Reason. The national press swarmed the small town of Dayton to cover the trial; it also became the first trial ever broadcast on radio. While Faith vs. Reason was ultimately immaterial to the outcome of the case, we can be reasonably assured that the debate raged in campus dormitories across the country, as it had in the courtroom and on the steps of the courthouse. In fact, though Darrow got the better of Bryan in the battle of wits, Scopes was convicted, and the movement to ban Evolution in classrooms was still continuing in a number of states through 1927.

The AAAA formed shortly after the trial, and, it was understood, in reaction to it. The AAAA's aims, as stated in their charter, were more generally stated, but the tone was clearly confrontational, e.g. the association shall "publish and distribute scientific and anti-religious literature and conduct a general propaganda against the church and clergy" in order to "abolish belief in God." It was America's first explicitly atheistic organization. The "infiltration" of the schools was an obvious countermeasure to the spreading Evolution ban. The shock-value names of the groups listed above have a thematic consistency which suggests that the AAAA provided guidance in this direction, perhaps aiming to sensationalize the cause for quick effect.

How much of this did Richard understand when he became involved? It's probably a safe bet that he never imagined that within a week his name would travel to the four points of the compass, including his hometown.

Richard left Wisconsin at the expected time in June 1928, but without a degree, which explains the hint to *Dime Detective* that his "education didn't take." Perhaps H.J. was only willing to subsidize four years of college, regardless of the outcome; perhaps Richard's having a job waiting at the dairy made the actual degree irrelevant. His major was economics, probably what had been expected of him by H.J. in order to assume a meaningful position. We should note that H.J. continued to be more than simply the head of a successful local business. By 1928, he had been a director of the Illinois State Dairymen's Association, had traveled to D.C. to meet with the federal government as a representative of the Illinois Butter Manufacturers' Association, had visited other East Coast cities on business trips, and had addressed local and statewide organizations on the economics of the industry. He was a big-picture businessman and had probably envisioned grooming Richard to follow in his footsteps. But with Richard not having his heart in his studies, and thinking about books and writing, it fell to Edward to carry the torch for the next generation. Richard left Wisconsin, and Edward transferred to Columbia to complete the final two years for his business degree. He graduated in June 1930.

There's little evidence to indicate what Richard was up to in the year following college. Undoubtedly, he was back at home in Freeport. His *Dime Detective* comments suggest that he immediately turned to writing, but that may have been an approximation. We pick up his trail when he joined Edward in Manhattan at the end of the 1928-29 school year, and then when his first story appeared in *The Underworld*.

Richard entered a flourishing market. The pulp magazine field grew steadily over the first three decades of the 20th Century. The typical pulp in the first decade, Street & Smith's *The Popular Magazine*, for instance, offered a wide variety of fiction suitable for the whole family: mysteries for the adults, sports and adventure for younger readers. Slowly, the market fragmented into niches focused on single genres, or catering to different age groups. Street & Smith was the king of the trendsetters. *Detective Story Magazine*, beginning publication in 1915, was the first detective pulp; *Western Story* (1919) and *Love Story* (1921), likewise, blazed new paths. In the '20s, new companies came on the market to challenge the industry stalwarts, Street & Smith and the Munsey company. Some of the new companies, Fiction House and the Clayton Group, offered titles in multiple genres. Soon, where there had been a pulp magazine section on the newsstand, now there were separate sections for adventure, western, detective, love, etc. And then, by the end of the '20s, the individual genres had further split into super-specialized areas. Alongside the westerns were western romance titles. A new classification, the war pulp, started in 1926 with *War Stories*. Within a few years, *War Stories* shared shelf space with *Submarine Stories* and *Zeppelin Stories*. The air-pulp came about in 1927 with *Air Stories*. Soon there were multiple air titles, some specializing in stories of commercial aviation, some with air-war stories. The cover paintings on the pulps grew increasingly colorful and sensationalistic. The old-style pulp featured staid portraits; the fresher pulp covers depicted dramatic events at moments of peak action. The newsstand became a place of excitement, offering peeks into every corner of the imagination.

In May 1909, a newsstand which carried every pulp on the market had 14 titles available. In May 1919, that number stood at 22. In May 1929, when Richard visited New York, that number had nearly quadrupled to 83. Some of the magazines were over two hundred pages long. The vast majority of the fiction published in these many titles was original; that is, never before published. This growth industry in magazines begat a new army of writers to fill the pages. An intelligent person could set about learning the craft of storytelling, aided by magazines like *Writer's Digest* and *The Author & Journalist* which kept abreast of the rapidly-moving field, and expect to be published within six months to a year. There may never have been an easier time to break into print writing fiction. It was a fictioneer's paradise. This is the world that Richard entered, this was the gold rush. But, like most gold rushes, by the time you hear about it, it's already winding down. The end of this particular boom was the fateful Wall Street crash of October 1929, which happened anywhere from four to six weeks after the October *Underworld* with Richard's "Clues" went on sale.

Over the next few years, income drained out of the pulp business. A look at the changing newsstand would have given a picture of health. The mix of magazines changed with the times. New titles replaced failed obscurities. The total number of current titles averaged about 85 from the end of '29 through the early months of '32, and then took a precipitous decline to under 60 when Depression unemployment neared its peak. But the total number of magazines is a deceptive figure in these early Depression years. Income evaporated in more subtle ways. In the late '20s, most cover prices ranged from 15 to 25¢. Those prices began to drop. After the budget-priced Thrilling chain came on the market in late '31, the typical cover price in the industry hit a floor of 10¢. Additionally, the pulps thinned; 128 pages became the norm. Accurate figures are hard to come by, but with so many working-class people—bedrock pulp readers—losing their jobs, circulations declined, and companies failed, explaining the drop in titles in 1932. Some publishers increased the pressure on the writers' brigades by mixing in reprinted fiction, for which very low rates were paid to the original authors; thus shrinking the market for original fiction even more. Multiplying all of these variables together meant that there was simply less money flowing to the authors. Many writers had become accustomed to living on a nice 2¢ a word, or more. They thought they had found their calling, even those, frankly, who were not overly talented. For them, the downdrafting market provided a rude wake-up. After the Crash, the pulps quickly became a penny-a-word market for the vast majority of contributors, even many seasoned pros. Richard could not have foreseen any of this, of course, so we will assume that he entered the world of professional wordsmithing with all the zeal his youth commanded.

We can't assume that every manuscript Richard put in the mail sold to the first publisher who received it. Some stories may have gone to several publishers before finding a home; some may never have sold. Some may have been revised on the recommendations of an editor, and then sold. If Richard had kept a log of his writing activity, we could step through his career with greater accuracy. Needless to say, if such a log existed, it's no longer available. Therefore, we will simply trace his career as best we can following the publication order of the stories, knowing that the fullest version of the history is lost to time.

The second Credicott story to appear was "Death Painting," in the January 1930 issue of *The Dragnet Magazine*. At 6,000 words, it was more than double the length of "Clues," with more involved plotting. Most remarkable for a beginner, the story received the cover illustration, a striking image in purple and black which perfectly captured the story's hook: *"A beautiful woman found hanging in front of her own portrait—strangled to death!"* Richard's name was top-billed, putting him above Armitage Trail, who would become well-known as author of the novel *Scarface*, from which the classic 1932 gangster film was adapted. As with all of Richard's stories, "Death Painting" was carefully crafted, but that's no guarantee of a sale. In "Death Painting," Richard had zeroed in on a key ingredient required for a detective pulp story: the need for novelty—an unusual murder, a strange clue, sinister circumstances—to grab and hold the readers' interest.

Richard made a quick return in the February issue of *The Dragnet* with "Murder Behind Murder." The story opens with anger and conflict, then quickly reveals its hook, "the Hatchet Killer," with all its ghastly implications. Reader involvement, curiosity and sense of foreboding is stoked within the opening sentences. This would have caught the attention of the editor who reviewed the manuscript. Many of them read the first and last pages of a story before committing to the rest. "Murder Behind Murder," while well-organized and intelligently written, does not turn out to be terribly interesting. It also includes, for Richard, an unusually sloppy mistake; halfway through the story, the first names of the two protagonist brothers swap (corrected in this volume). We know this, of course, because *The Dragnet's* editor passed the mistake along to the reader—and probably received a few tart letters in response.

The Dragnet was published by Magazine Publishers, the outfit that issued *The Underworld*. Like most of the other detective pulps, it followed the trend toward gangland fiction, as indicated by the front-cover banner: "Detective and Gangster Stories." In the October 1929 *Author & Journalist*, *The Dragnet* advertised a 1 to 3¢-a-word rate for stories. That was pre-Crash. By the June 1930 *A&J*, the top rate had dropped to 2¢. Assuming that Richard received 2¢ for the cover-illustrated "Death Painting," the payment would have been about $120, a far cry from the $11.50 he may have earned for "Clues." He would have to have believed that he'd already made it. Even at a penny it would have been a big step up. "Murder Behind Murder," with no cover illustration, was more likely to have earned a penny.

Richard appeared in two other pulps dated February 1930, *Real Detective Tales and Mystery Stories* and *Young's Magazine*. Three hits in one month is a lot in a career that only numbered eighteen (known) stories, and a lot for a newcomer. Twelve of his stories would appear in his first thirteen months as a writer, showing that he was seriously trying to establish himself.

Real Detective started life in 1922 as *Detective Tales*. In 1923, the publisher, located near Chicago, added *Weird Tales* as a companion magazine. Both were edited by former police court reporter Edwin Baird. In 1924, the magazines were spun off into separate companies, Baird going with the retitled *Real Detective Tales*. By 1930, he had written extensively on detective fiction for the writers' mags and was one of the better-known editors in the field. He had a stated preference for police stories, which Richard managed to blend with the gangster story in "The Racketeering Cop." Writing to an editor's tastes is one of the marks of a pro; it suggests that Richard had studied the writers' mags. Baird must have liked the story a lot, as suggested by his come-on blurb: "*Here is a police story by a new writer that ends in a whirlwind of exciting action.*" Indeed, it's an entertaining story with well-described action. Richard was mastering the lingo of the gang story, with its peculiar combination of extreme violence and tasteful understatement:

> Connors steadied himself. His left shoulder was numb; he could not move the fingers of his left hand. As the fan of bullets swept around to him, almost touched him, he fired twice. The deadly clatter ceased; the submachine gun slipped from nerveless fingers and clanged upon the pavement.

"The Racketeering Cop" demonstrates some of the moral ambiguities that would prove problematic to gangland fiction. Richard's cop protagonist, though sympathetic in the end, is, in fact, an accessory to murder and a racketeer, both of which he gets away with, in violation of the '30s ethic that "crime does not pay." It's also Richard's shortest story, and may only have netted him a penny a word, or about $22. But he was selling—and making editors happy.

We've subtitled this volume "crime stories by Richard Credicott." Technically, "A Strange Wife," from *Young's Magazine – Snappy Stories*, is not a crime story. We could bend over backwards and argue that adultery, the theme of the story, is a crime against marriage and morality; but, in truth, "A Strange Wife" is Richard's only known story outside the crime pulps, and is included here for completeness.

Young's, named after founder C.H. Young, and one of the earliest pulp magazines on the market, ran regularly as a monthly from April 1903 through September 1933. By the late '20s, it was following the trend toward "sophisticated" fiction, brief stories exploring the sexually daring lives of flappers and bon vivants. Magazines like *Young's* were another branch of genre specialization. What is a "snappy" story; or a "lively," "saucy," or "spicy" story; or a story labeled under any of the other similar terms used to describe these magazines? It usually involved big city swingers living for the night life, looking for love in a permissive environment of promiscuity and adultery. *Young's* editor Cashel Pomeroy stated his policy in the August 1929 *Writer's Digest*: "We want what is known as the clean 'sex story.'" "Clean" implied that sex could only be alluded to with hints and winks, as in this passage from "A Strange Wife":

> Terry was the perfect lover. Other men were dull, clumsy clods beside him. They were only awkward toyers with love, ignorant of all the subtle nuances in the art of love. Not Terry; he knew every corner of a woman's heart; knew how to thrill her, how to caress her, how to wake ecstasy in her heart with a kiss.

The backdrop of "A Strange Wife" is the theater world, which implies New York City although the location is unspecified. Perhaps the idea to write such a story came from the May visit to Manhattan, and a night at the theater where a "row of silk-clad girls" doing "an involved dance" left an indelible impression. In an August 1930 blurb, Pomeroy insisted that his stories "must have an air of craftsmanship and good technique in storytelling." Richard certainly hit the mark with "A Strange Wife." It's a quality example of the type of story to be found in *Young's*. Richard knew where he was going, building to the suspenseful scene that yields the dénouement. He's as adept with the clean sex story as he is with tales of gangsters.

The lives of Richard's characters contrast with the expected pattern of behavior in Freeport; "A Strange Wife" suggests that adultery leads to greater happiness for its married couple:

> Other women who loved one man uninterruptedly did not know the real thrill of love. They fell into a state of pleasant boredom that

lasted forever. But to lose Terry, and then to have him come back to her—each time it was as if she were but a young girl first experiencing the raptures of passion with her first lover.

It follows that marrying the girl next door, in a town like Freeport, and remaining faithful throughout a lifetime, would not achieve the same level of "snappiness." Richard's "strange wife" has found a way to rewind the clock over and over. Her fear—of "a state of pleasant boredom that lasted forever"—may echo Richard's fear, and may describe his desire to break free of convention by becoming a writer.

Richard may have written other stories for the snappy magazines; they're incompletely indexed at this time, so it's difficult to say. But with seventeen crime stories and only one sex story to his record, it's clear where his real interests fell. *Young's* offered a cent-a-word, the same as the crime pulps, so there was enough incentive to write more sex stories had his tastes gone in that direction.

In this period, Richard may also have been splitting his time by working at the dairy. Other than his success in getting published, we have one other item of evidence that indicates he considered writing his primary occupation. The 1930 U.S. Census, which counted the Credicott family in April, listed Richard's occupation as "Author, Detective Stories." What did H.J. think of Richard's writing career? We can only speculate—based on his reaction to the Circle of the Godless incident—that he understood his son's need to sort out his own fortunes. And Richard could show that he wasn't a dilettante, both with his published work—and the checks. H.J. may even have admired him; Richard's freelancing demonstrated the kind of entrepreneurial boldness that H.J. had employed in expanding the dairy.

With his next story, Richard jumped with both feet into the new world of the gang pulps. In the late '20s gangster stories had become an almost obligatory component of detective magazines. They were even creeping into other genres, e.g. the air pulps featured air-gang stories. It was the aforementioned Harold Hersey who went the next step in specialization by publishing magazines solely devoted to gangster fiction. Hersey left Magazine Publishers in mid-'29 and, with financing from Bernarr Macfadden—the famous health and fitness guru, and magazine magnate—started the Good Story Magazine Company. Hersey had a prior relationship with Macfadden, having managed his lucrative string of confessional magazines for most of 1927.

Hersey's philosophy was to introduce a wide variety of titles and let the market quickly pick the winners, as opposed to taking losses while nurturing magazines to success. He also aimed at contemporary themes and tastes. Thus, during a small blizzard of magazine introductions, Hersey gave birth to *Gangster Stories*, its first issue having a cover date of November 1929; and *Racketeer Stories*, February 1930. To simplify the distinction, racketeers were the brains of the mobs, gangsters the muscle. Prohibition had entered its twilight years, with the consequence of the law in creating new empires of racketeers and gangsters, combined with its all too obvious failure to curb alcohol consumption, the subject of considerable public discussion. Hersey's timing proved sound: the gang pulps were immediate hits.

Into the heat of the moment came Richard, his "Gangster Love" appearing in the fifth issue of *Gangster Stories* (March 1930). It was his first full-fledged gangster story and, at 6,500 words, his longest story to date. Some of the most entertaining writers in the gang pulps, like headliners Anatole Feldman and Margie Harris, spat out the chiseled language of the underworld like they were born to it. Richard displayed a similar knack for the genre. His dialogue is vivid and violent:

> "What are you going to do with him?" asked Rose.
> Bascone's lips drew back from his teeth. "Do with him?" he exclaimed. "We're going to play with him for a while. We're going to get all the dope on where his booze is hid so we can knock it off. Then we're going to bump him off. Fill his stomach so full of lead he'll sink to the bottom of the river and never come up."

His action is vivid and violent, as well:

> [Spot Taylor] still held the automatic in his right hand. As he fell to the floor with Bascone on top of him, he turned its muzzle against the gang leader's side and rapidly pulled the trigger six times. Bascone's body was paralyzed from a bullet in the spine before they hit the floor, and Spot rolled out from under him and sprang to his feet.

And the story resolves its central conflict in a satisfying way. It was exactly the kind of stuff Hersey was looking for. With this one story, Richard showed that he had found a better home for his talents than the story of deduction. His detective stories feel like the work of a promising, but as yet undeveloped, writer. His gang stories arrived as a thoroughly finished product.

Though he would be a near-regular in the Hersey gang pulps for a time, "Gangster Love" was to be Richard's only appearance in the flagship *Gangster Stories*. When he introduced the line, Hersey initiated a unique pay scale for his contributors based on the circulation of the magazine: 1¢ a word, up to 50,000; 1.5¢ for 50,000 to 75,000; etc. *Gangster Stories* was selling about 40,000 copies a month, so Richard's check would have been $65. Another Hersey title, *Flying Aces*, hit 90,000 in the same period, which suggests that *Gangster* had more upside, and that perhaps Hersey split the market by putting out the similar *Racketeer Stories*. If so, it cost Richard the $32.50 the extra half-cent would have brought in.

Of note, "Gangster Love" would have been on the newsstands when Hersey's gang pulps received a rude reaction from John S. Sumner, the New York censor. As executive secretary of the New York Society for the Suppression of Vice (NYSSV), Sumner was authorized by the state legislature to investigate citizen complaints about the display or sale of indecent products, which then led to enforcement action by police and prosecutors. He became most well-known for harassing booksellers for carrying works—by James Joyce, D.H. Lawrence, and others—that are now considered classics of literature. Newsstands and magazines were a particular source of attention, as well, especially the so-called "sex magazines" which offered risqué short stories—tame by today's standards—and sometimes nude photography. (*Young's* seems to have belonged to an in-betweener class, toeing the line of permissibility but never stepping over it; by policy, it was less racy than its sister pulp, *Breezy Stories*.) Sumner, and his enforcement operatives, created a lot of trouble for the magazine trade, raiding distributors, confiscating and destroying thousands of unsold issues, arresting and prosecuting news dealers.

On February 20, 1930, the *New York Times* reported that *Gangster Stories* and *Racketeer Stories* were being removed from sale in the state of New York—Sumner's sole jurisdiction—under threat of action by the NYSSV. A citizen had complained and Sumner had found the magazines in violation of the state's vaguely defined morality statutes. The specific law, on the books for thirty years, banned "magazines devoted to or chiefly made up of bloodshed, lust or crime." Sumner complained that "Gangsters always triumph at the end of the adventures described in both magazines." The nationally-distributed magazines never missed an issue, though they may have been impossible to buy in New York for a month. Behind the scenes, Hersey and Sumner came to an accommodation—the wording of which has not been discovered—and the magazines continued. Obviously, the glorification of criminals would have been the central problem. Hersey would have agreed that criminals would not profit in the end, and that gangsters could get away with killing their rivals, but not with killing cops. The reality may have been that Hersey did some hand-waving and apologizing while waiting for Sumner to lose interest and move on to the next "miscreant."

The February story was picked up by the national media and reported in newspapers across the country. But, like the Circle of the Godless story, the coverage was brief and short-lived, passed along to readers as much for its sensationalistic value as its newsworthiness. The two controversies sit well together in the always compelling "early signs of the collapse of civilization" category.

Did Richard know about Hersey's problems? No coverage could be found in the *Freeport Journal-Standard*; however, the affluent family may well have subscribed to a Chicago newspaper that did cover the story. In any case, if his "With the Censors" cartoon in the *Siren* is any indication, he probably would not have minded. He might have viewed censorship against Hersey as another battlefront in the war against overbearing governmental authority, as symbolized by Prohibition and events like the Scopes trial.

With his next story, "Murder From Behind," Richard was back with Magazine Publishers, in *Detective-Dragnet Magazine* (June 1930). *Detective-Dragnet* debuted with an April cover date; it wasn't a new magazine, just a retitling of *The Dragnet*; the "Detective and Gangster Stories" banner was removed from the front cover, as well. Following Hersey's dust-up with Sumner, Magazine Publishers applied a bit of cosmetic discretion to make *The Dragnet* look less like a gang pulp on the newsstand, to fend off potential problems. Inside, the contents hadn't changed; *Detective-Dragnet* advertised "Detective, Gangster and Crook Stories" on the Table of Contents, and the stories themselves met the promise.

The title "Murder From Behind" sounds awfully similar to "Murder Behind Murder" from the February *Dragnet*, but the story is quite different. It's a gang story from the police point-of-view, making it more like "The Racketeering Cop." It probably garnered another penny-a-word paycheck. It might have dawned on Richard that the penny-rate had turned into a de facto standard, barring unexpected luck. There would be no headlines to mark the end of an era, but the gold rush was over. Richard would have figured out that the most reliable way to make more money was to sell more or longer stories.

Harold Hersey introduced two new gang pulps, both debuting with June-July issues. They weren't bimonthlies; Hersey's projections, as he'd announced in the October 1929 *A&J*, called for ten-issue-per-year schedules; this required two double-dated issues. The two new titles were *Gangland Stories* and *Mobs*. Hersey didn't try to differentiate them, only saying that they would use material similar to *Gangster* and *Racketeer*. It was basic marketing; the differentiation was all in the label. Perhaps he thought that by emphasizing the world of the gangs, rather than individuals, he would avoid further charges of glorification. His lurid editorials, in both June-July issues, made clear his contempt for gangsters, e.g. "Criminals are like beasts of the jungle. . . . It is, indeed, a grotesque commendatory [sic] upon modern civilization that the jungle should be put at our very doorsteps" (*Mobs*). Both new pulps had essentially similar titles, another example of letting the market pick the winner. *Mobs* was the loser, getting a quick hook after two issues, while *Gangland* lasted fourteen issues before merging with *Racketeer* in 1932.

Richard appeared in both issues of *Mobs*, making him, along with two other minor writers, Bill Beyer and Robert Donaldson, the only figures to do so. Richard was overshadowed in the June-July issue by newcomer Margie Harris and veteran Perley Poore Sheehan; and in the August issue by Anatole Feldman, who was busy filling all of Hersey's gang pulps with colorful forty-page epics. Feldman was a prime example of the working pulp writer. His prose was a little loose, but there was a lot of it, all reliably entertaining. Richard was a fan of Feldman's first Big Nose Serrano story, demonstrated by his fan letter printed in the August 1930 *Gangster Stories*:

> DEAR MR. HERSEY:
>
> Since I'm in the writing game myself, I don't ordinarily write editors telling them what I think of stories. But Anatole Feldman's "Serrano of the Stockyards" [*Gangster Stories*, May 1930] has made me break my rule.
>
> It's a marvellous story! Wonderful character, action, and plot. Good humor, alternating with tense dramatic action, and at times almost poignant drama. I try to put fast action in my own stories for you, but Feldman's got us all beat!
>
> I'm hoping to see some more novelettes—book-length—about Serrano.
>
> Sincerely,
>
> RICHARD CREDICOTT,
> 1467 S. Carroll Ave.,
> Freeport, Ill.

Richard would get his wish; the popular Big Nose returned for another eleven adventures over the next five years.

Richard's first story for *Mobs*, "A Gun Moll's Revenge," was his longest to date at 6,600 words. It opens with a grisly discovery:

> Sergeant Rebholz, of the city homicide bureau, gazed down at the dead man moodily. Duke Darrand bumped off—how the newspapers would roar! Duke Darrand—the racketeer king and the emperor of the underworld, who ruled with an iron fist, richly rewarding those who served him and ruthlessly wiping out those who crossed him. Duke Darrand—the youthful, intelligent and debonair millionaire gangster who maintained a great estate in Florida and was accepted by society there, who was a member of the boxing commission and was known the country over as a sportsman.
>
> And now he had been found dead in a ditch like any cheap gorilla or greaseball! "Bumped off!"—the words that could be used as the epitaph of almost every gangster.

The passage concludes with language echoing Hersey's operatic anti-gangster editorials. Hersey would have loved it: toss a bone to the censor and then get on with the blood and guts. And a good tale it is, bristling with action. He'd also hit on an element that was fast rising in popularity: a moll—a tough-talking, hardboiled gangster's consort—in a prominent or starring role. "Gangster Love" featured a moll, but as a subordinate character. Hersey never stated a preference for moll stories in his writers' mag solicitations, but it's clear from the stories themselves, and especially the cover paintings, which often featured hard chicks with guns, that molls were a selling point. A.A. Wyn, chief editor of Magazine Publishers, and Hersey's nearest rival in the gang story field, was more forthcoming. He stated in the June 1930 *A&J* that, for *Detective-Dragnet*, "Woman interest may be included, but the leading character should be a man." A soft statement, but by the September *Writer's Digest*, he'd significantly amended his needs: "Our policy encourages woman interest, especially of the gang girl or moll type." With an October 1930 cover date, a small outfit, Real Publications, took moll interest—and genre specialization—to its logical extreme by producing *Gun Molls Magazine*, which managed to last nineteen issues into 1932. But not everyone savored the ascendance of the tough chick. John S. Sumner said, in his condemnation of gang pulps: "I especially resent the women who lead the gangs."

Richard was hitting his stride. He'd not only found his voice—his gangster prose was exemplary for the genre—but he was staying abreast of market trends. He was undoubtedly devouring the gang pulps as a student and fan, as well as keeping up with the writers' mags. In the next issue of *Mobs*, he reached his apotheosis with "The Big Shot's Moll." At 15,500 words, it more than doubled his longest story to date. Like Feldman, he was giving Hersey what he wanted—and more of it.

Incidentally, a passage in the story gave us our title for this volume:

> If she only had a machine gun, she might be able to do something.
> An automatic pistol is a puny weapon in comparison.

Richard's heroine, Babe O'Connor, is tough, but sympathetic, in character a cut above her perfumed rivals:

> Babe was keeping herself clean—something unusual in the underworld, where conventional morality is almost unknown and women often pass freely from man to man. She knew the fate of these women: they might live in luxury for a time, but in the end they sank down and down, to the lowest levels of existence. Unless they luckily came to a sudden death, they died in unspeakable squalor and poverty.

Babe finds that she is not immune from descending into the underworld's version of Hell. She's cast out of her own gang, taken for a ride; she's doped in an opium den. Richard delivers on the implicit promise by finding words for the "unspeakable" squalor:

> On one bunk a bedraggled woman lay unconscious, her head and one arm hanging out. In other bunks were thieves, dips, cheap racketeers and gunmen. A sailor sat nervously on the edge of one bunk, anxiously watching a Chinaman who was cooking a pipe for him at a small table.

The story peaks in a crescendo of female empowerment, as only a machine gun can facilitate it:

> Rat-a-tat-tat-tat!
> Three of the men fleeing from the building went down under the hail of steel-jacketed bullets. The others whirled about to face this new menace.
> Rat-a-tat-tat-tat!
> Her submachine gun spewed a stream of death again. More of the men went down. In a moment only one man remained upon his feet. He raised a submachine gun to fight her with her own weapon, sent a barrage of bullets kicking about her.

"The Big Shot's Moll" is one of Richard's best, an epic of moll mayhem. It's fast-moving, evocatively described, and ends with a moral that would have brought tears to Sumner's tortured eyes.

The Underworld underwent a turbulent financial history. In early 1930, it returned to the control of its 1927 founder, J. Thomas Wood. He immediately went $80,000 in debt which resulted in money owed to authors and other creditors. When Richard appeared in the September issue with a 6,000-worder, "His New Dress Suit," *The Underworld's* problems had all been resolved. However, the story is a throwback to Richard's early efforts, which suggests it may have been sold during the turmoil, then delayed in publication; with an accompanying delay in payment to the author. If so, it was a sign of things to come. "His New Dress Suit" is a well-written mystery with a good premise, but an unsatisfying ending. Its gang element is minimal and tangential. And it was probably a half-cent-a-word sale, half of what he was probably getting from Hersey for his first-rate stuff.

In November, he was back in business with two strong gang stories in Hersey pulps. His first for *Racketeer*, "The Big Shot's Weak Spot," is a great one, short, to the point, scrubbed of sentiment, with a hint of mischievous glee. It delivers its violent plot developments like a series of quick left jabs, then finishes off with a right hook of a moral in the closing paragraph. If Aesop had written a gangster fable, it could have been "The Big Shot's Weak Spot." Hersey gave it a prominent mention on the cover.

Richard had another first appearance in November, in *Gangland*, with the 7,200-word "Racketeer's Choice." It opens with a thumb to the eye of authority:

> Chris Thorp brought Dion O'Reilly's rumbling cavalcade of five booze trucks into New York without a hitch, despite the fact that it was in the middle of the afternoon and probably thousands of people saw them as they thundered down First Avenue. When they reached the lower East Side, they turned upon a dirty side street and disappeared through the sliding steel doors of the gang warehouse that fronted the river.

Of course, the law comes through in the end, thus making the story safe for Democracy, but the overall feel, as in many gang stories, was of a gangland that operated as if law and enforcement was largely irrelevant, thus reflecting the prevalent view among the public. For the longest time, Congress ignored the vast problems wrought by Prohibition, reluctant to admit that the Great Experiment had been a disaster. That started to change in 1930; the first hearings on the efficacy of Prohibition were held in February.

This ends the productive period of Richard's writing career. These last two stories were his eleventh and twelfth professionally published works. Over the rest of his career, only six more stories would be published in a two-and-a-half-year period. He was abandoning the effort to establish himself as a professional, perhaps letting his writing degenerate into hobby status. The likeliest explanation is that he had figured out he couldn't be productive enough to draw a real income, a stark contrast to the lure of a steady paycheck from the dairy. Brother Edward had graduated from Columbia in June 1930, and returned home to join the dairy. Robert W. Moren left the University of Wisconsin in June, as well; like Richard, he logged four years of college, but earned no degree. Moren joined Edward at the dairy. Richard may have felt pressure to become the Third Musketeer, to hold on to his birthright.

In March 1931, Richard returned to *Detective-Dragnet* for the first time since the prior June. That 1930 appearance roughly coincides with a change of payment policy from Magazine Publishers. As editor Wyn stated in the June 1930 *Author & Journalist*: "payments [are] made twenty days before publication. So closely do we work to this schedule, however, that regular writers receive their checks approximately one month after acceptance."

Wyn, obviously feeling the effects of the market downturn, was splitting the difference between the industry-standard, author-friendly "pay on acceptance" policy, and the exploitive "pay on publication" policy employed by marginal publishers. This suggests that Richard abandoned Magazine Publishers as a prospective market, favoring Hersey's pulps. The outlook was further roiled in early '31, when Hersey switched to straight "pay on publication." If Hersey had been sitting on Richard's last submission, he would certainly have been annoyed—as would any other contributor undergoing the same treatment. Further submissions to Hersey would have seemed futile, with the potential to turn Richard from contributor into creditor. This may have swung the pendulum back to Wyn, but half-heartedly, if Richard had soured on writing as a regular profession.

The March 1931 story, "Gangland's Back Pay," is one of his best. Its lead is the ruthless "Al Nucci, beer baron, alcohol king and overlord of the underworld." Nucci, like his creator, is a philosopher:

> "I know I'll get mine some day, but I like it. I'm ready to take my dose of lead when it comes along. I'll have to, whether I want to or not. I'm in the racket too deep to get out. The mob wouldn't stand for that. They'd turn against me if I tried it."

The story then proceeds to put his prophecy to the test.

Richard is then absent from the pulps until "Alibi's Holiday" in the October 1931 *Detective-Dragnet*. This story drew praise from August Lenniger in the December *Writer's Digest*, in "New Horizons for Mystery Stories," an article on A.A. Wyn's evolution of *Detective-Dragnet* into an action-oriented detective pulp. Lenniger cites ten stories from the September through November issues, but "Alibi's Holiday," with a lengthy plot synopsis and analysis, is the most prominent, comprising a fifth of the article. Lenniger begins his analysis with: "Mr. Wyn asked me to point out particularly the *human* element in this story; it provides a realistic, sympathetic touch that grips the reader's emotions." If Wyn had been hoping to keep Richard on the roster, the attempt failed. It was to be his last story for Magazine Publishers.

Richard was back in the Hersey pulps a final time, with a short 4,200-word piece, prophetically titled "The Last Deal," appearing in the November-December 1931 *Racketeer*. It's a decent effort, if not at the level of his best. With the Hersey switch to "pay on publication" earlier in the year, it's entirely possible Hersey had been sitting on "The Last Deal" for many months. The delay, if combined with a smaller than expected paycheck, would have told Richard that Hersey's pulps had peaked in 1930 and were now in decline, lending the company an air of unreliability. It would be thirteen months before he appeared in print again.

His third and last story for *The Underworld* (December 1932) was "Tick o' the Clock," a 5,000-word short, a private-eye story with gang overtones. It's well-constructed and concludes in exciting fashion, making it the best of the three. One passage describing the detective may have been a close description of Richard himself, if we substitute "crime writing" for "detective work":

> Criminology was his sole absorbing interest in life. He had a natural flair for detective work and an intuition which, supplemented by a keen reasoning mind and a capacity for hard work, had already enabled him to make somewhat of a name for himself, though he was still young.

Richard had another appearance in the same month, with "The Three Horrible Heads" in *Dime Detective Magazine*. This story is interesting for several reasons. At 12,000 words, it was his second longest to date, suggesting a serious return to writing after the year-long hiatus. It earned the cover illustration, his first since the January 1930 *Dragnet*. And it showed him switching gears again, writing for a new trend in pulp stories, the detective-horror hybrid.

Dime Detective was the star magazine for a new chain, Popular Publications. Led by veteran pulp editor Harry Steeger, Popular launched on the market with four titles dated October 1930. One, *Gang World*, was a direct threat to Hersey's empire, and probably ate into his sales. After mixed results with the initial titles, which were priced at 20¢, *Dime Detective* was launched with a November 1931 cover. Putting *Dime* in the title was an obvious attempt to draw the newsstand browser's eye to the new financial reality, that most pulps were going to be 10¢ products. The strategy worked. As Steeger recalled in 1977, "We made enough money to keep going but it was not until we started *Dime Detective* that the profits really began rolling in." Hersey, by contrast, priced his forbidden-pleasure gang pulps at a quarter, and stubbornly held on to the high sticker. *Racketeer* and *Gangland* dropped to a still-high 20¢ with their May-June 1931 issues; *Gangster* never went below a quarter.

As for the detective-horror trend, it evolved over several years. *Detective-Dragnet* started introducing detective stories with a weird element in 1931. The best example is Paul Chadwick's Wade Hammond series, which debuted in the September 1931 *Detective-Dragnet*. In 39 stories, which continued into 1936 (when the magazine had been renamed again, to *Ten Detective Aces*), detective Hammond faced off against a dizzying variety of weird villains and situations. By the end of 1931, *Detective-Dragnet's* editor, A.A. Wyn, had barred gangster stories, and instead called for "a new type of detective adventure story in which atmosphere plays an important part; in which the writer can unlimber his imagination within reasonable bounds."

Dime Detective began life with stories that stressed action over deduction, i.e. detectives that used their fists as much as their brains. In the September 1932 *Writer's Digest*, Steeger made his first explicit request for detective-horror material: "We want detective stories of mystery and action with a slight horror twist." By mid-'33, the desire for horror was heavily emphasized: "Don't submit any deductive detective tales. The shadow of horror to come must be cast darkly over every page" (*Writer's Digest*, October 1933).

(We should note that Universal studios undoubtedly influenced and amplified this trend with their new cycle of distinctive horror films, starting with *Dracula*, released February 1931; *Frankenstein*, November 1931; and *The Mummy*, December 1932.)

"The Three Horrible Heads," appearing only three month's after Steeger's initial request, shows that Richard was still keeping abreast of changes in the pulps, either through recreational reading or the writers' mags. The detective-horror trend may have inspired him to jumpstart his career with new enthusiasm. (Which doesn't explain the more conventional "Tick o' the Clock.") Though it's never excessively gory, the theme of severed and shrunken heads in "Three Horrible Heads" gives it more than a twist of horror.

Popular offered its contributors a penny-a-word-and-up at this time. If we assume that making the cover of the December issue merited a penny-and-a-half, Richard would have earned a nice $180.

Richard's next detective-horror epic for *Dime Detective*, "The Ghoul of Murder Manor," appeared in the June 15, 1933 issue (the magazine switched to bimonthly publication in March), and it also earned the cover illustration. The gap from December to June 15, between the two *Dime Detective* appearances, merits attention. Our first assumption might be that he had taken particular care with the story, which was the longest of his career at 17,800 words. But another variable is Popular's payment policy in this period. In the March 1933 *A&J*, Steeger announced that the company would be "paying on publication for approximately two months." This suggests a cash-flow crunch that prevented Popular from stockpiling purchased stories through paying on acceptance. The projected two months, however, turned into a year. "The Ghoul of Murder Manor" was to be Richard's last story for *Dime Detective*, and his last published story—period. It's yet another example of him tacking in another direction right after the time his publisher stopped paying on acceptance. If Richard had been grappling with the question of whether it was possible to make a career of pulp-writing, the continuing whiff of financial instability would not have helped. How could you make a living at it when the publishers were holding your pay in abeyance? And it wasn't just Hersey, whose Good Story chain went under in 1932, Magazine Publishers, and Popular. Nineteen-thirty-two was a terrible year for the national economy and most of the pulp publishers experienced difficulty. Some of them even stiffed their contributors, although this wouldn't have been the case with any of Richard's markets. In due course, the pulp-magazine business would stabilize. Richard's bad luck was to enter the field in the hardest stretch of years until the early-'50s when the pulps entered their terminal decline.

The irony is that Richard's career ended at its peak of success. His stories were getting longer, his plots more complicated; he was producing trendy material of great value to his publisher; two consecutive submissions had made the cover of *Dime Detective*; and his word-rate may have jumped up accordingly. At a penny-and-a-half, "The Ghoul of Murder Manor" would have earned $267, probably equal to a couple months' pay at the dairy. To further the irony, his writing exploits finally caught the attention of the *Freeport Journal-Standard* (June 16, 1933):

RICHARD J. CREDICOTT HAS STORY IN CURRENT ISSUE, DETECTIVE MAGAZINE

The current issue of the *Dime Detective* magazine contains a 30-page story by Richard J. Credicott, of Freeport, entitled "The Ghoul of Murder Manor." The story is the closing one in the publication and is illustrated. Mr. Credicott has had a wide variety of stories accepted by several publications and is quite versatile in his writings.

Was it the case that Richard had already thrown in the towel when this story appeared? And how did the story get into the paper? Obviously, someone familiar with Richard's record was behind that concluding sentence. The record is silent.

What do we make of Richard Credicott's writing career? Eighteen stories—mostly shorts—in less than four years is not much for a pulp writer. His total output was about 122,000 words (with total earnings, given our word-rate estimates, of $1,400, about equal to an average year's salary in the early '30s). The field would be defined by million-word-a-year men who could compose fiction on a typewriter as fast as many of their readers could absorb it off the printed page. It didn't have to be textbook stuff; it only had to deliver genre thrills in a reasonably coherent package. Richard clearly took time with his stories, outlined them carefully, probably subjected them to multiple drafts. He might have thought, going in, that that was the formula for success. That would have been the point of view of a studious, meticulous person. But the publishers wouldn't have paid him more for a better class of writing unless he had developed an unmistakable reader following—unless he was selling magazines. His meager output was too dispersed for that. There seems no doubt that he could have succeeded as a professional writer, had he the patience, had his luck in timing been better. His natural talent is unmistakable. He immediately moved ahead of the thousands of contributors who may have understood the English language but didn't have the first clue about telling a story. If he had learned to write faster—and with less pride in the outcome—if he had had the stomach for that—he could have made pulp writing his business. Instead, he stands as a case study in the obstacles to becoming a pulp writer during the early years of the Depression.

Richard's life doesn't end with "The Ghoul of Murder Manor," of course. He worked for the dairy along with Edward and Robert W. Moren. H.J. Credicott remained the general manager. The precise nature of Richard's work during the '30s isn't known, but it's clear that the three young men were the heirs apparent to the business. They would have grown into H.J.'s and Robert Moren Sr.'s middle management.

Richard's recreational life turned to other pursuits. The one that left a long public record was his interest in contract bridge, a card game which came into fashion in the mid-'20s. The game is played by four players consisting of two partnered pairs. It appears that Richard was introduced to the game by his mother Clara. She was active in bridge as early as 1930. Richard's heavily documented involvement begins in February 1933, which must have been very near the time that he stopped writing. Did he finally surrender gang pulp and detective-horror to contract bridge? We have only the coincidence to guide us.

On February 23, 1933, eighteen pairs competed in Freeport's first annual duplicate contract bridge tournament at the Top Notch restaurant. Clara and her partner won the East-West division. Richard and fellow Class of '24 Pretzel, Henry J. Raepple (pronounced "ripple"), won the North-South. The playoff, for the championship of all Freeport, was held at the Credicott home on March 10. H.J. served as one of the official observers. Let's hope he didn't have to cover his eyes as Richard and Raepple walked away with the prize, two silver cups with the emblem of the United States Bridge Association.

In May, Richard and Raepple played in a tourney at the Palmer House, Chicago. In three matches, they had a seventh and two fourths, in a field of over two hundred players. The ingenuity of their play earned special mention from the tournament director. In October, Richard supervised a tournament at the Hotel Freeport, under the auspices of the new Freeport Bridge Association. In February 1934, Richard hosted the F.B.A. championship at the Oak Brand Creamery. For refreshment, buttermilk, Eskimo pies, ice cream and cake were served. Raepple and partner won the tourney; Richard and partner finished fifth. In 1934 and '35, Richard, Raepple, and other F.B.A. players traveled to Dubuque, fifty miles west, for tournaments.

Bridge, obviously, was a serious and addictive hobby. Richard and Raepple stayed active in bridge for decades, now and then as partners. Raepple wrote a bridge column for the *Journal-Standard*, contributed to national bridge magazines, and was considered instrumental in popularizing the game. So who else was Henry J. Raepple? He became Richard's best friend. Richard's son, Dave, remembers Raepple as something of a "mystery man." That description may derive from Raepple's unmentionable past. If bridge and gang pulp made for a unique aesthetic mismatch, even more so did bridge and criminal gang activity. While Richard had written about fictional gangsters, his partner, strangely enough, was an actual reformed gangster.

Raepple's story sprang to life in September 1925. He'd quickly returned to Freeport from the University of Illinois, where Richard had been a fellow freshman. Raepple may already have dropped out. Back in town, he linked up with two other Pretzels, Harry Commons, Class of '23, and Beloit College dropout, whom he'd known for eight years, and Robert D. Schroeder, Class of '24, whom he'd known for four. Raepple appears to have been the linchpin, as Commons and Schroeder were only recently acquainted.

Brief insights into Raepple, Commons, and Schroeder come courtesy of the *Polaris*. Richard and Raepple were probably pals, since Raepple supplied numerous illustrations to the '23 book, the year that Richard was Art Editor. They were cartoons and full-page illustrations, quite similar to the work that Richard had done. For the '24 book, Raepple succeeded Richard as Art Editor. Raepple was in the Latin Club with Richard, their senior year; in the Spanish Club, under President Credicott; and joined the Credicott brothers and Robert W. Moren in the Radio Club. Commons and Schroeder were apparently uninvolved in school activities with the exception that Commons played three years on Freeport High's stellar football team.

Senior photos in the *Polaris* were always accompanied by an editorial quote meant to characterize the person in a few words. These are usually amusing and, given the fates of these three Pretzels, a bit ominous. Commons: "He had a head to contrive, a tongue to persuade, and a heart to execute any mischief." Raepple: "Genius is a capacity for evading hard work." Schroeder: "Einstein couldn't puzzle him." At any rate, on with the tale . . .

The trio of Raepple, Commons, and Schroeder rented an apartment in Freeport's Tarbox Building, which immediately turned into a bachelor vice nest, littered with empty hootch bottles and poker chips. The boys enjoyed a highball with their card game. At least some of the illicit liquor had been

Polaris photos of Raepple, Commons, and Schroeder.

obtained for them by Thelma Symens, wife of a "magnetic healer" who had offices in the Tarbox. Two bottles of whiskey were purchased by Thelma from a local man, George E. Ott, for "four or five dollars a quart." Eventually, though, the state charged Thelma with selling liquor. The trial took place on her nineteenth birthday. Commons testified that the liquor had been "rot-gut whiskey"; Schroeder described it as "vile bitter-tasting stuff"; while Raepple "did not offer any particular characterization of the beverage."

Thelma's trial jumps ahead of the plot, but it supplies a probable motive—extreme dissatisfaction with the hootch—for why the trio decided to blackmail Mr. Ott. The initial idea had been Schroeder's. They obtained all the necessary tools: a rented typewriter, a set of skeleton keys, a "30-30 lugger pistol" purchased for $18. They had a phone installed in their Tarbox "offices" under an assumed name. Raepple wrote the extortion note, which included this flavorful passage:

> Have met and done away with better men than you will ever hope to be. They tried to cross us and we give them a wooden overcoat for their pains. We know all about your little bootlegging business and we have samples of your stuff, and signed statements by two reliable witnesses, who have bought your liquor, rotten artificial whiskey to boot.

The blackmailers set the price for peace at six hundred dollars. They signed the note with a skull and crossbones. The trio went to Ott's residence where Raepple opened the front door and threw the note inside. Ott, however, took no action.

They turned their attention to another victim, Frank Haegele, a prominent manufacturer, who Schroeder claimed was commonly known to be selling liquor. They decided to put him on the spot for a cool grand. Raepple's vicious extortion note, wrapped around a railroad spike, was thrown through Haegele's front window. Excerpts follow:

> We know that you have been bootlegging, and we have samples of your liquor. If there is a slip anywhere all Freeport will hear about

your disgrace, you will be placed arrest, you will be both fined and placed in the federal penitentiary, your whole life will be ruined. We do not trifle, and by —— we mean business. . . . We got all the dope on your liquor deals and it all goes to the cops, we are going to mail the whole story to the Journal-Standard. . . . You have the thousand bucks or by —— you will be a dead man. Our whole gang is watching every step you take and if you don't want to get shot, pay up. . . . The cold cash is the only thing that can save you, and if you think more of a thousand dollars than your life and family, why don't pay. . . . The minute anything goes wrong Monday night there will be a couple of dead men in Freeport. We could blow your head off any night. . . . If you haven't got one thousand let us know what kind of a casket you want.

The skull and crossbones having proved insufficiently intimidating, the note was signed with a bloodstain. Five days later, another note, which included a threat to blow Mrs. Haegele's head off, was left in a bottle. Haegele had nothing to do with bootlegging, but afraid for his family's safety, he agreed to pay off. There followed an evening of miscommunication. The unholy three, driving around in a used sedan rented from the Freeport Buick Co., actually confronted Haegele on the street, ironed out the confusion, and collected the thousand bucks, which they split three ways.

A third victim, S.E. Raines, the local superintendent of schools, received notes but events overran the fruition of that plot. It was the fourth victim, Leroy Balles, who brought the gang crashing down. He received three extortion letters, two typed out by Raepple, one lettered in pencil by Schroeder. Early the subsequent Sunday morning, using the $18 "lugger," Raepple fired shots into the air outside the Balles home. Balles contacted the police. When the gang later made a threatening phone call to Balles, the police traced it to the Grace Episcopal Church, where Raepple and Commons were arrested. One of them drew a gun on the police, but didn't fire. They were initially

The End

Art by Henry Raepple, 1923 Polaris

charged with carrying concealed weapons. When Schroeder, the youngest of the three, was rounded up, he became the first to confess, concluding his remarks with touches of philosophy and theology:

> For the past several years I have had a tremendous mental struggle to decide between altruism and egotism. At last I have found that egotism and Nietzsche are all wrong.
> I have a hard path before me—to live down my wrong—but with God's help and a little application of practical Christianity I will do it.

After the story broke on November 10, it was front-page, big-banner news in the *Journal-Standard* for several days. Richard was away at college when it all went down, but he must have heard about his former classmates in due course.

After Schroeder's collapse, the confessions of his cohorts soon followed. It came out that all three were students of Nietzsche. Their shocking behavior drew comparisons with Leopold and Loeb, the two University of Chicago students who, in 1924, murdered a fourteen-year-old boy in an attempt to commit a perfect crime. Leopold and Loeb had been adherents of Nietzsche, as well, considering themselves to be—in Nietzsche's terminology—supermen. Clarence Darrow defended the pair in the widely-publicized court case. It wouldn't be the last time a Darrow case sent ripples all the way to Freeport. . . .

Thelma Symens went to trial first, a mere six days after the case first broke. A jury found her guilty of selling alcohol. On recommendation of the State's Attorney, the court imposed a fine of $100, sparing her a jail sentence in return for cooperation in helping the state prosecute "higher-ups" in the local bootlegging racket.

Commons presaged the outcome of the main event by saying: "I intend to treat the public fairly by taking my punishment without any quibbling about technicalities, and I expect the public to treat me fairly in the future if I am able to make good." On December 17, 1925, the anticlimax was stamped official. Each of the three supermen pleaded guilty to four counts of extortion. They were sentenced to one-to-twenty-years in the state reformatory at Pontiac. Eligible for parole after eleven months, they were freed on a technicality after fifteen. Raepple's father was buried in August 1926 while his son sat behind bars; a hidden cost of the crime. According to the 1930 Census, Commons became a traveling salesman. Schroeder, curiously, listed his occupation as "Magazine Writer"; no corroboration could be discovered.

Admittedly, the tale is tangential to Richard's biography, but irresistible nonetheless. A real-life Freeport gangster story. It evokes some of the special flavor of the Jazz Age. If parents had nightmares about their children listening to wild music, guzzling hootch, and dancing like dervishes, how much more must they have feared the subversive, ruinous influence of Nietzsche and Darrow? In the long run, it didn't matter. By 1933, Richard and Raepple were two young men in their late twenties, behaving responsibly, channeling their need to stand above the crowd into the game of Bridge.

The Oak Brand Creamery remained successful under H.J.'s leadership as general manager. He retained his position of prominence in the industry, serving as president of the American Butter Institute, director of the Illinois Dairy Products Association, director of the Freeport Chamber of Commerce, and similar positions. The 1948 Polk City Directory for Freeport lists Oak Brand with H.J., Richard, Edward, and Robert W. Moren as the four principals; Richard was listed as general manager. H.J. turned sixty-nine in 1948 and must have given Richard the first shot at succeeding him. He died on April 27, 1949, "after a long illness." The funeral was held at St. Mary's Catholic Church. He was survived by his wife Clara, both sons, and a grandson, Richard's son David. His estate was bequeathed in full to Clara.

Richard, Edward, and Robert all were married along the way. On October 11, 1942, Richard married the former Frances M Hirst (no middle *name*) (July 1, 1907 - March 1985), her second marriage. She and Richard had been schoolmates at Freeport High. She participated in drama in high school. She married schoolmate James Pollock in 1926, divorced him in 1939. The Pollocks had been active in Freeport bridge circles, which must be where she became acquainted with Richard. After the marriage to Richard, they played bridge, sometimes as partners; she was also active in the Women's Society of Christian Service and the Freeport Garden Club. Their only child together, David Edward, was born in 1948.

*Richard & Frances,
ca. 1942*

After H.J.'s death, Edward became general manager of the dairy. Richard, like his father, took a leading role in the industry, serving in several positions including president of the Illinois Association of Ice Cream Manufacturers. He belonged to the local Rotary Club, along with Edward.

On June 17, 1969, Richard and Raepple won a YMCA bridge tournament. Frances and her partner finished second. For the two men, it may have been the last time. Raepple died of a heart attack on November 22. The *Journal-Standard* noted that he had published a commercial newspaper in Miami,

Florida; and had worked for Boeing in Seattle during WWII.

Over time, the business of the creamery diminished. In 1977, Oak Brand discontinued making ice cream and sold the distribution network; they retained the butter operation, with a work force halved to ten employees. Edward explained the decision: "management is getting old and we're trying to retire." The Oak Brand Building—the central operation—went on the market later in '77, which may indicate the final dissolution of the dairy.

Richard slipped away on February 20, 1991 and left the treasure that we've unearthed eight decades after it was buried in some rather obscure magazines. This volume will remain a tribute to his life and talents.

LITERATURE

1922 Polaris

CLUES

A finger print, a cigarette butt, a hair, a button, a scrap of paper—every thief leaves his clue. In this case it was—

THE YELLOW RAYS OF A FLASHLIGHT cut through the darkness of the library and fell upon the opened doors of a wall safe. The great house was dark and silent; the only sounds were the monotonous ticking of the hall clock and the occasional whisperings of the two men who knelt before the safe.

Dan Gordon, who held the flashlight, opened the inner doors of the safe and turned the light on the compartments. He was a short, wiry man, scarcely five feet two inches in height, with narrow hunched shoulders and the face of a pug. He was an expert cracksman, and such safes as this were mere toys which he opened by touch.

He pulled out one of the drawers and chuckled when he saw in the bottom a glittering profusion of gems.

"Let's have the bag, Mike," he whispered.

Mike Tracy, who knelt beside him, drew from his pocket a small leather sack. He was as different from Dan as it was possible for him to be. He was a giant, standing over six feet three inches in height, and was built in proportion. He was of a gentle, almost timid nature, and followed Dan unquestioningly in every exploit that the latter undertook. The two of them had become known in the underworld as the "Twins," and they were much respected, for Dan's brains and Mike's strength made an almost perfect combination.

Dan lifted a diamond necklace from the plush covered bottom of the drawer and let it slip slowly through his fingers so that its many facets cascaded with fire. Then he reluctantly slipped it into the bag which Mike held out and followed it with the other jewels.

"If that tip was right," said Mike in an almost inaudible voice, "Nelson oughta have some real jack here, too."

Dan looked quickly into the other drawers which contained for the most part stocks and bonds. These he left undisturbed, for he knew the difficulty and danger of disposing of them. In the last drawer he found a packet of bills fastened together with tape. He flipped them through his fingers—they were all of large denomination.

Dropping the bills into the bag after the jewels, he took out a handkerchief and carefully wiped every part of the safe that his fingers had touched. He used gloves for most of his work, but in the actual opening of a safe he had to use his bare finger tips.

Suddenly there was the sound of a stair creaking. Instantly Dan snapped off the flashlight and they froze. They drew their automatics and strained every sense to find whether the noise had been a natural one or had been caused by someone descending the stairs.

They stood thus for five minutes. The only sound in the silence was the ticking of the clock.

"False alarm, I guess," grunted Dan finally. "Let's beat it."

He swung the door of the safe shut and put the bag of loot in his pocket.

They had just turned toward the open window through which they had entered when there was a second creaking noise in the hallway just outside the door leading to the library. They whirled about, their automatics in their hands, but the blackness was so intense that they could see nothing.

Several seconds passed and Dan was almost ready to believe that it had only been his imagination, when a voice roared out:

"Hands up!"

There was a click of a wall switch and the lights flashed on.

In the doorway, not six feet from Dan and Mike, stood a heavy-set man of medium height. His left hand was on the wall switch and his right hand held a pistol leveled at them. He had a bath robe thrown over his pajamas and had apparently just risen from his bed. They recognized him at once as Emery Nelson, a wealthy philanthropist and the owner of the house which they were robbing.

Dan's and Mike's automatics spat fire at almost the same instant and the air of the room rocked with the thunder of the detonations. Both bullets struck Nelson full in the chest, and the force of the blow sent him back against the door frame.

His pistol dropped from his nerveless fingers and clattered on the floor while over his face shot a look of surprise and consternation. Then his knees buckled under and his body pitched to the floor.

There was a scream from the upper floor of the house, followed by the sounds of shouts and running feet.

"Beat it, Mike!" exclaimed Dan. He ran across the room and sprang through the window, alighting on his feet on a gravel driveway that ran along the side of the house.

Mike followed him more slowly, for he had difficulty getting his great bulk through the window. Together they hurried down the driveway, skirted the garage, and stepped into the alley.

In the house behind them lights were flashing on in the second story and a woman screamed hysterically for the police.

They ran the length of the alley, treading lightly so that they made as little noise as possible. At the farther end they stopped in the shadow of a building, put their automatics away and straightened their clothes. Then, when they saw that no one was watching, they stepped to the street and sauntered along as though nothing had happened.

A few minutes later they climbed to their room on the third floor of an old rooming house. Dan went to the bathroom and hid the sack containing the money and jewels in a secret hiding place under the floor beneath the bathtub; then he returned to their room.

Mike was seated despondently upon the bed, his face wrinkled with worry.

"That's the first time I ever knocked off a guy, Dan," he said.

"Aw, forget it," replied Dan. "It won't be your last one." He dropped into a chair and tipped it back against the wall.

"But what if the dicks get us? They'll send us to the chair."

"Don't let that work on yuh. They're not going to find us."

"But we mighta left some clues."

"Not on this job. We didn't leave any finger prints or nothin'. They haven't got any way of tracin' us. Nelson's croaked and can't identify us, and no one else saw us. We got off this job clean, I tell yuh. The cops won't know where to look."

"Are yuh sure of that?" Mike looked up pleadingly.

"Hell yes! What's eatin' yuh, Mike—yuh lost your nerve?" He brought his chair down with a jerk and looked searchingly at him. "What you need is a good drink."

He took a bottle of whiskey from a dresser drawer and poured out half a tumbler full for him. Mike downed it with one gulp and mechanically lit the cigarette that Dan offered him.

"Why, say," continued Dan, warming up to his subject. "They ain't got a chance in the world of findin' us. The only way they ever could would be if we shot off our mouth and some rat got an earful an' squawked on us. But we're safe there.

"We'll beat it outta town in a coupla days and keep our traps shut. How could they get us anyway? All they know is that some guys cracked the safe and shot Nelson. They ain't got finger prints or nothin'. Only two bullets. An' no one saw us."

"Mebbe," replied Mike laconically.

"We're in real luck. We're sittin' pretty now. There's twenty grand in cold cash there, and we oughta get twenty more on the stones."

Dan poured out a drink for himself. The more he thought of the night's work, the more elated he became.

They had been in the room for about two hours when there was a sudden rapping on the door. Mike jumped to his feet, terror written on his face.

"Who's there?" called Dan.

"Sergeant Lewis. I want to talk to you boys for a minute."

"My God!" groaned Mike. "They found something."

"Shut up!" snapped Dan. "Don't be a sap. They haven't got anything on us. It's probably about something else."

He unlocked the door and an officer entered the room. He planted solid feet in the doorway, put his hands on his hips and looked at them sinisterly.

"Well, well. How's the Twins? Haven't seen you boys for quite a while."

Dan met the other's gaze boldly, but Mike's eyes fell.

"Well?" said Dan, finally breaking the silence.

"I guess you know why I'm here, boys," said Sergeant Lewis.

Dan gulped, then found his voice.

"What d' yuh mean? We haven't been doin' anything."

"No, I guess not." Sergeant Lewis's lips tightened into a grim smile. "You only bumped off Emery Nelson and walked off with about forty grand. That's all."

Dan's heart gave a bound at the mention of Emery Nelson. Had there been some leak of which he had not thought? It seemed impossible, but here was the police. His throat was suddenly dry and he felt the cold sweat on his forehead. He thought desperately of escape, and glanced at the window out of the corner of his eye.

"I don't know what you're talkin' about," he mumbled, moistening his lips with his tongue.

"Maybe so. But I'll just take you two birds along to the station." Sergeant Lewis started forward.

At that moment panic seized Dan.

He suddenly whipped out his automatic and pressed the trigger. But Sergeant Lewis had his revolver out just a second sooner. The guns roared almost simultaneously, but the bullet from Sergeant Lewis' gun struck Dan's hand so that his gun was knocked aside and the bullet thudded harmlessly in the wall. The blood spurted from his hand and he dropped the automatic with a cry.

Almost instantly Mike shook off the lethargy that had been holding him and leaped on Sergeant Lewis from the side. One blow knocked the revolver from his hand and sent him staggering against the wall. Mike closed in on him, battering at him with blows of terrific force. He was fully six inches taller than the policeman, and for a moment there seemed to be no doubt of the outcome.

Dan hopped to a corner of the room, holding his shattered right hand in his left, and screaming advice to Mike. He held himself ready to kick Sergeant Lewis in a vital spot if the opportunity presented itself.

The two men blundered against a table and sent it rolling to the corner of the room, the glasses and bottles on it falling to the floor with a crash.

Mike's apparent advantage quickly disappeared. Sergeant Lewis had been a professional boxer before joining the police force, and he was fully able to give and take blows, even from an opponent of superior height and weight. He kept Mike at arm's length, knowing that if those huge arms got around him, they could crush his chest like an egg shell.

Mike left himself almost entirely open, depending rather upon the force of his blows than skill to carry him to victory. Sergeant Lewis suddenly sent a rain of blows against his unprotected chin, and then finished with two quick jabs to the solar plexus. Mike gasped and sank to the floor, groaning convulsively.

Sergeant Lewis relieved him of his gun and snapped handcuffs on his wrists. Dan's wound was bleeding badly, so Lewis tore a strip from the sheet and bound it about his hand. Then he picked up Dan's automatic from the floor and put it in his pocket with Mike's gun.

"These'll be enough to send you birds to the chair, all right," he commented grimly. "We got the two bullets that killed Nelson, and Crosby can tell whether they were fired from these guns. And I guess they were, judging by the squawk you made."

"I thought yuh said we got off clean," snarled Mike at Dan.

"Come on now," ordered Sergeant Lewis, jerking Mike to a sitting position. "We'll run along now."

"Listen, sarg," pleaded Dan. "How'd yuh come to pick us up? We didn't leave no clues, did we?"

"Only two bullets."

"Two bullets? How'd yuh know it was us that fired 'em?"

"I told yuh they could trace the bullets," whined Mike.

"Shut up," commanded Dan. "How'd yuh do it, sarg? How'd yuh find out who we were just from two bullets?"

"That was easy. The two of you only stood five or six feet from Nelson when you shot him. You both fired at the same time.

"Now those two bullets hit Nelson's chest not more than two inches apart and on the same level. Well, one of them went slightly downwards through his body, and the other slightly upwards. That meant that one gun was held a little below the level of his chest and the other a little above it. That was certain, because we knew that Nelson hadn't moved between the firing of the two shots— he couldn't have, since they were fired at the same time. D'you get me?"

"Yeah. But what does that get yuh?" Dan's forehead wrinkled as he puzzled over the problem, and the blood dripped unheeded from his hand.

"The rest's simple. The guy that held the rod below the level of Nelson's chest and shot upwards was short—not more than five feet four; and the guy that shot down was tall—at least over six feet. So all I had to do was look for a pair, one short and the other tall. And right away I thought of the Twins, and you birds sure fit. And it's lovely of you being right here and waiting for me to call."

DETECTIVE *and* GANGSTER STORIES

DRAGNET

JANUARY

20¢
25¢ IN CANADA

DEATH PAINTING
by Richard Credicott

The **HIGHWAY** *to* **HELL**
by William H. Stueber

CROSSED CROOKS
by Kennie MacDowd

MACHINE GUNS
by Armitage Trail

Cover painting by Alfred G. Skrenda

DEATH PAINTING

A beautiful woman found hanging in front of her own portrait—strangled to death! A baffling, cold-blooded murder—yet the solution lay in the discovery of some tiny paint stains.

AS DETECTIVE SERGEANT DEWING STARED AT THE DEAD FIGURE before him, his eyes opened wide. Accustomed as he was, in his profession of detective and hunter of criminals on the homicide squad, to seeing murder in all its gruesome forms, he had to admit that this murder was unique in his experience.

He stood in the great arched door of Phillip Marsden's private art gallery, his arms akimbo, his head thrust forward and raised slightly. Behind him Detective Dittmar, a huge bulk of a man with a heavy jowled face and sleepy eyes, peered over his shoulder in open-faced astonishment.

"Wow! Lookit that, sarge!" exploded Dittmar.

"Shut the door, Jake," ordered Dewing, advancing into the room.

Their feet sunk noiselessly into the thick carpet. When Phillip Marsden, the eccentric multi-millionaire, had added this art gallery to his home, he had spared no expense to make it complete. It occupied an entire wing of the house and was two stories in height; on both sides there were high mullioned windows and it was lighted at night with a great chandelier. It was furnished only with an ottoman in the center of the room.

The opposite wall contained a deep-set niche that reached almost from the floor to the ceiling in the shape of an arch. Before it hung two heavy drapes which had been pulled back to reveal the ghastly sight behind them. In the niche hung a large painting, a life-sized, full-length portrait of a beautiful young woman. And hanging before the painting, so as to almost conceal it, was the dead body of the same young woman!

She wore a shimmering silver evening gown, sheer silk stockings and jeweled slippers, while diamonds glistened upon her fingers and a long rope of pearls hung across her breast. But her once beautiful face was blue and contorted with agony. About her neck was looped a wire which was fastened to the top of the niche so that her body swung free of the floor.

"What d'yuh make of this, sarge?" asked Dittmar at last, pinching one of his jowls between his thumb and forefinger.

Dewing walked across the floor to examine the hanging figure more closely. The lithe grace with which he moved bespoke a carefully trained body and great strength. His angular face was youthful—he was not more than thirty, though his rise in the detective bureau had been rapid as a result of his unusually developed powers of observation and his keen analytical ability.

He was well-acquainted with the career of the murdered woman, Mrs. Marsden. As Coleen Derling she had been the favorite of the stage world several years ago. She had finally captured the heart of the multi-millionaire Marsden and had settled down to a married life with him which was far from being staid, for her name was linked with many different men.

Dewing finally abandoned his inspection of the body. "It's a cinch, Jake," he said, "that this wasn't the work of any ordinary crook. Look at the rings she's got on. They must be worth a fortune. And that pearl necklace—they're perfectly matched."

"Yeah, it's goin' to be a tough nut to crack," replied Dittmar lugubriously. "My guess is that some nut did it."

"You may be right. Well, see if Dr. Benson's here yet."

Dittmar lumbered to the door and soon returned with the medical examiner, a small thin man with a perpetually weary air.

"Have you seen Marsden, doc?" asked Dewing.

Dr. Benson scarcely glanced at the hanging figure as he set down his bag. "Yes. And I'd say that he's either insane now or is fast becoming so. Dr. Upton is staying with him."

"Can you take it down?" he asked, after giving the body a cursory examination.

Dewing cut the wire and Dittmar carried the body to the ottoman.

"She died of strangulation," announced Dr. Benson. "Though whether death was caused by the wire about her neck I can't say now."

"You mean that she may have been dead when her body was hung before this picture?"

"It's possible. My reason for thinking so is that the wire does not seem to be drawn particularly tight about her neck. I can tell you definitely when I've made the autopsy."

"It isn't important," said Dewing. "What about the time of death?"

"She's been dead approximately two hours."

Dewing took out his watch. "That'd make the time of her death around eight o'clock," he said. "It's just a few minutes after ten now. Well, if your men are here the body can be removed, doc."

When the body had been removed, Dr. Benson left to take care of Marsden so that Dr. Upton would be free to talk to Dewing. Dr. Upton appeared in the door of the art gallery, walking with a firm tread. He was a tall, grey-haired man with a heavily-lined, kindly face.

Dewing motioned him to the ottoman. "How is Mr. Marsden, Dr. Upton?"

Dr. Upton shook his head sadly. "This ghastly affair was too much for him. He's temporarily out of his head. I hope that you are not intending to try to question him."

"We may not have to trouble him," said Dewing. "As I understand it, you were present when Mrs. Marsden's body was discovered, and I'm hoping that you will be able to give us all the information that we'll need."

"I'll do my best, Sergeant Dewing. What did you want to know?"

"First tell me how you happened to find the body."

Dr. Upton stroked his chin with long nervous fingers as he concentrated upon his narrative. "I had made a tentative appointment with Marsden for this evening to discuss a matter of business. Several things came up which delayed me, so I didn't get over before nine thirty. As soon as we had concluded the business, Marsden—"

"What was the business?" interrupted Dewing.

"Marsden was purchasing one of my paintings for his gallery—'The Sleeping Boy' by Rembrandt. When we had completed the arrangements, he insisted that I see Van Iperen's new painting of Mrs. Marsden."

"Van Iperen?"

"Yes. You've heard of him, I suppose. He's a Belgian and one of the best known artists on the continent. Marsden engaged him to come to America solely to paint Mrs. Marsden. The picture, he said, had been finished but a few days ago and had just been mounted."

"Go on."

"Marsden and I came into this room to see the picture. He was very much excited, and repeated several times that I would be amazed at the beauty of it. When he pulled the drapes back and I saw Mrs. Marsden's body hanging there, I was paralyzed for a few minutes. As soon as I regained control of myself, I made a swift examination, but I saw that it was too late. She had been dead for at least an hour." Dewing glanced at the niche in the wall thoughtfully. "How did Marsden take it?" he asked. "What were his reactions?"

Dr. Upton frowned and seemed reluctant to answer. "Really," he answered evasively, "I was so much shocked myself that I scarcely noticed."

Dewing let the point pass. "Now, Dr. Upton, I'd like to ask a few more questions. This is coldblooded murder of the most horrible kind. It isn't ordinary murder at all. The most probable motive that could lie behind it is revenge; but not revenge so much on Mrs. Marsden. If someone had wanted to kill her, they would have killed her in the easiest and most effective way. They didn't, so we will assume that the motive was to get revenge upon Mr. Marsden. And they did it in the most terrible way—they killed his wife and hung her body before her newly completed picture where they knew that Mr. Marsden was likely to happen upon it by accident. Do you follow me?"

Dr. Upton puckered his eyes and nodded. "I think so," he said. "You mean that the murderer, or murderers, wanted to play an ironic joke upon Marsden. It's reasonable."

"You knew Mr. and Mrs. Marsden quite intimately, didn't you?"

"I know Marsden fairly well, having lived beside him for fifteen years. I have attended Mrs. Marsden professionally, but never became friendly with her, and I know no more about her than the ordinary gossip."

"Do you know of any enemies of Mr. Marsden who would be capable of doing such a thing?"

Dr. Upton spread out his hands in a hopeless gesture. "Enemies? Of course he had enemies. A man of his wealth and disposition has hundreds of enemies. But I couldn't point out a single one of them and honestly say that I suspected him."

Dewing probed him farther, but could not overcome the other's reticence. "Have you any theory at all, Dr. Upton?" he asked finally.

"I'm afraid not."

Dewing raised his eyes at the doubtful tone in the other's voice. "Now I'm going to be frank with you," he said. "I believe that we both have the same thought. When I said that the motive of this crime was revenge, I was wrong. There is another possible motive which I did not want to mention then. And that is—madness!"

Dr. Upton scratched his chin reflectively. "You've hit what I had in mind exactly, Sergeant Dewing," he replied. "I didn't want to advance such a theory myself, but it had occurred to me and I was inclined to accept it. Marsden's reactions were deucedly strange—you heard him for a minute when you arrived. The truth is that he wasn't normal before he looked at the picture. He was almost insanely insistent that I see it, and, as I said before, he assured me that I was going to be very much surprised."

"I hold the theory only as a possibility," said Dewing. "But it's logical.

Here are the grounds for such a theory. Mrs. Marsden was by no means a—er—conventional woman, and if what I have heard is true, she gave Mr. Marsden plenty of cause for jealousy. He was of a jealous temperament, was he not?"

"Extremely so."

"Then isn't it possible that his jealousy may have grown so great that he would kill his wife rather than let another man have her? It has been done before. Particularly is this possible if he were unbalanced."

"It's fantastic, sergeant, but no more fantastic than the crime itself."

"Well, we'll see Mr. Marsden now," said Dewing. "He may be in a saner frame of mind."

When they approached the library in which Dr. Benson was keeping Marsden, they heard peal after peal of laughter.

"The man's mad!" exclaimed Dr. Benson, coming out of the library to meet them. "Stark, raving mad."

Marsden was a short fat man with an almost round head nearly devoid of hair. His face was flabby and his tiny eyes had lost their focus and seemed to be protruding from their sockets. When he saw them he jumped up and began to shout. "She's dead, I tell you, she's dead!" he cried. "No one will ever have her now!"

Dewing gave up any idea of questioning him. Dr. Benson and Dr. Upton conferred together for a moment and decided to have him taken to the psychopathic ward for the night.

During the conference Marsden had remained silent. Perhaps he heard the doctors' decisions, for he suddenly sprang to the library table and tore open a drawer. Steel glinted in his hand as he raised a revolver to his head.

Like a flash Dewing sprang at him. There was a roar as the revolver discharged, but he had reached the other's wrists and turned them upwards so that the bullet buried itself harmlessly in the ceiling.

Dewing tried to wrest the revolver from him, but Marsden had the strength of a madman. Abruptly he released his hold upon the wrist and grasped his fingers. A quick twist, a jerk, and Marsden was prone upon the floor with Dewing straddling his back. The revolver dropped from his fingers as his arms were twisted behind him.

Dittmar came to life and snapped a pair of handcuffs on the man and lifted him to his feet. Dr. Benson promptly took charge of him and hurried him away.

"I'm afraid that that proves Marsden's guilt beyond a shadow of a doubt," sighed Dr. Upton. "Alternate fits of triumph, then profound dejection over her death."

"It looks that way," acceded Dewing.

He sent Dittmar to look over Mr. and Mrs. Marsden's private letters and possessions and set himself the task of questioning the servants. They all agreed that the relations between Marsden and his wife had been very bad. Their knowledge of the movements of the two for that evening was very meager. One of the maids had helped Mrs. Marsden dress at seven thirty and had seen her go to the garden for a walk, as was her custom. The butler had seen Mr. Marsden disappear into the library at seven o'clock, but did not know whether he had stayed there or not. He had not seen him again until Dr. Upton called at nine thirty.

Dewing gave the grounds a superficial examination and found in a tool shed the ladder which had probably been used to hang Mrs. Marsden's body before the picture. The chauffeur had been in his rooms over the garage all evening waiting for Mrs. Marsden to call for the car, and had seen no one near the tool shed.

When Dewing returned to the house he found Dittmar waiting with a sheaf of letters in his hand.

"I've sure got the dope on Mrs. Marsden," he crowed. "Wanta look them over, sarge?"

"Not now. Just give me the gist of it, Jake."

"Well, she had one bad affair with Victor Thomas. There's a couple of letters here from him. He says he's gonna bump himself off if she don't run off with him."

"That so?" said Dewing. "Let's hear some more about him."

"I don't think you need to consider him, sergeant," interrupted Dr. Upton. "I happen to know that he's in South America now. But what's your interest in these men? Do you think that any of them might be involved? I thought that you had come to the conclusion that Marsden was guilty."

"He's guilty, all right, I guess," answered Dewing. "But you never can tell. We have to examine every phase of a murder before we adopt any particular theory. Go on, Jake."

Dittmar thumbed through the letters. "There's some here from John Nelson."

"John Nelson? Don't bother about him. He died several months ago."

"Then there's half a dozen from Karl Gustin."

"He's the painter, isn't he?" asked Dewing of no one in particular.

"He is," put in Dr. Upton. "But I hardly think he could be involved. He spent most of the evening with me. I'm having my living room redecorated and he's going to furnish the murals."

"He was with you at eight o'clock?"

"He was with me from seven o'clock to eight thirty."

"That lets him out then. Don't bother about the rest, Jake. We aren't getting anywhere. Take them along with you and look them over. If any of them look promising, you can turn them over to me. I think that we're through here now. C'mon, Jake, let's beat it."

The next morning Dr. Benson sent his report on the autopsy to Dewing. Mrs. Marsden had died by strangulation previous to being hung before the picture.

"A lot of good that does us," growled Dewing, throwing the report upon his desk.

Detective Dittmar was ensconced in a swivel chair with his feet cocked up on a desk and his small eyes in his fat face closed tightly. He yawned deeply, stretched his arms and blinked several times.

"An' with Marsden crazy as a loon," he commented. "I dropped in at the psychopathic ward this mornin' an' they was just gettin' ready to take him to the Central Hospital. He was clear outta his head."

"Say anything about killing his wife?"

"Naw. All he said was that there wasn't nobody that was goin' to have his wife now. I tried to pump him, but he didn't know anything, an' the docs cut me off quick."

"I'm not settled in my mind yet that he's the one that did it. C'mon, big boy. Stir yourself. We'll run over to Marsden's place and look it over."

Dewing saw nothing in the grounds about the Marsden residence that he had not observed the previous night. They searched the art gallery again, but it offered no clues. They found that if the murder had been committed in the garden it would have been easy to attain access to the gallery by means of a side passage.

They were wandering through the garden when Dewing suddenly grasped Dittmar's arm.

"Just a minute, Jake, before you set your feet down, look at those marks on the cinders."

Just ahead of them the smooth rolled surface of the cinder path had been disturbed.

"Looks kinda like somebody mighta been roughin' it up," admitted Dittmar.

"It sure does. Let's look around a little."

They crouched down and carefully examined the cinders and the surrounding grass. Then Dewing gave a triumphant cry and held up a small gold disk. There was a tiny hole pierced through the edge of it from which hung several links of a gold chain.

"It's an art prize," he explained. "Mm-m. There's some initials and a date on the back. 'K.G. 1921.' Now, Jake, how do you suppose that got here?"

"Looks like there'd been some kind of struggle an' one of the guys dropped that." His sleepy eyes brightened suddenly. "Say, sarge, mebbe that's the guy that croaked Mrs. Marsden. She was walkin' in the garden, you know. He killed her here an' then took her in the art gallery an' strung 'er up."

"Exactly what I was thinking. And what do the initials 'K.G.' suggest to you? Karl Gustin, of course. He's an artist and he'd be likely to have something like this."

"Yeah. But he was at Dr. Upton's then," objected Dittmar.

"Well, it's not very far over here, is it? Not more than a couple of hundred feet. He might have slipped away without Dr. Upton's noticing it. C'mon; we'll run over to Upton's."

The butler ushered them at once into Dr. Upton's office.

"Good morning, Dr. Upton," said Dewing. "I hardly expected to find you in at this time, but I took the chance. I supposed that you would be at your office."

"I'm always at home now," replied Dr. Upton genially. "I retired from regular practice quite a number of years ago, though the habit's so strong with me that I still keep my office here for anyone who cares to see me. Well, I suppose you want to see me about Marsden. You've probably heard that I had him transferred to the Central Hospital. I'm afraid that the poor fellow is completely insane. As soon as possible I'll have him committed to a private sanitarium that I'm connected with where they may be able to do something for him. I don't suppose that under the circumstances he'll be prosecuted, will he?"

"Probably not," replied Dewing. "But it wasn't that that I called to see you about. I wanted to ask you about Karl Gustin."

"Gustin?" Dr. Upton elevated his eyebrows in surprise. "What about him?"

"You said that he was with you from seven until eight thirty last night. Are you quite certain that he was with you all that time?"

"Yes. He was here. Why do you ask?"

Dewing opened his hand and displayed the gold piece that he had found. "Do you recognize this?" he asked.

Dr. Upton examined it closely, but said nothing.

"You see the initials upon the back?" continued Dewing. " 'K.G.' Who could this have belonged to but Karl Gustin? I found it on a cinder path in Marsden's grounds. The cinders there had been scuffed up as though there had been a struggle. Now Mrs. Marsden was last seen alive last night in the garden. If Gustin could have slipped away without your knowing it, he could easily have overpowered Mrs. Marsden, hung her body before the picture and returned to your home in a few minutes."

"Why—why I'm almost certain that he was here all the time," stammered Dr. Upton.

"Almost certain—what do you mean?"

Dr. Upton frowned. "When I said that he was here, I didn't mean to imply that I was with him all during that time. As a matter of fact a patient interrupted me once and I left him for a few minutes."

"How many minutes?"

"I really don't know. I hadn't thought of it before. It seemed absurd to me to think—just a minute. I have the patient's card here. I may be able to recall from that." He rose and took a card from a filing case. "Let's see. It was Arthur Ranson, an old patient of mine. I had an appointment with him, but had quite forgotten it until he arrived. I was with him about half an hour."

"At what time?"

"From about fifteen minutes to eight until twenty minutes after."

He tossed the card upon the table. Dewing glanced at it. At the top was the patient's name and there was one brief line of writing.

"Then you don't actually know where Gustin was during that half hour," persisted Dewing. "He could have slipped out of the house and back again without your knowing it?"

"If it comes to that—I expect so," confessed Dr. Upton a little angrily. "But it's absurd to suspect him. When I left him he was working on some drawings and on my return they seemed much nearer completion."

Dewing rose to his feet. "Well, you've told me what I wanted to know," he said. "It looks bad for Gustin. He'll have a lot of explaining to do. C'mon, Jake, we'll run up to headquarters for a minute and then see what Gustin has to say. Thanks very much, Dr. Upton."

After a brief stop at police headquarters, they sped to one of the older sections in the city, frequented mostly by artists and writers. When they got out of the car, a patrolman approached them from the door.

"You cert'nly got here quick, Sergeant Dewing," he said. "It's hardly two minutes since I phoned headquarters."

Dewing stared at him. "What do you mean?" he rapped out.

The patrolman gaped at him. "Why you come on the suicide, didn't you?" he asked.

"Suicide? What suicide?"

"Mr. Gustin's."

"He's dead?" The news was so startling that Dewing could not grasp it for a moment.

Just then a car drew up behind the police car and Dr. Upton got out.

"Hello, Sergeant Dewing," he greeted them. "I thought that I'd run over and see Gustin with you if you don't mind. I'm absolutely certain that he had nothing to do with Mrs. Marsden's death, and I'd like to be on hand to see him prove it. Since he was with me at the time of her death I feel rather responsible."

"He's dead," said Dewing. "He just committed suicide."

He sprang up the stairs closely followed by Dr. Upton, Dittmar and the patrolman. They burst into Gustin's apartment, which was little more than a large studio furnished with a few chairs, a desk and a cot.

In the center of the floor lay a man upon his back. He wore dirty unpressed clothes and a paint-stained smock. There was a bullet hole in the center of his forehead and in his right hand he held a revolver.

Dr. Upton made a swift examination of the body. "He's been dead only a few minutes," he announced. "He fired the bullet directly against his forehead and died instantly."

"When did this happen?" Dewing demanded of the patrolman.

"Not more'n three or four minutes ago. I was walkin' by on the other side of the street when I heard the shot. I could tell by the sound where it come from, so I came right up. Nobody answered, so I walked in an' found him like this."

Dewing walked about the studio thinking deeply. So they had run the murderer down at last. Gustin's suicide was an almost certain confession of his guilt.

He looked at some of the paintings that hung upon the walls. They showed decided evidence of genius. From a back window he looked down upon a rickety fire escape that descended to a narrow courtway opening upon an alley. He turned his gaze back into the room.

"I guess we got the right guy this time," said Dittmar, emerging from a corner with a waste basket in hand. "Look what I found." He took several torn pieces of paper, spread them flat upon the desk and arranged them so that they formed a single sheet of paper.

It was evidently the beginning of a letter which had been started, then torn to pieces and thrown into the waste basket. Dewing read:

"Dear Coleen, I cannot endure this agony any longer. You loved me once. Now you do not even let me paint you, but go to Van Iperen, who can never hope to portray your real beauty, for he does not love you as I do. My hate for your husband is growing so great that I do not know whether I can control it. I would rather have you dead than continue as we are—"

"You see, sarge," went on Dittmar, "Gustin was the bird that bumped off Mrs. Marsden. Marsden was a false alarm. He just went nutty outta grief. Mebbe Gustin found out that we were onto him an' decided to bump himself off before we got here."

"I guess you're right, Jake," admitted Dewing.

"It doesn't seem possible," cried Dr. Upton. "I could have sworn that Gustin remained in my house from seven until eight thirty. If this is true—and I can hardly believe it yet—I owe you an apology, Sergeant Dewing, for trying to lead you off the track."

"We all make mistakes," replied Dewing dryly.

He noticed a square of canvas lying face up upon the floor. It was a half finished portrait of Mrs. Marsden, and the paint was still wet as though Gustin had been working on it shortly before he committed suicide. He picked it up and looked at it closely. It was a beautifully done likeness of Mrs. Marsden, but the vivid colors of one eye and the nose had been smudged as though some one had brushed against it. He set the picture upon an easel, wondering how it happened to be upon the floor, for the rest of the studio was in perfect order.

"C'mon, Jake," he said suddenly. "We'll move the body over on the couch."

There he examined every inch of the man's clothing, but found nothing more interesting than dried paint and grease spots. Dewing considered the problem. Then, as he looked about the room, his eyes suddenly narrowed.

"I've changed my mind," he announced abruptly. "Gustin didn't commit suicide—he was murdered!"

There was a chorus of exclamations.

"What d'yuh mean, sarge?" asked Dittmar. "Why there ain't no question about it. Wasn't he found with the revolver in his hand right after the shot?"

"But that revolver was put there by the murderer after he had killed Gustin. And the murderer was—*you*, Dr. Upton!"

Dr. Upton whirled about. His face worked angrily. "What do you mean, Sergeant Dewing?" he demanded. "Are you mad?"

"I repeat that you murdered Gustin, Dr. Upton," said Dewing grimly. "You and Gustin together killed Mrs. Marsden and when you learned that we were on his trail you were afraid that he would betray you.

"I can't prove that you helped Gustin murder Mrs. Marsden, but I can prove that you murdered Gustin. I'll tell you first how you did it. When I told you that we were going to question Gustin, you knew that you were lost. Then I mentioned that we were going to headquarters first, and you figured that that would just give you time to kill Gustin and escape before we got there. With Gustin dead your secret would be safe.

"You left your car somewhere near here and came up to this studio the back way by the fire escape. You found him working on a picture. You took this revolver, held it against his forehead and fired it; then put it in his hand to make it look like suicide. You went out the back way again, got into your car, and arrived here just a moment after we did. I suppose that in coming back here you thought you would kill any possible suspicion that we might have against you."

Dr. Upton's face was white. "You're insane," he croaked. "Where's your proof of this fairy tale?"

"Here's the proof—and it'll be enough to convict you. Gustin was working on a painting when you came in—there it is." Dewing pointed to the painting which he had found on the floor and had put upon the easel. "After you shot Gustin you stepped back and knocked that painting off the easel. When I found it on the floor I noticed that the paint on the eye and the nose had been partly rubbed off. I examined Gustin's clothes, but there wasn't a sign of fresh paint on them. I figured that that paint had to be somewhere, and I found it. Look!"

He caught Dr. Upton's arm and whirled him about. Dittmar and the patrolman could see on the back of his left shoulder a smudge of paint, the exact pattern of the paint that had been rubbed from the portrait! It was faint, but it was easily discernible.

Dr. Upton lost all of his calm. He stood trembling, his face drained of all its color, looking like a caged animal.

There were footsteps in the hall. Dittmar went to the door and talked a moment with an old woman, then turned and spoke to Dewing.

"Here's a woman, sarge, that says she saw a guy leave this room right after the shot."

The woman broke in before Dewing could say a word. "They're a saying that poor Mr. Gustin shot himself, but he didn't. I was upstairs when I heard the shot—I live right next door—and I looked out the window wondering what on earth had happened. Then I saw a man come out of Mr. Gustin's room and run down the fire escape."

"What did he look like?" asked Dewing. "Like this man?" He pointed to Dr. Upton.

The woman surveyed him with doubtful eyes. "I couldn't rightly say," she said. "I didn't see his face. It might be him. What I did see was a big spot of paint on his shoulder. Don't you believe that poor Mr. Gustin killed himself. He was—" She broke off and screamed abruptly.

Dr. Upton had suddenly torn a revolver from his pocket and thrust it against Dewing's back.

"Put up your hands!" he barked. "Every one of you or I'll kill you."

Four pairs of hands were quickly raised.

"Yes, I killed Gustin," roared Dr. Upton. "But what are you going to do about it? I helped Gustin kill Mrs. Marsden also. I wanted to revenge myself upon Marsden. I trusted him and gave him my fortune to invest. He cleaned me out by crooked work. And why? So that he could force me to sell my painting, Rembrandt's 'Sleeping Boy,' to him. I sold him the painting and got his money for it, but I got my revenge when he found his wife's dead body."

He glared at the four of them, but they made no answer. Dewing looked obliquely at Dittmar, who stood at the other side of the room, and nodded slightly.

"Upton!" roared Dittmar suddenly.

Startled, Dr. Upton glanced over at Dittmar without, however, removing his revolver from Dewing's back. To have Dr. Upton's attention distracted for just a fraction of an instant was all that Dewing wanted.

His body whirled about, pivoting upon his right foot, pushing the revolver to one side. His left hand swung down in an arc, clamped over the revolver and twisted it away from him.

A shot rang out, but it ploughed into the wall. A jerk and the revolver fell from Dr. Upton's fingers and clattered upon the floor. With a stride Dittmar crossed the room and pinned Dr. Upton's arms to his side. Dewing ran his hands over his clothes to see that he had no more concealed weapons, before releasing him.

"Tried to pull a fast one, didn't you?" jeered Dittmar, picking the fallen revolver from the floor and pocketing it.

Dr. Upton dropped heavily into a chair, all the fight suddenly gone from his face. "You've got me," he muttered. "I give up."

"You had a clever scheme," said Dewing reminiscently. "But you made two errors. You took out your patient's card when I asked exactly what time you examined a patient last night. You said that Arthur Ranson was an old patient, but there was only one entry on the card, which meant that you had had only one consultation with him. I wondered about it at the time. That card was only a fabrication on your part, wasn't it?"

"You're correct," replied Dr. Upton, smiling crookedly. "I made it out so that I would have an alibi."

"Well, that point remained in the back of my mind. Then when I found Gustin dead just before we got here, I thought that it was a strange coincidence. The first thought that flashed into my mind was that you had warned him by phone, still thinking him innocent. But when I found the smudge on the painting, and no trace of fresh paint on Gustin's clothes, I became suspicious. So I looked at you and found the corresponding smudge. Now tell me—why did you pick such a peculiar form of murder?"

"That was Gustin's idea. He proposed it to me when he learned that I was planning to kill Marsden. He wanted her death to be an ironic joke, and it suited my purposes. He was madly jealous of Van Iperen's portrait of Mrs. Marsden. He was—" He fell back in the chair, deathly pale.

The shrill siren of the patrol wagon drawing up in front of the house burst upon their ears.

"It was a slick scheme, all right," commented Dewing. "Well, here's the wagon. We might as well be going."

"Too late," said Dr. Upton weakly.

Something in his voice caused Dewing to whirl about and stare at him. "What's the matter?" he cried, alarmed at the expression of agony on the doctor's face.

A shudder ran over Dr. Upton's frame. "Poison," he whispered faintly. "You didn't think to search me for the weapon a doctor knows best. I took it when you thought I was wiping my mouth with my handkerchief."

"Quick! Get a doctor!" Dewing shouted at Dittmar.

"It's too late," said Dr. Upton. "I'll be dead in—in—"

With that his body crumpled and slid silently to the floor.

MURDER BEHIND MURDER

*A shake-up faced the Detective Bureau if they failed to bring
in the Hatchet Killer.*

DETECTIVE LIEUTENANT DAVIES SLAMMED THE TELEPHONE RECEIVER down upon the hook and gave vent to explosive curses.

"Sergeant Blake!" he roared.

At the sound of his voice the heads of the detectives in the adjoining room swung around sharply as though they were on pivots. One of them dropped a cigarette and leaped to his feet. He was young and powerfully-built; he looked intelligent, though he was far from being handsome, for early in his beat-pounding days his nose had been smashed, and there was an ugly bullet scar across his cheek. Sergeant Blake looked tough and he was tough. Nevertheless, his brawn had come to some kind of compromise with his brains, and Lieutenant Davies counted him one of the best men upon the homicide detail.

"Come in an' shut the door," snapped the lieutenant.

Blake followed him into the office and shut the door softly. He saw that his superior was boiling with anger, and at such times it was well to step quietly.

"And now—what in blazes have you birds been doing about the Hatchet Killer?" demanded Lieutenant Davies.

"Why, everything possible, sir," answered Blake evenly. "All we can do is wait for a break."

"Waiting for a break!" Lieutenant Davies snatched a newspaper from a pile on his desk and waved it in Blake's face. "Lookit this! See what they're saying while you're waiting around? They've got this damn Hatchet Killer spread all over their dirty sheet."

Blake stood rigidly at attention, but the veins stood out on his angular forehead and the bullet scar flamed red. "But what can we do, lieutenant?" he protested. "This Hatchet Killer isn't any common crook; he's a nut. Why would any ordinary crook want to go around choppin' up women just for a little two-bit jewelry when he could just as well stick 'em up?"

Davies waved his hands in eloquent despair. "Hell, man. Supposing the Hatchet Killer is a nut—that don't make no difference. What does make a difference is that he's killed three women and one man. I don't care if he's an ordinary crook or not. We've *got* to get him."

"But how 're we gonna lay our hands on him? We don't know what he looks like. John Leidler musta got a good look at him when he killed this Wagner girl, but the Killer got him cold. The only other guy that's got a look at him was so far away he couldn't describe him except to say he looked like a motorcycle cop. For all we know he might be a cop."

Lieutenant Davies smashed the newspaper which he still held down upon his desk in disgust. He started to speak and then stopped.

"We're doin' everything we can," continued Blake doggedly. "But what 're we gonna do? We can't search the whole city for him. Even if we did, we wouldn't know him when we got him. We've got men patrollin' Riverside Park where he killed the three women and the fellow. They're there night an' day, an' they stop everybody that looks suspicious an' search 'em. If this Hatchet Killer tries to pull off any more stuff he won't have a chance—"

"Yaah!" sneered Davies. "He won't have a chance, eh? Why you poor prune, he just pulled another job."

"What the hell!" gasped Blake. "In the park?"

"No, about five hundred feet south of it. He got in the Cochrane place last night and killed Arthur Cochrane in his library. Chopped his head all up with a hatchet. They didn't find him until this morning, though, and I just now got word of it."

Blake whispered a fervent curse to himself. He knew what this would mean. The Hatchet Killer had sought his former victims in Riverside Park, but if he now began to enter homes at random and kill their occupants, it would create a reign of terror. Not only that, but Arthur Cochrane was wealthy and socially prominent, and the uproar over his death would be so much the greater. If the press and the public had been frantic before, they would now be hysterical.

Lieutenant Davies's face softened and lost its harshness. He dropped his hand upon Blake's shoulder and said:

"Now listen, boy. I'm putting you on this case, too. I'm depending on you to do the best you can. I know you can't do the impossible, of course.

But—damn it! When I think of this mess I get so mad I don't know what I'm doing, and I fly off the handle."

"I'll do all I can," promised Blake.

"And another thing. The commish was around to see me an' the chief last night. He don't blame us, but he says that we've either got to get this Hatchet Killer or there's gonna be a shake-up in the department. And that means you an' me an' everybody else. You may find yourself back in harness before long. Now get going, lad."

A motorcycle officer standing at the door of the Cochrane mansion took Blake and his assistant Charlie Allen inside to the library. There they found Dr. Leary, the assistant medical examiner, waiting for them. Blake examined Arthur Cochrane's body, which lay back in a Cogswell chair, an open newspaper across the knees. He was a small, slight man well over fifty years of age. His head had been cut repeatedly by slashing blows which ran from the upper left to the lower right. The blood had run down across the face from the cuts so as to make it almost unrecognizable.

Blake stared at it stolidly for a few moments, then turned to the medical examiner and asked: "Well, what's the dope, doc?"

"He died about midnight," answered Dr. Leary. "Death was probably instantaneous, for the body shows no sign of struggle. There are seven cuts upon the head, only three of which penetrated all the way through the skull."

"It was done with a hatchet, wasn't it?"

"I should judge so. The instrument had a straight, sharp edge three inches in width."

"You say it was sharp an' it only cut through the skull three times? You wouldn't have to hit very hard with a sharp hatchet to go through the skull, would you?"

"In my opinion, none of the blows were struck with any great force."

Blake picked up the newspaper which lay across Arthur Cochrane's knees. A pipe lay between this man's legs. The tobacco in the bowl had been half smoked, and there was a sprinkling of ashes across the trousers.

"It looks to me," Blake muttered to Allen, "like he was smokin' his pipe an' readin' the newspaper when the Hatchet Killer come in. When he saw him, the pipe fell outta his mouth or his fingers an' he dropped the newspaper across his knees. Then the Killer got him before he could move."

He turned his attention to the room itself. Although it was a library, there were bookshelves only on the inside wall. The other three walls were composed of large casement windows, one of which stood open.

"The Hatchet Killer came in the window," said the motorcycle officer, noting the direction of his gaze. "The lock's broken an' yuh c'n see footprints outside."

Blake leaned out of the window and examined it. There were marks where a tool, evidently a chisel, had been inserted to force it open. He looked down at the flowerbeds five feet below the sill of the window. It had rained the evening before, so that the cultivated earth of the beds was almost muddy. Clearly defined in the soft earth was a double set of footprints—one approaching the window and the other receding.

Blake gazed at the footprints thoughtfully, then turned his attention to the rug upon which he was standing. Apparently he did not find what he was looking for, for he dropped to his knees and examined the rug more closely. Allen regarded him with a puzzled frown.

"That's funny," Blake said at last, standing up. "If the Hatchet Killer got in the window, his feet shoulda been muddy, an' there isn't a sign of mud on the rug." He scratched his bony chin reflectively. "Oh, well, let's not git to thinkin' any quicker 'n we have to." He grinned and turned to the motorcycle officer. "Who found the body?"

"Mr. Cochrane's brother, Norman Cochrane. He's waitin' in the next room if yuh wanta see him."

Norman Cochrane proved to be an even smaller man than his brother. In appearance he might almost have been his twin. He was pacing nervously about the drawing-room, his face haggard, when Blake entered.

"This is horrible, Sergeant Blake," he groaned after Blake had introduced himself. "I can hardly bring myself to believe that it isn't all a nightmare. And to think that my brother was lying dead in the library all night and we didn't know it."

Blake paid little attention to the man's grief. "You found the body, didn't you?" he asked.

Norman Cochrane shuddered, as though to rid himself of the frightful memory. "Yes. I—I found it. When I came down this morning breakfast wasn't ready, so I stepped into the library intending to get a magazine. Then I saw him and—I hardly recognized him at first—" His voice trailed off into silence.

"You didn't touch the body, did you? I mean you didn't move the newspaper that was across his knees, did you?"

Norman Cochrane shook his head. "I left the room at once and ran to call the policeman on the corner. I didn't go back into the room. I could see that he was dead."

"I see. Did you hear anything last night?"

"No. I went to bed early and fell asleep at once."

"Who else was in the house? Any relatives or servants?"

"I was Arthur's only relative. The cook and the butler sleep in the back of the house, and the chauffeur has a room over the garage. But they didn't hear anything—I've already asked them."

Norman Cochrane put his hands before his face as though trying to shut out the horrible picture of his dead brother. He pressed the backs of his hands against his eyes. Then he took his hands down and Blake saw that tears trembled in his eyes.

"You must catch this Hatchet Killer, sergeant," he pleaded. "If—if it will help any if I offer a reward, I'll do it."

"I hardly think that'll be necessary, Mr. Cochrane," said Blake. "We'll get him soon enough. It's only a question of time."

He spoke with an assurance that he was far from feeling. He recalled all the cases of maniacal murderers that he had heard of. Often they had been captured, though sometimes it had not been until after they had committed a dozen or more horrible crimes. Yet in many other cases the insane criminal had never been captured: he had either tired of murder, or his insanity had changed its direction, or the insanity had been temporary and had ultimately disappeared.

Blake questioned the cook and the butler, learned nothing, and then set out with Allen to examine the grounds about the house. They stopped first at the footprints in the flowerbed beneath the library window.

"D' you notice anything funny about these footprints, Charley?" Blake asked.

Allen bent his lank form over and squinted at them. "They look okay to me," he confessed. "Mebbe though the Killer didn't get in this way. It's muddy, all right, and if he come this way he shoulda left some mud on the rug like you said." Suddenly his face brightened, and he added: "Unless mebbe he took off his shoes."

Blake laughed harshly. "That's a hot one, Charley," he sneered. "The Hatchet Killer walks up to the window, breaks it open, climbs up on the window sill, takes off his shoes an' jumps in the room. What d' you think Norman Cochrane was doin' all this time? Think he was blind and deaf? With all that happening, he wouldn't be readin' a newspaper."

Allen's face fell. "It don't sound right," he admitted.

"And another thing. The guy that made these footprints just walked up to the window, broke it open an' walked away. If he climbed in an' out there'd be more of 'em. An' look how high the window is: it's an easy five feet. If he jumped or dropped outta the window, there'd be deeper prints where he landed."

"Yeah, I guess you're right," conceded Allen. "But I don't get the idea."

They were interrupted by a man padding up behind them.

"Say, what're you guys doin' here?" he demanded.

They turned about and saw a tall, heavy-set man with broad stooped shoulders regarding them suspiciously. He wore a smartly pressed uniform, polished leather puttees and a chauffeur's cap pushed back on his low forehead. There was a snarl on his thick lips and his eyes were glinting menacingly.

"What's it to you?" snapped Blake, sticking out his battered face pugnaciously. "If you wanta know, I'm a sergeant of detectives. Now who're you, an' what are you doin' here?"

The man's face instantly lost its belligerency when he heard the word "detective," but it retained all its surliness. "Oh, awright," he said. "My name's Hart. Peter Hart. I'm the chauffeur here."

He stared at them for a moment, then turned and started to walk away.

"Sa-ay. Wait a minute," cried Blake. "What's your hurry? I wanta ask you a few questions."

Peter Hart stopped, half turned around and mumbled something under his breath.

"D' you hear anything last night about midnight?" asked Blake.

"Naw."

"Well, then; did you *see* anything?"

"Naw. I was in bed." When Blake asked him no more questions, he turned without a word and shambled toward the garage in the rear.

Blake looked after the retreating form, his eyes snapping and his lower lip protruding. "Wow, but is he one tough baby," he breathed. "What wouldn't I give for a chance to walk over his map."

He and Allen turned their attention back to an examination of the grounds about the house. When they reached the long low mud bank which led down to the water's edge, Allen gave a cry of astonishment. There was a double row of footprints in the soft earth where a man had evidently walked halfway down the smooth slope of the bank, only to stop and retrace his steps.

"The same guy made these that made the footprints under the window," announced Allen triumphantly. "They're the same size, an' the heels are worn away in the same way."

They walked out to the point at which the prints stopped and Blake squatted on his heels to examine them.

"Yeah. You're right, Charley. It was the same guy," he said. "But there's something funny about them. Look how deep the toe marks are on these two prints. And the left foot is way ahead of the right."

He stood up and placed his feet in the same relative position. He teetered on his toes, frowning. "Why would anybody want to walk halfway down the bank, then turn around an' go back?" he demanded.

"Mebbe it was dark an' he couldn't see where he was goin'," offered Allen.

Suddenly Blake grinned broadly. "I've got it!" he cried. "He threw something in the river. He walked halfway down the bank so he'd be sure to throw it far enough out in the water so nobody'd see it. Yup, that's exactly the way anybody'd stand to throw something."

Allen looked from the prints that Blake had made in assuming the position of throwing, to the prints that they had found. "But what would he wanta throw in the water?" he objected.

"Who knows—mebbe a hatchet." He looked at the river. "If we could drag it here, we'd soon find out."

"It don't look so deep," said Allen. "I don't think it's more 'n two or three feet here. The water's clear enough so that we could see the bottom if we had a boat."

Blake turned and stared at the garage. It was three stories in height, and was set back only a few feet from the water's edge. The first story, or more properly the basement, opened upon the river and had a roller track leading to the water. The second story, or the main floor, opened flush with the driveway and was used for the cars, while the upper floor comprised the living quarters of Peter Hart.

Blake tried the basement door, hoping to be able to get out a boat, but it was securely padlocked. He went around to the front of the garage to see whether Hart had a key to the lock, but the latter was not in evidence. He called to him but received no answer. Feeling sure that Hart must be in his rooms, he pounded upon the door of the stairs that led to his quarters.

After a minute Hart came clumping down the stairs. "What d' yuh want?" he grumbled, glaring at Blake.

"Is there a rowboat here?"

"There's one in the boat-room." Hart stood still, making no motion either to produce a key or to unlock the door for him.

"Well, can you get it out for us?" snapped Blake. "We wanta use it."

Hart mumbled something that Blake could not understand. But he set out around the side of the garage, fumbling in his pocket for a ring of keys. He produced them and thumbed them over as he selected one of them.

As he fitted the key into the padlock, Blake started. Something stirred in the recesses of his memory as he saw Hart hold the key in his left hand to turn it. He observed a gold ring of a peculiar pattern upon the little finger of Hart's left hand, and a strange light came into his eyes.

Hart swung the door open. "Here she is," he said, turning and disappearing around the side of the garage without offering to help them.

Allen stared after Hart. "Well, of all the hard-boiled eggs I ever saw!" he fumed. "Wouldn't even help us get this crate out."

The two of them seized the heavy rowboat and threw their weight against it. It moved slowly until they got it upon the roller track to the water, down which it coasted easily. Blake got in the front of the boat and Allen took the oars, rowing in a circle directly opposite the point at which they had found the footprints on the bank.

Suddenly Blake called: "Stop, Charley. I think I see something."

While Allen held the boat stationary in the slowly moving water, Blake took off his coat and rolled up his right sleeve. He plunged his arm into the shallow water, groping about on the muddy bottom until his fingers encountered a hard object.

He withdrew his arm from the water and held up a new hatchet. The blade was shiny, though the cutting edge was covered with a dark red crust and bits of matted hair. Allen stared at it as though hypnotized.

"This's it, Charley," exulted Blake. "This's the hatchet they used to bump off Arthur Cochrane. It's got a straight sharp edge three inches wide just like Doc Leary said. An' there's blood an' hair on it."

He shook the water from it and wrapped his handkerchief about the blade. "Mebbe there's fingerprints on it. It's been in the water about nine hours, but I guess if there was any prints, they'd still be there."

They went on to search the entire bottom within a range of one hundred feet of the footprints upon the bank, but they found nothing more. Finally they returned to the boathouse and put the boat away.

"And now, Charley," said Blake, "we're gonna search this garage from the top to the bottom."

"What for, sarge?" asked Allen in amazement. "What're you lookin' for?"

"Mebbe another hatchet," answered Blake noncommittally. "I've got a hunch that we might find something, though mebbe I'm just nuts."

They went through the boathouse thoroughly, even emptying a keg of nails to be certain that there was nothing concealed in it, but in the end they had not found what Blake was searching for. When they went around to the front of the garage, Blake glanced up at the windows of Peter Hart's quarters, and he could have sworn that he caught a glimpse of a face peering down at them through the curtains.

They searched the garage as thoroughly as they had the boat-room, moving boxes and tools and poking into chests. Blake tipped back an old box filled with pieces of pipe and gave a cry. He held up a second hatchet!

"Lookit, Charley!" he exclaimed. "Here's the hatchet the Hatchet Killer used."

Allen looked at it in bewilderment, then stared questioningly at Blake. "How'd you know that, sarge?" he asked.

"Look at the blade: it's been wiped off, but you can still see the blood stains. An' look how the edge is nicked. You remember the Wagner case? The Killer missed her once an' hit the park bench. From the cut in the wood I could tell that the Killer's hatchet had a rounded blade with a nick near the end. You saw that cut; I've got it down at headquarters now. Watch."

He lifted the hatchet and brought it down on a workbench. "You see!" he said triumphantly, wrenching the blade from the grip of the wood. "It's just the same. That cut in the park bench was just the same as the fingerprint of this hatchet."

Allen pushed his hat back and scratched his head, puzzled. "I guess it's the same hatchet, all right," he admitted. "But what—"

"Don't you see it yet?" demanded Blake. "Peter Hart is the Hatchet Killer!"

"Wh—what!"

"It's simple. He lives only a coupla hundred feet from Riverside Park, an' it'd be easy for him to sneak over there, pull off some job, then run back here an' hide. Remember that the one man that saw the Hatchet Killer from a distance said he thought he had a uniform like a motorcycle cop's? Don't Hart wear a chauffeur's uniform with leather puttees?"

"I begin to get the drift," confessed Allen. "He's the guy, all right. But how in thunder did you come to hook him up with this Hatchet Killer?"

"Didja see how he held the key when he unlocked the padlock? He had it in his left hand. I noticed when we first saw him that he had on a uniform, and I thought he acted kinda suspicious. Then, when I saw he was left-handed I thought of the Hatchet Killer right away. I knew he was left-handed because in all his killings the direction of the cuts ran down towards the left. If he'd held the hatchet in his right hand they'd 've run down toward the right. Then I looked at him closer an' I saw a funny gold ring on his little finger. I didn't get a close look at it because he didn't hold still, but I could swear it's one of the rings that the Hatchet Killer got from Mrs. Foote."

"Sa-ay!" exploded Allen. "I knew I didn't like that guy! I thought he smelled funny." He glanced menacingly at the door which led up to Peter Hart's rooms. "Let's go up an' collar him."

Blake opened the door without knocking this time and they started up the stairs, Allen at his heels. At the top was a second door, which he swung open.

He stepped into a small living room scantily furnished with a small table and a few chairs. Through an open door he could see an even smaller bedroom beyond. Peter Hart was seated in a chair looking out of the window, but at the squeak of the opening door he swung around and leaped to his feet.

"What the hell!" he roared, his lips drawing back into a furious snarl. "What're you doin' here?"

Blake stood in the door, while Allen peered over his shoulder.

"So you're the Hatchet Killer," he said slowly in a biting tone of voice. "I thought—"

He made a sudden dive across the room. Hart had leapt towards an open table drawer, and before Blake reached him a revolver flashed in his hand. But as he raised it Blake seized his wrist and twisted it sharply with both hands. There was a roar as the weapon exploded, but the bullet passed between Blake's legs and the revolver clattered a moment later upon the floor.

Hart snarled and sent a blow crashing against Blake's chest that threw him back against the room's single window. The chauffeur was fully half a head taller, and he had the strength of a mad ox. He turned toward the door, but started back when he saw Allen leap into the room with a revolver in his hand.

With a roar he whirled about and dived for the window. Blake sent his fist smacking against the chauffeur's unprotected chin, but it had no effect. Allen raised his revolver, but had to hold his fire for fear of hitting his sergeant.

Then Hart's huge bulk hit Blake and bore backwards. The chauffeur's arms wrapped about his and held him helpless. His back hit the window and shattered the glass, splintered the frame. He tried to hold himself from toppling out through it backwards, but he could not.

Their arms about each other, they fell through the air. Their bodies turned slightly so that they both lit upon their sides, the force of the blow almost paralyzing Blake's right arm, though they fell upon soft grass which absorbed some of the shock.

Hart sprang to his feet at once, but Blake threw out a foot and tripped him. As the chauffeur fell to the ground Blake leaped upon him, seizing his wrist with one hand and turning it half around in a ju-jitsu hold. With his knee he pressed against the man's elbow, pinning his entire arm to the ground. He had him at his mercy—if he tried to escape he could snap the bones of his arm with a twist.

Without waiting to take the stairs, Allen leaped from the window after them and lit close beside them. He grasped Hart's other arm and twisted it behind him. Blake brought the arm that he held back and Allen snapped handcuffs on them.

Together they jerked the chauffeur to his feet. All the fight was gone from him, and it was evident that he had lapsed into complete madness. His eyes were rolling wildly, he was muttering incomprehensible words while the froth drooled from his twitching lips.

The noise of the shot had not passed unheard, for a moment later Norman Cochrane, the motorcycle officer and a patrolman came running from the house. When they saw the chauffeur with his hands handcuffed behind his back and the light of madness in his eyes, they stopped, amazed.

"Well, here's your Hatchet Killer," said Blake.

At this announcement Cochrane almost seemed to lose control of himself from fright. He backed away from his brother's chauffeur, his face white.

"Wh—what?" he chattered. "You don't mean—"

"He's the Killer, all right. There's no doubt about that. We've even got the hatchet that he did all the killing with."

"Why—why—he looks as though he's mad!" cried Cochrane.

"He is. He was half insane, an' when we found the hatchet an' pinned the goods on him, he went completely off his nut." Blake began to massage his right shoulder gingerly.

"But—but—he looked all right," protested Cochrane. It was evident that this new development had almost unnerved the little man. "To think that we had this madman in our house all the time and didn't know it! If I had only guessed, I might have saved my poor brother from his horrible fate. But I never thought—"

Blake left him then and searched Peter Hart's room. He returned with a handful of rings, bracelets, wrist watches and other jewelry that the Hatchet Killer had taken from the bodies of his three women victims.

"Charley," he said to Allen. "You run Hart down to headquarters in the bus. I'll be down in a few minutes with the motorcycle officer. If Lieutenant Davies isn't there, get hold of him somehow an' see that he's there."

They put Peter Hart, who had fallen into an apathetic silence, into the back of the squad car and the patrolman got in beside him.

Blake turned to Cochrane. "Will you ride down with 'em, Mr. Cochrane?" he asked. "I'd like you to be there when we make out the charges against him." He turned to Allen. "And, Charley, don't make out the charges until I get there. It won't take me more 'n a few minutes to get there."

But it was thirty minutes later before the motorcycle officer swung into the private driveway behind headquarters. Blake leaped out of the sidecar and made his way to Lieutenant Davies's private office. He carried under his arm a small wooden box.

The lieutenant seized his hand and wrung it enthusiastically. "This is a wonderful piece of work, sergeant!" he cried. "Allen has been telling me all about it. And I'm going to see that you get all the credit that you deserve."

"Thanks, lieutenant," said Blake dryly. He deposited the box that he was carrying upon the desk.

"You've got the hatchets there?" asked Lieutenant Davies.

"Here she is." Blake took the hatchet that he had found in the garage from the box and laid it upon the desk. "There's fingerprints on the blade if you need 'em. And here's the jewelry." He emptied a handful of jewelry from his pocket upon the desk. "Hart's still got one of the rings on his finger, though. I didn't take it off. D' you want it?"

Lieutenant Davies nodded, so Allen stripped the ring from the chauffeur's unresisting finger and laid it on the table beside the hatchet.

"There's enough evidence there to send Hart to the chair," said Blake. "Though I don't guess he'll ever see it." He looked over at the chauffeur who stood at one side silently, his head hanging between his shoulders, his eyes dead and a dribble of saliva on his chin. "They'll put him in the nut house quick."

"I'm afraid so," sighed the lieutenant.

Blake turned to the desk sergeant who had entered the office and stood at one side.

"Well, Tony, you can book Hart on the Mrs. Carter, the Mrs. Foote, the Miss Wagner and the John Leidler killings."

"Put down the Arthur Cochrane one too, Tony," added the lieutenant.

Blake smiled grimly and shook his head. "I was just coming to that, lieutenant. You can book Norman Cochrane with that!"

Davies's mouth dropped open and a look of utter astonishment crossed his face. Allen stared at his sergeant to see whether he had gone mad. If any of them had looked at Norman Cochrane's face, they would have seen it go a greenish-white.

"Why—why—" sputtered Davies. "Sergeant Blake! What's the idea of this tomfoolery? Have you gone mad?"

"Not so's you could notice it," retorted Blake. "If you don't believe me, take a look at Cochrane's face!"

Lieutenant Davies slowly swung his gaze around to the latter's face. He gasped. For Norman Cochrane's face was a mask of terror, and it was not the terror of an innocent man accused of a crime, but the terror of a guilty man found out!

"You want proof?" asked Blake. "Here it is." He took from the box a second hatchet, the hatchet he and Allen had retrieved from the river's bottom. "Here's the hatchet he used to kill his brother. Don't touch it: there's some fingerprints on it. I haven't tried them, but they're his all right. He bought it at Haskin's Hardware Company two days ago. I called up every hardware store in town until I found one that remembered selling him a hatchet."

"But—this is hardly believable," protested Lieutenant Davies.

"Maybeso, but I can prove it before any jury. You want more proof? Did Allen tell you about the footprints beneath the window and on the river bank? Here's the shoes that made 'em. I found 'em in a closet in his room, hid behind some boxes. You can still see traces of mud on the sides. I also found the chisel in his room that he used to break open the library window. It fits the marks perfectly." Blake put a pair of shoes and the chisel on the desk.

Lieutenant Davies was convinced. He turned to Cochrane and rapped out a single word: "Well?"

Cochrane grew almost chalk-white, and he had to lean against the desk for support. He tried to speak and choked on his words.

"D' you wanna confess?" asked the lieutenant. "We've got the goods on you; you can't get out of it. It'll go easier on you."

For a moment Cochrane's lips twitched as he tried to speak, then a torrent of words broke out. "Yes, I'll confess! I did it! I killed him! I was bankrupt and he wouldn't give me a cent to help. I've always hated him, and he always hated me!"

Lieutenant Davies called in a police stenographer who took down his confession. Cochrane signed it when he had finished; then he and Peter Hart were taken from the room.

"Boy, I want to shake your hand!" cried the lieutenant. "I don't see how you ever did it. Allen told me the whole thing while we was waiting for you, an' I never once thought of him being guilty."

"It wasn't much," objected Blake, grinning embarrassedly. "I just thought the whole case looked fishy, even when you first told me about it."

"Well, tell us how you did it. I still don't know how you figured it all out."

"Why, in the first place," explained Blake, "I thought it looked funny that the Hatchet Killer should murder a man. So far he had only killed women for their jewelry. Of course he killed John Leidler, but we knew he killed Leidler because he tried to protect Miss Wagner. Then when I saw the body, it looked even fishier. For one thing Arthur Cochrane was smokin' a pipe an' readin' a newspaper when he was killed. The pipe was between his legs an' the newspaper was over his knees, just where he'd dropped them. If the Hatchet Killer had come in the room, he would never have sat there and waited to be killed. He'd 've jumped up an' tried to defend himself. Of course he might not 've looked up from the newspaper until too late, but the chances were he would. So it looked as though he musta known whoever it was that killed him.

"The next thing I noticed was that all the cuts on his head ran from the left down to the right. This meant that whoever killed him was right-handed. Well, I knew the Hatchet Killer was left-handed, because on the four people he killed the cuts were in just the other way. Dr. Leary told me two more things that didn't hook up right. First, that the hatchet that killed Arthur Cochrane had a straight sharp edge. I knew that the Killer's hatchet had a rounded, dull edge. Second that none of the cuts were very deep. Now in these other four killings, the cuts had been very deep, almost cutting the head in two.

"When I got that far I was pretty puzzled. Then when I found how the footprints had been faked under the window, I figured that it must be an inside job. I didn't know that Norman Cochrane had done it, but I suspected it. For one thing he coulda walked up close to his brother with a hatchet behind him without his brother suspecting him. The second reason that I suspected him was because I knew the man that did it wasn't very strong, because the cuts in the head weren't deep, and Arthur Cochrane fitted in there. Then we had some luck an' discovered that the real Hatchet Killer was the chauffeur."

Blake paused a moment and grinned. "That just about knocked Norman Cochrane off his pins. Anyway it gave me a chance to go through his rooms by sending him off to the station. You see, I wasn't sure yet that he killed his brother."

"Piece of luck nothing," growled Lieutenant Davies admiringly. "That was real detective work figuring that Hart was the Hatchet Killer. Allen told me how you did it, and I've got to hand it to you. I think that both of 'em must be nuts. I'll bet they both end up in the booby hatch."

"Maybeso," agreed Blake. "But you've got to admit Cochrane had a brilliant idea. You see, he figured he hid his murder behind all these others."

Connors wagged the revolver at Phillips. "Not so fast, big boy," he warned. "You forget about that popgun of yours . . .

. . . an' run along an' tell Martello an' Rico what I said."

THE RACKETEERING COP

Here is a police story by a new writer that ends in a whirlwind of exciting action.

"GET THIS, PHILLIPS," SAID DETECTIVE SERGEANT CONNORS. "I'm through with you an' Martello." His cold blue eyes glinted as he stared at the gangster who sat opposite him at a small table in the pool room.

"Aw, don't get hard now, Connors," pleaded Denny Phillips. "There's no call for makin' a squawk. You're gettin' good dough, an' there's plenty more. Yuh play along with us an' you'll be sittin' pretty."

Connors shifted his huge bulk to a more comfortable position in the straight-backed chair. He dropped a hamlike hand upon the greasy table and the glasses jumped. His massive, clean-shaved typical police face was almost impassive; only the firm set of his thin lips and his narrowed eyes betrayed his intense determination.

"To hell with the jack!" he growled. "It's Donovan I'm thinkin' of. You guys bumped him off."

"I ain't denied it, have I?"

"An' you think you can get away with stuff like that? Think you can knock off a cop any time you want to?"

"I told yuh already, Connors, it was an accident."

"Accident, hell! There wasn't no call for you shootin' him down. Why didn't you take the pinch? You probably could've fixed it. Why didn't you let Donovan run you in?"

"What? With ten grand worth of alky on the truck?" snorted Phillips. "Yuh must think we're nuts."

"Martello could've stood that," replied Connors.

"Yeah. Think he's gonna toss away ten grand in alky, th' truck an' five or six grand more to fix it up for one damn' flattie? Not much. An' where was you when it all happened? You're the guy that was gonna see that Donovan was outta th' way when we run th' booze in. You was gonna see that he was at th' other end of his beat. What d'yuh think Martello's been passin' th' protection jack to yuh for?"

"I couldn't help that. He changed his beat an' I couldn't find him in time."

"Well, what're yuh kickin' about then?" sneered Phillips. He leaned forward suddenly. "C'mon, Connors. Let's forget about it."

Sergeant Connors' eyes became grim. "I ain't forgettin' about it. I told you I'm through with you, an' I mean it. You an' Rico an' Martello take the lam tomorrow."

"An' if we don't?"

"I'll pull you on the Donovan killin'."

Phillips laughed harshly. "You're outta yer head!" he cried. "Yuh know what it means to you, Connors."

"I know, all right."

"It means you take th' rap, too."

"Well?"

"Aw, hell! You've gone batty. Lissen, Connors. You're in it as deep as we are. If you try to give us th' works, it's th' big house for you, too."

"It's okay with me," said Connors grimly. "I'm not goin' to see a cop croaked an' do nothin' about it. By rights I ought to run you three birds in. But I'm in it as deep as you are. I'll compromise an' say nothin' if the three of you beat it outta town an' stay out. But if you stick around—well, it's the rap for all of us."

"Ain't that nice!" jeered Phillips. "We hit th' rails an' leave you here sittin' pretty. I suppose you got Nelson fixed. He'll give you a bigger rake-off on th' booze, will he?"

"You're talkin' through your hat, Phillips. I ain't got any hook-up with Nelson. If he wants to take over the mob an' run things when you three clear out, he can do it. Me, I'm off the racket. From now on, I'm goin' straight."

"Yeah. That's a lot o' hooey an' you know it. Where d'yuh think you'll get off at buckin' Martello? If yuh don't quiet down a little, he'll put yuh on the spot."

"Tell him to go ahead," invited Connors. "But he'd better be quick about it, because tomorrow I'm goin' to pull him."

"You're damn' right we'll go ahead!" cried Phillips, springing to his feet. His hand darted to his rear pocket, but stopped at the magical appearance of a large revolver in Connors' hand.

Connors waggled the revolver at Phillips. "Not so fast, big boy," he warned. "You forget about that popgun of yours an' run along an' tell Martello an' Rico what I said." He lumbered to his feet and stowed his revolver away. "Well, so long, Phillips. Hope I don't see you again." He went to the door in heavy strides that shook the floor.

Phillips snarled impotently for a moment, then flung after him, "When they're tuckin' you under th' sod, you won't feel so gay."

"Mebbe," agreed Connors placidly.

He lit a cigarette with spadelike fingers and crushed the match into tiny splinters before he threw it away. Then he turned toward police headquarters.

"Hey, there, Connors," called a voice as he entered the front office. "Come here a minute."

"Oh, hello, Hanson." Connors dropped into a creaking chair. "What's on your mind?"

Lieutenant Hanson swung his lean form around in the swivel chair and cocked his feet up on a chair. "The chief's sure worked up about Donovan," he remarked. "What do you think about it?"

"I don't know. What do *you* think?" Connors took a cigar from a pocket in his bulging vest and cut off the end with his thumbnail.

"Well, I don't know. My idea is that one of the booze gangs pulled it off. It don't look like the work of stick-up guys. The trouble is no one seems to have been around when Donovan was shot."

"That makes it kinda hard," said Connors. He lit his cigar and puffed at it slowly.

"The chief's as crazy as a bedbug. He swears he's going to cook the guys that got Donovan. He's been raking the city all day and has had nearly every crook in town on the pan and sweated them."

"Get anything?" Connors tried to look up casually from a close study of his cigar band.

"Not yet. And I don't think he will unless some stoolie comes across."

"Which ain't very likely."

"Not if it was one of the booze gangs," agreed Hanson. "The only clues the chief's got are the bullets they took out of Donovan. You heard about them?"

Connors shook his head.

"There were a couple of bullets from a .45-caliber Colt automatic and one from a .38-caliber revolver. All the chief has to do is to find the guns that fired the bullets."

"Not much chance," observed Connors.

"Not much. But I sure hope he gets the birds that did it. It means the chair for them if he does."

"Well, mebbe he'll get 'em," said Connors, with little enthusiasm.

Late that afternoon Sergeant Connors sauntered down the street toward the rooming house in which he lived. The sinking sun left the other side of the street in shadow and threw a red glow upon his face.

He was almost unconscious of his surroundings. Tomorrow, things would come to a showdown, for, unless Martello and his two lieutenants had left town, he meant to arrest them.

He roused himself abruptly at the sound of two screaming voices. Some fifty feet ahead of him two gangsters were brawling.

"You will, will yuh?" snarled one of them.

"Who's gonna stop me, yuh lousy rat?" shouted the other, catching the first on the point of the jaw with a stiff jab.

Immediately Connors set out for them. A police officer is always a police officer, even when off duty.

Coming from the opposite direction, a large black limousine edged over to the curb near Connors. Some sixth sense warned him and he paused in his stride long enough to swing his head around. In a flash he recognized the driver of the car as Martello, and he saw Phillips and Rico in the back seat.

With grinding brakes, the car skidded to a stop. Phillips leaned to an open window and raised from his lap a sub-machine gun. Its evil barrel pointed directly at Connors' breast.

He was being put on the spot! The fighting gangsters were only a lure to attract his attention long enough for his body to be riddled with bullets. Martello was desperate. He did not want to abandon his mob and the prosperous racket he had built up.

The sub-machine gun spat fire. A death-dealing stream of bullets shot from its muzzle and its clatter filled the confines of the narrow street.

But, huge as Sergeant Connors was, he was far from being clumsy. As Phillips pressed the trigger, he dropped and dived forward. The stream of lead punctured the spot where he had just been and drummed against the brick wall behind him, sending out a shower of chips.

Connors sprawled on the curb and somersaulted to his feet a little to the rear of the car. His police revolver appeared in his hand.

A bullet crashed through the rear window of the car, striking his left shoulder and almost spinning him around with the force of the blow. Through the cracked window he saw the grim face of Rico. Connors' gun roared once and the face slipped from view, a gaping hole in the forehead.

In the meantime Phillips was leaning from the window, trying to swing the sub-machine gun around so that he could point it at Connors. He had not taken his finger from the trigger and bullets spewed from it in a circle of death.

Connors steadied himself. His left shoulder was numb; he could not move the fingers of his left hand. As the fan of bullets swept around to him, almost touched him, he fired twice. The deadly clatter ceased; the submachine gun slipped from nerveless fingers and clanged upon the pavement.

The car leaped forward. Martello, with the death of his two lieutenants, was apparently giving up the attempt on Connors' life. Connors swayed on his feet, for the bullet in his shoulder had become an agony, but he took careful aim at one of the rear tires and pressed the trigger.

There was a second explosion as the flying bullet struck the tire. The car swerved around, crashed against a steel telephone pole, sending out a shower of broken glass. A figure catapulted from it, automatic in hand.

Connors aimed a fourth shot, but it missed. He felt a searing pain in his side and he fell over. Martello had gotten him.

He groaned and hitched himself to his hands and knees. A third bullet ploughed through the flesh of his left arm and almost threw him over again. He cursed and raised himself upright on his knees, his face deathly white with the effort.

He threw up his revolver and drew a bead on Martello. Bullets whipped about his head, but he was unconscious of them. He pressed the trigger once, twice, until it clicked upon an empty chamber.

Martello spun around and fell upon his face. Connors slowly put away his weapon and rose to his feet. He stood motionless for a long time, fighting to regain control of himself. Then he walked toward Martello.

There was the shrill scream of a police siren, a squad car sped down the street, skidded to a halt. Plainclothes men piled out, weapons in hand, and closed in upon the wrecked car.

"You're too late—I guess," said Connors. "I got all of 'em."

"God, man! You're wounded!" cried a voice that he recognized as Lieutenant Hanson's.

As Connors looked down at Martello, things began to whirl before his eyes and he sat down abruptly on the curb, refusing all offers of assistance. A hurried call was sent for an ambulance.

There was a gurgle from the prostrate man upon the sidewalk. One of the detectives turned Martello over upon his back and Connors saw that he was still alive.

"My God! It's Martello!" gasped Hanson.

"Yuh got me, Connors, but—" A cough racked Martello's frame.

"What is it, Martello?" asked Hanson, leaning down over him. "If you've got anything to say, spill it quick. You're not going to live long."

For a moment Connors forgot the pain of his wounds. It had come now. Martello was going to reveal his connection with the gang and his indirect connection with Donovan's death. It meant disgrace for him, disgrace and a prison sentence.

"I croaked Donovan," mumbled Martello. "Me and Rico did it. An' Connors, he—he was—" his voice faded out.

"Yes, yes. Go on," urged Hanson, leaning even closer to the dying man's lips.

"Connors, he—he—" Then Martello shuddered and was suddenly still.

"He's dead," announced Hanson. He stooped and disengaged the gun from Martello's fingers. "And I guess that this is the gun he used to kill Donovan. It's a .45 Colt automatic."

"An' here's a .38 that Rico had," said a detective, emerging from the interior of the wrecked car.

Everything seemed to be going around before Connors' eyes. Martello, Rico, and Phillips were dead; Donovan was avenged. Martello had meant to betray him, but he had died before he could do it. Now he could go straight.

"Boy, you pulled a sweet one!" declared Lieutenant Hanson. "But what made them pile on you?"

Connors thought rapidly. "I don't know," he said. "Unless mebbe it was because I'd been nosin' around on the quiet checkin' up on 'em. I kinda had a hunch they was the birds that got Donovan, an' they musta heard I was after 'em an' decided to put me on the spot before I could make a pinch."

A STRANGE WIFE

THE ORCHESTRA BURST INTO A CRASHING FINALE and the curtain slid down as a row of silk-clad girls did an involved dance. The audience clapped, began to rise to their feet and to file out.

Olga Andray, the lead, smiled mechanically as she did her step before the cast behind her. The rich voluptuousness of her undulating body was a lure that held the eye of more than one man in the audience. She knew that there would be at least a dozen notes from various men asking to have the privilege to escort her to any place that she might care to go.

The curtain fell for the last time. Olga whisked from the stage, pushing her way imperiously through the other members of the cast.

"Nancy!" She slammed the door of her dressing-room. "Has Terry been here? Did he say that he would meet me?"

"Yes, *mad'moiselle*. He was here half-hour ago and say he be back."

Olga hurriedly slipped from her costume and wiped the grease-paint from her face. Terry had suggested that they go to the Palais Rouge to-night, and she wanted to be ready for him.

Years of stage life had hardened her, had given her a veneer of sophistication that made her heart an almost impregnable fortress. She sat in it calmly, coldly, watching with contemptuous eyes the men that milled about her, maddened by the invitation of her flesh. She accepted what they offered her—jewels, clothes and cars—but never left her stronghold.

Never, that is, until she met Terry. He had sent in his card one night and she had chosen it almost at random, only ascertaining first that he had the money to indulge her expensive whims. She had found him, dark, debonair and handsome—a welcome relief from the aged, almost ossified, millionaires that are an actress's bread and butter.

Almost immediately she had found herself enormously attracted to him. He aroused a passion in her breast that she had never known before, a passion that on an irresistible tide swept her from her fortress and left her helpless. His caressing touch upon her arm was enough to set her pulse pounding.

Terry was the perfect lover. Other men were dull, clumsy clods beside him. They were only awkward toyers with love, ignorant of all the subtle nuances in the art of love. Not Terry; he knew every corner of a woman's heart; knew how to thrill her, how to caress her, how to wake ecstasy in her heart with a kiss.

There was a knock on the door and the maid admitted Terry. He was in evening dress—a tall, dark, princely figure. His black hair had on the sides just that touch of gray which was needed to set off his smooth, handsome face. His thin, sensitive nose, with the slight hook, above the closely-trimmed black moustache, and his erect military carriage, gave him an aristocratic air.

He stood silent before her, with that air of deference to her beauty which was a tribute almost peculiar to him. His eyes caressed her body, warming upon her gown with the black-metal sheen which hung almost to her ankles.

"Ah, darling," he said in a low, throaty voice, "you are like a black opal to-night!"

For a moment his eyes lost their focus and he recalled a magnificent black opal that he had seen that afternoon at Tiffany's. Yes, Olga was as beautiful, as precious, as that. Perhaps he would get it for her.

Olga gave a slow smile and laid her hand upon his arm. On one of her fragile fingers glittered a ruby ring that he had given to her.

"Nancy! My wrap!" she called, without turning her head.

He adjusted the wrap and followed her to the stage door. A chauffeur sprang from a Rolls-Royce and held the door open. She sank into the luxurious cushioning with a sigh and leaned against Terry's shoulder.

Terry had everything, she reflected; wealth, a Park Avenue apartment and social position. Her lips drew down a little wistfully, a strange expression for her face.

Lately a strange thought had taken possession of her, a thought that she would never have believed possible for her; for she was thinking that she would like to have Terry for always, that she would like to be his wife. She smiled ironically at herself. She—*she* who had thought that no one man could ever satisfy her, who had laughed at the idea of being faithful to one man, who had repulsed millionaires—*she* wanted to have one man for herself, to be his alone!

She had given herself to Terry soon after they met, as a matter of course—such things were really quite casual; but with her it had been quite different this time. She had not expected the passionate response which she had made, she had not counted upon being overwhelmed by the emotional storm that he roused in her. Love—love which demanded marriage and scorned all halfway measures—had always been foreign to her.

Perhaps, if Terry had not had a wife, he would have married her. She was not sure. That he was married had not troubled her at all in the beginning; in fact, she preferred to play with married men. Their association with their wives usually made them think that they knew all about women, and so made them easier prey to her wiles. Married men, having had a taste of happiness in their homes, are more eager in their search for it elsewhere, and more willing to pay for it.

It was with amazement that Olga realized that she was becoming jealous of Terry's wife; jealous, even though she had Terry's love, and so should have despised the deceived woman.

But Mrs. Randolph had Terry, his home, his wealth, his social position, his security—and his name! Olga wanted more than Terry's love a few nights of the week after the theatre; she wanted Terry all of the time.

A divorce? Well, why was it not possible? Terry loved her—of that she was sure. She knew that Mrs. Randolph was a beautiful woman, for she had seen her picture often in the rotogravure section of the newspaper, but she was sure that Terry did not love her.

Yet she hesitated to ask him to get a divorce, though the temptation was growing stronger and stronger. She hoped that he would propose it himself. Perhaps, if she made sly suggestions, asking him how he could endure to live with his wife, he might come around to it.

At the Palais Rouge night club the head waiter greeted them obsequiously and showed them to a quiet table in a corner. Terry ordered champagne, which was produced almost instantly. The waiter poured out two glasses for them.

Olga sipped the effervescing liquid, then toyed with the narrow-stemmed glass while she looked about her at the various diners. She saw one, a middle-aged woman dressed in stylish clothes that only looked dowdy on her. The familiar spectacle; a woman losing her beauty and trying desperately to retain it by wearing over-stylish clothes and resorting to beauty specialists.

She set the glass upon the table and gazed fixedly at the clouds of small bubbles that formed in the sparkling liquid and broke upon the surface. Where would she be when she was as old as this woman? The best of her beauty would be gone and her stage career would be ended. She had little money; her expensive manner of living left little over. Butterflies do not store for a winter day.

It made her melancholy to think in this vein; she must not allow herself to continue. Abruptly, she seized the glass and drained the champagne at a gulp.

"Come on, Terry," she smiled; "let's dance."

When they returned to the table after the dance, the mood had quite left her. She leaned towards Terry, her dark eyes slanting and slumbrous with passion, listening as he talked.

"I have news for you, Olga," he said at length. "My wife is going to Boston for a week's stay."

Olga's eyes brightened. "Then, you can come over every night, can't you?" she asked.

"Unless unexpected business comes up, yes," he answered. "And I have a little trip planned for the day after to-morrow. We'll go to Atlantic City for two days' stay."

"But the show?" Her face fell.

"I'll arrange that with Burton. What's the use of my owning the show unless I can have a few privileges?" He smiled pleasantly.

Olga returned from Atlantic City more determined than before that Terry should be her husband. She mentioned nothing of the matter to him, though, for she was still undecided as to what to do.

That night Terry did not get to the theatre until almost thirty minutes after the show. He had been detained by a business conference, so that he still wore his street clothes.

"We'll run up to my apartment while I change," he explained.

Olga wandered through the rooms of his apartment while she waited for him. In the library she found a large portrait over the fireplace and recognized it at once as Mrs. Randolph. She stared at it while hate and fury worked in her heart until she wanted to tear the picture from its frame and stamp it upon the floor.

This was the woman to whom Terry belonged, who bore his name. If she would only die so that Terry would be free! Or if Terry would only divorce her!

She curled her lip and turned away from the portrait, throwing herself into an over-stuffed armchair. How comfortable and luxurious it was in this apartment! How wonderful it would be to live here with Terry!

There was the sound of footsteps in the hall. She glanced at the door, wondering whether any of the servants had returned, though Terry had said that they had all been given a holiday.

A woman walked past the open door, then halted as she saw the light in the room. She stepped into the doorway.

Olga sat up abruptly; for, though she had never seen Terry's wife in the flesh, she recognized this woman at once as Mrs. Randolph. Her body went cold, then a warm flush ran over it. Her chance had come now! Terry's wife was ignorant of her and probably thought her husband a paragon of probity. Now was the time to show this woman what Terry really was, to prove to her that Terry had been unfaithful to her. Surely she would divorce him then.

She would not try to conceal the fact that she was Terry's mistress; she would boast about it, taunt her with it.

Mrs. Randolph paused in the doorway for only an instant, and a barely perceptible flush of surprise crossed her well-bred face. She was beautiful, Olga admitted to herself; even more beautiful than her pictures showed her. They could not present the rich color and vitality of her smooth cheeks, the vivacity of her brilliant blue eyes, and the softness and sheen of the brown hair that waved about her face.

Then Mrs. Randolph advanced into the room and stopped near the table. Olga expected to see humiliation, consternation or despair upon her face, but she was not prepared for what occurred.

For Mrs. Randolph said in a well-modulated tone, even smiling a little.

"You are Olga Andray, I suppose?"

Olga rose to her feet. "And you are Mrs. Randolph, I imagine," she said. She also smiled, for she was determined to lose nothing in the matching of weapons that she knew would come.

"You are correct. I am glad to find you here, Miss Andray; I have wanted to meet you for a long time."

"You have been wanting to meet me?" repeated Olga, gasping with astonishment. She could not understand Mrs. Randolph's attitude. But, perhaps, she still did not suspect that she was Terry's mistress; perhaps she had only heard of her as an actress in Terry's theatre. Well, she would soon learn the truth. Olga gloated a little over the pain of the disillusionment that this woman would feel.

But before she could speak again, Mrs. Randolph went on.

"Why, of course! You are my husband's mistress, aren't you? A woman can be excused for a slight curiosity concerning her husband's mistresses. She has a very natural interest, if for no other reason than to find whether she suffers by comparison."

Her eyes swept over Olga, taking in every detail of her body and dress.

Olga had been caught doubly unprepared this second time and she listened open-mouthed. This was not even indifference. It was a situation which she felt almost helpless to cope with. If she had been met with mad fury or despair she would have known what to do.

The lines about her mouth hardened.

"Yes, I'm Terry's mistress," she snapped, feeling vastly inferior to this other woman who was so calm and self-collected. "What are you going to do about it?"

"Do?" Mrs. Randolph echoed the word with surprise. "Why, nothing, of course! I hope you haven't mistaken my interest for resentment."

A ray of hope shone through Olga's confusion.

"You don't love Terry, then?" she asked. Perhaps this strange wife would be willing to divorce him.

"Love Terry? Of course I love him."

"But—but—" Olga floundered almost helplessly. "But after this you'll divorce him, won't you?"

"Never!"

Footsteps sounded in the hallway and a man's voice sang out:

"Olga!"

"We're in here, dear," responded Mrs. Randolph, hardly raising her voice.

His white face appeared in the doorway.

"Judy! My God! You here?" he cried.

"Come right in," invited his wife. "You got my telegram, didn't you? I was forced to cut my visit short a few days."

"No; it must be at the office. I haven't been there all day." He stood like a man dazed, his eyes traveling back and forth between the two women.

"Do come in, Terry," insisted his wife again. "We're just in the midst of a most interesting discussion. I'm sure that it'll interest you also."

He came in, groped for a chair with one hand as though he could not see it, and dropped heavily into it. Beads of sweat began to appear upon his forehead and his teeth were tightly clenched.

"Miss Andray tells me that she is your mistress, Terry," remarked Mrs. Randolph conversationally. "If she will pardon my saying it, she is really very much prettier and more charming than I had imagined."

"Don't talk like that, Judy," pleaded Terry.

Olga was still dazed, but she saw that things were going against her and she made an effort to collect her wits. Then it occurred to her that her opportunity had come now.

"Terry! Won't you go away with me now?" she begged, plucking at him.

He looked up at her with haggard, uncomprehending eyes.

"What do you mean?" he croaked.

"You love me, Terry. Let's go away together."

He stared at her as though he did not understand what she said.

"I love you, Terry. Please come away with me," entreated Olga. "She doesn't love you; she doesn't want you."

The import of what she was saying dawned upon him and he rose slowly to his feet. His eyes glittered and his teeth drew back from his lips in a snarl.

"You get out of here!" he blazed.

She stumbled back, dumbfounded, from the menace of his eyes.

"Terry!" she faltered. "You don't—mean—"

"That's exactly what I mean," he said, putting equal emphasis upon every syllable. "I'm through with you. Get out!"

Olga glanced at him with unbelieving eyes, unable to understand. She made no motion to leave, so he took her arm and pushed her through the apartment. He took her down to the car and bruskly ordered the chauffeur to take her to her apartment.

When he returned, his wife was in almost the same position that he had left her. But her face was not serene and smiling now; it was grim, and her eyelids drooped.

"Judy, Judy!" he cried abjectly. "Can you ever forgive me?"

She sank into a chair and covered her face with her hands.

"Oh, Terry, how dared you bring this woman into our home?"

"Darling, I was mad. But that is all over now; I swear to never have anything to do with her again."

Judy remained implacable. But as Terry grew more passionate a thrill shot through her. It was always like this. Terry tired of her after a few months and wandered as most men do, or would like to do. And she tired of him in almost the same length of time. She grew so sick of him that she scarcely wanted him to touch her. She became completely indifferent and only wanted him to leave her alone, though she never told him this. No, he thought, with masculine simplicity, that she loved him at all times.

When he became sated with her, he turned his attention to other women. For a time she cared nothing about this. Then her interest in Terry would return, and with it would come raging jealousy against the woman Terry had chosen to love. Once before this she had surprised Terry and his mistress together and had made a scene, pretending that she was heartbroken.

Always Terry returned to her in time, cured again of his wandering; and invariably she forced him to court her again, to win her love again. When he had won her, they had passionate moments together, moments as passionate as the first ones that they had known.

This was what she lived for, this real ecstasy of passion. Other women who loved one man uninterruptedly did not know the real thrill of love. They fell into a state of pleasant boredom that lasted forever. But to lose Terry, and then to have him come back to her—each time it was as if she were but a young girl first experiencing the raptures of passion with her first lover.

Terry was the perfect lover, but even perfect lovers tire one at times. But reunited after his lapses, he never failed to give her an overpowering thrill; he proved again to her that she was the only woman in the world that had the power to hold him.

"Darling, darling," murmured Terry in her ear, stroking her curling brown hair, "you know that I love you, that you are all the world to me!" He pleaded with her with passionate intensity.

He took from his pocket a small box and opened it. Upon a cushion of cream plush lay a magnificent black opal with a long spun-gold chain.

Judy took it and held it to the light. It scintillated with all the colors of the spectrum, constantly changing as she twisted it in her fingers. A bauble of living fire.

"It's for you, dear," he whispered. "I got it to give you upon your return."

She knew that it had been meant for Olga, but it made it none the less precious and beautiful.

She stretched out her arms to him.

"Take me, Terry," she said.

Gangster Love

*A damned queer way to show love—laugh at a guy when
he's lying hog-tied on the floor, while a fat slob lays hands
on his girl, right in front of him!*

Spot Taylor stood in the darkness of the wide doors of the Western Garage
and looked out at the night traffic that eddied toward the theatre district.

The headlights of passing cars momentarily lighted up his thickset,
powerful body and threw moving shadows across his angular face. He wore
expensive flashy clothes that set off his broad shoulders; his craggy chin was
smooth-shaven and his black hair was combed back from his forehead.

He stood in his habitual posture, with his feet wide apart and his right
hand resting inside his coat flap. In this position, with his hat pulled down
over piercing black eyes, he looked somewhat like the familiar picture of
Napoleon.

He did not do it for effect, but because with his hand inside of his coat, a
.45 Colt's automatic swung in a shoulder holster just a few inches from his
fingers.

Spot Taylor could not tell when he would be in deadly need of a weapon.
Death might come spitting at him in a hail of lead at any moment from the
shadows or from a passing car.

As the leader of the most powerful and feared booze gang in the city,
there were dozens of men in rival mobs that would shoot him on sight.

Of course he was heeled, for he never went unguarded; two cannons lurked near him—one outside to scrutinize passers-by and the other behind him, each ready to throw away his life in the protection of his.

A tall Swede moved up from the lighted rear of the garage where he had been superintending the loading of a fleet of great trucks with alcohol and whiskey for the suburbs and small towns surrounding the city.

"Got the stuff ready, Spot," he said. "How about puttin' on a double crew of gorillas?" He squinted up at the dark moonless sky. "This'd be a fine night for Ruby Bascone to try a little hijackin'."

Spot cursed softly to himself. "Go ahead, Slam. And see that each wagon gets two choppers."

Spot's eyes hardened as he stared out into the night, but his face remained almost immobile. Yet inwardly he was seething with anger. When Millio had ruled the River Rats there had been comparative peace between the two mobs.

Then a dope-crazed gangster had killed Millio and fiery, impetuous Ruby Bascone had assumed command of the River Rats. He had lost no time in breaking the tacit agreements between the two mobs that the city was to be divided into two districts, and he had been muscling in on Spot's territory, mowing down his men and hijacking his booze trucks.

Spot had done his best to effect peace between them. He knew that there was no profit in warfare between them; it disrupted their business and put them in bad with the police and the federals. As long as they were quiet, and paid plenty of protection money they could go about their business undisturbed, but putting men on the spot and hijacking trucks was bad business. The newspapers inevitably raised a stink and the police had to shut down on them, and before it had all blown over a great deal of money had slipped past their fingers.

But Ruby Bascone could not see this. He was crazed with a desire for power, and he wanted to rule the city's underworld alone. He loved the fireworks more than the money; he had repeatedly hijacked Spot's trucks, thrown pineapples into his night clubs, cut down his men with machine guns. It was war, and war to the finish.

"The city isn't big enough for the two of us," Spot said to Slam Larsen. "Ruby's going to get me in the end unless I get him first."

Slam lit a cigarette and asked: "You found where Ruby hangs out yet, Spot?"

Spot shook his head. This had been one of his greatest difficulties in his war with the River Rats. They operated chiefly upon the river, which snaked its way through the eastern part of the city, carrying their liquor in fast launches and unloading it here and there into small fast trucks.

Despite the spies that Spot had sent out, he had been unable to learn where the headquarters of the River Rats were located.

Slam Larsen started to speak again but, seeing Spot's mood, he remained silent. He returned to the back of the garage and superintended the arming of the trucks. A few minutes later they thundered out the front doors and turned to the west, armed men in both the front seats and in the tonneaus, submachine guns ready for battle.

Spot looked after them thoughtfully as they were swallowed up in the darkness. He felt sad, though his face gave no evidence of it. Tomorrow morning was to be the funeral of Manuel Murray, one of his closest lieutenants. Murray's body had been found in a lonely country ditch, his chest riddled with bullets. The coroner's jury had rendered a verdict of "death inflicted a person or persons unknown," but there was no doubt in Spot's mind nor the newspapers that the River Rats had put him on the spot.

Suddenly Slam Larsen seized his arm. "Look, Spot!" he cried, pointing to a black sedan racing down the street from the west.

Spot recognized it at once. It was the armored, bullet-proof car which Ruby Bascone used whenever he left his headquarters. Spot's fingers closed on the grip of his automatic, half drawing it from his shoulder holster. But to shoot at the car was useless. Its only vulnerable part was the tires.

The car was traveling at over sixty miles an hour when Slam Larsen first sighted it. But as it drew closer to the garage it was forced to slow down by a truck turning onto the road from a side street. When it passed in front of the garage it was barely moving, and a street light illuminated the interior of the car so that they could clearly see its occupants.

Spot's lips parted in amazement. For in the back, sitting beside Ruby Bascone's bulking figure, was Rose Willard! Spot could clearly distinguish her slender rounded form, the black hair peeping from beneath the red hat that he had bought for her only the other day, the smooth oval of her face with the brilliant brown eyes and the splash of red that was her mouth.

Spot stared after the car as it disappeared in the traffic, his mind dazed. Rose Willard, his girl, his moll as all gangland knew, was riding with his worst enemy, Ruby Bascone!

His whole body went cold. At the thought of her treachery his legs began to tremble. For five years Rose had been his girl. He had showered her with money, giving her all the clothes and jewels that she could possibly desire. And now she was throwing him over for a grease-ball like Bascone.

Spot recalled that two years ago, before the death of Millio, and Bascone's ascent to power, Bascone had made a play for Rose. But she had turned him down flat and Spot had beaten him up to teach him better manners. Was she deserting him now because she believed that his power in the underworld was waning?

Slam Larsen, too, stared after the car, his eyes open wide. He whispered a fervent curse and looked apprehensively at his chief. Spot's two guards had their guns out and were waiting for orders. They had recognized Rose and knew that this called for war. Spot's prestige alone demanded it.

"Run out the car," rasped Spot, withdrawing his hand from his automatic. His face was white with anger.

In a moment a uniformed chauffeur raced up from the rear of the garage in a Lincoln sedan. Spot, Slam Larsen and one of the guards got in the tonneau while the other guard sprang in the front seat beside the driver.

"To the hotel," ordered Spot.

The car shot down the street to the Willmouth Hotel, which Spot owned and utilized as the headquarters for his gang. It came to a stop in the private entrance upon the turntable. Spot leaped out and hurried into the lobby. There seemed to be an unusual excitement, for men were clustered about in groups talking excitedly. A man ran up to him.

"Listen, Spot. Dope Manners is up in your room. He wants to see you right away. It's about Rose."

As Spot stepped into the elevator he glanced back into the lobby. He saw that everyone was looking after him. From their strained attitudes he knew that they had already learned what Rose had done. And he also knew what they were thinking. Such an insult, which was an insult to the whole mob, could be wiped out only by death. Death spitting from guns.

In his office upon the tenth floor he found Dope Manners waiting for him. He was a small man, scarcely five feet in height. He had no official connection with the gang, for Spot did not use dopesters, knowing them to be too unreliable, but he was tolerated about the hotel for he was occasionally useful in doing small jobs.

"Lissen, Spot," he whined. "I saw Rose get in the car wit' Bascone. She— Say! Don't!" He writhed in Spot's grasp, for Spot had put out a hand and seized his shoulder with iron fingers.

"Out with it!" snarled Spot. He was in no mood to be taunted with Rose's treachery.

"All right," gasped Dope, as Spot relaxed his grip a little. "I saw 'em. I saw the whole thing. An' Rose had to get in Bascone's car."

"What's that?"

" 'S the truth. Rose was walkin' down the street about half a block ahead of me. I saw Bascone's car run by me an' stop near her. I yanked out my gat an' started to run up, knowin' there'd be trouble. Three gorillas jumped out an' stuck their rods in her back. Then one of 'em threw her in the car an' it got away before I could get there!"

Spot released Dope Manners and tossed a hundred dollar bill to him, telling him to get out. If Rose had been forced into the car, she had not betrayed him. While it relieved him to knew this, it made action so much the more urgent. He had to get Rose out of Bascone's hands before she was injured, even though he had to search out every member of the River Rats himself and torture her whereabouts from them.

He ordered Slam Larsen to send three fully armed cars cruising through the river district. There was small hope that they would find her, but they might pick up some member of the River Rats that they could screw information out of.

Spot paced about his office nervously. It irritated him that he could hear his two guards talking quietly together outside of the door. He stopped before the window and looked out across the city that lay below him. In the distance he could see the twisting river shining silver in the moonlight, dark warehouses, wharves and buildings lining its banks.

His black eyes narrowed to mere slits and his lips drew back from his teeth in a snarl. Somewhere in those buildings Rose was imprisoned, and he was helpless to aid her. His own sense of impotence maddened him.

Unable to endure the inaction any longer, he took an elevator to the lobby. His two guards descended with him and followed close behind him. Slam Larsen came up to report that the scouting cars had reported nothing as yet, and that he had sent half a dozen spies on foot through the river district.

Spot wandered about the lobby, trying to distract himself, but he could think of nothing but the fact that Rose was in Bascone's hands. It seemed suffocatingly hot to him, and he went to the side entrance of the hotel for some fresh air. When his two guards fell in beside him, he turned on them angrily.

"Beat it," he growled, wanting to be alone for a few minutes.

He set off down the darkened street at a rapid pace. The cool night air and the fresh tang in the air seemed to refresh him a little and to help clear the confused thoughts in his mind. He walked block after block, paying little attention to where he was going.

"Hey, Spot," whispered a shrill voice behind him.

He whirled about, his hand automatically jerking his pistol from his shoulder holster.

"It's only me. Butch Capper."

A man slouched from the shadows. Spot recognized him as a cheap pickpocket. As far as he knew, Butch was connected with no mob, but worked entirely alone.

"What d'yuh want?" snarled Spot. "Make it quick."

"I heard Ruby Bascone got yer moll."

Spot's lips tightened and his eyes blazed, making him look like an angry cobra about to strike. "Well?" he said, jamming his automatic in Butch's stomach.

"Hey!" protested Butch, flinching. "I got some dope for yuh. I'm for yer mob, I am. I saw where Bascone took her."

of flesh, his thick lips dropping open and an expression of fear printing itself upon his face. This quickly gave way to anger that brought the blood flaming to his cheeks.

"Why—damn you!" he snarled. "You dirty double-crosser!"

Rose laughed harshly and turned a little so that Spot could see that she held a small .25 caliber Colt automatic in her hand. Bascone's lips twitched and he took a step towards her.

"Do you think you can get away with stuff like this?" he roared.

"Not so loud," warned Rose, "or I'll season you with hot lead. I don't want your gorillas down on my neck. And keep your hands away from your pockets."

She moved to one side so that she was out of the range of Spot's vision. Again he heard that faint tinkling sound. Then suddenly Bascone leaped toward the position where Spot judged Rose to be. There was a shot. The bullet splintered through the panels of the door above his head, so he knew that Bascone must have knocked up Rose's pistol in time to save himself.

Spot jerked open the door and sprang into the room. Ruby Bascone had his arms about Rose and was pressing her to his barrel-like body. Her automatic had dropped to the floor.

He leaped forward and his shoulders writhed as he sent his left fist crashing to the side of Bascone's head. Bascone fell back, mouthing curses, and Rose slipped from his arms. But, quick as a flash, he had thrown himself upon Spot, his huge weight bearing him down.

Spot stumbled and tried to break away. But Bascone's fat arms had a grip of iron and they were wrapped about his arms, pinning them to his sides.

Spot's great strength was no protection against this catapulting mountain of flesh, and his knees crumpled and he fell upon his back, the rival gang leader still on top of him. He felt his ribs crack and his breath was knocked from him.

But he still held the automatic in his right hand. As he fell to the floor with Bascone on top of him, he turned its muzzle against the gang leader's side and rapidly pulled the trigger six times. Bascone's body was paralyzed from a bullet in the spine before they hit the floor, and Spot rolled out from under him and sprang to his feet.

Rose staggered to him, her disarranged black hair streaming down over her shoulders. "Spot, we've got to get out of here," she cried. "They'll kill us!"

He looked at her grimly for a moment. She had betrayed first him and then Ruby Bascone. He ought to kill her for her treachery, but he had not the heart to do it.

"Where is this place?" he asked, still trying to get back his breath.

"It's an old warehouse on the river. The Sholsky place. You've never been able to find it because they only come here by boat."

He had not time for more questions, for he heard the sound of running feet in the hall. As he whirled about, two men burst in the door. One of them had a revolver in his hand and the other was tugging one from his hip pocket. Spot and the first man fired together, but it was the gangster that went down.

Then Spot's trigger clicked emptily and he saw that the gun was jammed. There was no time to try to clear it, for the second gangster had his pistol half way out of his hip pocket. Spot reversed his automatic and brought it crashing down on the gangster's head.

"Quick, Rose," he called, working desperately to get the jammed shell out of the automatic, "how do we get out of here? They'll all be down on us in a minute."

She slipped a small box in her coat pocket, grabbed up the small automatic that he had dropped, and ran out of the room ahead of him.

"Down the stairs here, I think," she called after her.

Spot raced down the dark stairs after her. The air echoed with shouted questions and exclamations. A man appeared on the turn of the stairs. Before Spot could get his gun into action, Rose had put a bullet squarely in the middle of his forehead, and the man's body tumbled down ahead of them.

At the bottom they found themselves in a vast storage room piled high with boxes and crates. In a fleeting glance Spot saw that much of it was liquor—bottled whiskey, alcohol and beer. On one side sliding doors large enough to accommodate trucks opened into smaller rooms. Rose hesitantly went through one of these doors and wasted valuable seconds trying to find the light switch.

"Shut the door and lock it," she directed. "I'm not sure about this other door. Ruby Bascone showed me everything in such a hurry that I'm not sure that I can manage it."

Together they slid the doors shut. Men piled down the stairs, their guns flashing fire in the semi-darkness of the storage room. Spot slipped the locking iron bar across the doors just in time, for a dozen men threw themselves simultaneously against the other side of the door.

On the other side of the small room in which they found themselves was a second set of garage doors. They were of heavy steel, triple-bolted, and with auxiliary padlocks.

"This opens—on—the street," grunted Rose, tugging at a bolt.

Spot lent her his aid and the bolt slid back. The doors had evidently been built to stand a siege from without, for it had almost the strength of a bank vault door. Together they began releasing the triple-locking mechanism.

Behind them men battered and pounded on the locked doors through which they had just come. Then there was a silence. A man's voice shouted from a distance: "Keep back!" Then there was a tremendous roar and the very walls of the room rocked and heaved.

Spot glanced back at the doors which separated them from the gangsters. They were twisted and splintered, but they still held. They were using dynamite on them!

He returned desperately to his work. The doors behind him would not stand more than one charge such as the last. He was confronted at last by a single padlock which locked a bar. He jerked at it, but it did not give. In the distance a man's voice rang again: "Keep back!" The second charge of dynamite was about to be fired.

He put the muzzle of his automatic against the keyhole of the padlock. He fired twice and the clip was empty.

But the padlock gave this time to his savage jerk and he slipped it from its hasp.

There was a second crashing roar of the explosion of the dynamite. A blast of air struck him and almost whirled him from his feet. The garage doors behind him were shattered and there was a gaping hole through it.

"The light!" cried Spot, throwing up the bar which the padlock had held.

Rose fired a single shot at the electric light bulb in the center of the ceiling and it was darkened. And not a moment too soon. There was a chattering roar and a steady streak of fire from the wrecked doors. A machine gun!

It was so dark that the machine gunner could not see their location. He started a deadly fan of bullets moving across the room from one side to the other. Spot and Rose threw their weight against the heavy doors and pushed. Slowly they creeked open, even as the steel hail crept closer to them.

The rain of bullets spattered on the opening steel doors, ricocheting in all directions. It almost touched Spot's elbow. Then together they burst through the doors and sprawled on the pavement while the bullets screamed over their heads.

They crawled on their hands and knees to one side so that they would be out of the range of the bullets; then they rose to their feet and began to run. They were on a narrow, badly lighted street, and on both sides of them towered the dark silent walls of the warehouses, while one end of the street debouched into a pier on the river bank.

They headed toward the distant street that ran parallel to the river. Behind them men poured out of the door which they had just left, their guns slinging a stream of lead after them.

They swung out upon the main street. Spot looked desperately about for some means of escape. He beckoned to a lone taxi cruising down the street. The taxi started for them, then, hearing all the shots, started to speed past them. Rose stepped from the curb and leveled her automatic at him. The taxi driver gave a wild look at her, then skidded the cab to a stop.

Rose jumped into the cab and Spot followed.

"Step on her, buddy," rasped Spot, "if you don't want a bullet in your guts."

The driver needed no encouragement. Half a dozen of Bascone's men dashed out of the side street, their revolvers blazing. He stamped upon the accelerator and the car leaped forward, throwing Spot back into the seat.

A bullet crashed through the rear window and threw a shower of splintered glass over Rose. Then the taxi whipped around the first corner and was out of range. But it was not until the driver had gone six blocks and was sure that there was no further danger that he slowed down to less than forty miles an hour.

Spot leaned forward and handed a bill to the driver that made him gasp. "Willmouth Hotel, and make it snappy," he said.

The driver glanced around at him; then a light of recognition came into his eyes. "Okay, Spot," he said, and stepped on the accelerator again.

When Spot settled back into the seat Rose threw her arms about him. Spot pushed her savagely away from him, his black eyes glittering dangerously.

"What's the idea?" he inquired sarcastically. "You threw me over for Bascone. I don't know why the hell you threw him over then. Have you decided that you didn't play the right guy after all, eh?"

Rose drew away from him and looked straight into his eyes. Her hair fell over her shoulders and her breast was heaving tumultuously. Spot thought bitterly that she had never seemed more beautiful or desirable than at this moment.

"Spot, you don't believe that," she said slowly, evenly. "Oh, don't you understand? Don't you see what I was trying to do?"

"I see all right." His face became black. "Don't think that I'm going to forget easy how you double-crossed me or how you laughed when Bascone kicked me. Not by a damned sight."

"But—but—Spot! I did it for you. Can't you see?" she pleaded. "You weren't getting anywheres against Ruby Bascone. He was putting your best men on the spot and hijacking your trucks. And you couldn't get at him because you didn't know where he was located. I knew that he wanted me; he had tried to make me before, and I thought that if I—let him think—that I was double-crossing you— Oh, can't you see?" The tears began to well from her eyes.

Spot grasped her shoulders in his hands and looked at her incredulously. "Do you mean," he asked, "that you went with Bascone just so that you could find out about him?"

Rose nodded vigorously. "Yes. I thought that just as soon as I found out where his headquarters were, I'd escape somehow and come back and tell you. And it wasn't really so dangerous. I had a gun with me. If he had tried anything, I would have shot him. When you came in, I was just going to escape, only he knocked my gun out of my hand."

"Why—" Spot stared at her for a moment longer; then he took her into his arms.

When he released her a few minutes later, she stroked his cheek with one hand. He felt something cold and looked down at her fingers. There was a large ruby ring on the third finger of her left hand.

"Say, take that ring off!" he exploded.

"Why, sure, Spot." She slipped it from her finger. "Do you want it? Ruby Bascone gave it to me. I've got lots more."

She reached into her pocket and took out the small box that Spot had seen her slip in when they were leaving Bascone's room. The lights were dim in the back of the taxi, but when she tipped back the lid he could easily see the glittering profusion of rubies that filled it.

"You got those from Bascone?" he gasped.

She nodded again. "I made him show me all around the place and dance with me a lot when he took me there. When I couldn't stall him off any longer, he took me to his rooms and showed me his collection of rubies. Then he started to attack me. I decided that it was time to escape then, so I pulled my gun on him and started to pick up the rubies he'd spread out on the table. But he jumped on me and I wouldn't have got away if you hadn't 've come. When you were working with your jammed gun, I picked up the rest of them and put them in my pocket."

He put his arms about her again and drew her very close to him as the taxi drew up in front of the Willmouth Hotel.

MURDER FROM BEHIND

Detective Lieutenant Merriam was in the tightest pinch of his life. Finger prints, incriminating papers and an eye witness pointed to him as the killer of a gangster boss. The shadow of the electric chair loomed big—

DETECTIVE LIEUT. STEPHEN MERRIAM STOOD IN THE DARKNESS looking at the house. The heat of anger throbbed in his brain and glittered in his eyes. One of the hands thrust in his coat pockets fingered a revolver.

"Hell!" he muttered furiously to himself. "I might as well get it over with."

With a heavy tread he started across the street toward the house. It was a gray-stone building on a fashionable avenue, set close between other houses on a bank that sloped down to the dark river. At one side of it and in the rear was a thick-walled, one-story addition without windows on either the front or the side.

He rapped sharply on the heavy steel door of this addition and waited impatiently. After a pause a small barred grating slid back and an eye peered out.

"What the— Is that you, Steve?" growled a voice.

The door opened and a very fat man stood framed in it. He was Tony Carrozo, the leader of the most vicious booze and dope gangs in the city. The flesh hung on his face in folds, but with none of the geniality and good humor generally seen in fat men; rather it was the coarse, blubbery face of a Satan grown heavy with idleness.

"Yeah, it's me," said Merriam.

He stepped into the entryway and Carrozo shut the door, making sure that the night lock caught. They passed on into a room which had been fitted as an office, with a glass topped desk at the farther end. Behind the desk the hot summer air flowed in the open windows which looked down upon the river where the lights of boats glistened upon the oily water. They were quite alone; the only other door which opened into the house proper was closed.

"What's the idea, Steve?" demanded Carrozo angrily, clipping his words with a vehemence that made his chin shake. "I thought I told you never to come here. There'd be a helluva squawk if anybody saw you."

"Yeah, I guess there would," said Merriam ironically.

"Well—what the hell! You want to get fired from the force?" Carrozo puffed as he lowered his bulk into the chair behind the desk.

Merriam's eyes smoldered.

"You should worry," he rasped. "I've been worth plenty to you." He dropped into a chair and faced Carrozo across the desk.

"I should worry, should I? What's the matter? Have you gone nuts? You want to get the can tied to you?"

Carrozo's heavy jowled face took on an expression of menace. His small red eyes almost hidden in the fat began to glint dangerously.

"Lissen," growled Merriam, trying hard to control the rage boiling up in him, "don't you talk about tying the can to anybody. It's me that's tying the can to you. D'you get me? I'm through with you and your dirty work!"

"Huh? Whaddayuh mean?"

"You heard me. I'm done with you. I've had enough of this damn stool pigeoning from you. They're beginning to suspect a leak down at Headquarters now."

Carrozo's face began to redden under the fine perspiration.

"You're talking big, Steve," he sneered. "Why you poor prune, you're dumber than I thought you were! You want to take the rap, eh? Don't think I wouldn't give it to you. One squawk outta you and I'll turn you over to the Federals. With the stuff I got on you on the croaking of Marty Crellor, the narcotic agent, it'd mean the chair for you."

The sweat began to stand out on Merriam's forehead. He knew that Carrozo had him, and had him right. How many times he had cursed himself for a fool! Carrozo had offered him big money to ride the booze trucks for him, and a dick's salary is small. How was he to know that the trucks were carrying dope on the side? One night there had been a raid by Federal narcotic officers and, after a pitched battle in which Merriam had not participated, the truck had escaped, leaving one of the Federal detectives dead. It was all on paper, in Carrozo's safe. The gang leader had only to turn it over to the government and he was done for. The evidence had even been framed in such a way that Carrozo did not enter and so that Merriam alone seemed guilty of the killing.

Ever since then Carrozo had been blackmailing him. Not for money, of course, but for information. Merriam had a trusted position in the Police Department so that he knew the activities of everyone from the moll-buzzers to the bomb squad. He had been able to warn the gang leader again and again of impending raids so that he had been able to come out of trouble with clean skirts.

But now he was through. He had been a square cop for years before prohibition laid its tainting hand upon the police force, and it went against his grain.

"Maybe so," he answered. "But if I have to take the seat, there might be some other guys sitting down with me."

Carrozo brought his fist down on the desk with a crash.

"Are you trying to get tough with me?" he roared. "Why you cheap precinct elbow! Lissen, and get this straight! You're not done. I've got the hooks in you, and they're gonna stay right there. You try and get out and I'll lay you down on some spot with a wreath of lead. I won't wait for the Federals to cook you."

"Like hell you will!" shouted Merriam.

He gripped the edge of the glass topped desk with both hands, fingers flat on the top and thumbs hooked underneath, so hard that his nails grew white.

"Shut up!" yelled Carrozo, heaving himself to his feet. "You lissen to me now, and lissen good! You start spilling your guts and you're done for. You don't declare yourself out in this game. You stick and play ball, whether you want to or not. Why you lousy tin-eared bull! If you don't—"

At this instant Merriam lost the last vestige of his control. His eyes shone madly as he jumped to his feet. His hand tugged the revolver from his pocket, jerked back on the trigger.

Carrozo saw his intention too late. He sprang back, his knees hit the edge of his chair and buckled under him.

"Steve! For God's sake—"

Hardly aware of what he was doing, a red mist before his eyes, Merriam pulled the trigger. The reverberating roar of the explosion brought him back to his senses.

Carrozo sprawled in his chair, his head hanging over the back. On the expanse of his white silk shirt a splotch of blood was slowly spreading. His huge body was completely inanimate.

"Good Lord!" cried Merriam. He had not meant to shoot. He had torn out the revolver with the vague idea of attempting to intimidate Carrozo.

He crossed around the corner of the desk and grasped one of the arms that hung over the arm of the chair. There was no pulse in the wrist. The bullet had entered his chest directly over the heart, killing him instantly.

Merriam dropped the wrist and stared at the figure. He felt no remorse for having killed the man. He had only cheated the state's electrician out of a well-deserved job. Justice was served, perhaps unethically; and thousands of people, the victims of his racketing and extortionist plots, would be thankful.

He glanced hurriedly about the room. He had left no trace of his presence. He slipped the revolver into his pocket and let himself out the private entrance. The lock clicked shut behind him.

Merriam had scarcely settled himself in the assembly room at Headquarters at a game of blackjack when Captain Brown, Chief of Detectives, burst in.

"Steve! Hell's busted loose! Carrozo's just been bumped off!"

The card game was summarily abandoned as the detectives leaped to their feet.

"Where?" cried Merriam.

"Out at his place. Harmack, the uniformed bull out there, just phoned it in. He was on his beat when Carrozo's chink came running out yelling that he'd been killed. Steve, you and Reilly jump out there quick. I'll be out as soon as I can get hold of Brennan and Steiner. And I'll see if I can locate Doc Hoffman. There's gonna be hell popping when this gets out!"

Merriam was dazed for a moment. Then he smiled grimly to himself. This was a break for him. Assigned to the case of the man that he had just murdered!

"Let's go, Dan," he said to Reilly, his brother-in-law and partner. "See you later, Cap."

They took a police car and raced to Carrozo's home, where they found Harmack, a uniformed patrolman, stationed at the front door of the gray-stone building. He admitted them and they questioned Kuo Chong, Carrozo's Chinese servant.

"My jus' now go out to mail some lettahs. I come back an' knock on doah. He no ansah! I go in—find him dead!"

"Yeah?" grunted Merriam. "Where is he?"

Kuo Chong chattered volubly as he led them through the hall and into Carrozo's office. The scene had not changed. Carrozo lay back in his chair in the same position in which Merriam had left him. The blood had seeped farther down on his silk shirt and was drying a darker red.

"Cripes!" said Dan Reilly. "So they got the old boy at last! He lasted a long time. Well, there ain't nobody gonna shed any tears over him."

"Yeah, he lasted a long time," agreed Merriam. "But when these Big Shots fade, they fade fast and completely."

He made a pretense of examining the body and the room. He speculated with Reilly on the way in which the killer had gotten into the room. Yet all the time he felt like an actor in some strange farce.

He did not remember the papers in the safe until he began this examination of the room. Then he felt a moment of panic; if they were found, and they certainly would be, he would be charged with the Crellor killing, and suspicion might run on him for Carrozo's death. He had to destroy them.

He tried the door of the safe, but it was locked. He went through the desk drawer, hoping that he would find the combination written some place for safe keeping. In the end he found it. It was written in pencil on the top inside of one of the drawers almost out of sight.

He twirled the dial through the combination. After a moment the tumblers fell into place and the door swung open. He quickly riffled through the contents of the drawers, found the papers which implicated him in the killing of the narcotic agent. But how was he to destroy them with Dan Reilly watching? He knew that Reilly would be loyal to him if he explained the situation, but he did not want to do this.

Then he remembered seeing a brief case in one of the desk drawers. He took it out and crammed the papers in the safe into it. When he got back to Headquarters, he could pick out the ones he wanted and get rid of them.

He glanced once more about the room to see whether he had forgotten anything. Captain Brown would be along in a few minutes and he must leave nothing which would implicate him. This was to be one more case which would go down in the police records as "unsolved."

Then his eyes fell upon the glass top of the desk. And in a flash there came back to him a picture of himself sitting before that desk, his fingers gripping the top tightly. There would be a perfect record of his finger prints on the desk, and Brennan, the finger print expert, would be certain to find them.

He put the brief case upon the desk top and took out his handkerchief to wipe his forehead.

"Hot, isn't it, Dan?"

"Yeah, it sure is," agreed Reilly.

Then, sure that Reilly's eyes were not on him, he put his hand with the handkerchief wadded up in his palm down on the top of the desk and began to rub it.

"Here! What're you doing?" snapped a voice.

He whirled about to see Captain Brown just coming in the door, closely followed by Brennan and Steiner, the photographer.

"What's the idea, wiping off that desk?" demanded Captain Brown.

Merriam looked down foolishly at his handkerchief. "I wasn't noticing what I was doing, Cap," he apologized.

"Huh! You're getting damn careless," snorted the captain. "Well, what's the dope?"

"Not much yet. This is just another gang killing."

"Any idea who did it?"

"Nope. It looks a little like Scollo's work. This is gonna he a hard case to crack."

"What's the brief case?"

"Some papers I took out of the safe. I'll look them over when I get back to the station."

"I'll take a look at 'em."

Captain Brown opened the brief case and ran through the papers swiftly. Then he gave a low whistle. Merriam's heart went cold, for he saw that the captain was examining the papers which exposed his connection with the killing of the Federal detective.

When he had finished reading the papers, he looked up at Merriam, his eyes both hard and sorrowful.

"This is gonna be a hard case to crack, huh?" he sneered. "Well, it looks like I know who did it."

Merriam went white.

Reilly gasped. "Who did it, Cap?"

"Your side-kick here. Merriam."

"What in thunder—" Reilly stared open-mouthed at his chief.

"You're slick, you are, Merriam," said Captain Brown. "And to think how I trusted you!" He wagged his head sadly. "I've been suspecting a leak for a long time. I thought it was funny that things seemed to spill outta the station so damn easy. I suspected just about everybody but you.

"Probably I never would have thought of you if I hadn't got a call just before I left the station now. Some bird called up and said he heard a shot here, and then saw you run out a minute later. I thought it was all boloney, but what do I find when I get here? You're trying to rub something offa the desk. Finger prints, probably. Then I look through these papers and find you was in that bumping off of Marty Crellor. Don't it begin to kinda look like maybe you croaked Carrozo? We'll damn soon find out. Brennan, take the prints on this desk. We'll see what he was trying to rub off."

The finger print expert dusted off the desk with a powder, bringing out clearly a series of prints just on the edge of the glass top.

"Whoever made these prints, Captain, was sitting in this chair here. He grabbed the edge of the desk like this—" Brennan sat down in the chair and illustrated without touching the desk. "They couldn't be made that way by anybody standing up."

Captain Brown's weather beaten face became more grim and forbidding. "Reilly, did Merriam sit down in that chair after you two got here?"

Reilly looked almost sick as he answered the question. Not only had he married Merriam's sister, Mary, but he had been his partner ever since he had entered the plainclothes department from the uniformed force, and there was a close bond of affection between them.

"No, he didn't, Cap," he said.

At this moment Patrolman Harmack pushed a small man in a chauffeur's uniform into the room.

"Here's a fella, Captain Brown, that wants to see you. He claims he saw something."

"Well?" growled the captain.

"My name's Hardy," said the man. "I'm a chauffeur for Mr. Ostermann three houses down. Well, about half an hour ago I was sitting in the car waiting for the boss to come out, when I heard a shot. Then a minute later a guy comes running outta this house and hikes down the street."

"Would you know this guy if you saw him again?"

"Sure. I got a good look at his face."

"Is this the man?" Captain Brown pointed at Merriam, who was standing at one side so that the chauffeur had not seen him.

The little man's eyes widened. "Yeah, that's the guy, all right. I couldn't make no mistake about him."

The grim look on Captain Brown's face deepened as the web wove closer about one of his most trusted men. "Brennan. Compare Merriam's prints with these on the desk."

Merriam made no protest as the finger print expert rolled his fingers on an inked pad and then on a sheet of paper.

"They're the same, Captain," announced Brennan.

"Uh-huh. Well, I guess this case is cracked wide open. We'll do down to Headquarters now."

Lieutenant Merriam had been in the box many times before when he questioned prisoners. It was an inside room at Headquarters with no windows, and it was practically sound-proof. But this was the first time that he had ever sat in the prisoner's chair.

Assistant District Attorney Grebel, hastily summoned from his bed, was questioning him, anxious for a confession so that the solution of the murder could be announced simultaneously with the news of the murder in the morning papers. Captain Brown stood against the wall watching, refusing to take a hand in it. Sergeant Murphy had his broad back against the door.

But Merriam said nothing in reply to Grebel's questions. He knew that they had all the evidence against him that they needed, but it would help him none to confess, and it might injure his case. They would not dare to use physical violence on him, for he was still a member of the police department and was entitled to some consideration. All they could do was to attempt to wear him down by threats and persuasion.

"Listen, Merriam," pleaded Grebel, "we've got the goods on you. You haven't got a chance in the world of beating the rap. You might as well come clean. Maybe we could fix it up so that it would look like self-defense or something like that. There isn't anybody going to get hot about Carrozo's being croaked."

"You get nothing out of me," said Merriam, "until I see a lawyer."

At this moment there was a knock on the door.

"It's Doc Hoffman," announced Sergeant Murphy, opening the door.

"You've got the bullet?" asked Grebel.

The medical examiner threw a curious glance at Merriam sitting under the powerful light but did not come in. He handed a little lead pellet to District Attorney Grebel.

"Here she is. I found it lodged, against the spine. It passed directly through the heart."

"Okay," said Grebel, and the doctor left.

But Merriam was leaning across the table gazing intently at the bullet in Grebel's fingers. An expression of amazement spread over his face.

"Let's see that bullet a minute, Grebel," he asked.

The district attorney hesitated a moment; then passed it to him.

Merriam examined it with growing astonishment that was clearly portrayed upon his features. For the bullet was not the one which he had fired!

He had shot a .38 cartridge, but this was a .32. For a few moments his mind could not comprehend this fact. Why—that meant that he had not killed Carrozo! The gang leader had been killed by a bullet from some other gun.

Merriam's keen mind set to work at once on this problem. The shot had certainly entered Carrozo's body from in front—hence whoever had fired the shot had been standing behind him. And from the fact that he had not heard the shot, a Maxim silencer must have been used on the weapon. Even a Maxim silencer makes some noise, particularly on a high-powered gun, but if it had been fired at almost the same time that he had fired his revolver, he would not have heard it. And his own bullet, then, must have gone through the open window behind Carrozo's back.

If only he had the revolver which he had fired. But it was reposing in the bottom of the river where he had dropped it on the way back to Headquarters. It would be almost impossible to find it. And he could not prove possession of it, for he had taken it from a crook who he had picked up during a raid.

His mind assembled the facts with lightning speed. If the killer had stood behind him, that meant that he had entered by the private entrance, and that he had a key to the door. Probably he had been standing in the dark entryway when he had fired the shot. But Merriam happened to know that only Carrozo's lieutenants had duplicates of the key. Perhaps the killer had been a member of Carrozo's gang.

But, if the chauffer had not seen anyone but himself leave the area, where had the killer disappeared to? He remembered the bank that led down to the river in the back. He must have slipped out of the door immediately after firing and escaped by the back way.

But this knowledge helped him in his present predicament not at all, nor was it likely to. He was headed straight for the chair, for he could not expect the police to believe and investigate such a fanciful story.

"Cap, you say somebody called you and said they saw me leave Carrozo's place. Do you know who it was?"

Captain Brown shook his head. "No. He didn't give any name. Whoever it was had a shrill voice, kinda like a kid's."

One added clue to the identity of the killer. A shrill voice. For it must have been he who had phoned Captain Brown.

Merriam looked about the room desperately. In jail these facts would be useless to him. Outside, he could follow them up and perhaps find Carrozo's killer.

Abruptly he sprang to his feet and sent his fist crashing against Sergeant Murphy's jaw. The policeman went down like a poled ox. Before the other two men could do more than cry out, he was through the door and running down the corridor.

Captain Brown roared like a bull as he dashed after him. Merriam whipped around a corner, darted into the detective squad room. The man at the switchboard looked up with blank astonishment.

With two strides he was across the room. The window was open. He threw his feet through it, lowered his body as far as he could, and then dropped. A breathless fall through the air as he fell fifteen feet; then the soft cinders in the alley beneath his feet.

Over his head Captain Brown's head protruded from the window.

"Stop him!" he shouted.

Merriam darted down the alley, past the open door that led into the headquarter's garage, and out into the street. A coal truck rumbled past. He made a dash for it, leaped into the body and crouched down.

Merriam paced impatiently about the little room that looked down into a littered courtyard. Twenty feet away the El tracks ran level with the window, and cars roared past, shaking the very house with their vibration.

On the dirty bed several morning newspapers were spread out. The headlines read:

CARROZO KILLED BY POLICE LIEUTENANT
Lieutenant Merriam captured but makes daring escape from police headquarters

There were large pictures of Carrozo, of the house and office in which he had been killed, of Lieutenant Merriam in uniform. Commissioner Shaw denounced the murder, and denied reports that Merriam had killed Carrozo in their drive to rid the city of "hoodlums." Police Chief Lungren assured the public that Lieutenant Merriam would be in custody within twenty-four hours. The police dragnet was out and the city was being raked with a fine tooth comb.

Merriam chewed savagely upon a cigar. He stiffened whenever he heard a step upon the stairs, momentarily expecting to hear Reilly's knock upon the door. He had taken the risk of phoning to him and asking him to meet him there late that afternoon.

At last it came. "Steve?" asked a voice. "This is Dan."

He opened the door and Dan Reilly walked in.

"Mary is frantic, Steve," he said. "For God's sake, why'd you have to kill Carrozo?"

"I didn't kill him."

"What!"

"It wasn't me that croaked him."

"Why—you just about as much as admitted that you did, Steve."

"I thought I did. But when I saw that bullet that Doc Hoffmann took out of him, I knew that I didn't." He went on to explain the circumstances and his theory.

Reilly sat as though stunned.

"Lissen, Dan," said Merriam. "We got to get the guy that did it. I can't hide here forever. They'll get me sooner or later. And you know it means the chair for me if they do."

"But what the hell can we do? Cripes, you know what chance there is of getting anything in these gang killings. We don't catch five out of a hundred. I might be able to pick up something from a stool, but I doubt it. You didn't see the guy that did it. It might be Druggan's mob, or maybe the Scollo mob, or even somebody on their own."

"I got a scheme that might work."

"Spill it."

"Well, we know a little about this bird that bumped Carrozo. We know that he had the key to the door. The way I figure it, it was somebody in Carrozo's gang. He came in to kill Carrozo and found me there. When I went off my nut and banged away at him, he fired at the same moment. Then he beat it out and called up Captain Brown. And he's got a shrill voice."

"That ain't much to work on, Steve."

"Maybe not, but it's the best we've got. Here's my idea. You get hold of Ray Douglas and pump him—or better yet bring him up here where I can talk to him. He was the closest to Carrozo in the mob. He'd know who would want to bump him."

"You're crazy, Steve! Douglas'd kill you! Carrozo's whole mob 'er shooting off their mouth that you're not going to live to reach the chair."

"I don't think so. I got Douglas's kid brother out of a bad jam once. He was a straight kid, and Douglas will listen to me. You go out and get him, Dan. Bring him up here about nine o'clock. I'll still be here if Brown don't pick me up before then."

The lights in the courtyard winked out as the night advanced. Merriam sat slouched in a chair before the window, staring at the dark mass of the El tracks and the lighted cars flashing by. An unlighted cigar, chewed almost to shreds, hung from his lips.

Then the sound for which he had been waiting came—the creak of the stairs and Dan Reilly's knock on the door. Reilly and Ray Douglas, a hard-eyed gangster, entered.

"Hullo, Ray," said Merriam. "Hoped you'd come."

"Dan here says you didn't croak Carrozo," said Douglas.

"I didn't. Do you think I'd be asking you to come up here if I had? Hell, if I'd bumped him, I'd be taking it on the lam on the first rattler."

Douglas looked at him searchingly; then relaxed. "I believe you, Steve. You were square with my kid brother, Jim, and I think you're square with me."

"Take a seat," invited Merriam. "I want to talk this thing over with you."

Douglas sank into the preferred chair while Merriam and Reilly sat down upon the bed.

"You know," began Merriam, "how things stand with me, Ray. If I get picked up, it means the hot seat for me. I wouldn't have a Chinaman's chance of beating the rap. With a smart lawyer I might be able to get off with life—but what the hell!"

"Yeah, they got you right, Steve. But what do you want me to do? Help you take it on the lam? I can get you out of the city, if you want. I'll stake you. Damnit! I'd be glad to. I'm not forgetting what you did for my kid brother."

"No, that isn't it, Ray. What would I do if I took it on the lam? I'm a cop, I couldn't be anything else. I'd go nuts if I tried to learn anything else. I'd rather take it on the chin than that."

"Then where do I come in?" puzzled Douglas.

"Just this. I want the dope on Carrozo. I'm gonna find who croaked him."

Douglas scowled. "You got a fat chance, Steve. If you didn't do it, it might be one of Scollo's rods, or maybe Druggan's."

"No, I don't think so. I believe it was somebody in your mob." He went on to tell him the deductions he had made.

"It sounds reasonable," admitted Douglas. "But there aren't more than six of us got the key to Carrozo's office."

"Well, then it's one of you six."

Douglas chewed his lip reflectively. "Maybe there's something in it at that. You say this bird that called Captain Brown had a shrill voice?"

"Yeah."

"Well, it might be Jack Millar. But, hell!—he wouldn't do it!" Then his face brightened. "By God! I'll bet it was Dope Claybaugh!"

"Thunder!" Merriam stared at Douglas. "Why didn't I think of him before? I sent him up for a five spot once. He's had it in for me ever since. He's just the kind of a rat that'd do something like that."

"He had a key. Carrozo used to think he was the nuts, though I couldn't see it. He's been having trouble with Carrozo lately, and one of the boys was telling me he was slated for a ride."

"Did he know it?"

"I think he guessed it."

"He fits, all right. He hangs out around the Blue Sky night club, doesn't he?"

"Yeah. He's got a room at 576 Devon."

Merriam stood up.

"Well, thanks, Ray. You've helped me a lot. You'll lay off of Dope, won't you? I want to handle him myself."

Douglas jammed on his hat. "Sure, Steve. If you want any help in doing it, give me a ring."

When he had left, Merriam looked triumphantly at Reilly.

"Boy, I'll bet a plugged nickel Dope is the bird we want. He had it in for me. Well, we're gonna get him and find out. If he did it, he's gonna spill if I have to beat his teeth out. You get hold of Bill Thomas and pick me up here at two thirty tonight. He keeps his bus on the stand over at the Draxler Hotel."

At three o'clock, before dawn had begun to light up the sky, Merriam and Reilly crept up the stairs at 576 Devon. When they reached the third floor, they stopped before a door at the end of the hall. It was locked, but a few minutes work with a lock pick and Merriam had it open.

Upon the bed, covered only with a sheet, lay the thin form of a man, breathing heavily in sleep. Without a moment's warning, they threw themselves upon him. Merriam straddled the man's chest, pinning his arms to his side under the sheet. What was meant for a shriek, turned out to be only a gurgle as Reilly rammed a handkerchief in his mouth. In a few minutes they had him trussed up tight.

"Now to see if we can find a gun with a Maxim silencer," said Merriam.

They searched the room thoroughly, but found no sign of a revolver. In the pocket of a pair of pants thrown over a chair they found a key which Merriam judged would open the door of Carrozo's office. And hidden under the mattress were several bundles of morphine.

They wrapped a blanket about Dope Claybaugh and tossed a suit of clothes in it. Then they carried him down the fire-escape in the rear of the building. In the alley Bill Thomas was waiting with his taxicab.

Swiftly the taxi whirled through the city and out into the country. It finally stopped before a little cottage built in the woods upon the bank of the river. They carried the captive into it and dumped him upon a cot. Reilly deposited a paper bound box upon the table.

"Here's some grub Mary fixed up for you, Steve."

"Thanks. I can use it, all right. You tell Mary not to worry about me. You and Bill come back tomorrow night unless I call you first. Dope ought to spill his guts by then."

When the cab had left, Merriam took the bonds off Claybaugh, leaving only the ropes about his ankles. Then started the long vigil to force a confession from him. He did not make the mistake of trying to extract it by physical torture. There was a much better method. Dope Claybaugh was a morphine addict, and if deprived of his drug for only a day, he would be a shrieking maniac ready to turn his own mother over to the police for a bundle of the precious drug.

For the first few hours, Dope did little other than curse Merriam. He stoutly denied that he had had anything to do with the murder of Carrozo, but the more he denied it, the more certain was Merriam that he was guilty.

But as the hours passed, as dawn came, then daylight with the blinding summer sun and the overpowering heat, and finally the twilight, Dope's courage oozed from him. His system was beginning to demand imperatively the drug to which it was accustomed. He cursed, shrieked, had convulsions, and was out of his head part of the time.

At last he broke down.

"Hell, yes!" he screamed in his shrill voice. "I did it! Gimme a shot, won't you? I'll go nuts. Yeah, the gun had a silencer on it. . . . Yeah, it's hid in the eaves' trough on the roof. Just go to the top of the fire-escape—"

Merriam gave him just enough of the powder then to stop the worst of his agony. He did not give him a full dose for fear that he would gain a dope addict's courage and repudiate his confession.

At eight o'clock Reilly and Bill Thomas showed up.

"I got him," Merriam announced grimly. "He broke a couple hours ago. We'll take him back now."

The cab drew up in front of Headquarters and the three of them walked into the lobby and took the elevator up to the third floor, where they went directly to Captain Brown's office.

"What the hell!" Captain Brown gasped. "Millar! Jones!"

The two detectives bounded into the room, their guns out when they saw Merriam.

"Cripes. We're not going to hurt you," protested Reilly.

"Here's the guy that croaked Carrozo," said Merriam, pushing Dope forward. "And here's the gun he did it with." He placed a .32 caliber revolver equipped with a Maxim silencer upon the desk.

Captain Brown gaped from one to the other of them.

"What's coming off here?" he inquired. "I don't get this. Are you stringing me?"

Merriam explained Carrozo's death to him.

"You've got Dope dead to rights. This is his gun, and you can get Major Laylan to check it with the bullet you took out of Carrozo. He's confessed, and he'll do it again if you want him to. C'mon, you!" He impelled the dope fiend forward. "Speak your piece!"

"I did it! I did it!" screamed Dope, on the verge of collapse. "Gimme a shot, won't you? I'm going nuts—"

Merriam cuffed him into silence.

"I still don't get this," puzzled Captain Brown. "You thought you croaked Carrozo, but you missed him and Dope here was behind you and did it with a rod equipped with a silencer. Is that the way it stands?"

"Yeah." Merriam spoke tonelessly. He felt no exultation in having cleared himself of the Carrozo killing, for the captain still had the papers which implicated him in the Federal killing.

Captain Brown seemed stunned as the full import of this struck him. Then he asked:

"But what about Marty Crellor, the Federal dick?"

"That was a frame. They used my gun and left it there. I didn't know there was dope on the truck. I didn't take any part in the battle. Dope'll tell you that."

"How about it, Dope?" asked the captain.

"Yeah, that was a frame—and a sweet one. Merriam didn't know anything about it. But can't you gimme a shot? I've gotta have it! I'll go nuts! I'm—"

"Jones, take him out," ordered Captain Brown, "and have Doc Hoffman give him a shot to quiet him down. Then stick him in a cell to cool off a bit. I want to see Grebel before I fix up the charges. Give him a ring and tell him to run over as soon as he can." He turned back to Merriam then. "Hmmmm. So that business of Marty Crellor was one of Carrozo's frame-ups, eh? You don't deny that you were on the truck though, do you?"

"No. But I'm ready to stand the rap for that. I can't prove anything."

Captain Brown looked straight into his eyes for a long minute. Then he swung about in his chair and opened a safe set against the wall behind him. He took out a sheaf of papers bound together with a rubber band.

"These're the papers on that," he said.

Then he slowly tore them across again and again, until they were only fine bits, and dropped them into the wastebasket. He rose and grasped Merriam's hand, his eyes suspiciously moist.

"Steve, as far as anybody is concerned, those papers don't exist! They haven't been given out to the press, nobody knows about them, not even Grebel, and I've never heard of them! We need coppers like you in the department. Maybe your hands were dirty, but they're clean now, if I know anything about you. We need men that can take it standing!"

A Gun Moll's Revenge

"We're gonna get those rats to-night! The same papers that say Duke is dead are gonna say Shorty Hastler and his whole mob are wiped out!"
—So swore Duke Darrand's woman.

"HERE HE IS, MISS," SAID THE MOTORCYCLE OFFICER. "Right where I found 'im."

He pointed his flashlight into the dark ditch that bordered the highway and pressed the switch. A beam of light fell upon a huddled, blood-drenched figure that lay in the bottom. The fashionable coat and vest across the man's chest had been shredded with bullets; the face had been shot into an unrecognizable pulp. Paula MacKinnon stepped forward a little so that she could see the figure. There was scarcely any change of expression upon her beautiful face. The darkness hid the slight quivering of her full red lips, the sudden tightening of her black eyes.

"It's him," Paula said dully. "It's Duke."

Sergeant Rebholz, of the city homicide bureau, gazed down at the dead man moodily. Duke Darrand bumped off—how the newspapers would roar! Duke Darrand—the racketeer king and the emperor of the underworld, who ruled with an iron fist, richly rewarding those who served him and ruthlessly wiping out those who crossed him. Duke Darrand—the youthful, intelligent and debonair millionaire gangster who maintained a great estate in Florida and was accepted by society there, who was a member of the boxing commission and was known the country over as a sportsman.

And now he had been found dead in a ditch like any cheap gorilla or greaseball! "Bumped off!"—the words that could be used as the epitaph of almost every gangster.

"Taken for a ride," muttered Sergeant Rebholz to himself. "They all get theirs, sooner 'r later. An' what a ride!"

He looked at Paula MacKinnon. She took it coolly. To look at her one would never guess that she had been Duke Darrand's moll, his sweetheart!

Rebholz knew the three men who stood behind Paula—what cop didn't? There was Chopper Cramer, and in the rear Nick Burlio and Jazz Maier, three of Duke Darrand's chief lieutenants. A chill ran down his spine as he looked at their grim faces. A picture rose before his mind of spitting machine guns and roaring bombs, of hell let loose upon the city. Duke's death was a thing that would have to be avenged with death.

He shook his head a little as he stepped into the ditch and knelt beside Duke's body. He began to go through the pockets and cursed softly when his hands became covered with blood. He had seen the bodies of many gangsters and racketeers who had been taken for rides, but he had never seen a body which had been so viciously mutilated. Literally hundreds of bullets must have torn through the man's head and chest. Only Duke's clothes and the papers in his pockets served to identify him.

The medical examiner arrived just as he finished his search. He gasped when he saw the body.

"My God, sergeant," he cried. "I've never seen anything like this before!"

He conducted a perfunctory examination, allowed the police photographer to take several flashlight pictures, and had the body placed in an ambulance to be taken to the morgue.

Chopper Cramer stood for a moment looking after the ambulance disappearing into the darkness. Then he turned to the motorcycle officer and asked: "You found 'im, Frankie?"

"Naw." The officer jerked his thumb towards a lighted farm house that stood on the top of a hill. "The farmer there saw the whole thing. He sent in a call an' they chased me out."

"What happened?"

"He said he was in bed when he heard some shots. He looked outta the window an' saw a big black car standin' beside the road here. There was two guys standin' beside it shootin' down into the ditch. He thought they had machine guns. They kept that up for about two minutes; then they jumped in their car an' beat it."

"Didn't see who they was, did he?"

"Naw. He was scairt to go outta the house."

But Chopper Cramer had no need to ask who had done this. They both knew that it was the work of Shorty Hastler's mob, the only gang in the city which had not come under Duke's leadership. There had been an armed neutrality between the two gangs, but lately there had been rumors that Shorty Hastler had tired of this and was ready to break it.

"Well, thanks, Frankie," said Chopper, "for lettin' us know so quick. Guess we'll be movin' along now."

He crossed the highway to the black Lincoln limousine that stood on the other side and slid behind the wheel. Paula got in the front seat beside him and Nick Burlio and Jazz Maier got in the back seat. Their faces were wooden. Chopper started the engine, whirled the car around and gave it the gas as he headed back towards the city.

The motorcycle officer stared thoughtfully after the disappearing car as he shook a cigarette out of a pack. "There's sure gonna be war now," he said.

Sergeant Rebholz nodded. "An' I hope they get that dirty Shorty Hastler an' get 'im good." He took a handkerchief from his pocket and tried to wipe the drying blood from his hands. "He needs it. I never saw a guy chopped up like they did Duke."

For a few minutes there was silence in the car racing back towards the city. The only sound was the roar of the high-powered engine and the whine of the tires. Chopper Cramer bent low over the wheel as he pressed the accelerator almost to the floor boards. The pointer on the speedometer hovered above seventy—there was plenty of time, but he felt the need of speed to release his tense nerves. His lips moved soundlessly in curses.

Beside him Paula stared straight ahead at the twisting road with burning eyes. Her white teeth bit at her red lips. Her heart was a raging inferno of hate. Duke was dead. Duke Darrand, her lover, was dead. She did not see the road. Before her eyes swam the vision of Duke's body lying in the ditch, his head pounded to a pulp with machine gun bullets.

She felt no sorrow for him. There was no room for that now in her mind. The only thing that she could think of was revenge. Perhaps later, when Shorty Hastler had paid for this with his life and his mob had been wiped out, there would be time for sorrow. But not now.

At last Chopper spoke. "Tonight?" he asked.

There was no need for him to say more. They all knew what he meant.

Nick Burlio and Jazz Maier in the back seat growled their assent. Paula nodded grimly. Her fingers caressed the butt of the .32 automatic that hung in a special clip holster beneath her left arm. She longed for the chance to pump her steel-jacketed messengers into Shorty Hastler's guts.

When Chopper reached the city he slowed down to a bare sixty. He whipped the car expertly through the crowded night traffic and drew up, with a blast of his horn, before a garage. Instantly an armed guard threw open the doors and the car slid inside.

The news of the happening had already leaked out. "Did—did they get Duke?" asked the guard.

Chopper nodded and they started up narrow stairs. At the top they went down a long narrow passageway. They could hear dance music. On one side of the passageway were small slits that looked into the Tropical Gardens, Duke Darrand's famous night club to which came the elite of the city's night life. Two armed guards were stationed at these slits, ready to quell the least disturbance.

At the end of the hall was a suite of rooms, one of which had served as an office for Duke Darrand. Here they found half a dozen men gathered—all members of the mob. Their faces were questioning.

"Well, they got Duke," said Chopper.

A growl ran around the room. Paula looked about and saw black angry faces. She knew that every one of these men would have willingly laid down his life for Duke, and that now they would give their lives for revenge.

And as for herself, well—hadn't she been Duke's moll? And hadn't he treated her as square as any man could treat the woman he loved? She had lived for him. Now, if need be, she would die to see that he was avenged.

But Chopper was speaking. He was telling them how Duke's body had been found. When he had finished, he stopped and looked around at them with blazing eyes. Now that Duke was dead, he was the gang leader, and he issued orders.

"We're gonna get those lousy rats tonight," he rasped. "The same papers that say that Duke is dead are gonna say that Shorty Hastler an' his whole damn mob 're wiped out!"

The chorus of approving grunts left no doubt that he would be willingly obeyed.

"We'll crack down on their Third Avenue headquarters," continued Chopper, "an' give 'em the works. They won't be expectin' it now. They'll figger we'll hold off a while. But we won't. We'll mop them up so clean that there won't be nobody left to bury 'em but the city." He turned to a guard who stood at the door. "How many men we got here tonight, Tony?"

"There's fifteen watchin' the floor an' the garage. But give me an hour an' I can round up fifty cannons easy. There's ten of 'em comin' in on the trucks in half an hour or so."

Chopper counted the men in the room. "We got enough right here, Tony. There's eleven of us here. Take seven men off the floor an' send 'em in. Then jump down an' get three cars ready."

The guard opened the door and the crash of the orchestra music reached their ears. A moment later men began to dribble in.

Chopper took a key from his pocket and opened a built-in steel cabinet which covered one entire wall of the room. This was the arsenal. Inside were racks of sawed-off shotguns, high powered rifles, Thompson sub-machine guns, and all types of revolvers and automatic pistols. There were shelves filled with boxes of cartridges, loaded automatic pistol and sub-machine gun clips.

He took a sub-machine gun from the rack, caressed it with loving hands, then laid it upon a table. "Two choppers for each car," he said. "An' take along plenty of ammunition. We may need it. Any o' you boys want anything? Help yourself."

Paula took an extra clip for her .32 automatic and dropped it into her coat pocket. She hesitated as Chopper took down a box of pineapples, specially-built bombs manufactured for them by their explosives expert. He gave two of them to both Nick Burlio and Jazz Maier and took two himself. Before he returned the box to the shelf Paula took two more and put them in her coat pocket.

"Everybody ready?" asked Chopper. He gave explicit directions for the attack; then they tromped through the hallway and down the stairs to the garage.

Three Lincoln limousines were drawn up in a line ready for them, a driver behind each wheel. Chopper Cramer, Nick Burlio and Jazz Maier each took command of one car. Paula did not wait while they distributed the men between them. She sprang into the trim roadster that Duke had given her, started the engine and whirled out of the garage.

She raced the car across the city at break-neck speed. She grazed fenders, missed street cars by inches and plunged through traffic lights set against her. The street lights sped past her in an almost unceasing blob of light. A police squad car turning upon the boulevard took up her chase with screaming siren, but lost her in the jam of traffic.

When she reached Grant Street, she stopped the car just before its intersection with Third Avenue. She got out and turned down the avenue towards the building which the Hastler mob used as their headquarters. It was an old four-story brick structure with a dirty radio shop on the first floor. There were lights in the windows on both the second and the third floors—almost the only signs of life upon the street.

Paula looked up and down the street, but there were no signs yet of the cars that Chopper was sending out to raid Hastler's headquarters. She had outdistanced them. But they would be along in a few minutes and she would have to hurry.

She entered the building beside the Hastler headquarters and walked up four flights of stairs. There a trap door at the top of a ladder opened upon the roof. It was fastened with a rusty padlock which Paula broke open by hitting it a sharp crack with the butt of her pistol. She pushed the trap door back and stepped out upon the roof.

The roof of the Hastler headquarters was a few feet lower and she jumped down to it. There was a trap door in the center. She tried it carefully. It was not locked, and she pulled it back a few inches. But there was nothing beneath it but impenetrable blackness and she replaced it.

She went to the edge of the roof and looked down. Half a block away, almost hidden by the darkness, stood an unlighted car. From the plans that Chopper had made she knew that it contained Nick Burlio and his men. Chopper himself was to come from the other direction, while Jazz Maier was to take the rear entrance. They had forgotten the roof, but she had set herself to guard that and to see that not one of Shorty Hastler's mob escaped in that direction.

She hid behind a chimney at the edge of the roof from which she could survey the trap door. She took out her automatic and snapped off the safety. From her position she could shoot down anyone attempting to escape by means of the roof. Hastler's mob would be caught like rats in a trap.

Paula hoped that some of them would attempt to escape through the trap door. It would give her infinite satisfaction to be able to shoot them down. She would be able to feel then that she had done something to avenge Duke's terrible death. . . .

Then she started. She heard the scraping of feet. There was a squeak as the trap door was lifted. It was pushed back by an arm and a head came into view.

Paula sighted her automatic and her finger tightened upon the trigger. She would send one of them to hell. But something stopped her, held back her finger. There was a strange grin upon the man's face. It was not the look of a man fleeing from death. It was the smug, self-satisfied grin of a man that had done something smart, that had put something over on somebody.

While she held her fire uncertainly he crossed to the edge of the roof so that he could look down into the street. He leaned over the parapet, keeping his head well back so that he could not be seen from below. The stronger light filtering up from the street fell upon his face. He was grinning like an exultant Satan. He chuckled loud enough so that she could hear him.

Paula was suddenly sure that something was terribly wrong. The alarm had not been given—why then had this man come up out of the trap door, and why was he looking down into the street as though he knew what were going to happen? Had the Hastler mob been warned of the raid in time to escape? Was this only a trap?

The man started across the roof, climbed to the next one and continued across that. If she were going to fire, she could not wait much longer. She suddenly decided that she would not kill him, but that she would follow him.

He disappeared. He had dropped to a lower roof. Paula stepped from behind the chimney and followed him. She was just in time to see a trap door slam down over his head. She raced to the trap door and raised it a few inches. She heard steps descending stairs and a man's whistle echoing hollowly through empty halls.

She followed the man through the trap door and started down the stairs after him. The building seemed to be entirely deserted, for there was utter silence and there were no lights behind the rows of doors.

The echo of a door slamming rang through the halls. From the sound she guessed that it was the outside door and that the man had reached the street. Throwing caution to the winds, she raced down the remaining flights of stairs. She must not lose this man. He might get away from her in the street.

But she opened the outside door cautiously when she reached it. The man might have stopped directly in front of it. Luck was with her. He had crossed the street and was standing beside a telephone pole looking back at the building which he had just left. She shut the door behind her and paused in its shadow.

The Lincoln car in which Nick Burlio had set out was not far from her, parked against the curb. Farther down the street, a sub-machine gun under his arm, Nick Burlio was running, with six men behind him, toward the Hastler headquarters. And coming from the other direction, with more men behind him, was Chopper Cramer. Paula knew that Jazz Maier was approaching the rear door at the same moment.

Chopper raised his automatic and fired once into the air. It was the arranged signal. His men converged with Burlio's, threw themselves against the door to Hastler's headquarters and crashed it in. Instantly they poured up the stairs, disappearing from her sight. The raid was on!

A minute passed without sound. Two minutes. By now there should have been the roar of gunplay as Chopper's men closed in on Hastler's. But only the rattle of a trolley car on the next street disturbed the deep silence of the night.

Paula's gaze swung around to the man who stood across the street. There was the same satanic grin upon his face. A premonition of danger seized her. This was a trap. She had an impulse to run to the building and call Chopper's men out.

Suddenly there was a thunderous roar that shook her eardrums. The ground heaved under her feet and a blast of air whirled her back staggering. A great sheet of flame leaped from the windows of all three stories of the Hastler headquarters, licking the buildings on the other side of the street. Shattered window glass rained down upon the street. A great portion of the roof leaped into the air, then slid down into the street, crushing a car parked at the curb.

It was a trap!

Paula leaned weakly against the side of the building, almost sobbing with rage. She understood it all now. Shorty Hastler had planned all this. He had figured that they would raid his headquarters as soon as they discovered Duke's dead body, so he had abandoned them and honeycombed them with explosives. They were probably wired so that Chopper's men would set them off in some way when they were well inside.

Flames burst from the windows again. There was a roaring as the building began to blaze. People rushed, screaming, from the buildings surrounding it. From somewhere a policeman's whistle shrilled. Paula gazed at the flames as though hypnotized. Her heart was like lead in her breast. She saw a picture of what the inside of the building must look like. The force of the explosion must have torn Chopper's men to shreds. If any of them had escaped alive, the flames would burn them to death. They would not have a chance.

Duke was dead. Chopper Cramer was dead. Nick Burlio and Jazz Maier were dead. All of the mob's best men rubbed out in a night. And somewhere in the city Shorty Hastler was probably laughing. . . .

The raging flames painted the street red. And things went red before Paula's eyes, red with the mad hate that burned within her. The man still stood across the street, laughing at the flames. Paula's hand slipped inside her coat, half pulled her automatic from its holster. At this distance she could easily put a bullet through his evil heart. . . .

There was the wail of a siren as a police car dashed up. A squad of motorcycle officers whipped around the corner. The ringing clang of a fire engine, then another. They came from all directions.

Two men stumbled from the burning building, their clothes burnt from their bodies. They collapsed upon the sidewalk and lay still.

Paula crept across the street, her automatic half out of its holster. The man turned and started down the street. She could have shot him at any moment. But she did not. It was not the police that stopped her. She did not give a thought to them. It was the thought that his death could not possibly atone for the death of Duke, and of Chopper, and of all the others. No, she would follow him. He would go to Shorty Hastler's new headquarters. When she had learned where they were, she could gather together what was left of the mob and take her revenge.

The man turned the next corner and she lost sight of the fire. She followed him carefully, keeping far enough behind so that he would not notice her. He apparently had no suspicion that he was being watched for, after traversing several blocks, he turned into an alleyway without a backward glance.

Paula hesitated at the entrance of the alley. If the man dodged into some dark doorway, he might easily escape her. She had to follow him, even here. She started after him, keeping in the deepest shadows.

Suddenly he disappeared through what seemed to be a door set in a high board fence. She hurried forward, running lightly on her toes. She heard a door open, then shut. She stopped before the fence and located the door through which he had gone. She looked for a crack or a hole in it so that she could see what lay beyond, but she found none.

She tried the door. The latch clicked and the door swung back. She was looking into a small area perhaps thirty feet square which was littered with rubbish. On three sides was the high board fence; on the fourth side a four story building with steps leading up to a door and a rickety iron fire escape leading down from the roof.

She slid through the fence door, crossed the area, climbed the few steps and listened at the door. There was only silence.

She started to turn back. She would gather together what men she could and they would raid this place. If Shorty Hastler were hiding here, they would search him out and kill him.

Then she stopped, electrified. A car was lurching down the alley. It skidded to a stop on the other side of the fence. "Run in an' tell Shorty—" rang out a voice. Then steps and the slamming of a car door.

Paula cast about desperately for some hiding place. But there was not even a barrel behind which she could conceal herself. She would be trapped if she remained where she was. There remained only one possibility—to attempt to escape through the house.

She opened the door at which she had been listening and breathed a prayer of thanks that it was unlocked. She found herself in a dimly lit hallway typical of the crowded boarding houses. There were rows of doors on both sides of her, but the few that she tried were locked.

The voices grew louder outside and she knew that the men were approaching the door. A hand rattled the door knob. Desperately she seized the only means of escape that offered itself and darted up the stairs that led to the second floor. At the top she found herself in a second dimly lighted hall. At one end shone the red electric light bulb that indicated the fire escape.

She had escaped for the moment, for the men who had entered the building did not come up the stairs. But she heard the sound of voices through a door. Despite the danger of her position, she paused to listen to them.

"Yup," said a voice. "It got th' whole bunch of 'em. It was fixed jus' right. Chopper Cramer an' Nick Burlio an' their gorillas was all inside."

There was raucous laughter. Then the clink of glasses and the gurgle of liquid being poured out of a bottle.

"You got 'em on the run, Shorty," boomed a voice. "Duke's mob is all busted to hell now. What's left we c'n mop up in two days."

"You shoulda seen it, though," continued the first voice. "The explosion nearly blew the front outta the building. The flames shot outta the window clear acrost the street. Two guys comes outta the door, but they was done. The clothes was burned all offa them."

"Good work, boys, good work," crackled a voice that Paula recognized as Shorty Hastler's. "With Duke an' his mob outta the way, there's big dough in front of us. An' I don't mean maybe."

The blood surged madly through Paula's brain. Now was her chance. Her hand slipped into her coat pocket and closed around one of the bombs. She could throw open the door, toss in the pineapple and wipe out these murderers at one crack. Blow their stinking carcasses to bits. Send them to the hell that they deserved.

Yet she hesitated. She knew the destructive power that was in this little metal container. It would not only annihilate everyone in the room, but it would blow out the walls and bury her under them.

Before she could decide, two pairs of feet pattered up the stairs. She darted down the hall, searching for some hiding place. None offered itself. In desperation she opened the first door that she came to and flung herself inside.

There was a curse. A man had been sitting in a chair tilted back against the wall beside the door. He had a heavy revolver in one hand. The front legs of his chair came down on the floor with a crash. He sprang to his feet.

But almost as quickly as her mind took in these details, Paula acted. Her hand lifted her automatic over her head and brought it down with all the strength that was in her arm. The heavy butt struck the man's forehead and he grunted hollowly. As he tottered, she struck him again. He collapsed, sliding his length upon the floor and turning over upon his back. She knew that he was definitely out.

Quickly she shut the door and put her ear against it. The footsteps had reached the top of the stairs, paused a moment, then entered another room. She breathed a sigh of relief. She knew that the men must have heard the overturning of the chair, but apparently they had found nothing suspicious in the noise.

There was a muffled noise behind her. She whirled about, her automatic raised, her finger pressing the trigger.

Then the muzzle of the automatic slowly dropped and she gasped in amazement. For she confronted a strange figure. On the other side of the room was a large easy chair in which was tied the figure of a man. Ropes had been bound about his arms and chest and legs so that he could not move. From behind a rag tied about his face so that it covered his mouth, muffled groans were coming.

"Duke!" she cried.

The man writhed in his bonds. His eyes stared at her with a mingled expression of amazement and relief.

For a moment Paula was paralyzed with astonishment. She could not understand this. She had thought that Duke was dead. Had she not seen his body riddled with bullets? But here he was alive. Then the explanation flashed upon her. It had been someone else whom they had found in the ditch. It had been someone dressed in Duke's clothes and with Duke's papers in his pockets.

And she understood too why the man's face had been shot to a pulp. It had been a plant. Shorty Hastler had had the man's face shot away so that they would think he was Duke.

She sprang across the room and seized the gag across Duke's face. She untied it and jerked the wadded handkerchief from his mouth.

Duke Darrand, his handsome face white and twisted with pain, tried to speak, but his voice was only an understandable croak.

"O Duke! Duke!" half-sobbed Paula. "I thought you were dead!"

She tried with fumbling fingers to untie the knots of the ropes about his chest, but the stiff rope resisted her fingers and tore her fingernails.

"Knife—his pocket!" gasped Duke, nodding to the figure on the floor.

Paula found a small pen knife in the man's vest pocket. With this she began to saw at the ropes. They resisted tenaciously, but at last the strands that held his arms parted. He took the knife from her and began to finish the job himself.

"Duke! What happened?" begged Paula. "We found a body in the ditch—and we thought—"

"It was a trap," explained Duke tersely, beginning to regain the use of his tongue. "Shorty Hastler and his men jumped me when I left Delmonico's tonight. They brought me here. They told me they were going to plant some guy that looked like me. They took my clothes off for him and gave me these rags."

Paula noted for the first time that he was wearing a dirty, baggy suit of clothes. The ropes about his chest parted and he leaned over to saw at the bonds which held his ankles. In the next room they could hear voices and shouts of laughter. The man upon the floor was stirring restlessly, groaning.

"They said," continued Duke without looking up, "that they were going to muss up his mug with a Tommy gun so that the mob would think it was me. They had some scheme, but they didn't tell me what it was."

The last ropes about his ankles parted and he leaped to his feet. He staggered slightly and had to lean on Paula, for the ropes had been so tight that they had almost cut off the circulation in his body.

"Duke," said Paula, turning her face away, "their scheme worked. They got—the boys."

"What?" Duke seized her shoulders with both hands. "Not Chopper and Nick and—and—"

"Yes, they got them all. I think they got Jazz too. They didn't have a chance." She told him then how they had rushed into the trap that Shorty Hastler had set for them, and how they had all been wiped out by the explosion. And then how she had come to be here.

Duke's face grew black and his head drooped. "Oh, my God!" he muttered fiercely. "The dirty rats! The dirty rats!"

Paula threw her arms about him. "But they didn't get you, Duke," she cried. "I've still got you. We'll get away somehow and get the boys together and come back—"

He straightened abruptly, and she saw that his eyes were burning madly. "We'll—get—them," he said. "We'll get them for this. They made a mistake when they didn't bump me off. They figured they'd hold me here so that they could learn where all my stations were. They thought that they could torture me into telling them where I kept my jack. But we'll get away now and—" He did not finish.

"I've got two pineapples here," said Paula.

"Good. We may need them." He crossed the room to the figure of the man upon the floor and picked up the revolver which was still in his limp fingers.

Suddenly there were footsteps outside and the door swung open.

"Shorty says to bring Duke in," sang out a voice. "He wants—"

The man stopped short in the doorway as his eyes fell upon Duke and Paula facing him. His mouth dropped open with surprise when he saw the guard stretched out on the floor, unconscious. But it was only for a moment. His hand streaked to his armpit and came out with an automatic.

But he never got a chance to fire it. Both Paula's and Duke's guns barked. The man, struck squarely in the forehead by both shots, fell back against the frame of the door and slid to the floor.

Instantly there was pandemonium. In the next room there were shouts and the sounds of chairs being hastily pushed back. From somewhere a woman shrieked.

"Quick! We've got to get out of here!" cried Duke.

Paula sprang through the door over the body of the man that they had just shot. In the hallway a man leaped from the door of the room next to theirs. A single shot from her gun sent him spinning and reeling along the wall.

Duke was upon her heels. The stairs to the lower floor were cut off from them. More men came piling out of the room, guns in hand. Together they downed the second two men that came out of the door. Shots spattered past them, ripping through the plaster and sending out showers of little chips.

More doors opened at both ends of the hall. They were just at the foot of the stairs that led to the third floor. They ran up them. At the top Duke turned around just in time to plug one man starting up after them.

Paula glanced up and down the hall looking for some avenue of escape. At the farther end a red electric light bulb shone feebly. The fire escape. But before they could reach it, the men would have swarmed up the stairs after them.

Duke was standing at the head of the stairs shooting down at the mass of men climbing up.

"Duke! Get back!" shouted Paula.

She pushed him back with her left arm and seized one of the pineapples in her pocket with her right. Her fingers sought the release pin and snapped it back. She threw it.

There was a roar that almost split their ear drums. A sheet of flames leaped up. The walls of the house rocked and shuddered. The stairs collapsed, the railing toppled over, the floor upon which Paula and Duke had been flung heaved upwards, then settled as though it were going to fall through to the next floor.

They struggled to their feet. At the bottom of what had been the stairs lay a few bodies almost covered with wreckage. A man screamed with agony.

"The fire escape!" shouted Paula.

They ran toward the back of the hall. Part of the floor had been torn away and they had to leap over the gap. Duke seized the door which opened upon the fire escape and wrenched at it. But the force of the explosion had twisted the walls so that it was wedged fast.

He cursed and grasped the handle with both hands, tearing at it. It creaked and slowly slid open. At the other end of the hall a door swung open and a man sprang out. A bullet whined past their ears and splintered the panel of the door.

Together they reached the fire escape. It had been almost torn from the side of the building and it hung out drunkenly, swinging back and forth. They stumbled down it, their feet crunching on bits of broken glass that covered it.

A gun roared above them. It was the man that had fired at them from the end of the hall. Duke turned his gun upwards and fired twice. The man screamed. His gun rattled upon the iron steps and thudded past them. Then his body slipped, fell through a hole in the railing. It fell past them, twisting in the darkness, one heel striking the railing near Paula's head. There was a crash as it hit the ground.

They reached the bottom of the fire escape. It ended ten feet above the ground. Duke jumped. He fell upon some scattered tin cans and almost sprawled full length from the force of the drop. Paula jumped after him and he caught her arms, breaking the force of the drop for her.

At the same moment a man burst from the back door of the building. Duke aimed his revolver and pulled the trigger, but there was only an empty click. Then the man was upon him and they fell to the ground, locked in each other's arms.

"They're out in back!" roared a voice from inside the house.

Duke twisted over, broke the man's hold and sent his fist crashing square against his jaw. The man folded up upon the ground.

Paula seized his arm and they began to run toward the door which opened upon the alley. Glancing back over her shoulder, Paula saw a group of men gather in the hallway and start out the door after them. She knew that they would not have time to escape. Before they could reach the alley, they would be mowed down by bullets.

"Down, Duke!" she cried. Her fingers snatched the second pineapple from her pocket and snapped the release pin. As she turned about shots sang past her. As she threw the bomb she caught a glimpse of Shorty Hastler's stocky figure among the men pouring out of the doorway.

An instant later there was a roar, a blast that picked her up and threw her through the air against the fence.

The bomb had exploded just inside the door. The walls of the building exploded out, crumpled down like a house of cards. A rain of bricks flew through the air. The iron fire escape, torn entirely away from the building by the second explosion, crashed full-length into the area, its outer end tearing down the high board fence.

Flying bricks and bits of wood almost covered Duke. Painfully he heaved his shoulders and crawled from beneath them. Grasping the twisted fire escape which lay just before him, he pulled himself to his feet.

He looked at the building which he had just left. Almost the entire rear wall had been torn out. He could see the floors sagging down. A flame leaped up from the wreckage and shed a red glow over the scene. He saw a body lying at the side, the head almost torn from the body. Despite the way in which the features had been mangled, he recognized that it was Shorty Hastler. Well—he had paid for his crime.

But Paula—where was she? Had she been killed by the explosion, crushed by the falling fire escape? He staggered about the area, almost sobbing with agony. If she were dead. . . .

His feet stumbled over a body at the foot of what was left of the fence. He bent over to examine it. His hands touched warm flesh, long hair.

"Paula! Paula!" he cried.

He fell on his knees beside her, gathering her into his arms.

THE BIG SHOT'S MOLL

Buck Garvey wanted The Big Shot's Moll to rat, but she wouldn't! Buck Garvey's dying words were: "She wanted me to rat on the mob!" And the Big Shot believed Buck Garvey!

I
YOU KNOW TOO MUCH!

BUCK GARVEY'S FINGERS TWITCHED as they slid across his vest toward the automatic pistol slung in his shoulder holster. His small eyes, between the slits of his eyelids, burned redly with the light of a killer who is ready to murder.

"Then yuh won't do it, huh?" he snarled, leaning across the little table so that he was balanced almost on the edge of his chair.

Babe O'Connor drew back from the leering face which was so close that she could feel the hot breath upon her cheek. She surveyed Buck with scornful contemptuous eyes. Her head, with the bobbed golden curls, the beautiful blue eyes and the full red lips set in a perfect face, was held high. Her lithe sensuous body was very tense and straight in her chair.

"How many times," she cried furiously, "do I have to tell you that I won't! Hasn't there been enough bloodshed already without starting a new gang war? Anyway, I'd rather die than double-cross Big Shot's mob. I'm no rat!"

Her body almost trembled with the force of her anger. It gave her a wild beauty, as of some sleek untamed creature of the jungle. Her blue eyes became as gray and as hard as steel.

Babe had always distrusted Buck Garvey. Even though he was the cousin of Big Shot Stacey, and was the chief lieutenant of Big Shot's mob, there was something elusive and furtive about him that made her uneasy. She had the feeling that he would be loyal to Big Shot only as long as no one else offered him a bigger price for his loyalty. And now her intuition had proved correct—he wanted her to help him betray the gang!

Of course, she had always known that Buck wanted her. He had asked her again and again to become his moll; and she had refused him just as often.

Babe was keeping herself clean—something unusual in the underworld, where conventional morality is almost unknown and women often pass freely from man to man. She knew the fate of these women: they might live in luxury for a time, but in the end they sank down and down, to the lowest levels of existence. Unless they luckily came to a sudden death, they died in unspeakable squalor and poverty.

It is true that Babe was not of the underworld, though she lived upon the fringe of it. Her father and mother had died before she was fifteen, leaving her to fare for herself. After a few years as a waitress in various lunchrooms, she had caught the eye of a theatrical producer and had been given a chance in a cheap dance revue. Her natural ability, together with her striking blonde beauty and long arduous hours of practice, had made her a successful dancer. She might have been a star—but she had not been willing to pay the price, and she had resigned herself to playing lesser parts.

It was there that Big Shot Stacey, the leader of one of the largest and most powerful gangs of the city, had found her. He had promptly sought her out and offered her a place in one of his night clubs, at many times the salary she was receiving. She had accepted when she found that he expected nothing of her but her work.

But, despite her own determination, she had as promptly fallen in love with Big Shot. Tall, big of body with great broad shoulders; a cheerful face and a ready grin; black hair curling across his forehead—he was the only man that had ever attracted her.

Men of Buck Garvey's type—gunmen, racketeers and gangsters—buzzed about her like flies. But she knew the tragedy of their lives; that most of them were dope addicts or would some day be so; that they were utterly untrustworthy; that their lives were usually ended in prison, or in the electric chair, or at the end of some other gunman's flaming gun; and she had turned them all away.

Big Shot, even though he was at the head of a gang, was different from these men. There was something wholesome and attractive about him that had instantly attracted her.

But if he loved her, he gave no sign of it. Still, she knew that he liked her, and she often dared to hope that some day, some day he might. . . .

"You're a nice kid, Babe," he often said, stopping beside her to fondle her golden curls as she danced in the Red Dragon. "Keep going the way you are, and—"

He had first placed her in the Whoopie Rendezvous night club. She had been an immediate success there, and it was not long before he transferred her to the Red Dragon and put her in charge of the entertainment and the music.

With the growing prosperity of the mob, Big Shot had purchased a farm just outside of the city limits. The farmhouse, a great colonial building located at the end of a long lane off the state road, he had turned into a fortress to serve as the headquarters of the mob. With its barricaded windows, its heavy steel doors and its armed guards, it was practically impregnable from the attack of any but an army.

At the head of the lane, just off the state road, was the Red Dragon, the most elaborate and exclusive club that the gang maintained. Only the elite of the underworld, and of the social and political world, could gain entry there.

Babe had been there to-night, rehearsing a new dance with the orchestra, when Buck Garvey approached her.

"C'n I see yuh pretty quick, Babe?" he asked. "I wanta talk to yuh."

"Sure, Buck," she answered, signaling to the orchestra to stop. "I'm going to run up to headquarters in about half an hour. I want to go over a new scheme with Big Shot. Be all right if I see you then?"

The first guests were straggling in when she left at eleven o'clock. She jumped into her roadster, ran the eighth of a mile back along the lane to headquarters. Buck met her at the door and took her into a private room.

There he broached his plan to her. He and a number of others were tired of Big Shot's domination of the mob, and he proposed to take over command himself. He had made a temporary alliance with Tony Ruso, Big Shot's most powerful competitor in the city, and together they planned to make a sudden raid upon headquarters, wipe out Big Shot and his most faithful men, and bend the rest to his will.

"You're crazy, Buck!" cried Babe, when she heard the plan. "You couldn't do it!"

"I couldn't, huh?" sneered Buck. "Well, I'm going to! It'll be easy. Lissen. I'm gonna get the guards off on one side, then open the door for Ruso's gorillas. You take care o' Big Shot. I don't mean bump him off—we'll do that; but get him off upstairs somewhere where he can't do nothin' till it's all over. See?"

Babe flushed red with anger.

"You know damn well I'm not that kind of a rat, Buck!" she flung at him.

"Aw, don't get sore, Babe. Big Shot's gotta go sometime. An' it might as well be now. C'mon, now. Why can't you an' me hook up together? I'll give yuh anything yuh want. Yuh know I'm crazy about yuh. I want yuh fer my moll. We c'd go a long way together. An' with you helpin' us, we c'n work this slick."

"I told you no once!" spat Babe.

Buck pleaded, cajoled and threatened, but Babe remained adamant. She had seen too often the results of gang wars. The roar of pistols, several bodies found on country roads, and a new gang leader in power. And then, in a few months, it began all over again. There seemed to be no limit to human greed and ruthlessness. A gang leader's throne was an insecure one. And she had no desire to mix herself in any gang.

But to betray Big Shot—it was unthinkable. Though she was not a member of his mob, she owed her allegiance to him. And infinitely stronger than that—she loved him.

"Then yuh won't do it, huh?" cried Buck finally, losing his temper.

Babe flung her reply in his teeth again. Her hands clenched the edge of the table until her knuckles were white. Even though she were to die by inches, it would be impossible for her to betray Big Shot.

And she knew that she was staring into the eyes of a killer. She saw his hand creeping toward his automatic beneath his arm pit. Unless she immediately accepted his proposition, she knew that he meant to kill her.

"Then yuh know too much to live!" rasped Buck, his fingers leaping like the dart of a snake to his gun.

There was no time for Babe to draw the little automatic that was slung under her arm. Before she would even be able to get its muzzle from its clip holster, she would be riddled with bullets.

Buck's automatic never left its holster. Quick as thought, Babe jerked her arms forward, throwing the table against Buck's chest. Caught off balance, he fell backwards.

And in the split second before he could regain his balance, her automatic streaked from its holster and was spitting death at him. Three times she sent bullets crashing into his chest before he fell from the chair and sprawled upon the floor.

She leaped to her feet and stood staring down at him, ready to fire again if necessary. But Buck was done. One of the bullets had struck his spine and he was paralyzed. His chest heaved and blood frothed on his lips.

Babe stared down at him, terror-stricken. It had happened so quickly that she scarcely realized what she had done. It was the first time that she had ever killed a man, or even fired a shot at one. The little automatic had been given to her by Big Shot, and she had worn it for her protection at his insistence.

There was a shout in the corridor outside the door. A figure burst through the door, wrested the automatic from her unresisting fingers.

"What the hell!" he breathed, bending down over Buck.

She saw that it was Ray Meyers, one of the headquarter guards.

"He wanted me—to double-cross the mob, Ray," she said.

Feet pounded down the hall. More men came through the door.

"Buck!" cried a voice.

Babe looked up to see Big Shot falling on his knees beside Buck Garvey. But now his usually genial face was very grim.

"Babe plugged him, Big Shot," offered Ray. "Here's her rod. She was still holdin' it when I come in. I took it away from her."

On the floor Buck groaned, tried to speak.

"Quick! Get Doc Shapley," ordered Big Shot.

"It's too late," muttered Buck painfully. "She got me. Through the lung. I'm done for."

Big Shot seized Buck's hand. "Buck! What happened?"

Buck's eyes had fallen shut. But at the question they opened. He stared up at Big Shot; then over at Babe. An evil light came into them.

"She wanted me to rat on the mob," he mumbled, his voice growing rapidly weaker. "Wanted me to double-cross yuh fer Tony Ruso. When I wouldn't, she plugged me. Damn her!"

Then he died. But his open dead eyes remained fixed on Babe in an accusing stare.

II

Sentenced to Death

Big Shot sat with his elbows upon the desk in his office at headquarters, his head sunk dejectedly into his hands. His curling black hair fell down across his forehead. His fingers concealed his down-cast face.

Babe O'Connor a traitor? He could scarcely believe it. Why—he had loved her! And he had thought that she loved him, or at least cared for him.

Yet in the other room, a grim reminder of it, lay Buck Garvey's body covered with a sheet. And before him on the desk was the .25 Colt automatic which he had given Babe and practically forced her to wear. He had loved his cousin as though he were his brother, and he had trusted him in everything. Now—now he was dead by the hand of the woman whom he had thought some day to marry.

A shudder ran through him. Sometimes he hated his gang and his work. It made beasts of men and women. To kill and be killed. Money flowed like water, and life was almost as cheap. Though gold poured into one's lap, it robbed one of everything finer in life.

Often he had wished that he and Babe might leave it all and go to some quiet peaceful place where they could live happily without the eternal fear of some gunman's bullet in their back. But now the life had gotten Babe; she was the murderess of his best friend; she had sold her soul to the most vicious gang leader in the city; she had been willing to knife him in the back.

He lifted his head and looked at his lieutenants who sat about his desk in a circle. They were waiting for him to speak. Babe O'Connor sat in that circle, but it was as a prisoner.

Babe's eyes were traveling from face to face about that circle. And in each face she saw disgust and anger. She knew that they had the supreme contempt for her that any gangster has for a rat or a stool pigeon.

There at Big Shot's right was Olie Jensen, the mob's chief engineer and the caretaker of the arsenal, his usually good-natured face set in a puzzled frown. Babe knew that the tall Swede had liked her, though they had seen each other seldom. Beside Olie, on her left, was Jake Swartz, the manager of the great fleet of trucks that carried their liquor in and out of the city and to all the neighboring towns.

On her right the suave, handsome Al Feraro glowered at her; he was in charge of the hundreds of Italians who cooked out alcohol and made the wines and finer beverages. And then, on Big Shot's left, was the flat-faced Fred Pabst, leader of the mob's gunmen and musclemen.

She looked at Big Shot. He had dropped his head back into his hands so that she could not see his face, but she knew how he was suffering. Her heart grew heavy within her. Buck Garvey's last dying words had condemned her with him. She had the hopeless feeling that it would be useless for her to tell him or the others the truth—they would only disbelieve her.

Fred Pabst broke in upon the silence, growling:

"I say bump her off, Big Shot."

"She's guilty as hell," added Jake Swartz.

The other two lieutenants said nothing. Big Shot looked up again, looked full at Babe with an accusing damning stare that struck her to the heart.

"Well, Babe," he asked wearily, "what've you got to say?"

Babe held her head high and tried to appear nonchalant. The light from the chandelier shimmered upon her golden curls. The only sign she gave of the stark despair within her was a slight whitening and trembling of her red lips.

"What's the use?" she inquired. "You wouldn't believe me anyway."

"You're damn right we wouldn't believe you!" grated Fred Pabst. "You double-crossing rat!"

"Shut up, Pabst," ordered Big Shot. "Let's hear what she's got to say. Maybe she had her reasons."

"They better had be good ones," added Al Feraro.

Babe took a deep breath. She knew that she would not be believed, and that death was hanging over her by a thin thread. But she had to warn Big Shot. Buck Garvey had sold himself to Tony Ruso, and he had said that other members of the gang had also. Even though she could not save her own life, she might be able to put him on his guard against Ruso.

"You want to know? I'll tell you!" she flashed. "Buck told me that he wanted to see me about something, and I told him that I would meet him here. When I got here, he took me into the room. There he told me that he had hooked up with Tony Ruso, and that he was going to kill you and take over the mob. He wanted me to help him and—"

She broke off. She was going to add that he had asked her to be his moll, but she could not say it. Not before Big Shot. They all knew that she worshipped him.

"Anyway," she continued, "I told him to go to hell. Then he started to pull his rod and I had to kill him."

"Yeah!" snarled Fred Pabst. "You damn dirty little liar! Buck Garvey was one o' our best men, an' you know it. You're jus' tryin' to lie your way out."

"She's the one that sold out to Tony Ruso," put in Jake Swartz. "Didn't Buck say so himself? She wanted him to rat on us, an' when he wouldn't, she plugged him." He looked straight into her eyes and added: "An' yuh know damn well that's so, Babe."

Big Shot looked down at his desk. He picked up Babe's small automatic and fingered it while he considered. Then he said:

"Call in Ray Meyers, Jake. We'll see what he's got to say."

Jake Swartz stepped to the door and called out, "Meyers!"

The gunman, who had been waiting outside, stepped in and shut the door behind him.

"Now, Ray," began Big Shot. "Tell us just what happened."

Ray Meyers looked at Babe and licked his lips nervously.

"Well, I was goin' down the hall when I heard Babe yellin'. I thought that was kinda funny, an' I stopped an' listened a minute. I heard her say: 'Then yuh won't do it, huh? Yuh know too much to live!' Then there was three shots. I jumped in the door an' she was standin' over Buck with her rod in her hand. I took the gat away from her, an' then the rest o' yuh come in."

Babe leaped to her feet.

"Why, you lousy little kike! You—"

"That's what yuh said," persisted the gunman. "I heard yuh all right."

"Oh, you rat!" choked Babe, looking as though she were going to spring upon the man and tear him tooth and nail. "Then you were in with Buck! You sold out to Tony Ruso with him. You're in—"

"Shut up!" roared Big Shot.

Babe looked at him appealingly, but she saw no mercy nor belief in his face. Ray Meyers' lie had been the last thing needed to condemn her forever in his eyes. She was crushed. She had not expected Meyers to help her, but she had not suspected that he was in the conspiracy with Buck.

She sank back into her chair. The horrible irony of the situation struck her, and she almost laughed hysterically. Big Shot's mob was faced with the most dangerous test in its existence, it was undermined with treachery, and she, the only one who knew this and might be able to help them, was not believed and was branded a traitor.

"All right, Ray," said Big Shot. "Get out."

The gunman threw a last malignant and triumphant glance at Babe and slunk out of the room. But Babe was the only one that saw the triumph in his eyes—the others were looking at her.

"She's guilty as hell," declared Jake Swartz for the second time. "Her story don't even stick together. If Buck Garvey had been gonna rat on us—which ain't possible—an' reached for his rod to plug her, she wouldn't be here now. Buck could beat anybody on the draw, let alone a cheap twist like her."

"Listen, Big Shot," pleaded Babe desperately. "Can't you believe me? You've got to. I can't help how it looks, Buck was double-crossing you. And Ray Meyers was in on it with him. He was lying to save his own skin. He lied about what I said. It was Buck that said that. It's not that I care so much about myself. It's you and the mob that I'm thinking about. If there are rats in the mob—and Ray Meyers is one of them—you've got to find out who they are. Just because Buck is dead won't stop this!"

But she could see that Big Shot was listening to her, wearily, unbelievingly.

"What's the use of lying, Babe?" he asked. "You can't get out of this jam that way. Buck was my best man, and he wouldn't lie to me when he was passing out. A man doesn't lie at such times."

He stopped and looked around at his men. They were all staring belligerently at Babe.

"I say bump her off!" rasped Fred Pabst. "We've had enough of this wah-wah."

Big Shot was silent for a few moments. Then he said:

"Well, I'm going to leave it up to you, boys. I can't decide what to do. Buck was my cousin, and Babe—" He broke off.

But Babe knew what he meant, and every man there knew. It wrenched her heart so that tears almost burst from her eyes. He meant that he had cared so much for her that he couldn't judge her.

"Well, Jake?" he asked.

"Take her for a ride!"

"An' the quicker the better," added Fred Pabst. "Yuh can't kill a rat too quick."

"Put her on the spot," chimed in Al Feraro.

Only Olie Jensen hesitated. But when they all looked at him questioningly, he nodded his head.

Death! Babe faced it bravely. There was not a break in her face as they pronounced it on her. No man was ever going to say that she was a coward.

Silence. Big Shot had hidden his face behind his hands again. They waited for him to speak. When he finally looked up, Babe saw that his face was haggard.

"Babe," he said slowly. "You're washed up. But I'm going to give you one chance. One chance."

The men muttered. All except Olie Jensen, who looked hopeful.

"If you come clean, Babe, I'll let you take it on the lam. You can take your roadster, I'll give you five grand, and you can beat it out of here. Go someplace where we'll never see you again. But I warn you that if you ever come back, you'll be shot on sight!"

When Babe replied, she looked straight into his eyes without flinching. It was he that looked away.

"I can't come clean," she said, "because this is a frame-up. You're taking the word of men like Buck Garvey and Ray Meyers against mine. So—you might as well kill me now and have it over with."

"It's your only chance," pleaded Big Shot.

Babe did not answer. It was taking all her courage to maintain her pose. She had to bite her lower lip to keep it from trembling.

"All right then. Well—who wants to take the ride?"

"I'll do it," offered Fred Pabst. "An' damn glad to see that a rat gets hers." He leered at Babe.

"Okey. But"—and Big Shot's voice almost broke—"get it over quick."

III
TAKEN FOR A RIDE

THE BIG TOURING CAR SHOT AWAY FROM HEADQUARTERS and roared down the lane toward the state road, its powerful headlights cutting a wide swath through the darkness.

In the back seat sat Babe, her golden curls flying in the wind that whipped around her head. Her immobile face masked the black sorrow and despair that lay behind it. Her last ride! The ride of all rides!

The cold bore of an automatic pressed in her side. Ray Meyers sat on the seat beside her, twisted sideways so that he almost faced her, his eyes never leaving her. He was the executioner, and it was his duty to guard her until they reached the spot.

Fred Pabst guided the car expertly, stepping on the accelerator savagely so that it leaped ahead with its power. Once he glanced around at Babe and laughed harshly.

The car approached the Red Dragon at the head of the lane. It was almost midnight, and cars were turning into the parking place in a steady stream. The lights shone eerily upon the great molded dragon's head that hung out over the entrance. Above the roar of the motor Babe could hear the blare of the orchestra.

Inside was gayety, laughter and music. Couples were dancing, rejoicing in the ecstasy of life, careless of the morrow. That was where she should be now, coming out upon the stage in her pirate costume, dancing happily, the orchestra playing a gay lilting tune. . . .

But instead, she was riding past with an automatic pressed in her side, riding to her death. All this gayety would go on, but her lifeless body would be lying in some lonely country ditch. The horrible death of a traitor.

A sob rose to her throat and choked her. Life was so sweet and delicious. She had braved death before, but she had never thought it would be like this.

Then, as the car turned upon the state road and the sound of the music grew dim behind her, she half-turned for one last look.

"Careful," growled Ray Meyers. "One move outta yuh an' I'll fill yuh with hot lead. I'd do it now, only I don't wanta smear up the cushions."

Then he gave a taunting laugh in which Fred Pabst joined.

"Boy! We sure pulled this off slick!" exulted Pabst. "For a coupla minutes there, when I saw Buck was plugged, I thought we were goners."

"It looked bad," agreed Ray Meyers. "But Big Shot never tumbled. He thought so damn much o' Buck, I guess he never thought he could rat on him."

"Buck was a damn fool for even tryin' to make Babe. I told him he was crazy, that he was a damn fool, but no, he hadda try it. He'd gone nuts on her. Well, he got himself sunk for it."

"Anyway, he played straight with us."

"Played straight? Whadda yuh mean?"

"Well, he didn't squawk on us, did he? If he had, we'd 'a' been goners. Buck knew he was done for, but he stuck with us."

"Be yourself," jeered Pabst. "Buck didn't stick with us. He wanted to get back at Babe for what she did, an' that was the only way he had."

Babe's blood was boiling with anger as she listened to them. She had suspected that Fred Pabst was in the conspiracy against Big Shot when he chose Ray Meyers to help him take her for the ride. She remembered how bitterly he had been against her for her "treachery," and how he had been the first to demand her death.

They rode in silence for a time. Before them lay the dark mass of the city, criss-crossed by paths of light, a dome of light over it. From the distance echoed the shrill of the trains. Through the dark masses of clouds moving slowly across the sky occasional stars shone.

Fred Pabst turned the car on a side road that would take them around the city. They did not want to put her on the spot too near the Red Dragon, so they were taking her to some dark lonely road on the other side of the city.

"Big Shot gives me a laugh," went on Pabst. "He's so damn cocky. It warmed my guts to see the way he got hot over Buck's passing out."

"An' his guts are gonna get warmed to-night—with hot lead." Ray Meyers guffawed loudly at his pun. "Sa-ay! Ruso won't call it off to-night jus' because Buck got bumped, will he?"

"Hell, no! It's all fixed for four o'clock this morning. A punk like Buck Garvey ain't gonna make no difference. Ruso's gonna have his whole mob ready. With you an' me to open up the doors, it ought to be a pipe."

Babe had to grit her teeth to keep from breaking in upon their boasting. She wanted to tell them that they had not won the battle yet. But in the bottom of her heart she knew that Big Shot would have little chance against them. He was prepared for any attack that might come from the outside, but not for traitors in his midst.

As the car whipped through the darkness and the cool air bit at her cheeks, Babe's brain gradually cleared. Her boiling emotions subsided and she took a firm grip upon herself. She was not dead yet, she told herself. She began to scheme calmly. There was only one man guarding her. If she could catch him off his guard for only a moment, she might be able to take advantage of it and escape.

Though she kept her face straight ahead, she began to watch Ray Meyers narrowly. Just the slightest relaxation of his vigilance might give her an opportunity. If she lost—well, she had lost. Death would only come a few moments sooner.

But no chance offered itself. She knew that at the slightest suspicious move upon her part Ray Meyers would fire. He would take no chances. He was watching her like a hawk.

"It won't be long now," flung back Pabst jocularly as he turned from the main road to a little frequented one on the other side of the city. He was already slowing down the car, looking for a place to stop.

"How's it feel to be bumped off, Babe?" jeered Meyers.

"Not so hot, eh?" chuckled Pabst. "Though it's a shame to knock off a good-lookin' broad like you. I wouldn't mind havin' you to myself for a while. But hell! Business is business." He sighed mockingly.

He slowed down, almost stopped; then caught sight of a light in a farm house and continued on. Babe saw that if she were to do anything, she would have to act quick. She had only a few more minutes of life. For the first time she spoke.

"Why, you dirty little grease ball!" she spat. "Think you're getting to be somebody now, huh? I wouldn't wipe my nose on you!"

"Don't think I wouldn't take you if I wanted you," retorted Pabst, somewhat nettled by the scorn in her voice. "Only I don't want you, see?"

Babe laughed. "You don't want me, huh? As if you haven't followed me around like a sick dog with your tongue hanging out! But you know better than to touch me. You knew that you were nothing but a rat, Pabst."

"Yaah!" sneered the gunman. "You talk big! You'll make a pretty-lookin' stiff, you will. You see them trees at the top o' the next hill? When we get there, I'm gonna blow a nice big hole right in the middle o' your mug!"

Despite herself, Babe shuddered. She had only a few moments now. But she flung at him:

"Well, I won't look half as bad then as you do right now, you flat-faced baboon!"

There was a muffled snort of laughter from Ray Meyers. Fred Pabst choked with anger, for his lack of facial beauty was a sore point with him.

"You're nothing but an ugly, flat-nosed ape," snapped Babe, "standing up on your hind legs and letting out a big grunt. You're a pain in my guts. And there isn't a decent-looking girl in the town that can stand your mug around!"

Pabst exploded into a string of curses. Ray Meyers was trying with poor success to keep his face sober. He glanced up at Pabst to see how he was taking Babe's razzing.

It was the chance she was waiting for, and had made for herself. As quick as a flash of lightning, her left elbow snapped up and caught Meyers a crushing blow on the nose that drove his head backwards. Both of her hands fell upon the automatic pressed against her side and jerked it away.

There was a roar as his finger constricted upon the trigger. But the bullet sped harmlessly through the top of the car. Pabst yelled and stamped on the brakes.

Then Babe wrenched the automatic from Ray Meyers' fingers and turned it against him. He screamed and lunged for the weapon.

She fired once, twice, three times. Meyers stiffened; then fell back into the corner of the seat and rolled upon the floor.

"Damn you!" roared Pabst.

The brakes were shrieking as the car slowed down. He steered with one hand while with the other he tugged at a revolver in his coat pocket.

Babe turned the automatic on him and pulled the trigger. But even as she did so, she saw that it had jammed on the third shot, for the breech block was back.

She dropped the gun and leaped over the door of the car. She flew through the air, her body twisting over and over. She caught a glimpse of stars in the clouded sky, of the dark mass of the car speeding away from her with squealing brakes, of the ground leaping up at her.

Then she lit upon her side on soft earth and rolled over several times before she could stop herself.

As she sat up, the car came to a stop seventy-five feet farther down the road. A dark figure leaned out over the side and fire stabbed the darkness from a shiny object. She heard the spurt of bullets striking the ground about her.

Leaping to her feet, she scaled a dirt bank behind her. Then she was over a fence and was concealed in the expanse of a field of waving grain.

IV

CAPTURE

IT WAS MORE THAN AN HOUR LATER that Babe stood in the shadow of a doorway in the heart of the city. There was the reassuring feel of an automatic pistol in the clip holster under her arm. She had pounded on the door of Pop Markovitz, the fence, until she had roused him so that she could replace the gun which Ray Meyers had taken from her.

What lay ahead of her? She did not know and she could not guess. If she stayed in the city, she was facing almost certain death. She was an outcast; Big Shot's mob would certainly kill her if they found her, and she would be little more safe from Tony Ruso's gang.

Her better judgment told her to take it on the lam, as Big Shot had suggested. She could go to some place where she was not known and start life anew. But it went against every instinct in her to turn tail and run like a coward. For one thing, it would be abandoning the only man that she had ever loved.

No, she had to stay. Ineffectual as she was, she still might be able to help Big Shot.

She turned from the doorway of Pop Markovitz's clothing store and started down the street. Her feet were leaden. Her ears were deaf to the noises of the city about her. She did not see the cruising taxis and the cars that whined past her.

And so she did not notice the black Lincoln limousine that passed her, slowed up and then stopped. By the time her dazed mind had taken cognizance of it, a figure had leaped from the rear door and was confronting her, the blue gleam of an automatic pistol in its hand.

"Big Shot!" she gasped.

The light from a distant street lamp made his figure seem even taller so that he towered over her. His face, beneath the brim of the low-pulled black hat, was half in shadow, but she could see how grim and haggard it was.

The man whom she loved!

She saw his finger tightening upon the trigger. She knew that in another moment his pistol would spit fire and that lead would tear through her heart.

"You double-crossing hell-cat!" he rasped.

The bore of the automatic centered upon her left breast. But she stood silent, her arms at her side, waiting calmly. Death was sweeping down upon her, but she would meet it without faltering or flinching. She would show Big Shot that she knew how to die.

But as she waited, nothing happened. Slowly his finger relaxed its pressure upon the trigger. Then his arm fell to his side, the pistol held loosely.

"Babe. I can't—I can't!" he whispered hoarsely. "I ought to plug you, but I can't. You bumped Buck Garvey and Ray Meyers and ratted on us, but I can't kill you. Because"—and his voice dropped so low that she could scarcely hear the words—"because, no matter what you are now, I once loved you!"

Her heart leaped. The words that she had been waiting for for so long! That he loved her. She forgot that he had branded her a traitor and had sent her for a ride. She knew only that she loved him, and that he said he had loved her.

She took a step toward him. Surely he would listen to her now.

Instantly he drew back, his face set in hard lines.

"Babe, it's too late now. I thought once that you cared for me, but if you had, you would have waited for me. I thought that you were wonderful, something better than you are. No, there's no use of your pretending now just because you happened to have changed your mind. You've ratted, and you know it. You've sold yourself to Ruso. I won't plug you now, though

God knows that I ought to. But I warn you again: get out of town, and get out quick! The first time that any of my men see you, they're going to shoot to kill. If you stay around here, your life won't be worth a plugged nickel. Or run along to Tony Ruso. Maybe he can hide you somewhere."

He turned back toward the waiting car.

"Big Shot! Wait!" called Babe frantically. "I tell you I didn't rat! Listen to me. Fred Pabst and Ray Meyers were both in with Tony Ruso. They talked about it when they took me for the ride. Ruso's going to raid your headquarters at four o'clock this morning. Pabst is going—"

But Big Shot was not listening.

"I warn you again, Babe," he flung back over his shoulder, "get out of town!"

Then he leaped into the car and slammed the door behind him. The motor roared, cutting off the last words that Babe said, as it slid off.

She stared after it as it whipped around the corner.

She sobbed to herself. "He won't listen! He won't listen! He won't believe me. And at four o'clock—"

A horrible feeling of utter helplessness in the face of disaster shook her. Then out of this grew a single thought, a single determination that burned in her brain.

She would get Tony Ruso. She would kill him. It might not be too late yet. She had almost three hours before her. If she could get to Ruso, she would kill him even though it cost her her life. Life as it was, was not worth living. And perhaps if she did kill Ruso, Big Shot would see that she was not a rat, and that she really loved him.

She started grimly for the Ruso headquarters. She did not know how she would penetrate into them, but she must manage it in some way. Somewhere she would find Tony Ruso, and she would pump bullets into him until her gun was empty and his evil life was wiped out.

At length she saw the Ruso headquarters in front of her. There, bordering upon the alley in the center of the block, was the Ruso Flower Shop, with the Ruso Central Garage beside it. The flower shop was dark now except for a single light that shone dimly in the rear, but the garage was brightly lighted. She knew that in the basements beneath them were Ruso's hop joints, with a myriad of small rooms fitted with bunks and with Oriental attendants ready to sell and prepare any kind of dope.

Farther down the street was the dim sign which announced the Plaza Amusement Palace, run in conjunction with a hotel, which was the center of Ruso's vice dens. Ruso was in control of the entire dope and vice trade of the city; Big Shot Stacey had never cared to touch either of them, profitable as they were.

As she drew closer to the flower shop, she suddenly shrank back into a doorway. A car had turned into the alley and had stopped close against the building, a car which she recognized as the touring car in which she had been taken for a ride!

A figure leaped from it and disappeared in a door at the rear of the flower shop. But in the momentary glimpse that she had caught of it, she had recognized Fred Pabst!

Leaving the doorway, she hurried into the alley and melted into its shadows. Above the flower shop there were lighted windows on both the third and the fourth floors of the building.

Minutes passed as she scanned these windows. One of them on the third floor was momentarily obscured as a man stepped up to it to pull down the shade. But in that split second she was certain that she could make out the ugly features of Tony Ruso, a cigarette hanging from his lower lip.

She would have shot him then if she had had the time. But in the instant it took her to recognize him, the shade was down and he was gone.

A red mist seemed to dance before her eyes. Her blood pumped furiously through her veins. This was the man who had caused all the trouble. The lust to kill him became an obsession with her. But now that she had located him, she had to find some way to get at him.

She doubted whether she could enter by the same door which Pabst had used. There would certainly be guards, and only blind luck would enable her to pass them.

Her eyes fell upon the fire escape which zig-zagged to the roof. True, it did not pass within ten feet of the window at which she had seen Tony Ruso; but it would surely open upon some hallway or room from which she could gain access to Ruso's room.

However, the fire escape drop was ten feet above the ground. But luckily Pabst had parked his car directly beneath it, and, by standing on the top, she would be able to reach it.

Without hesitation, she crossed the alley and climbed up upon the car. The leather top sagged beneath her weight, but it held her.

Standing upright, she grasped the lower landing. It was the work of a moment for her to swing herself up on it. Years of dancing had made her body strong and supple.

There she paused, listening to find whether she had been heard. She was hidden in the darkness, though shafts of light fell through the windows over her head and shone upon the wall of the building on the opposite side of the alley.

Having assured herself that she had not been seen, she started to creep up the steps. She could hear a faint murmur of voices behind the window at which she had seen Ruso, but she could not make out the words.

When she reached the landing on the third floor, she cautiously raised her head so that she could gaze through the window. It opened upon a dimly lit hall running the width of the building. Cutting that in two was another hall running the length of the building. The room which she sought should be somewhere to the left of her; perhaps opening upon the very hall into which she was looking.

She slid up the window slowly, noiselessly. Half up, she stopped and listened again. The murmur of voices was louder, but she could not yet understand what was being said, though she thought that she recognized Fred Pabst's voice among them.

She drew her automatic from its holster, slipped off the safety catch, and slid through the window.

She put her ear against the first door to the left. Yes, that was Fred Pabst's voice that she heard. And the other was Tony Ruso. She had heard his voice once when he had come to the Red Dragon to confer with Big Shot.

Her hand fumbled for the door knob. She would throw open the door, shoot down Tony Ruso and Fred Pabst before they knew what was happening. Then, perhaps, she might be able to escape by the fire escape.

But as her fingers started to turn the knob, there was the sound of a door shutting in the longitudinal hall, and then of footsteps. A figure came into view at the intersection of the two halls.

"What the hell!" shouted the man when he saw her slim body pressed tight against the door. "Babe O'Connor!"

His hand streaked to a shoulder holster. Babe's automatic erupted into fire twice, and he crumpled to the floor, shouting brokenly.

It was the signal for bedlam to break out. Shouts echoed in the various rooms. Another man ran down the hall. Babe jerked at the door, trying to fling it open so that she could at least get Tony Ruso before she was killed, but she found it was locked.

A man appeared at the intersection of the two halls, stared down at the wounded man, then dodged back as one of Babe's bullets nicked his arm.

A door opened behind her. Even as she whipped about, arms closed about her chest in a vice-like grip that pinned her arms to her side. She struggled like a wild beast, trying to turn her automatic, but a crushing grip upon her wrist forced her to drop it.

Then the door in front of her opened and Tony Ruso stood framed in the doorway, an enormously thick and squat figure. He gave a grunt of surprise; then grinned wolfishly so that his face looked like a disfigured gargoyle.

"Well, well," he chuckled. "If it ain't little Babe O'Connor come to bump me off! Come right in!"

He smirked, stood aside and made a sweeping gesture of welcome with his hand. Standing behind him she saw the flat-faced Fred Pabst.

V

DOPED!

"ALL RIGHT, SET HER DOWN, KARL," ordered Ruso. "An' get out."

The man who had seized Babe from behind set her feet upon the floor and released her; then left the room.

Babe held herself erect by an effort of will. She felt sick with disappointment, not that she had been captured, but that she had failed in her effort to kill Tony Ruso. She looked contemptuously from Fred Pabst's leering face to Ruso's hideous features; then looked away from them.

"How in hell did you get here?" asked Pabst.

"Through the window," interjected Ruso impatiently. "She came up the fire escape."

His eyes traveled up and down her figure gloatingly. They devoured the white curve of her neck, the gentle swell of her breast, the graceful symmetry of her hips and legs. They dwelt longest upon the ivory oval of her face, upon her blue eyes that stared defiantly past his head, and upon her crown of golden curls.

"Lemme bump her off," suggested Fred Pabst hopefully. "She's caused us too damn much trouble already. She finished Buck Garvey an' Ray Meyers, an jus' about shot our plans all to hell. Lemme put a load o' lead in her guts." He reached for the revolver in his coat pocket.

But Ruso laid a restraining hand upon his arm.

"Not so fast, Pabst," he warned. "She's a damn good-lookin' broad. They don't come like this very often."

Pabst cast an oblique glance at Ruso and smiled knowingly.

"Oh, I see. Well, I don't blame you. But watch out for her! She's a hell-cat!"

Ruso put a dirty hand under her chin and tipped her head back. Instantly Babe's hand shot out and hit him a stinging blow on the flat of his cheek.

"Keep your dirty paws off me!" she snapped.

Ruso fell back from her cursing. He scowled and rubbed his cheek where a red mark showed. Pabst by an effort composed his face.

"She's poison, Tony. She'd jus' as soon stick a knife in you as eat."

"So-o," drawled Ruso venomously. "So-o. I've got the medicine that tames cats. I've been needin' a few more skirts in my joint in Chicago. We'll see how she likes it there."

He sprawled into a chair, stretching his short legs out and sinking his chin upon his barrel-like chest. From this position he squinted up at her calculatingly.

At his words, a cold chill prickled her flesh and her heart seemed to stop beating. She had come prepared for death—but not for this! Once in one of

Ruso's vice dens in Chicago, she knew that there would be no escape. There would be only the unspeakable horror of infinite degradation. . . .

Pabst took a bottle from a table and poured out three drinks.

"Have a drink, Babe. Might as well be friendly. No? Well, suit yourself."

He sipped his drink, but Ruso tossed his off at a single gulp, smacking his thick lips. Then the gang leader eyed Babe again.

"So you're the twist that wanted to be Big Shot's moll, eh?" he inquired sarcastically, lifting his eyebrows high above his slit eyes.

In spite of herself, Babe flushed. Her eyes rested for a fleeting second on his gargoyle face and an angry retort rose to her lips, but she restrained it.

"The Big Shot ain't so hot now," continued Ruso. "He's jus' about at the end o' his rope. One, two more hours an' he's gonna have lead poisoning. An' have it bad. We're gonna fill him so full he'll sink in the river outta his own weight.

"Yup, the Big Shot's all washed up. When we get through with him, there won't be nothin' left. At four o'clock we raid his headquarters. With him not expectin' it, an' with Pabst here to open up for us, it'll be a cinch. Well, he's gonna find out somep'n, an' pretty damn quick! He's gonna wake up with a gat screwin' in his guts. He's been runnin' this burg jus' a little too long, only he don't know it yet."

He folded his hands over his stomach in self-satisfied comfort. Pabst grinned and picked up the drink which Babe had refused.

"An' do yuh know what you're gonna be doin' when Big Shot bumps off?" inquired Ruso. "No? Not even curious, eh? Well, I'll tell yuh in case you're jus' kinda bashful about askin'. You're gonna be doped to the gills. You're gonna be so dead to the world yuh won't know nothin' about it till it's all over. An' then tomorrow you're off for Chi to the nice little place I got in mind for yuh. You'll be so hopped up that when yuh get to work there, you'll think you're enjoyin' yourself. You'll like it there, oh yes! How's that strike yuh, eh?"

"You talk big, wop," said Babe.

"Yeah?" The grin faded from Ruso's face. "Karl!" he roared.

The man who had first captured her appeared in the door.

"Tie her up," commanded Ruso. "An' make sure yuh do a damn good job."

"Okay."

Karl disappeared through the door and returned in a moment with a coil of rope. He proceeded to tie Babe's hands firmly behind her back, and her ankles together. She managed to kick him in the stomach, but only got a cuff on the side of her head for her pains. In the end she was firmly trussed up, held upright by one of Karl's hands about her neck.

Ruso poured out a quarter of a tumbler of whiskey, added as much water; then took a small green medicine bottle from a table drawer.

"Knock-out drops," he commented as he poured a little into the tumbler. He stirred the mixture and added: "An' you're gonna drink this."

Babe set her lips tight together and glared at him. If he wanted her to take it, he would have to force it down her throat.

"Open up," ordered Ruso, holding up the glass. "Pretty please. No? Open her, Karl."

Karl jabbed a thick finger between her lips and ran it back along her gums. She clamped her teeth tightly together, but the pain of the pressure of his finger against the hinge of her jaw was intolerable, and her mouth dropped open.

Ruso laid one hand on her forehead and pushed her head back. With the other he poured the mixture into her mouth. She gasped and almost strangled as the whiskey bit at her throat, but most of the liquid ran down her throat.

Ruso set the glass back upon the table with a click.

"In ten minutes you'll be in bye-bye land for the rest of the night. If yuh have any dreams, yuh can think of us pluggin' Big Shot. When yuh wake up, it'll be all over an' you'll be on your way to Chi. Ready to go to work for me there. Well, up with her, Karl. We'll take her to the cellar."

Karl seized her with rough hands and threw her over his shoulder. Her head hung over his back on a level with his waist. She had to tip her head far back to see anything but his legs and the floor. But as they left the room, she saw Fred Pabst grinning after her maliciously.

With Ruso leading, they went down three flights of stairs, ending in a long corridor rank with the smell of stale opium smoke. As they went down it, they passed many doors opening into small rooms. Through the doors she caught glimpses of bunks filled with the scum of humanity, the dregs of the underworld.

Two Chinamen padded past who gave Ruso a sing-song greeting. Through one door she saw a luxuriously furnished room with well-dressed men and women lying on couches—the elite of the social world caught up in the toils of drugs in their mad search for new thrills.

"In here," said Ruso, opening a door.

They entered one of the dens which she had seen. On one bunk a bedraggled woman lay unconscious, her head and one arm hanging out. In other bunks were thieves, dips, cheap racketeers and gunmen. A sailor sat nervously on the edge of one bunk, anxiously watching a Chinaman who was cooking a pipe for him at a small table.

Then they passed through another door and she was dropped roughly on the floor. She saw that she was in a small, low-ceilinged room with a single door opening into the den through which they had just passed.

"Sweet dreams," said Ruso.

The door shut and she was alone.

She struggled fiercely with the ropes that held her, jerking and twisting them in an attempt to loosen them. But they only bit harder into her wrists and ankles and refused to give an inch.

Already she could feel the effects of the knock-out drops. A languor seized her body; a drowsiness took possession of her; she wanted only to relax and to drop off to sleep. She tried to fight off the feeling, but she could not.

She rolled desperately around her small cell, searching for something with which to saw the ropes about her wrists. The floor was quite bare; there was no help there.

Tomorrow—where would she be tomorrow? Where would Big Shot be? Dead, and she would be on the way to disgrace. She almost wept in the agony of the moment. If only she were not so utterly helpless, if she could do something. Even death at the hands of Fred Pabst would be preferable to this.

But the drug was slowly and surely taking possession of her. In one or two minutes she knew that she would be unconscious. . . .

She rolled over and over, trying to shake off the deadly stupor that was submerging her. Now she could scarcely feel the pain of the ropes about her wrists and ankles. Her mind was slipping, sinking into darkness. . . .

In a last effort, she lay upon her side and drew her knees up to her chin. She strained her bound wrists, attempting to draw them over her hips. She could not. She was so sleepy that she could not seem to muster the energy.

Yet, impelled by almost an obsession not to be conquered, she fought on. She turned her hips sideways, jerked and tugged. Now her wrists were half over. Another jerk and her wrists slipped over her hips, then over her heels.

Her hands were still tied together, but they were in front of her!

Biting her tongue between her teeth to keep conscious, she sat up upon her heels. She put her hands to her face, stuck the fingers of her right hand down her throat. She retched, but so numb was she that she could scarcely feel her fingers. She pushed her two middle fingers farther down her throat.

Then, almost automatically, she vomited. But it was too late. The drug had already taken effect. She tried to hold her head up—it fell upon her chest. Her body relaxed; she fell sideways upon the floor. Blackness closed in upon her. . . .

VI

THE PRISONER IN THE OPIUM DENS

SLOWLY CONSCIOUSNESS RETURNED TO BABE. Her eyes opened and saw only blackness about her. She was vaguely aware that she could scarcely move.

She did not know where she was nor what had happened to her.

Then it came back to her in broken snatches: Buck Garvey's treachery, her being taken for a ride, her escape and her capture. . . .

How long had she been unconscious? What had happened while she was lying there helpless? Was it after four o'clock? Perhaps Big Shot was already dead, traitorously shot down by the men whom he had thought to be his loyal friends.

Sensation returned to her body. She was a mass of shooting, blinding pains. Her arms were numb, so tightly were her wrists tied together. When she tried to sit up, her cramped muscles would scarcely hold her weight.

She had to get free. Perhaps it was not yet too late.

She attacked the ropes about her wrists with her teeth, pulling and jerking at them. One lip cracked and she tasted blood, but she still kept on. Yet it seemed a hopeless struggle; the ropes were heavy and stiff, almost as tough as wire.

But in the end one of the strands of rope gave a little. She worked frantically, and was finally rewarded by being able to pull out a loose end. In five more minutes her wrists were free and she was chafing them, trying to restore their circulation.

As soon as she was able to move her fingers, she started on the ropes about her ankles. They yielded more easily and presently she was free. For a time she did nothing but hobble about her low-ceilinged prison, flexing her muscles and searching for a weapon. She found nothing.

She tried the door, but it seemed to be locked. Applying her eye to the crack at the side of the door, she saw that it was fastened by a single latch. If she had a thin piece of metal, she might be able to stick it through the crack and lift the latch.

She hunted through the tiny cell again for something that would serve this purpose. When she was just about to give up in despair, her fingers touched the lower hinge on the door. The wood was rotten with age and the screws had been loosened so that the hinge was only half fastened.

She hooked her fingers behind it and pulled. It gave a little, but even when she threw her full strength against it she could not jerk it free.

She attacked it with her foot, stamping on it with her tiny heel. At last, with a rasping as the screws were pulled out of the wood, it fell loose and she pulled it free.

She inserted the flat edge of the hinge in the crack of the door and pried up against the latch. It did not give. She twisted the hinge violently, pressing it tight against the side of the door to get leverage. The latch slowly slid up with a sharp grating of metal on metal. Then the door swung inward.

Babe advanced into the den and shut the door behind her. She looked about to see whether she had been heard, but the only sound was the deep asthmatic breathing of the bedraggled woman that she had first seen. The occupants of the bunks were dead in drugged dreams. The corridor outside was silent. The mingled odor of stale opium smoke, sweating bodies and filth almost choked her.

She saw the sailor lying half on his side with his back to her in one of the bunks. There was a bulge in his hip pocket which had the familiar outlines of a revolver.

"I'll have to get that revolver," she decided. "I can't tell what I'll meet when I leave here, and it's worth the chance."

She tip-toed to his bunk and looked down at him. His mouth hung half-open in a fatuous smile. His breathing was deep and regular. Evidently he had taken the pipe which the Chinaman had been preparing for him.

Slowly she slid her hand in his pocket, keeping her eyes intently on his face, watching for the least sign that he was disturbed. But his deep breathing continued uninterruptedly as she drew out a nickel-plated revolver.

Suddenly she froze. There were steps in the corridor outside, soft shuffling footsteps.

Quickly she slid into an empty bunk and hid in the shadows. She was not a moment too soon, for a Chinaman came through the door and looked about suspiciously. He made a turn of the room, muttering to himself in a querulous sing-song voice.

Then he stopped before her bunk and peered in at her. Though Babe did not know it, it was the gleam of her golden curls that had given her away.

He started to give a frightened exclamation, but stopped in the middle of it as the heavy barrel of her revolver crashed down upon his forehead. The breath wheezed from his lungs as he slid to the floor.

She crept from the bunk, her eyes darting about the room to note any sign that the other occupants had been alarmed. But there was no move from the riff-raff in the bunks, and the only sound was the asthmatic breathing.

The Chinaman lay sprawled upon the floor, his eyes shut and a tiny trickle of blood flowing across his yellow forehead. Babe seized his arms and dragged him across the den and into the cell which she had just occupied. It took her only a few minutes to tie him with the ropes which had been used on her, and to gag him with a piece of cloth torn from his voluminous shirt. Then she shut the cell door and latched it.

Cautiously she peered out into the corridor. The disturbance had apparently passed unnoticed, for there was no one in sight. But from what direction had she come? She had been so dizzy that she had not noticed.

She crept noiselessly down the hall to the right, the revolver held ready in her hand. She passed the half-open doors of two more dens in which she saw bunks filled with sleeping people. In one room a Chinaman was preparing a pipe for a man lying upon his side in a bunk, but neither of them saw her as she slipped past the door like a shadow.

Then the corridor turned to the right, and narrow, unlighted stairs led upwards to the left. She chose the stairs and climbed them, stepping carefully on the sides of the treads so that they would not squeak. When she reached a door at the top, she stopped and listened.

There was the murmur of voices on the other side. At least two men were speaking together, but she could not understand what they were saying. She hesitated as to what to do. They might block her escape in that direction, but, on the other hand, she did not know what she would encounter if she retraced her steps and adventured farther down the corridor below.

In the end she decided to go through the door. She would have the advantage of surprise; if they offered any resistance, she had the revolver and could try to fight her way through them.

Abruptly she threw open the door and sprang through it.

"Stick 'em up!" she shouted.

Two men seated before a desk whirled about and their mouths dropped open. They hesitated, but only for a moment. Babe's revolver was covering them unwaveringly and the expression on her face argued no delay. Their hands shot up over their heads.

"Don't shoot, sister," said one of them. "You got us."

The other man bent forward and stared at her face. "It's Babe O'Connor!" he ejaculated.

"Stand up an' turn around," ordered Babe grimly. "And if either of you two birds makes a move for a gat, I'll plug you both."

They obeyed with alacrity.

"Don't yuh worry 'bout us, Babe," said the first man. "We ain't gonna take any chances with yuh. You're too damn good a shot for us to wanna monkey with. I seen yuh in that act where yuh shot all the corks off the bottles."

She frisked them, removing several automatics, a snub-nosed revolver and a long knife.

"Nice lot of artillery you got here, boys," she said. "Maybe I'll need it."

She stepped back to take stock of her position. They were in a glass-windowed office which looked out over the broad floor of a garage on both sides of which cars and trucks were lined against the walls. It was brilliantly lighted, but seemed to be quite deserted except for these two men.

Her eyes fell upon a Western Union wall clock. It was only five minutes to four! There might still be time for her to do something. She had been unconscious for only little more than an hour and a half. Her stringent measures had at least been partially effective by getting some of the drug out of her system.

"Has Ruso left?" she asked.

"Yeah," answered one of the men. "He pulled out ten minutes ago. Took jus' about everybody in the mob with him."

Ten minutes! Then he must already be there. And Big Shot was entirely unsuspicious. She looked at the clock again, and the minute hand seemed to be racing around toward the hour.

Through the glass door which opened upon the floor of the garage she saw a coil of electric wire.

"Careful," she warned. "One move and I'll plug you."

She opened the door with her left hand, reached out with her foot and dragged the coil of wire into the office.

"What's on the other side of that door in front of you?" she asked.

"Inside office," grunted one of the men.

"Open the door and march in. And watch your step!"

The first man lowered one arm to open the door; then immediately raised it again. They walked into the inner office and Babe followed them, carrying the coil of wire.

"Now down on the floor, you on the left. And you tie him up." She tossed the coil of wire to the other man. "Make sure you do a good job."

When the first man was tied, she forced the second man to lie on the floor beside his companion and she tied him herself. She tested the bonds of both and then gagged them.

She saw upon a desk a Type C drum for a Thompson submachine gun. Near it were a dozen empty cartridge boxes. She picked up the drum and saw that the outer edge had been dented so that it could not be used.

If she only had a machine gun, she might be able to do something. An automatic pistol is a puny weapon in comparison. But it was too late now to get one from Pop Markovitz.

Her eyes fell upon a steel cabinet in the corner of the room. She opened it and found a rack where weapons had been kept. In the bottom was a Thompson model 21A submachine gun. She took it out and examined it. It was in good working condition.

Upon a shelf at the top of the cabinet were half a dozen fully loaded Type C drums. She attached a drum to the gun, snapped back the actuator to cock it, and threw the lever to automatic fire. She felt thankful that Big Shot had once explained the action of the gun to her. Putting another loaded drum under her arm, she left the office.

But her heart sank when she looked at the wall clock in the outer office. The hands had crept around to three minutes past four. Unless Ruso's plans had failed, he was even now attacking the Stacey headquarters. And Fred Pabst had already betrayed Big Shot—perhaps had even killed him.

She ran across the floor of the garage and chose a rakish roadster against the wall. The key was in the ignition as she had expected. She slid into the driver's seat, dropped the submachine gun and the drum beside her, and stepped on the starter. The great car purred into life, and she swung it across the floor and out the open doors.

It was a race for life. Would she be able to get there in time to help Big Shot? She did not know. But if he were dead when she got there, she was going to avenge his death. Tony Ruso and Fred Pabst would never live to enjoy their victory.

The car shot across the city and onto the state road at express speed. She stopped for nothing. She saw the lights of the Red Dragon looming up before her; then she swung into the lane and was past it.

As she approached headquarters, she saw cars parked around it. There were flashes of fire in the darkness. Men were shooting down from barred windows on the second floor. The intermittent roar of a machine gun echoed through the night. . . .

VII

Two Gangs Meet

Babe brought the car to a quiet stop. She could see that Ruso had started his attack, though what the results were she could not guess. But it was evident from the continued gunplay that it had not been entirely successful.

She seized the submachine gun, tucked the extra ammunition drum under her right arm, and leaped from the car. But as she ran in front of it, and was momentarily outlined by the headlights, a bullet sang past her and zinged against the hood of the car. She saw the flash of the weapon that fired it in a second story window on the front of the building.

She quickly jumped back into the shadows. Evidently she had been mistaken at the distance for one of Ruso's men.

She advanced more cautiously toward the building. Between the great columns of the porch she could see that the steel imitation-wood doors were wide open. Through the doors she saw a mass of men milling in the large hallway, but she could not tell who they were.

A machine gun was roaring in short irregular bursts. There was the constant popping of smaller fire arms and the blasts of shotguns. Men shouted and screamed.

Babe crept on her hands and knees across the lawn to the porch. She carried the submachine gun and the extra drum under her right arm.

Overhead the heavy rolling clouds blotted out the stars and made her practically invisible, though the gleaming headlights of the cars parked at a distance from the house cut swaths of light through the darkness and patches of brilliance fell through the windows.

At the side of the porch she raised her head to a level with a window which looked in upon the great hall. It was entirely occupied by Ruso's men; and the leader himself, his gargoyle face a frenzy of rage and blood-lust, stood at one side roaring orders.

At the foot of the massive stairs that led up to the second floor stood the man she knew as Karl, a submachine gun at his shoulder. He was firing intermittent bursts up the stairs, in the middle of which two dead men sprawled. And from the top of the stairs there were less frequent answering shots.

"Ready now!" shouted Ruso. "Back!"

The men surged back from the staircase. Karl fell away from it after firing a short burst.

A man darted to the foot of the stairs, sent a glittering black object hurtling through the air before he leaped back. It disappeared at the top of the stairs; then there was a tremendous explosion. The roar almost deafened Babe. The windows shook and rattled; fragments of glass blew out; great pieces of plaster fell down from the ceiling of the hall, crashing upon the floor in a cloud of dust.

Ruso's men were using pineapples! Medium-powered bombs for hand-to-hand work. They would not dare to use the more powerful pineapples under the circumstances, for these would bring the very ceiling down upon their heads. But the less powerful pineapples would be very effective against any men lurking at the hall at the top of the stairs.

Babe started away from the window, bent upon circling the house so that she could judge the conditions and plan her attack. Her feet stumbled upon a man lying upon the ground. He groaned and writhed. She bent down over him. There was just enough light so that she could see that he was not one of Big Shot's men. His chest was punctured by bullets, his face was covered with blood.

She shook his shoulder.

"What happened?" she demanded.

The man was only half-conscious. "They got me," he moaned. "Through the chest. I'm done for."

She shook him more roughly. "Come to! What's happened here?"

He became more coherent. "Pabst let us in, but he slipped up somewheres. Big Shot an' most o' his men was up on the second floor. We couldn't get at 'em. An' they're still up there!"

He talked on, hysterically, repeating himself until his voice was only a whisper.

Then Babe understood the danger. Big Shot and his men were on the second floor, but they were probably without weapons. The arsenal was on the first floor, and with Ruso's men at the foot of the stairs they would not be able to reach it. They might be able to stand off Ruso's men for a short while, but ultimately they would be overwhelmed.

She looked through the window again. She saw Tony Ruso and Fred Pabst conferring together. She was tempted to raise the machine gun and mow them down. But, while she hesitated, it became too late. They crossed the hall so that they were out of the range of her gun.

"Ready! Get out!" came the roar of Ruso's voice.

The men retreated from the foot of the stairs. Several of them disappeared into the side rooms opening into the hall. Almost half of them, including Pabst and Ruso, ran to the back of the hall and vanished through a door there which led to the back part of the house. The remainder of them, with the exception of one man who held a metal object in his hand, ran out through the front door and across the lawn.

They passed within a dozen feet of Babe. She knew that as soon as they stopped and turned around, they would see her. She threw up the submachine gun, trained it on them and pulled the trigger.

Rat-a-tat-tat-tat!

Three of the men fleeing from the building went down under the hail of steel-jacketed bullets. The others whirled about to face this new menace.

Rat-a-tat-tat-tat!

Her submachine gun spewed a stream of death again. More of the men went down. In a moment only one man remained upon his feet. He raised a submachine gun to fight her with her own weapon, sent a barrage of bullets kicking about her.

But she presented a poor target as she stood in the darkness so that he missed her, while he was clearly outlined in the light that fell through the open doors. And as her bullets found him, drilled him through the heart, she recognized him as Karl.

She turned back toward the door in time to see the man who had been left standing there hurl something back into the building. He turned and fled down the steps, but before he reached the ground, there was a terrific explosion and he was picked up off his feet and thrown a dozen feet through the air.

The other explosion was as nothing compared to this one. The very walls of the building seemed to bulge and heave. The tremendous blast of air rushing out through the doors and windows threw Babe to the ground and rolled her over and over.

As she sat up, she looked back into the hall and saw that the stairway was blown to bits. The ceiling was collapsing, splitting into sections, spilling men.

She understood Ruso's tactics. Unable to dislodge Stacey's men from the upper hallway by the use of low-powered pineapples, he was using more powerful bombs, sending his men out of the house or into other rooms where the power of the explosive would not touch them.

Babe scrambled to her feet, still in possession of the machine gun and the extra drum which she had clung to frantically. She saw a figure rising from the ground not far away. It was the man who had thrown the pineapples. She riddled him with a burst of shot and he sank back to the earth.

Instantly she flew up the steps and into the wrecked hall. She saw that the entire ceiling of the long hall had collapsed. Wreckage lay everywhere; twisted broken timbers, bits of the stair railing, piles of plaster, broken furniture. She could look up to the very roof of the building, could see the doors on the second floor hanging drunkenly on their hinges.

Smoke and eddying plaster dust choked and blinded her. She stumbled over a body that lay near the door. It was Olie Jensen.

Other men were lying about, half covered by the debris, some of them horribly mangled. Evidently the explosion had caught most of Big Shot's men in the hall above as Ruso had planned.

Babe sobbed as she stumbled on, peering at the dead faces, fearing, dreading that she would find Big Shot among them.

Two of Ruso's men came out of a side room where they had hidden. They stopped when they saw her standing in the middle of the wreckage. Before they had recovered from their astonishment, her machine gun spat fire and cut them down.

The drum of the gun was empty. With almost a single motion she snapped out the old drum and clicked in the loaded one, pulling back the actuator to cock it.

"At 'em, Babe!" shouted a voice behind her.

Then Olie Jensen was beside her, an automatic in his hand. His face was covered with white plaster dust and a long smear of blood.

"Olie! I thought you were dead when I saw—"

The door opened at the rear of the hall and Ruso's men came rushing forward. They were met by an entirely unexpected hail of machine gun and automatic pistol bullets that downed half of them and sent the rest scurrying back through the door.

"That's the way to deal with rats!" shouted Olie.

They stood upon the wreckage like the spirits of vengeance. The wind which sighed through the open doors blew Babe's golden curls about a grim tense face in which blue-gray eyes blazed like white-hot steel. The Thompson gleamed dully at her side, its deadly bore pointed directly at the door in the rear of the hall, ready to spit death at any face that showed there.

"Where's Big Shot, Olie?" asked Babe, without taking her eyes from the door.

"He's here. But—I'm afraid they got him."

It was as though a cold knife stabbed her to the heart and was twisted in the wound. She paled and her knees felt weak. For some reason she had kept thinking of him as being still alive.

"Oh, they couldn't, Olie, they couldn't! He can't—he can't—"

But she was trying to argue against fate. She was trying to keep herself from believing what must be true.

"I'm afraid he's in this mess somewheres," said Olie. "He was right near the top o' the stairs when the explosion came. The only reason I got out was I was standin' near the front window lookin' out."

Babe looked about the wreckage. The explosion had destroyed most of the lights in the hall, of course, but there still were some wall lights upon both floors which miraculously lighted up the scene somewhat.

Near her feet she saw Jake Swartz, a bullet hole in his forehead and his revolver tightly clasped in his hand. He must have been dead when the explosion occurred. Not far from him was Lewis Merlitz, his legs almost blown from his body. And that man beside Merlitz—wasn't that Al Feraro?

Babe stumbled drunkenly over the debris, her mind sick with the horror of it, looking frantically for Big Shot, yet fearing and dreading that she might find him.

Then she saw him. He was lying half under a heavy timber, a pile of plaster almost covering his body. His mouth was open, his eyes staring upwards unwaveringly.

Dead! Oh, he could not be dead. It would be too terrible. She fell on her knees beside him.

"Big Shot! Big Shot!" she pleaded, as though the very force of her cry could bring him back to life.

Then his eyes turned down toward her. He was alive!

He stared at her dazedly for a moment; slowly the light of recognition came into his eyes. He pushed himself up on one elbow and the plaster bits slid off his chest, rattled on the floor.

"Babe!" he gasped. "You were right!"

She had no more thought for Tony Ruso. Big Shot was alive! She dropped the submachine gun and seized his hand.

"Big Shot, are you hurt?"

In answer, he sat up. Babe seized the heavy timber across his hips and tried to pull it away, but she could not move it. He reached down and easily threw it aside, leaping to his feet.

"They're in the back rooms, Big Shot," cried Olie Jensen. "I think they're bottled up back there. It's locked tight, an' they couldn't get out without the keys unless they break some o' the locks."

Even as he spoke, there was the sound of hammering in the rear rooms. Ruso was trying to escape!

Instantly Big Shot went into action. He picked up the Thompson that Babe had dropped and tossed it to Olie Jensen, then ran from the room through a door which Babe knew led into the arsenal. He was back in a moment with a flash-shaped object which he handed to Olie Jensen.

"Tear gas bomb," he explained. "I'll go 'round in back and guard it there. When I fire two shots, toss the bomb in and kill 'em as they come out. And Babe, you get back out of the way somewheres."

With that he dashed out the front door and disappeared into the darkness.

But Babe did not obey his command. She searched about her for some weapon. She finally picked the revolver from Jake Swartz's dead fingers, twirled the cylinder and found that it was fully loaded, then stepped up beside Olie Jensen.

Two shots sounded in quick succession from the rear of the building. It was the signal!

Olie Jensen swung his arm wide and the tear gas bomb sailed through the air, shot straight through the door behind which Ruso's men were hiding. Almost immediately a cloud of evil-smelling, choking gas came pouring out the door.

There were shouts behind the door, agonized cries as the gas bit at the men. A moment passed; then they came pouring out.

The submachine gun roared and the first men went down. But abruptly its clatter ceased. Babe saw Olie Jensen clutch at his shoulder, sway on his feet and topple to the floor. She brought her revolver into play. The next two men went down under that.

Then Fred Pabst burst from the door and leaped across the wreckage to escape the gas. Tears streamed across his flat face. He saw Babe and raised a gun. But she put a single shot through his forehead and felt a savage satisfaction as his body slid to the floor.

For a moment she thought that all the men had been driven out. But no. Another man staggered through the door, a handkerchief held over his face. The handkerchief slid down from the face. Behind it leered the twisted gargoyle face of Tony Ruso, his slit eyes staring straight at her and burning with a murderous light. Saliva was dribbling from his mouth and his breath was coming in tortured gasps.

Babe aimed the revolver full at his chest and pulled the trigger. The hammer clicked upon an empty cartridge.

Ruso was half way across the room now. She threw the empty revolver at him. He bobbed his head a little to one side on his bullet neck and it missed. Still he came on.

She began to retreat from him. Her foot caught on a timber and she sprawled on her back. She was held petrified with horror. Ruso seemed to tower over her like a stunted giant. His great hands stretched out in front of him, the fingers clenching and unclenching.

He fell on his knees beside her. His fingers wrapped in a crushing grip about her neck. She tried to scream, but her breath was cut off. His fingers were like bands of steel about her neck slowly contracting. Her lungs were racked with pain as she sought futilely to draw air into them.

Ruso's leering face seemed to be whirling about her. She felt a dribble of saliva upon her cheek. Blackness was closing in about her. Death was grasping at her with talon hands.

Almost her last thought was that, even though she had to die, she had saved Big Shot and proved her loyalty. He knew now that she was not a rat.

The darkness swirled blacker and thicker. The hands sank deeper into her neck. Then all was gone. . . . nothingness. . . .

"Babe! Babe!" almost sobbed a man's voice.

Her eyes opened and stared up into a formless face that was somehow familiar. And the voice—surely she should know that voice.

"Thank God, you're alive," said that same voice.

The face leaning over her became Big Shot's. And she felt his arms around her. She sighed happily to know that she was still alive and put her arms about him.

Not far from them, sitting upright with a hand pressed to one shoulder that was stained red, was Olie Jensen. He was smiling very triumphantly and rather foolishly.

"Lucky for you, Babe," he said, "that Big Shot got here in time. Ruso was chokin' you an' I couldn't do a thing to stop him."

Her eyes traveled down to a form that lay near her. It was Tony Ruso. From the drunken angle at which his head lay she knew that his neck must be broken. She could still see the imprint of Big Shot's fingers on that bull neck.

Abruptly Big Shot stood up, drawing Babe with him.

"Are you hurt, Babe? Can you stand up all right?"

"I'm all right. Only my neck hurts." She rubbed it gingerly.

"And you, Olie?"

Olie Jensen staggered to his feet. "Hell, there's nothing the matter with me!"

"We've got to get away from here quick. The police will be along any minute. We'll be in a devil of a boat if they catch us." He darted out of the hall and returned in a moment stuffing a stack of bills into his pocketbook. "I've got twenty-five thousand here. That ought to be enough to carry us for a while. We'll hit for Florida."

They ran out to the garage, where Olie wheeled out the Lincoln limousine.

Big Shot and Babe jumped into the tonneau, and Olie shot it down the lane toward the state road.

As they approached the Red Dragon, they saw that it was almost deserted. All of the cars which had been parked around it were gone. They had evidently fled when they heard the sound of the firing and explosions.

As they turned south upon the state road, they heard the shrill scream of police sirens coming from the city in the other direction. They had escaped just in time.

Big Shot knelt upon the seat and gazed out of the rear window for a time. He saw a squad of motorcycles dash into the lane, followed closely by three police cars. He could still see the glare of the lights upon the dragon's head suspended over the Red Dragon.

Then their car swept around a curve and it disappeared from view. Disappeared forever, he decided.

He sank back upon the seat and took Babe into his arms. With a little cry she slipped her arms about his neck, drew him closely to her. Now that it was all over, she was trembling.

"Babe," said Big Shot with fierce intensity, "I was crazy to ever suspect you of ratting on the mob. Why—if it weren't for you, I wouldn't be here now! And to think that I'd tried to send you for a ride! You might have been killed. And—and—"

"Oh, Big Shot, I—"

She stopped because his arms were around her so tight that she could scarcely breath. It hurt, but the pain was like a kiss.

"Well, that's over," he went on. "It's all over—forever. I'm through with the mob. It's dead, and I'll never bring it back to life. It doesn't pay. If the police didn't get me, some other gangster would in time. There's money—all that a man could ever want—but I'm through with that kind of money."

He was silent. He pressed his lips against her golden curls gently. Then:

"Don't you see, Babe? I love you! I've always loved you, from the first minute I saw you! Can't we get married tomorrow and go some place in Florida where we can be happy and forget all this that we're leaving?"

Babe smiled happily and nodded her head against his chest. She felt that her heart would burst with its happiness. Forgotten already was all the agony of the night. She saw ahead of her only vistas of years that stretched before them.

"Yes," she sighed, "yes." And she raised her lips to him for their first kiss.

In the front seat Olie Jensen nodded contentedly. He would follow Big Shot anywhere, but he was glad to get away from this gang warfare. He was glad, very glad.

HIS NEW DRESS SUIT

Another perfect alibi that failed to click.

LUCIA MUST DIE! Randall Morton repeated this to himself calmly as he stretched at his ease in his room. The hand that held the smoldering cigarette did not tremble as he plotted her death. His face was emotionless, and only the glint in his narrowed black eyes and the firm set of his thin, cruel lips gave any evidence of the terrible determination in him.

His eyes traveled to her photograph upon the library table. With an ironic smile he considered the perfect oval of her face with the curling, golden hair surmounting it. Through a trick of perspective, her large blue eyes seemed to look directly at him and her lips seemed to be about to break into a smile. Yes, she was beautiful; he had to admit that, even though he was tired of her.

He had loved her once, he supposed. But when love is past, and one looks back upon the dead ashes, it is hard to believe that there was once raging passion there. Love to him had never been more than a fiery desire which inflamed him to madness, and which, because of his wealth, he had never had any difficulty in satisfying. When he had tired of a woman, he cast her callously aside without a second thought, for the past lived only in the past.

But with Lucia Estrem it had been different. When he had said to her: "Well, we're through, Lucia," she had refused to believe him. He had expected that, of course, for woman's egotism makes it hard for her to believe that a man can tire of her.

When she had understood that he meant what he said, a new Lucia stood before him, a Lucia that he had never dreamed existed beneath the pretty, sensual exterior. When she found him impervious to and disdainful of her pleadings, she had changed so that he had scarcely recognized her. The soft mouth had become hard, her gentle blue eyes had narrowed until they appeared gray slits in her face and she had become a tigress.

"Randall," she had hissed through clenched teeth, "if you ever leave me, I'll kill you!"

Many women make that threat, but it is only out of their love for dramatics. With Lucia it had been more than that; she had snatched a revolver from a drawer and jammed the cold bore against his chest. Her finger had twitched on the trigger and one look at her convulsed face had convinced him that it needed only one more word to send a bullet crashing into his heart.

He had capitulated, of course; there had been nothing else for him to do before such dangerous fury. He had forced himself to make love to her, to assure her that he had not meant what he had said. But at that moment his indifference toward her had changed to black hate.

She was mad to think that by threats she could control him. He had never before obeyed anyone; opposition he had always crushed ruthlessly without a twinge of conscience, as ruthlessly as he was going to kill her. Death for her was the only way out. He could not run off and hide; he did not want to, and he knew that if she found him she would certainly kill him. It was either her life or his.

With his arms about her he had planned her death, discarding scheme after scheme. He knew that there were hundreds of men in the city, destitute or depraved men, who would kill for a few dollars, but he recognized the dangers of this method. He could not depend upon them to do a thorough job; they might blunder and implicate him. If they were successful, there was the danger of blackmail.

Now he had a plan that was faultless. With his cool, analytical mind he had looked at every angle of it and it sustained the closest inspection. To-night he was going to rid himself of Lucia in such a way that suspicion would never fall upon him.

At seven-thirty the doorbell rang and a messenger boy delivered his dress suit from the tailor. He took it to his bedroom and slipped it on. He had dismissed his man servant for the evening because he wanted no witnesses. He combed down his black hair, put on the white kid gloves which would guard against fingerprints, and in five minutes was spotlessly and impeccably dressed for the opera.

He stood in front of the door of his apartment and listened for a moment. Hearing no noise in the hallway, he quickly stepped out and closed the door noiselessly behind him.

Lucia's apartment was across from his at the other end of the hall. When he had loved her, he had thought this an advantage, but with his growing indifference, it had become a source of irritation. Now he was glad of the arrangement, for it fitted in exactly with his plans.

There were only two other apartments on the floor; opposite his room was a vacant one, and across from Lucia's was one occupied by Mr. and Mrs. Adler, a kindly old couple, wealthy and very much devoted to Lucia. He had carefully determined that they would be in for the evening, for their presence was essential to his plan.

He went down the hallway silently and entered Lucia's apartment, closing the door softly behind him. He was relieved to find that it was unlocked as usual. He glanced at the closet door in the entryway and smiled grimly; then passed into the living room.

A slim figure clothed in a silver evening gown ran to meet him. He mechanically took her in his arms and kissed her. He would have to keep up the pretense for a few minutes; then he would be free of her forever.

She took his arm and pulled him down on the sofa beside her.

"We've a few minutes before the opera, Randall," she breathed. "Just hold me in your arms and tell me you love me."

How women wanted to be told that they were loved, even though they knew it was but a pretense! They would rather live in the shadow of a past love than the reality of the moment. Though he found this irritating, he put his arms about her and made love to her.

At the same time his mind was functioning coldly, regularly, like a machine. He had first to relieve her mind of suspicion; then he could carry out his plan. If he went too fast, she might become apprehensive, and his success depended upon every detail working out.

He allowed himself to drift into a moody silence and he knit his brows in thought. He did not answer her questions and seemed very much preoccupied with some problem of his own. She noticed it and stopped, her eyes growing suddenly anxious.

"What's the matter, Randall?" she asked sharply.

He managed a start and a half smile and said:

"It's really nothing, Lucia."

She regarded him open-eyed, for his tone implied that he was hiding something.

"There is something the matter," she protested. "Tell me what it is." He saw suspicion growing in her eyes.

He remained silent for a moment, looking away from her.

"I haven't wanted to tell you, but I'm deucedly worried," he began at last. "Yesterday I received a letter that—was a threat. And another today."

"A threat?"

"Yes. It said that I was going to get mine. It warned me that I didn't have long to live."

"Do you think it's serious?"

"I'm afraid it is," he answered glumly. "The fact is, I'm almost afraid to go out."

"Why don't you inform the police?"

"I can't. You see, though there was no name signed and it was written on a typewriter, I'm almost sure that it came from Bumano's gang. I was buying some booze from them, you know, and tipping them off whenever any of my friends needed a little stuff. Last week I had a quarrel with them and I'm getting my stuff now from Gorman's gang."

"You really think they'd kill you?"

"Think they'd kill me?" he laughed. "Read the newspapers and find out."

"Isn't there anything that you can do?"

"Not that I know of. I got in touch with Gorman and told him about it, but he only laughed at me. Wouldn't do a thing. If I go out now, I take my chances on getting shot in the back." He looked morosely at the carpet.

She cupped her chin on her hands as she tried to figure it out. He looked covertly at her. Had he properly impressed her with the danger?

"I'd really like to go to the opera tonight, Lucia," he went on. "But I don't know whether it would be safe for you to go with me. I don't mind the danger so much myself, but I don't want to subject you to it. I'd feel a lot better if I only had a gun. But I haven't one on the place—" He stopped as though struck by a sudden thought. "You've got one, though, haven't you? Could you lend it to me until I can get one?"

He looked appealingly at her. He had gone on a very roundabout method to get her to give him the gun, but he felt that it was necessary that she give it to him willingly, and he knew that she would not do that if he asked her outright without explaining his reason.

"Why, certainly," she answered readily. "We'd better hurry, though, or we'll be late for the opera."

He followed her to the bedroom. She seated herself before a dresser and took a revolver from the lower drawer. The same one with which she had threatened him.

"Here it is," she said. "It's loaded."

He took it and threw off the safety. Now was the time! Everything had worked smoothly.

Something in his eye must have warned her, for she suddenly shrank back from him and raised her hands as if to protect herself. Her face became a mask of terror and she opened her mouth to scream, but no sound issued.

For just an instant he stood, the gun in his hand, looking down at her. An utter contempt for her swept over him. She thought she could hold him against his will by threatening him? He saw that she knew she was staring death in the face, and it send a wild thrill of exultation through him.

He jammed the revolver against her breast, pointing it slightly inward toward the spine, and pulled the trigger. There was a flash and the room rang with the roar of the explosion. The force of the blow threw her against the back of the chair. A look of blank astonishment crossed her face and her hands rose toward her wounded breast. Then her throat rattled, her hands fell to her side and she was dead.

He knew that he had to work swiftly for he had but a few seconds. Mr. and Mrs. Adler would certainly hear the shot and they would burst into the apartment in a few minutes at the most. He had to arrange the scene before he could leave.

He thrust the revolver into Lucia's right hand and hooked her first finger through the trigger guard. The gun had only her fingerprints, for he was wearing white kid gloves. He put one arm about her shoulders, the other under her elbow and lifted her to her feet. Her lifeless head fell over against him and he felt the brush of her golden hair on his cheek.

At the foot of the bed, and several feet from it, was a long ottoman. He carefully laid her body, face down, across the end of it so that her head hung over between the ottoman and the bed. Her right hand, still holding the revolver, he placed under her chest. He pulled back the edge of the heavy rug and hooked it under the toe of one shoe.

For one moment he surveyed the scene. It was perfect. No one could tell that it was not an accident. She had been crossing the room, revolver in hand, when her toe had caught on the heavy rug and she had fallen forward on the ottoman. The end of the gun in her outstretched hand had been turned so that it pointed directly at her and the convulsive clasping of her fingers had discharged it into her breast.

He hurried from the room. In the hall he heard excited voices and the sound of steps. It was too late for him to return to his room. Indeed, even if he had left directly after the shot, he probably could not have gained his room. But it did not matter; his carefully thought out plan had taken that into consideration.

He moved with calm precision without the slightest trace of excitement. In the entryway he slipped into the clothes closet and shut the door. He waited motionless in the darkness.

He recognized the voices of Mr. and Mrs. Adler approaching the door of the apartment. They pounded on the door.

"Lucia! Lucia!" called Mr. Alder. "What's happened?"

There was only silence. More pounding, then the apartment door was thrown open and Randall heard the sounds of their feet as they brushed through the entryway and went into the living room.

Mr. Adler called again, then gave a cry of horror. Knowing the two old people were in the bedroom and had found the dead body, he stepped from the clothes closet. The entryway was invisible from the bedroom, so that he ran no chance of their discovering where he had been when they entered.

He ran into the bedroom as though he had just come from his apartment. Mr. and Mrs. Adler were standing just inside the door of the bedroom, too horror-stricken to move.

"What's happened?" he cried.

This was going to be the hardest part of his plan to carry out. He had to pretend that he was horrified and broken-hearted over Lucia's death when he felt only triumph and relief.

Mr. Adler turned toward him, his face stiff with the shock, while his wife wrung her hands impotently.

"We heard a shot," he stammered. "We couldn't get an answer so we came in and we found her—like this."

Randall knelt beside Lucia and shook her shoulder, taking care not to disarrange her body.

"Lucia! Lucia!" he cried.

He stood up, masking his face with sorrow.

"She's dead," he announced dully.

Mrs. Adler began to cry and he gently urged the two old people into the other room and seated them on the sofa. He closed the door to the bedroom.

"This is terrible," he said. "It doesn't seem possible."

"What'll we do, Mr. Morton?" asked Mr. Adler tremulously. "Hadn't we better call a doctor?"

"It's too late. I'll call the police."

As he lifted the receiver, he stopped in horror. There was a smear of bright red blood across the back of the white kid glove on his right hand! If Mr. Adler had seen that, he was betrayed. But no; he was sure that neither he nor his wife had seen anything; they had been too dazed to notice a thing like that.

He spoke the number.

"Police Headquarters?" he called. "This is Mr. Randall Morton, at 1829 West Chestnut Avenue. Miss Lucia Estrem is dead. She was shot. . . . No, I don't know. I didn't get here until after it happened. All right."

He turned to the old couple. "The police and a doctor will be here at once. I'll be right back."

He went to his apartment and stripped off the telltale gloves. They were the only flaw in his crime, but it was not too late to remedy that. He wished that he could destroy them, but he did not have time for that. He opened a dresser drawer and thrust them back under a pile of shirts.

Now he had to force himself to act the part of the broken-hearted fiancé for the benefit of the police. No suspicion could possibly fall on him, but it would be best to act out his part. Both Mr. and Mrs. Adler knew that he had been engaged to Lucia, and he could not conceal it from the police. They may have known that he had quarreled with her, but then lover's quarrels are frequent, and he could say that they had made up. He had to smile at the thought; they had made up—but only so that he could kill her the more easily.

He returned to Lucia's apartment and sat down near Mr. and Mrs. Adler. How should he show his grief? He buried his head in his hands as though the tragedy had overwhelmed him.

Ten minutes later the police were at the door. A tall heavy-set man in plain clothes entered.

"I'm Captain Bennett of the Detective Bureau," he introduced himself. He jerked his thumb at a smaller man following him. "This is Detective Sergeant Andrews."

Randall introduced Mr. and Mrs. Adler and himself.

"Where's the body?" asked Captain Bennett impatiently.

"In there—in the bedroom."

They stomped into the room and Randall followed them to the door from which he could watch them. The two officers stopped just inside the door and swept the room with glances that took in every detail. Then Sergeant Andrews knelt beside the body and felt the outflung arm.

"Huh, she's dead all right, chief."

He lifted her left shoulder so that he could see the gun beneath.

"My gosh," he gasped. "Look at this."

Captain Bennett disengaged the dead woman's fingers and drew forth the revolver. His brow furrowed as he turned it over in his fingers. He broke it open and squinted at it.

"Just one shell been fired," he announced.

He looked down at Lucia. The evening gown was cut almost to the hips and there was no blemish on her back to indicate where a bullet had come out.

"Where's the wound, Andrews?"

The latter lifted her shoulder higher and pointed to a smear of blood on the silver cloth just beneath her left breast.

"Shot right under the heart."

Captain Bennett bent over and examined the wound closely; then straightened up with puzzled eyes.

"And look at that rug—how it's hooked over her toe," he said.

"Yeah. I saw that."

"Do you make the same thing out of this that I do, sergeant?"

"Yeah, I think so."

"Come on. We'll ask a few questions."

Randall moved back from the door to allow them to enter the living room.

"You found the body, Mr. Morton?" demanded Captain Bennett.

"No. Mr. Adler found it. I got here soon after he did and phoned the police."

"Oh. Do you recognize this gun?" He held out the gun that he had taken from Lucia's fingers.

"Yes. That was Miss Estrem's revolver."

"You're absolutely certain of that?"

"Yes. She showed it to me once. You can ask Mr. Adler. He might know."

Mr. Adler nodded agreement.

"Well, Mr. Adler," continued Captain Bennett, "how'd you come to find her?"

"I heard the shot."

"You heard the shot? Where were you?"

"In the apartment across the hall. I and my wife live there."

"I see. Did you know Miss Estrem well?"

"Quite well."

Captain Bennett looked quizzically at the grief-stricken faces of the two old people, then asked softly:

"Any relation of yours?"

"No. But—she was like a daughter to us, Captain Bennett."

"How long after you heard the shot was it that you investigated?"

"I came at once. I knew that something must be wrong. I could tell by the sound of it that it came from Lucia's apartment, and I investigated at once. We knocked at her door and got no answer, so we went in and found her dead."

"How did you know that she was dead?"

"We didn't. When we saw her body, we stopped dazed. Then Mr. Morton came running from his apartment. He touched her and said she was dead."

"Did you hear the shot, too, Mr. Morton?"

"Yes. I was in my apartment at the time also."

"Which is your apartment?"

"The one on the other side of the hall at the further end."

"And you came in the bedroom right after Mr. and Mrs. Adler?"

"Yes. I was just finishing dressing. The tailor had just sent up my suit and I was pulling it on when I heard the shot. I ran over as quickly as I could get my coat on."

"Did you know Miss Estrem well?"

"Quite well." He thought quickly. It would be better to tell the police that he had been engaged to her; they would find it out sooner or later, and it would seem better coming from him. "I—I was engaged to her," he went on in a choked voice.

Captain Bennett surveyed him with new interest.

"What was it, Captain Bennett?" implored Randall.

"It was an accident."

"An accident?" he echoed. A wave of exultation swept over him. The police had been completely deceived, then! Though, even when they were questioning him, he had no doubt that this was their belief.

"Yes. Did you notice how the body was?"

"I'm sorry; I was too dazed and upset to notice."

"The way I figure it out, Mr. Morton, is this: She was crossing the room with the revolver in her hand. Her toe caught on the rug and she fell forward. Maybe you didn't notice that the edge of the rug was hooked over her toe. Well, when she fell forward she put her hands down to catch herself. The end of the revolver hit the ottoman and was turned against her. She fell on top of it just as it went off."

Randall sank into a chair.

"It seems impossible," he murmured. "I can hardly believe it."

At this moment Dr. Barkley, the medical examiner, arrived. Captain Bennett introduced him; then took him into the bedroom. Randall watched them from the door as before.

Dr. Barkley made a brief examination of the body while Captain Bennett explained his theory.

"It looks probable," admitted the doctor. "Are you through with the body now? Let's move it to the bed."

The two detectives lifted the body and stretched it out on the bed. On the left side the blood had seeped through the silver fabric of the dress and left a crimson stain. The doctor cut the beaded shoulder straps and pulled the dress down so that he could examine the wound.

"Hm-m. The shot was fired at close range. That confirms your theory. It entered just beneath the ribs and probably grazed the heart. From the angle at which it entered, I'd say that it struck the spine. That'd explain why it didn't come out. I won't be able to give you the bullet until I've made the autopsy."

"No hurry, doc," said Captain Bennett.

Dr. Barkley reached down to pull up the dress over the wound when Sergeant Andrews stopped him with a gesture.

"Say! Look at this, chief!" he exploded.

He pointed at the smear of blood on the woman's chest.

"Well?"

"Yuh notice how it runs? There's a round smear o' blood just around the wound, then a long streak of it runnin' down across the stomach."

"That's so," admitted Captain Bennett, puzzled. "But what about it?"

"Yuh remember how she was layin' when we found her? Perfectly flat with her head hangin' over the edge. Well, if she fell down an' shot herself accidentally, the blood would have spread around the wound evenly. But it didn't; it ran down. That means that when she was shot, she was either standing or sitting!"

"I believe you're right!"

Randall felt a moment of panic. This was one thing that he had not thought of. She had been in an upright position for possibly ten seconds after he shot her; plenty of time for the blood to run downward from the wound. He reassured himself; the detectives would be able to make nothing of this. He was still safe.

"How about it, doc?" asked Andrews.

"You're correct there; I had entirely overlooked that. If it had been an accident, and she had been shot as she fell, it would have been impossible for the blood to run as it did."

"Where does that get us?" grunted Captain Bennett.

"It all depends," answered Sergeant Andrews. "Doc, did she die at once when the bullet struck her?"

"Probably not."

"She lived for a little while, eh?"

"Yes."

"How long?"

"Anywhere from two to fifteen seconds. Possibly longer. I can tell you with more certainty when I've made the autopsy and learned the exact course of the bullet."

"Could she have taken a couple of steps?"

"It's possible."

"What are you getting at?" interposed Captain Bennett impatiently.

"She committed suicide!"

"She did!"

"Yeah. This is the way I dope it out, chief. She was standin' right here." He moved over so that he stood in front of the chair in which Lucia had been sitting when Randall shot her. "She had the rod in her hand an' shot herself. Then she started stumbling forward an' caught her foot on the rug an' fell over like we found her."

"It looks okay to me," acknowledged Captain Bennett. "What do you think of it, doc?"

"I think he's worked it out correctly," agreed Dr. Barkley. "Now, if you don't need me any longer, I think I'll be running along. I'll turn in the result of the autopsy tomorrow noon." He took his instrument case and left.

"Now we gotta find why she did it," said Sergeant Andrews.

"I expect so, sergeant. Well, we'll have to ask a few more questions."

The two officers came again into the living room. Mr. and Mrs. Adler were still seated on the sofa and Randall had seated himself in a chair at their entrance.

"Our first guess was wrong," announced Captain Bennett. "It wasn't an accident—it was a suicide."

"A suicide?" protested Mrs. Adler blankly.

"Lucia would never have done that!" cried Mr. Adler.

"I'm sorry, ma'am," said Captain Bennett. "But that's what it is."

"I can't believe it. I can't believe it," wailed Mrs. Adler.

"You're certain of that?" demanded Randall.

"Absolutely." Captain Bennett went on to prove his assertion.

"No." Mr. Adler shook his head. "I can't believe it either. Why should she do a thing like that?"

"I don't know. I hope that you'll be able to tell me that."

"But she had everything in the world to live for."

"Was she in trouble of any sort?"

"She was perfectly happy. She had plenty of money and friends; she was in love with Mr. Morton and was engaged to him. She was perfectly happy, wasn't she, Margaret?" he addressed his wife.

"Yes—she was," agreed his wife. "If there had been anything the matter, she would have told me. She was like a daughter to me." She crushed a handkerchief to her eyes.

"Hm-m. But there must of been something," puzzled Captain Bennett. "Sergeant, go through that desk there and see what you can find."

Andrews went to a writing desk in the corner and began to go through the papers. Randall reflected with satisfaction that he had written no compromising letters which might turn up and embarrass him.

He had been a little frightened at first at the turn that the investigation had taken; in a moment his whole carefully buildup plan had crashed. He felt tremendously relieved when Sergeant Andrews had declared that it was suicide. He did not care what they thought it was, so long as it did not implicate him.

He wondered whether Lucia had told the Adlers of the quarrel they had had. Probably not. He had ended it on the same night that it began—at the point of a pistol. If the newspapers learned of it, they would be certain to blame him for the "suicide." He could imagine the headlines: "GIRL JILTED BY LOVER KILLS SELF."

But he was safe from any suspicion of the death. The only clue—the blood stained glove—he had hidden away. His alibi was perfect; he had just been dressing when he heard the shot. The Adlers could testify that no one had left the apartment and that it had been empty when they entered. No one would think that he had hidden in the tiny closet in the entryway until they had passed him.

"Well, Mr. Morton," continued Captain Bennett. "Do you know of any reason why she should commit suicide?"

Randall shook his head dumbly.

"Any—ah—quarrels?"

"Not recently. We got on quite well together."

"Was Miss Estrem in good health?"

"Yes."

Sergeant Andrews interrupted and held out a small, black leather book which he had taken from the desk.

"Just look at this, chief, it's a kind of a diary. Read what's on this page, will yuh?"

A frown gathered on Captain Bennett's forehead as he read the page.

"How do you explain this, Mr. Morton?" he demanded. "I thought you said you hadn't quarreled with Miss Estrem."

"What?" gulped Randall, leaning forward and trying to read what was written in the book.

"I'll read it to you. It's Miss Estrem's diary and it's dated a week ago. Here it is: 'Today Randall and I quarreled. He told me that he was through with me. I grew terribly angry and told him that if he ever did throw me over, I'd kill him no matter where he went. He changed his mind.' It's the last entry."

Randall silently cursed Lucia's passion for recording such things. He recalled now that she had once, several years ago, told him that she kept a diary. If he had only remembered that he could have taken it and saved himself this trouble. Still, it was not serious. He could explain it away, and they had no grounds to suspect him. They might believe that Lucia had killed herself because he did not love her, but they could not arrest him for that.

"It's true, Captain Bennett," he admitted freely. "I didn't want to mention it before because it would have given the wrong impression and it really didn't amount to much. I had been a little irritated with her and we had a slight quarrel. We made up at once and I can't imagine why she bothered to record it at all."

"You're certain that you haven't quarreled since?"

"Absolutely. We were on the best of terms, as Mr. and Mrs. Adler can tell you. If we had not been, they would have known, for Lucia confided everything in Mrs. Adler. You can see how unimportant it was when she didn't tell her. Why tonight I was taking her to the opera. As a matter of fact I was just dressing when I heard the shot."

"Yuh was just dressin'?" repeated Sergeant Andrews, leaning forward and eyeing him with sudden interest.

"Why, yes. I was rather late for I had to wait for a messenger to return my dress suit."

"Well, I guess that lets that out," said Captain Bennett, apparently rather disappointed that he had found no motive for suicide. "I'll make out my report now. I'll want you and Mr. Adler to help me for a few minutes; then you can go."

He took out a notebook and began writing while Sergeant Andrews disappeared. Occasionally he asked a question of Randall or Mr. Adler. Randall was intensely satisfied with himself; he had put it across without a single hitch. He was freed from Lucia forever.

Finally Captain Bennett shut his notebook with a snap and put it in his pocket.

"I'm done now," he said. "And you can go. One of the officers will take charge of the room."

Randall breathed a sigh of relief and started for the door. He felt the need of a good drink. Then he was stopped by the sudden entrance of Sergeant Andrews.

"Thought yuh were smart, didn't yuh?" blazed Andrews, gripping his shoulder.

Randall went white. What had happened? "What do you mean?" he cried, trying to twist from the other's grasp.

Mr. and Mrs. Adler watched the scene open-mouthed. Captain Bennett was stupefied by the strange actions of his subordinate.

"Here, look at this, chief," said Andrews, releasing Randall.

He unwrapped a newspaper and displayed—two white kid gloves, across the back of one a smear of blood.

"What's this all about?" asked the bewildered captain.

"Morton murdered Lucia Estrem!"

"Murdered her!"

He looked up at Randall, who had fallen back several steps at the sight of the gloves.

"I found this pair of gloves in Mr. Morton's room hidden in a dresser under some shirts," explained Sergeant Andrews triumphantly.

"You're crazy," sneered Randall, regaining possession of himself.

"Oh, I am, huh?"

Randall started for the door, but Captain Bennett barred his way.

"Just a minute, Mr. Morton. Let's get to the bottom of this thing. What's this you're saying, sergeant?"

"Morton murdered Miss Estrem and then hid these gloves in his room."

"I appeal to you, Captain Bennett," cried Randall. "How could I have murdered her when I was in my room? Mr. Adler testified that no one left this apartment after the shot was fired. And it was empty when they entered."

"How do you explain that, sergeant?" demanded Captain Bennett. "How could Mr. Morton murder Miss Estrem and still be in his apartment?"

"He wasn't in his apartment. He was right here in this one. He killed Miss Estrem and hid in the little closet in the entryway until Mr. and Mrs. Adler had gone past. Then he ran after them and they thought he had just come from his apartment."

"It's a lie!" flared Randall. But his courage was fast leaving him.

"If yuh look in the closet, you'll find footprints in the dust on the floor."

"Give us your whole theory, sergeant," commanded Captain Bennett.

"The way I dope it out is that," replied Sergeant Andrews, "Morton gets tired of Miss Estrem and wants to shake her, but he finds it isn't so easy as he thought, an' he finally decides to kill her. He goes in there tonight and gets her gun from her. Then he shoots her, puts the gun in her hand and lays her like we found her so it'll look like an accident. When Mr. and Mrs. Adler comes, he hides in the closet. Then he discovers the blood on the glove and hides them in his room before we get here.

"I got kind of suspicious when he said that he was just dressing when he heard the shot. I thought a minute and remembered the closet in the entryway an' I knew how he coulda done it. I looked in the closet and found footprints, an' then I thought I'd just take a look around in his apartment an' see if I couldn't find something. Well, I found the gloves."

"You're right, sergeant!" cried Captain Bennett. "You've done a nice piece of work there. But what made you suspicious of him in the first place? It looked all right to me."

"Yuh remember he said a messenger boy had just brought his clothes from the tailor an' he was puttin' them on when he heard the shot? Well, when I looked at him close, I saw that somethin' was wrong. If he had just put on the suit, it would have been brushed clean, but there was several golden hairs on the lapel of his coat."

Men didn't get out of Dion's mob. A few had tried it— and their bodies had been dredged out of the river weeks later. Yet this was just what Chris was trying to pull!

RACKETEER'S CHOICE

CHRIS THORP BROUGHT DION O'REILLY'S RUMBLING CAVALCADE of five booze trucks into New York without a hitch, despite the fact that it was in the middle of the afternoon and probably thousands of people saw them as they thundered down First Avenue. When they reached the lower East Side, they turned upon a dirty side street and disappeared through the sliding steel doors of the gang warehouse that fronted the river.

"Cripes, you gotta lot of nerve," said the guard who had admitted them. "Comin' around at this time of day!"

" 'S easy," scoffed Chris, jumping out of the cab of the first truck. "These wagons look like furniture vans, don't they? Nobody ever gives 'em a second look."

"But the cops?"

"Fixed. I had one of their stoolies give 'em a fake tip that Lawson's beer hustlers was going to screw a couple of loads through Hoboken. They're probably out there now cooling their heels."

The guard laughed.

"You got too many guts," he said. "You keep on like this an' somebody'll spill 'em for you, Chris."

"I don't think so," grinned Chris. "Nobody's ever going to get *me*."

The smile that twisted his lips had had a double meaning, could the guard but have known it. Chris wondered, a little ironically, what Dion O'Reilly would say if he knew that he was getting out of the racket. That this very night he was planning to take it on the lam.

But no, there was no need for him to wonder. He knew. Men didn't get out of Dion's mob. A few had tried it, and their bodies had been dredged out of the river by the police weeks later. If the Big Shot had the slightest suspicion of his intention, it meant the spot for him.

Nevertheless, he had made up his mind. Bringing in this load of liquor was his last job. O'Reilly had been muscling the mob into the dope racket, first in small driblets, and now in large quantities. It was the end for Chris. He had seen too often the pitiful wrecks that dope made of men and women, and he intended to have nothing to do with it.

And then—there was Lucy. The straightest kid he had ever met. She had been Lucy Andrews, one of the song and dance girls out in the Silver Moon night club. Chris had fallen for her, and fallen hard. Now she was Lucy Thorp. She wasn't the ordinary moll you could hook up with until you got tired of her. She played for keeps. They had ended up before a justice of the peace, with Chris clutching tightly in his hand a bit of white paper secured at the city hall.

Lucy wanted him to get out of the racket, and that was what he was doing. She had a car ready and, as soon as Chris had seen O'Reilly and had received his money for this trip, they were going to beat it out of the city, somewhere west where the gang leader couldn't touch them.

There, Chris hoped to get into some kind of police work. He knew crooks, and it was the one job for which he was really fitted.

"I like flaming rods," he had said to Lucy, "only I've just tumbled to the fact that I've been, on the wrong end of 'em. The next time I handle one, I want a piece o' tin on me."

The guard grinned after him as Chris made his way out of the warehouse, leaving the unloading of the trucks to the drivers and their guards. His slender youthful body was straight as a ramrod, with steel springs for muscles; his cleanly-chiseled face was tight-lipped and his blue eyes keen and intelligent.

He turned at once toward Heinie Muller's speakeasy, which was located on one of the dirtiest and most disreputable streets on the East Side. With its small windows, set below the level of the sidewalk and so covered with dirt and old signs that scarcely a ray of light entered, it looked like a joint of the crumbiest kind. Yet the average bum and cheap gunman would have been given short shrift if he had tried to enter—he would have quickly hit the bricks on his ear.

Not that any of them tried it. For Heinie's was a front for one of the most powerful mobs in New York. Its long narrow barroom was patronized only by the best rods and the slickest racketeers in the city. And in the back rooms on the upper floor, Dion O'Reilly, big shot of them all, ruled his push with an iron hand and a brace of choppers that brooked no opposition.

Chris swung down the steps, and pushed through the door. At his entrance the sprinkling of gunmen and killers standing at the bar and seated at the tables turned around and stared at him. A few of them greeted him boisterously.

He nodded to them and made his way past the dark booths to the back of the room. There he stepped through a hidden door in the wall and started up a dark narrow stairway.

It ended in a short passageway that was lighted only by one feeble bulb. The guard who stood before the door, revolver in hand, passed him on into Dion's office.

It was sumptuously furnished, with heavy carved-oak furniture that had the mellowness of years. His feet sank into a thick carpet that muffled every sound. There were no windows, and the light came from a great crystal chandelier.

Dion O'Reilly was seated at a desk. He tipped back in his swivel chair and regarded Chris from under beetling brows. He was short in stature, but his chest was like a barrel and his arms had the length and strength of a gorilla. He had a typical Irish face, with a short snub nose, blue eyes, and a bristling shock of red hair.

But there was more than Irish in him—a touch of the Slavic, perhaps, for he had a savage love for inflicting torture. Chris had seen him, when a single shot would have been sufficient, beat a double-crossing rat to a quivering pulp of almost lifeless flesh before he allowed one of his rods to end the man's agony.

"Well?" he barked.

"Got the trucks through okay, boss," reported Chris. "All five of 'em. They're down at the waterfront warehouse now, being unloaded."

"Any trouble?"

"A couple flats. The Morgan mob was all set to hijack us, but Tony tipped me off and I took the east route."

Dion O'Reilly's pug face broke into a black scowl.

"Damn that Morgan bunch!" His hairy fist crashed upon the desk top. "They're gettin' too cocky to live. One o' these days I'm gonna send up a bunch of the boys and mop up on 'em. But that's gotta wait. I won't be sendin' you up for any more stuff for a couple weeks. Here's your dough for the job."

He took out a billfold, counted out ten one hundred dollar bills and pushed them across the desk.

"Okay, boss," said Chris, stowing the money away in his pocket.

It had been a good week's work for him. This, with what he had already saved, amounted to almost five thousand dollars. It was enough—enough to take Lucy and him to Chicago or San Francisco and support them until he could pick up some kind of police work.

"When d'you want me on the job again?" he asked, repressing a smile at the thought that this was the last he would ever see of Dion O'Reilly's mug.

"Tonight. Hymie Cohen finally come across and agreed to supply me with all the dope I want at my own figure. He's bringin' the junk tonight by boat to the water front warehouse. I sent Ray Porter and Louie Webster to go along with him. There'll be half a million dollars worth of happy dust."

O'Reilly's eyes glistened at the thought. He went on to give Chris the details of the transaction.

"Okay, boss," said Chris when, the gang leader had finished. "I'll be on hand at fifteen to ten."

He left the office, went down the stairs and started across the barroom. He was exultant. In ten more minutes he could pick up Lucy and they would be on their way west.

But a man standing at the bar put his arm around his shoulders and stopped him.

"Whatza hurry, Chris?" he demanded. "Have a drink with me."

He saw that it was Guiseppe Anselo, a rod who had come from Chicago only a few weeks ago. He was slightly drunk.

"Sure, Guiseppe," said Chris, not wanting to get into a brawl at this time. He ordered a shot of rye, and Anselo doubled the order.

"Noticed yuh jus' come from seein' Dion," said Guiseppe. "You in on the big doings tonight?"

"Yeah. But don't talk so loud. You're pie-eyed, Guiseppe."

Guiseppe snorted with alcoholic indignation. "Pie-eyed, hell! It'd take more'n you to drink me under the table."

The bartender set the drinks in front of them. Guiseppe picked up his and toyed with it.

"There's gonna be some guys what won't like this bumpin' off to-night," he said thoughtfully.

"Yeah?" asked Chris. He didn't remember hearing about any smoke party scheduled for that night. "Why not?"

"Aw hell. This Ray Porter ain't such a bad guy."

Chris stiffened. The drink which was half way to his lips was held motionless. Ray Porter! Why, Ray was one of his best friends in the racket. He composed his face and downed the drink before he continued.

"Haven't heard much about it," he said. "Dion just mentioned it to me. Gonna bump him off when he gets in on that boatload of dope with Hymie Cohen?"

"Yeah." Guiseppe pounded on the bar for another drink. "Dion says he's been double-crossin' us with the Black DeVallo mob. Says he helped DeVallo hijack that truck load o' whiskey two weeks ago."

Chris nodded and stared thoughtfully at the layers of smoke wreathing about the electric light bulbs over the bar. Ray Porter scheduled for the spot? It stunned him. He seemed unable to think for a few minutes.

Though Ray had only been in the mob for six months, having blown in from St. Louis where, as talk had it, he had been hooked up with the Garcione gang, Chris had taken an instant liking to the laughing, good-natured young man. They had seen a great deal of each other, and Ray Porter was the only man that Chris regretted leaving in getting out of the mob.

Why, he remembered the night that Ray had gone with Lucy and him to the Golden Palace night club. Half a dozen of Black DeVallo's rods had raided the joint, bent upon wiping out the guests before they burnt it to the ground. Ray had sprang in front of Lucy and taken a shot in his shoulder which had been meant for her heart. But for his quick intervention, she would now have been dead.

He had to save Ray! He could not let him go unknowingly to his death.

But how? His first impulse was to try to warn him of the danger. Yet how could he do this? Ray and Louie Webster had gone to accompany Hymie Cohen back with the dope. It would be impossible for him to locate Ray until he returned, and then it might be too late.

His jaw set and his lips tightened as he made up his mind. His leaving tonight would have to be postponed. At ten o'clock he would have to be at the water front warehouse when the dope came in. He might find some opportunity for warning Ray, and even to aid him to escape.

He did not deceive himself that it could be easily done. Dion O'Reilly was a bad man to cross. The attempt to help Ray might mean his own death, but that was a chance he would have to take.

Abruptly he turned and left. In the west the sun was sinking redly in the chasm of street between the tenement houses. Its rays reflected from the banks of windows with a color that strangely reminded him of blood.

• • •

Fifteen minutes later he reached the little apartment that he had furnished for Lucy and himself. Lucy threw her arms about him and hugged him tightly.

"Oh, Chris, Chris!" she cried. "I've been so anxious for you to get back! I can hardly wait for us to get started and away from all this."

Chris kissed her hungrily; then held her away from him with his hands upon her shoulders. How pretty she was! The sun slanting through the little living room window made her coppery hair look like burnished gold. And her slim, delicately rounded body seemed so fragile beneath his rough hands.

"I've got everything ready, Chris," she said, her eyes shining with happiness. "See, everything's packed." She waved her hand toward the sofa, where two open suitcases lay, tightly packed. "And the car's outside, ready to go. By tomorrow morning we can be five hundred miles from here."

Chris did not answer, but gazed at her with somber eyes. He could scarcely bear to shatter her happiness by telling her what had happened.

But she saw that he was troubled, and her eyes clouded with alarm.

"Chris! Why don't you say something? What's the matter? Has Dion—"

Chris shook his head. "No, it's not that. But I've just learned that Ray Porter is going to be put on the spot."

"Wh—what?"

One hand went to her mouth, her knuckles pressed against her lips as though to repress an outcry.

"Yeah, Dion's chalked him up to be bumped off to-night." He went on to explain to her what he had learned.

"But—but, Chris!" she cried, when he had finished. "You've got to stop it! You've got to warn Ray. You can't let him be killed. Don't you remember how he saved my life? And what a good friend he's been to us?"

"I know," said Chris hoarsely. "But I can't warn him. He's on the boat coming in now, and I couldn't possibly reach him. The only thing I can do is to be on hand when it gets in at ten o'clock. And—well, you know what that might mean."

He peered anxiously into her white strained face.

"Yes—I know," she said slowly. "It means that if Dion O'Reilly has the slightest hint, he'll murder you."

Then, without a moment's hesitation, she continued:

"But you've got to do it, Chris! You've got to!"

Chris clasped her tight in his arms. "Good for you, Lucy!" he exclaimed. "I knew you'd say that. I'll be on hand at the warehouse at ten o'clock, and somehow or other I'll get Ray out of that mess. Then, as soon as it's over, I'll be back here and we'll start out."

"No," spoke Lucy quietly, "I'll go there with you. If there's any danger, I want to be in on it with you. We'll take the car, leave it near there, and then if we get away, it'll be ready for us."

"Lucy! You can't!" protested Chris, aghast. "I won't let you!"

"Try and stop me, big boy," she said gaily, squaring her shoulders. "I'm going, and you can't stop me. I know how to sling lead with the best of your cannon punks."

Chris evaded her eyes.

"But Dion would—"

"Dion wouldn't think a thing about it!" she cried. "I've been there before with you. And the two of us would have a better chance to warn Ray than just one of us would. Dion wouldn't suspect me, and I might be able to get to talk to Ray where you wouldn't."

Chris grudgingly admitted the truth of her logic. And in the end he agreed to let her accompany him.

"Maybe so," he said, as they were finishing their packing, "we could get Ray to go west with us. He's washed up with Dion now. I've got enough money now so that I could give him a stake. And I think if Ray had the chance, he'd probably go straight."

Before they left, at nine thirty, Chris took the automatic from his shoulder holster and inspected it. As an afterthought, he slipped an extra clip for it and a short revolver in the pocket of his coat. Lucy concealed a deadly little .25 caliber automatic in the bosom of her dress.

The Ford coupe which he had bought was parked outside. They packed their things in the back and drove it to within a block of the water front warehouse, where they left it in a dark alley. From there they walked to the warehouse.

It was a gloomy four story structure with windows only on the front. On the side it almost touched the water, being separated only by a narrow runway, and with a rickety wharf jutting out over the river on the street side.

Chris knocked on a small door beside the great sliding steel garage doors. A shutter drew back and an eye scrutinized them; then the door opened and admitted them.

They were in the great loading room into which Chris had driven the cavalcade of trucks, which were even now standing in a row against the wall. At one side a group of men were playing poker on a table set beneath a drop light. A dozen more gunmen and two flashy molls stood watching them.

A young man detached himself from the group and came over to greet them.

"Dion's waitin' for yuh in the office, Chris," he said. "Told me to send yuh in as soon as yuh come."

"Okay, Bartolli," answered Chris.

He left Lucy to watch the game and went into the little office in the front.

Dion O'Reilly and Guiseppe Anselo were seated at a table on which stood a bottle of whiskey and several glasses.

" 'Lo, Chris," Dion boomed. He was obviously in a good humor. "Here, have a drink." He poured out three glasses.

Chris dropped into a chair and tossed off the drink.

"All set for tonight, boss?" he asked.

He wondered covertly whether O'Reilly would tell him of his plans for bumping off Ray Porter. He did not think that the gang leader knew the extent of the friendship between them, and so there was no reason for him not doing so. But he dared not ask him anything about Ray for fear of giving himself away.

"Yeah," grunted Dion. He pulled out his watch and glanced at it. "Fifteen to ten. Time we got ready. Chris, you've got the same job you had before. See that the boys are stationed around and tell 'em to keep a damn good lookout for trouble."

"You expecting any?"

"I don't think so. But if Black DeVallo got wind of this, there'll be hell to pay."

Chris went out to the loading room and watched the card game until the hand had been finished. Then he interrupted it.

"Sorry to break up the game, boys, but the boss says we got to get busy. Hymie Cohen's coming in his speed boat in ten minutes, and his main boat is due at ten sharp."

He chose six rods, stationing two of them at the end of the street and the other four along the water front.

Then he rejoined Lucy, who stood before a door that opened on the runway along the river side of the building.

Six feet below them the dark oily water slapped against the foot of the runway. To their left they could see dimly the black mass of the wharf protruding out over the water, and far out the twinkling lights of boats, while almost lost in the gloomy distance were the pin pricks of light on the farther shore. The sounds of the boat whistles echoed hollowly on the sharp breeze that blew in their faces.

Lucy's eyes peered out across the darkness.

"Ray's out there somewheres?" she asked softly, so as not to be overheard.

"Yeah," assented Chris. "Unless Dion's plans fell through and Hymie Cohen don't show up."

Lucy gave a short sharp laugh. "And this is the night we were going to make our getaway!" She glanced behind her, at the gunmen and killers who stood about in groups. "We've got a fine chance of getting Ray away from this mob!"

Chris shrugged. "We've got to try. After what Ray did—"

He stopped as he heard two short shrill whistles far out upon the river.

"That's Hymie Cohen now! Hey! Bartolli, tell Dion that Cohen's coming!"

Bartolli ran to the office. A moment later Dion O'Reilly came out, followed by Bartolli and Guiseppe Anselo. He stopped beside Lucy and peered out into the darkness.

"I don't see Cohen," he said.

"Just got his signal," explained Chris. He pushed a button, and a red light over the door flashed two times.

Then he seized a submachine gun and ran out upon the wharf, followed by two gunmen.

They heard the subdued roar of a motor. A few minutes later a long narrow speedboat flashed out of the darkness, slowed down, and swung up beside the wharf. As one of the guards seized a rope thrown up and stopped the boat, four men stood up in it.

"Louie?" asked Chris, training the submachine gun on them.

"Yeah, it's me," answered the voice of Louie Webster. "Everything's okay, Chris. This is Hymie Cohen."

Chris lowered the machine gun as the four men clambered up on the wharf. He recognized the short fat man as Hymie Cohen, the dope runner. The other two men were his guards, and they kept their hands suggestively in their pockets.

Hymie Cohen laughed when he saw the weapon in Chris's hand.

"No need for the hardware, boy," he said. "Where's Dion?"

Chris led them across the wharf and into the loading room. Hymie Cohen and Dion O'Reilly greeted each other warily, as though they did not trust each other.

"You've got the stuff?" asked Dion.

"Yeah, it's out in the boat. Everything clear at this end?"

"Sure."

"And you've got the dough ready to pay for it?"

"Hell, yes!" exclaimed O'Reilly. "You don't have to be afraid of me, Cohen. I'm not goin' to pull a fast one on you. We're gonna do a lot of business together."

"Just wanted to be sure," chuckled Cohen. He turned to one of his gunmen. "All right, Izzie. Give the signal."

The man took a flashlight from his pocket, pointed it out into the darkness, and gave three long flashes, then three short ones.

Two minutes later a high-powered launch came sweeping in from the night. The pilot brought it up expertly against the runway.

As two gunmen leaped forward to secure the ropes that the crew tossed to them, a form leaped lightly to the runway. Chris's heart leaped as he recognized the tow head and lank form of Ray Porter.

"Hullo, Ray," he cried, clapping him on the back.

" 'Lo yourself," retorted the young man gaily. "How did your little jaunt turn out?"

Chris stepped closer to him. Now was his opportunity to warn him. But just as he was about to speak, a form pushed between them. It was Guiseppe Anselo.

"Trip okay?" asked Anselo grinning. "Didn't get seasick or nothing, did yuh?"

Chris choked back his words of warning. It would be suicide to do anything with Guiseppe Anselo at his elbow.

Then Hymie Cohen and Dion O'Reilly crowded past them and stepped on the boat. They disappeared into the cabin and returned, a few minutes later, with Dion carrying several small packages of dope.

"Gotta test your happy dust," Chris heard Dion say as they crossed the loading room and entered his office.

Chris gave up his attempt to warn Ray for the time being. Some of the other gunmen had joined him and Anselo and they were laughing and talking about the trip.

He walked over to the side, where Lucy stood watching.

"I couldn't do it," he groaned. "I think maybe Anselo suspects I might want to try something."

"But we've got to get to him," she said. "Perhaps I can get him off on one side."

"Be careful," begged Chris. "If Dion suspects, he'll bump off the three of us."

Then Dion reappeared in the loading room, followed by Hymie Cohen.

"Everything's fixed up, boys," he announced. "Get to work and load the stuff. Porter, you show 'em what to take off. Put it down in the vault. And Chris, you see that the stuff's stacked up in the vault and make a check on it."

Chris threw a warning glance to Lucy before he reluctantly descended the steps to the cellar. He opened the great steel doors of the vault, which were so cunningly concealed that they seemed a part of the brick wall, and began a check on the oil-bound packages of dope as soon as the men began to bring them down.

Though he worked calmly and efficiently, his mind was torn by anxiety. Did Dion suspect him, and had he sent him down here so that he would be out of the way when Ray was killed? Would he get back in time to warn Ray? Would they be able to make their escape?

When all the packages had been brought down and his check was complete, he rushed up the stairs with his figures. His eyes sought and found

Lucy. He read despair on her face, and he knew that she had failed.

Following the direction of her eyes, he started. He saw three figures disappearing through the door that led into the rear store rooms. One of them was Ray Porter, and with him were Bartolli and Guiseppe Anselo.

Ray was on his way to his death!

Chris glanced around desperately. Dion O'Reilly and Hymie Cohen were not in sight—they were probably in Dion's office. The other members of the two gangs were off at one side, where they had opened a case of liquor and were passing around bottles.

He crossed hurriedly to Lucy.

"Anselo asked Ray to go back with them to get out a case of special liquor for Hymie Cohen," she explained.

"Special liquor, hell! They're gonna kill him!"

He whirled and stared about the room. As far as he knew, there was no one there who knew why Ray had been taken into the rear room. Since Dion O'Reilly was out of sight, he would occasion no suspicion if he followed Ray.

He grasped Lucy's arm and pulled her toward the rear door.

"C'mon! We've got to help Ray. We'll get him out of this mess and beat it out the back way!"

Together they ran through the door and down the dark corridor. A shaft of light falling through an open door told them where the three men had gone. Chris drew his revolver as he plunged through the door.

Two seconds more and he would have been too late. He saw the three men standing on the other side of the room. Ray and Bartolli were close together, with their backs to the door. And just behind Ray was Guiseppe Anselo, with a revolver pointed straight at Ray's back! Even as Chris caught sight of him, he saw the hammer of the revolver go back for the fatal shot.

But before it had descended upon the cartridge, Chris fired. And his bullet sped unerringly through Anselo's head. Anselo tottered and fell forward. His revolver exploded, but the bullet ploughed into the floor.

"Ray! Look out!" shouted Chris.

But at the roar of the shot, Porter had whirled about, and he saw at once the significance of the revolver in Anselo's hand.

Bartolli was jerking a rod from his shoulder holster, but Chris dared not fire for fear of hitting Ray. Before Bartolli got into action, however, Ray sent a crashing right to his chin and sent him staggering back, to collapse against the wall.

From the floor Bartolli's gun smashed into flame and bullets singed past Ray. But almost as quickly Chris' slugs found him and tore through him. His body collapsed and the gun clattered from his hand.

"Quick, Ray!" shouted Chris. "Out the back door! Dion was having you put on the spot!"

Without question, Ray followed them out into the corridor. The three of them turned and ran toward the rear.

From the loading room came a chorus of shouts, the pound of feet. Then, the savage bellow of Dion O'Reilly's voice.

Chris reached the rear door and tore at it. It did not move. He stepped back so that the light could fall on it and saw that there was a heavy bar across it, fastened in place by a large steel padlock.

"Locked!" he gasped.

He turned the revolver on the padlock and sent three shots crashing against it. He tried to wrench it open, but it resisted him. It was too strong to be thus easily broken. This way was barred to them.

But what other way was there? There were no windows in any of the store rooms. The only other exit was out the front—and that was barred by Dion's gunmen.

"We can't get out here," he groaned. "Nothing short of a sledge hammer would break this lock."

"How about the second floor?" asked Ray. "There's windows in front, and we might be able to jump out to the street."

As they turned back and raced for the stairs in the center of the corridor, the door opened at the farther end and two men stepped in. Chris' and Ray's guns crashed at the moment and one of the men dropped while the other dodged back out of sight.

They heard, above the tumult from the loading room, Dion's voice roar, "Get out the choppers an' give it to 'em!"

They darted up the stairs. At the top Chris slammed the door shut and locked it. As he did so, he heard the pound of a submachine gun below. Steel-jacketed slugs splintered through the door, almost tearing it from its hinges.

"The front!" shouted Chris.

He seized Lucy's arm and they began to run toward the front of the building, where he could see the dim glow of windows.

But he had forgotten the front stairs. Before they were half way there, men burst up them. He saw the light glint upon a submachine gun as it erupted into spitting red flame. Bullets swept over their heads in a flaming arc.

He aimed at the machine gunner and pulled the trigger. He cursed as the hammer clicked upon an empty cartridge.

But at the same instant both Ray and Lucy went into action. Two streams of bullets converged upon the machine gunner and he went down sprawling, the spray of slugs from his weapon eating into the floor.

However, their escape in this direction was cut off. Another man was already reaching for the machine gun. More men crowded up behind him.

"Let's try the next floor!" shouted Ray.

They turned and raced back to the stairs. The door to the stairs from the first floor was breaking down as they turned up them. From across the front came the raking fire of the machine gun in another man's hands.

They reached the third floor just in time. Men came tumbling up the steps almost on their heels. And, between the roar of the gunfire, they could hear feet pounding up the front stairs.

Without a word, they raced to the top floor. Almost as if by plan, Chris and Ray seized a heavy packing case that stood near the head of the stairs and pushed it down on them. It fell a few feet then wedged solidly.

They turned and ran to the front stairs. Men were already pouring up. Chris snatched out his automatic and emptied it into their ranks. They fell back for an instant.

Then they repeated their procedure of stopping up the stairs by throwing large boxes down.

"That'll hold 'em for a minute, anyway," said Chris.

Suddenly they heard the throb of an electric motor and the scraping of wire cables.

"It's the elevator!" cried Ray. "They're coming up that!"

They ran to the elevator shaft, which is almost in the center of the building, pulled up the safety guard and looked down. They saw the cage slowly ascending toward them.

"Quick!" said Chris. "We'll push this heavy box down on it."

He indicated a large crate which was filled, if he remembered rightly, with heavy copper coils intended for a still. They threw their weight against it and slid it across the floor.

When it reached the opening, it hung for a moment; then toppled and fell. An instant later there was a terrific crash—it had hit the top of the ascending elevator cage.

This was followed almost at once by a second crash. Chris leaned over and peered down the shaft. He saw that the cable supporting the elevator had snapped and the cage had fallen to the basement.

"And now what?" he asked. "We can't hold out here. It's only a matter of minutes until they break through. I'm out of ammunition. How about you, Ray?"

"I'm out too," answered Ray.

"My gun's empty," reported Lucy.

They stared around hopelessly. The truth of what Chris said was evident. From the front stairs they heard the crash of what was probably a battering ram, breaking through the protection of the boxes.

"How about the roof?" suggested Lucy. "If we went up there and pulled the ladder after us, they couldn't get at us—at least not for a few minutes."

"Good girl," said Chris. "We'll try it."

He climbed the ladder to the trap door that opened upon the roof, pushed it back and stepped out. Lucy came after him, followed by Ray. Then, with Ray's help, they pulled up the ladder and laid it out on the roof.

For a moment they stood and looked about them. To the west they saw the banks of skyscrapers, rising higher and higher, their sheer black sides speckled with points of light. They could hear the horns of cars and the rattle of the elevated trains.

And in the other direction, to the east, was the blanket of darkness that lay over the river, blackness broken only by a few moving points of light.

Ray made a circuit of the roof and reported that there was no way by which they could reach the street. They were cornered there—safe until Dion O'Reilly's men reached them.

Chris put his arm around Lucy. She was shivering.

"This is a helluva game," he laughed ironically. "Here you are, Ray, one of Dion's best rods, and he tries to put you on the spot."

"And he would have, if it hadn't been for you," added Ray. "I didn't suspect a thing when Anselo and Bartolli asked me to go back with them to get out some liquor. You got there just in time to save me. I've got you to thank for it."

"Forget it. We'll all be dead in a few minutes anyway. It makes no difference one way or another."

Ray put his hand on Chris's shoulder.

"But it does, Chris. I appreciate what you've done. You've thrown your life, and Lucy's too, away in an effort to save me. I can't forget that."

Chris laughed again and drew Lucy closer to him. "Forget it," he repeated. "It's no more than you've done for me. I wouldn't have Lucy now if you hadn't taken that bullet in your shoulder when we went to the Golden Palace."

They were silent for a time, staring off into the darkness.

Ray walked over to the trap door and peered down it. Then he jumped hastily back as a bullet sang past his head.

"They're piling up boxes beneath the trap door," he reported. "A few more minutes and they'll have it high enough to get through. Then—*sowie!*—that'll be the end for us. If we only had something we could fight back with. But there isn't even a brick!"

Chris did not answer. He took out a package of cigarettes and offered Ray one. They both lighted up.

"Yeah, it's a helluva game," he repeated slowly. "Here I was just going to get out—and then this."

"Get out? What do you mean?" asked Ray.

"Just that." He gave a short sharp laugh. "I've got a little pile saved up—about five grand—and I was figuring it was time for me to go straight. Lucy and I was going to hit west tonight. We've got a little car, all packed, hid just around the corner."

"Good Lord!" cried Ray. "And you left that for—for me?"

Chris only shrugged. He drew Lucy a little closer to him. It was hard to look at death. They had had such wonderful plans. And particularly was it hard because he had drawn Lucy in with him.

"But—but—" protested Ray, plainly bewildered, "what were you figuring on doing?"

"You'll laugh, Ray," said Chris hesitantly, "but I was planning to go either to Chicago or San Francisco and get into some kind of police work."

Even in the darkness, he could see the queer look that crossed Ray's face.

"And you know," Chris went on, "we even thought of asking you to go along with us, Ray. You're one of the squarest guys I've ever known, and I wanted to see you get out of this racket. But it's too late now for anything."

Ray did not answer this. He walked close to the trap door and peered cautiously down it. Then he jumped back.

"They're coming up through now!" he cried.

Then, at the same instant, the comparative silence was broken by a rattle of shots that rose to an irregular roar. They came from down below, from the street level.

"Somebody's raiding the place!" exclaimed Chris.

He ran to the edge of the roof and peered down. Sixty feet below, in the street and on the narrow runway on the side, he saw the surge of bodies lit up by the flash of gunfire. Machine guns stuttered; then a bomb burst with an ear splitting roar.

"Black DeVallo's mob!" he screamed.

Out on the water was the dark shape of a boat coming in, then another. Guns crashed in a volley from their decks.

Suddenly a spray of bullet spat over his head. He glanced back and saw the head and shoulders of a man coming up through the trap door, a submachine gun in his hands. He leaped out upon the roof, and was followed by another man.

"Let's jump!" cried Lucy. "It's our only chance!"

In a split second Chris looked down at the water sixty feet below them and made up his mind. In another instant, if they remained where they were, they would die. And if they jumped clear of the runway below, they had a fighting chance.

He seized Lucy's hand and they jumped together. He felt bullets fan his cheek as they plunged downward. Then there was a sickening drop that caught at the pit of his stomach.

He saw the water flashing up at them. He felt the shock, the wrenching tear when they struck it. Lucy's hand was torn from his; then he sank down, down.

His lungs almost bursting, he struggled to the surface. His eyes were blinded by the water. His hands encountered a form. It was Lucy! He drew her to him and supported her in the water.

He was only dimly conscious that the roar of the battle was increasing. He heard the thunder of another bomb and the crash of a falling wall. Then Ray's voice, screaming from farther out in the water.

"Chris! Lucy! There's a boat out here!"

He turned on his side, still supporting Lucy, and swam in the direction of the voice. A moment later Ray was at his side, helping him with Lucy.

"Boat here—just a dozen feet," clipped Ray.

He saw the long slender shape of a small launch, a man standing up in it. They were beside it, and the man was pulling Lucy into the cockpit. Chris and Ray climbed in after her.

He turned a flashlight on them. Then, in the reflection of the light, Chris saw that it was a policeman. It was a police launch that had saved them.

A deep growl rose in his throat. After all they had gone through, to be caught by the police! He saw years of prison ahead for him—and for Lucy.

Abruptly he threw himself upon the officer and bore him down into the cockpit. If he could overpower him and capture the boat, they might still be able to make their getaway.

Then arms wrapped themselves about his chest and jerked him off the officer. Ray's voice grated in his ear:

"Hold it, Chris!"

The officer jumped to his feet and jerked out a revolver. But Ray's voice stopped him.

"It's me. Corrigan."

The officer hesitated, half lowered his revolver.

"Okay, boss," he said.

Ray released Chris and he stepped back.

"You're a cop?" Chris asked Ray bitterly.

"Yeah. Federal agent. Corrigan's my real name. I was sent here to break up the dope gang that's been running in so much stuff.

Chris waved a hand toward the battle that was still raging.

"A police raid?"

"Yeah. I had it scheduled for five minutes after ten, but something must have slipped. It looks like Dion O'Reilly and Hymie Cohen are done for, though. They're cornered there like rats. And there's enough evidence in the place to send 'em up for life, if they get out alive."

Chris' hands dropped to his sides. It looked like the end for him and Lucy.

"Well, what're you going to do with me?" he asked wearily.

"Boy," exulted Ray, "I've got a nice place all picked out for you! You said you wanted to go straight and get into police work. Well, how about joining up with the Federals? I've got a drag and can get you in. I'm going out to Chicago on some special work as soon as this is cleared up, and you could go with me. How does that strike you? Would you like to go?"

"Would I?" cried Chris. His hand found Lucy's and pressed it. "Would I? Say, you've got a new copper right now!"

Stories by Richard Credicott also appear in Gangster and Racketeer Stories, the other members of Blue Band Mob

A MAGAZINE OF UNDERWORLD LIFE

NOV.

Racketeer STORIES

25¢
30¢ IN CANADA

Don't Print That!
A Book-Length Novel by
WALT S. DINGHALL

Glycerined Gangsters
By HENRY LEVERAGE

The Big Shot's
Weak Spot
by
RICHARD CREDICOTT

Cover painting by R.C. Wardel

THE BIG SHOT'S WEAK SPOT

*Get wise to yourself, Barcone! One day someone's gonna
find your weak spot—and it'll be curtains for you and a mile
of flower wagons!*

BIG JACK BARCONE SAT AT HIS EASE IN CAPTAIN REGAN'S OFFICE. He was always
at his ease. A little matter like being called to Police Headquarters for
questioning concerning the death of Pete O'Malley, his friend and the chief
lieutenant of his gang, did not trouble him.

"You asked for me, Captain," he said. "Well, here I am."

He waved the hand in which he held an expensive Corona as he spoke. His fat figure was dressed in flashy clothes and a large diamond shone upon one of his fingers. He had an air of boastful assurance for, in his many dealings with the police, he had come to fear them not at all. He had one of the largest gangs in the city at his back; he had millions of dollars in the banks and in investments; and he brooked no interference from anyone.

Captain Regan smiled ironically, yet with a faint trace of amusement. He had been with the Police Department for years before the coming of the super-gangs with their hundreds of members, and his hair had grown white in the service.

"And you're all ready to spill your guts to me, I suppose," he said.

"Sure, sure," agreed Barcone, flashing a smile at Louise Hallston, who sat near the window. "I'm always ready to tell you anything I know, Captain. I've never held out on you yet."

Then he grinned openly.

Louise looked away from them, looked down toward the handbag she was twisting nervously with her fingers. Her beautiful face with its sweet expression, and the blonde hair which coiled about her head and shimmered in the sunlight that fell through the window upon it, gave her an appearance of innocence which was far from being her true nature. She had been a dancer and hostess in one of the most depraved night clubs of the city until Big Jack Barcone had found her. Now she was his moll.

But this time she could not share Barcone's little joke. Not when her heart was torn with rage and pain. For, though she was Barcone's woman, she had fallen in love with Pete O'Malley. And Pete lay in the county morgue with three bullet holes through his skull.

"Cut the comedy," growled Captain Regan, good-humoredly. "We both know you won't tell me anything you don't want to. And that probably won't be much! Now listen, Barcone, we both want to get the guy that croaked Pete O'Malley."

"Sure," agreed Barcone.

"And I want you to help me. Can't you forget this 'no-knowy-no-telly' stuff for a while? If you know anything, I'd like you to tell it. There's been too many gang killings lately, and the papers are beginning to squawk that it's bad advertising for the town. Though I don't see that they cut down on their crime news any."

"But what makes you think I know anything?" inquired Barcone, blowing a wreath of smoke toward the ceiling. "I only got wind of what happened to Pete this morning. I haven't had time to look around yet."

"Well, I don't know for sure that you do know anything," admitted Captain Regan. "But there isn't very much going on around here you don't know about. And you ought to have some ideas about this. Pete O'Malley was your man. You know how he stands with the different mobs, and who'd want to put him on the spot. I've got a hunch it was the Kendrick mob. The killing was right on the edge of their district, and I've heard it whispered around that they were out to get Pete. Now I'm going to show you what we've got."

He lifted a receiver from a desk telephone and called for the Bureau of Identification.

"Synder? You got the stuff ready on the O'Malley killing? Good. Bring it down now, will yuh?"

Sergeant Synder came in in a few minutes and handed him a large envelope.

"Here's the stuff, Cap'n. Rosenbaum said to tell you he went over the car again and there wasn't any fingerprints. And Harley'll have the diagram ready in half an hour."

When he had left, Captain Regan opened the envelope and took out two large photographs. He laid the first of them on the desk so that Barcone could see it.

Louise rose from her chair and walked over behind Barcone so that she could see it also.

It was a picture of a coupe parked beside the curb near a corner. The right door was open, and through the windshield could be seen a dark huddle of a figure over the steering wheel. In the background rose the gray outlines of a factory.

"This is the death car," explained Captain Regan. "This here is Ninth street, and this other is Monroe. Kelley, the bull on that beat, found it, and he didn't touch it until we got there. The engine was still running, though it was out of gear. Kelley didn't hear any shots. He didn't know anything was wrong until he said 'hello' and there wasn't any answer. Then he shot his flash through this open door and found the body."

Louise shuddered involuntarily as she looked at the picture over Barcone's shoulder.

"And here"—Captain Regan put the second picture beside the first one—"is a close-up of the body. We took this picture through the open door without touching the body. You see the three bullet holes through the side of Pete's head."

Barcone examined the pictures closely without offering any comment. Louise turned her head away, her eyes filmed with horror. She grasped the back of Barcone's chair to steady herself. This had been the terrible end of the man that she loved. Why, it seemed only a few hours since she had been in his arms!

She tried to compose her face to conceal the grief that almost overpowered her. She was afraid that Barcone or Captain Regan would notice her agitation.

She walked to the chair near the window, sank into it and looked out across the city's skyline.

"You see," went on Captain Regan, "Pete never had a chance. This is the way I figure it: he stopped near the curb, threw the engine out of gear and opened the door to talk to somebody; then whoever it was hauled off and plugged him. It was all over before he knew what was happening."

Barcone picked up the second picture and studied it. "What time did it happen?"

"Doc Mueller says right around eleven o'clock. Kelley didn't find him until almost twelve."

"Um-m-m."

Captain Regan leaned forward. "I'm going to tell you some more, Barcone. We pulled in Bugs Lewis."

"Bugs Lewis! What the hell! What's the idea, Captain? You're not nuts enough to think he did it, are you? Bugs and Pete have worked together for years. They've got an apartment together out on the North side."

"I know it. I didn't suspect him, but I wanted to find out if Bugs knew anything about it. He wasn't going to say anything, and we finally had to take him to the gym for a game of football. He came through, all right."

Barcone's fat face grew red with anger. He pounded the desk with his fist.

"You got your nerve, Regan!" he roared. "Haven't I told you to lay off my men?"

"Sure you have," answered Captain Regan cheerfully, placidly. "But I'm my own boss. There isn't any mob going to tell me what not to do. And this was such a temptation, you know. Anyway, after we played ball with Bugs for a while, he came through. Pete got a call last night about eight o'clock. He didn't tell Bugs who it was, but he went out in his car about two hours later. That mean anything to you?"

Barcone's anger was replaced by puzzlement. "You say he got a call? Didn't Bugs have any idea who it was?"

"Nope. He asked him, but Pete wouldn't tell him."

"Then I'll be damned if I know who it was."

Captain Regan pulled out a drawer and took out a small pill box. From it he dropped upon his desk two steel-jacketed pellets.

"Here's two of the slugs that did for him. The first one went right through his head and the window glass and we couldn't find it. This one here that's scratched went down more and we found it embedded in the door. And this other went down through his head and his neck into his body. Doc Mueller found it in the middle of his back. They're these nine millimeter Luger bullets."

He rolled them about on his desk with the tip of his finger. Barcone picked up one of them and examined it. Louise swung her eyes from the window and gazed at them fascinatedly.

"This is all we've got," went on Captain Regan. "There wasn't a single witness of it, or if there was, he hasn't showed up yet. Well, Barcone, what do you think?"

Barcone frowned heavily. "I'm telling you straight, Captain, I don't know any more about it than you do. If I did, I'd tell you. Pete was one of my best men, and I feel rotten about it. Hell, how should I know? I may be able to pick up something later. If I get anything, I'll let you have it. You know me well enough to know that I'm not going to let anybody put a thing like this over on me. But right now—I suppose you want me to say it was Kendrick's mob, huh?"

"You think it was them?"

"I told you once I didn't know. Your guess is as good as mine. It might be Scarfici's mob."

But Barcone's words lacked the air of conviction. Louise was suddenly convinced that he knew that it was the work of Kendrick's mob. He had so many lines of information that she felt he must at least have a strong suspicion, and the veiled hint in his words pointed directly toward Kendrick's mob.

Well, if they were guilty, they would suffer for it. Barcone would never rest until he had avenged Pete's death. If necessary, she would see to that. She had loved Pete, and she swore to herself that his killers must die.

"We got Kendrick," announced Captain Regan.

Barcone's eyes narrowed. "Yeah?"

"We dragged him out of bed early this morning. Same old stuff: didn't know anything about it; hardly knew Pete O'Malley; wouldn't croak a guy anyway."

"And you gave him the works?"

"Sure we gave him the works! But he wouldn't squawk no-how. We've got him, in the cooler now waiting for the next session. He was pretty heated when we got through working on him. If he was in on it, he'll break."

"Yeah, I guess he'll break," said Barcone. "He always was lousy."

"You think so? Don't kid yourself, Barcone. All you gangsters are lousy."

Barcone grinned broadly. Nothing could break through the shell of his egotism.

"You got me wrong, Captain," he protested with mock solemnity. "I'm no gangster. I'm in the lumber business."

"Sure you are!" smiled Captain Regan, wagging his white-haired head. "And some day you'll be laid out on a slab like Pete is now. The daylight'll be poking around in you finding out what made the wheels go 'round."

"Not me," boasted Barcone. "I've been in the game for six years, and I'm still going strong. It's just the guys without brains that get bumped off."

"Then you can expect an early funeral. If you had any brains you wouldn't be running a mob. You'd be in some honest business where your chances of living to middle age were better."

Barcone laughed ringingly. "You got a good imagination, Captain. Why, I don't take any chances. You ought to know that. The guy that croaks me will have to be a magician. I've got a better bodyguard than the president."

"Big boy, aren't you? But just remember that it only takes one slug to finish you. Just one little slug in the right place and you're done for."

"Sure. But before that little slug can get to me, it'll have to go through about three other guys."

"Maybe. And maybe there won't be any one there to take it for you when it comes. Get wise to yourself, Barcone. No matter what you do, you'll always have a weak spot somewheres. You can't help yourself."

Captain Regan stopped for a moment. His bluff, weather-beaten face grew almost philosophical as he continued:

"Every man has a weak spot somewheres. It's human nature—fate. Sometimes it's a woman, sometimes it's his best friend, sometimes it's circumstances over which he has no control. With the average man it doesn't matter—his life isn't at stake. But with a gangster, one slip means death. You think that you're perfectly guarded, with your armored cars and your gunmen, but there's certain to be a loophole somewhere in it. And someday somebody's gonna find your weak spot. And then it'll be curtains for you and a mile of flower wagons."

Barcone laughed again.

"Boy," went on Captain Regan, "the only smart gangster I ever heard of was Johnny Torrio. When he had his pile, he beat it to Italy. Why don't you try something like that?"

"Want me out of the city, do you?" jeered Barcone. "No, thanks, my dear captain. I like it here and I'm sticking. If you haven't anything else to say, we'll be running along. I've got business to attend to. I wish you luck with Kendrick. If you want to have him with a whole hide, you'd better keep him here."

Captain Regan followed them to the door,

"Sorry you won't take my advice. See you in the morgue sometime."

While they were waiting for the elevator, Louise asked:

"What makes you think that it was Kendrick's mob that killed Pete, Jack? I could tell from the way you talked that you did. Have you heard anything?"

"Don't it look like their work?" replied Barcone defensively. "It's too bad, too. Pete was a good man. We're going to give him a real send-off."

Louise was struck by a sudden doubt. Now that she had had time to think it over, it didn't seem logical to her. Pete had been the go-between for the two mobs, and he had told her that he was on good terms with Kendrick. Of course that would have given Kendrick a good opportunity to put him on the spot, yet she had heard no intimation of trouble.

She shook her head dubiously. "It's beginning to look funny to me, Jack. In the first place, that telephone call. You know that Pete O'Malley was too smart to let himself get put on the spot that way. If Kendrick had called him up and asked him to meet him, Pete wouldn't have gone without a guard."

"Forget it," grunted Barcone, scowling. "It was Kendrick's mob, all right. If Regan can't make Kendrick crack, I'll crack him wide open with lead when he lets him out. I'm going to mop up the streets with his mob. I've been holding my fire because I didn't want any trouble, but they asked for it, and they're going to get it."

The elevator stopped and they got in. As it started downward, Louise asked:

"And Captain Regan said that Pete was killed with Luger bullets, didn't he? You don't run across those very often. You've got a Luger, haven't you, Jack?"

"Yeah, I used to have one packed away somewheres. But you can buy them anywheres. That isn't worth much as a clue. Not unless you could find the gun that fired the bullet."

The elevator stopped at the lobby and they got out. Then Louise stopped.

"Didn't Captain Regan say Pete was killed at eleven o'clock?"

"Aw, come on," growled Barcone. "You act like this was a life and death matter to you!"

He took her arm and guided her out of the station. Several uniformed policemen stood outside the door, and one of them opened it for them.

At the curb stood his large limousine, a driver behind the wheel. Its thick glass was bullet-proof, and the body had been invisibly fortified with heavy steel plates.

Behind it was another limousine in which sat five of Barcone's men. They were his immediate bodyguard. And less in evidence, other men stood nearby on the sidewalk, and on the other side of the street, ready to jump in and save their chief if Kendrick's, or Scarfici's, or any of the other mobs of the city made a play for him. Barcone's boast that he was better guarded than the president was no idle one.

He opened the rear door to hand her in. But as she was about to step in, she stopped, a sudden suspicion crystallizing in her mind.

"Jack! Where were you at eleven o'clock last night?" she demanded. "You went out at ten-thirty and—"

A forbidding scowl blackened his face. "What're you trying to get at?" he rasped.

"Jack, did you know?" she almost screamed.

He tried to shove her into the car, but she jerked away from him.

"You killed Pete yourself!" she cried. "You knew that Pete and I—"

As she stared at him, she was suddenly certain. Then he had known about Pete and her. She saw it written upon his face. He had killed Pete so that he could have her alone.

"Well, what if I did?" he snarled, reaching out for her. "By God, I'm going—"

But with this sudden conviction, Louise went berserk.

Her hand darted to her handbag, snapped open the clasp, emerged with the gleam of a blue-steel automatic in her fingers.

"Hey!" shouted Barcone, lunging at her.

But she was too quick for him. As she sprang back from his reach, she lifted the automatic and her finger constricted upon the trigger. It erupted into flame and a single slug bored into his forehead.

An expression of blank amazement crossed his face. Then his knees gave way beneath him and he fell heavily to the sidewalk.

Louise gazed down at him for a moment with an expression of incredible fury and triumph on her face.

The gunmen in Barcone's second car stared at her, paralyzed with surprise. They had weapons with them, but this had been so quick and unexpected that they did not even think to use them. If it had been some other gangster attacking Barcone, his body would be already upon the pavement, riddled with bullets.

The policemen at the door gaped at the scene. They had heard the controversy between Barcone and Louise, but the outcome had caught them unprepared.

Louise was the first one to move. She leaped into the back of the car, slammed the door shut, and pressed her automatic against the driver's head.

"Quick! Get going!" she screamed at him.

The driver's head swung around and saw the gaping muzzle of the gun pointed directly at him. He gave a frightened yelp and obeyed her. The car leaped into life and jerked away from the curb with a roar. Almost crashing into another car, it straightened out and headed down the street.

"Step on it, Tony," she warned, "if you don't want a slug in the back of your head."

"Don't worry about me," he retorted, stamping harder upon the accelerator.

Whoo-oo-oo!

She heard the shrill siren of a police squad car. It rose and fell upon the air like a shriek. She glanced through the back window. There, hardly half a block behind them, she saw the bright orange of a Lincoln car.

"It's the cops!" she screamed in Tony's ear.

He stepped a little harder upon the accelerator.

The scream of the siren preceded them and cleared the streets as if by magic. Cars veered out of the way, people sprang back and watched the mad chase. The speedometer indicator crept up to seventy, to seventy-five—

The street grew narrower and Tony cursed. They were approaching the river. He could see the dark structure of the bridge looming up ahead of them. And upon the bridge, with its narrowed driveway, he could not dodge around the other cars. There was no time to turn off upon a side street.

He stamped on the brakes in an effort to cut down his speed. There was a huge truck just ahead of them. He cramped the wheel to the left in an impossible effort to get around it.

Yet he did. He shot by it at sixty miles an hour, missing it by inches. Then there was another car in front of him. He tried to straighten the car back—he could not do it.

The car struck the other one a glancing blow that deflected it further to the left. It bounced up across the sidewalk, smashed full-on into the bridge rail, demolished it. It tottered upon the brink for a moment. Tony hung lifelessly over the wheel; the steering post column had been driven into his chest.

Louise was thrown with terrific force against the back of the front seat. She screamed, reached for the right side door and tried to open it. It was jammed. She whirled about to the other door.

Even as she wrenched at it, the car toppled over, shot down engine first to the waters beneath the bridge. There was a tremendous splash. Then the car sank from sight.

Back at Police Headquarters, Captain Regan stood over the body of Big Jack Barcone.

"They all get theirs," he muttered, half to himself. "It's fate, and they can't escape it. They all have their weak spot—and with him it was his woman. And when that weak spot broke, it took only one little slug to finish him."

GANGLAND'S BACK PAY

"What's this—a bumping off party!"

Even brains and a mob of the fastest shooting red-hots in gangland can't keep a man in the racket forever.

AL NUCCI, BEER BARON, ALCOHOL KING AND OVERLORD OF THE UNDERWORLD, swung down the street with a quick, lithe stride. The sun sinking behind the sprawling tenement houses on the other side of the street threw a ruddy glow over his iron features.

Ordinarily, Nucci rode in a large car surrounded by armed guards. He ruled his powerful gang in a ruthless domineering fashion, and he was even more ruthless in dealing with his enemies. There were many who had cause to hate him and who would not have hesitated a moment to put a bullet in his back. A few had tried it, but they had been singularly unsuccessful.

Now, however, he was taking a short walk enjoying the crisp autumn air. He had just been to Spunello's soft drink parlor, where a bottle of excellent Chianti had made him feel very mellow and philosophical. He was carrying on a one-sided conversation with his single guard, Jimmie Bardonelli, as was often his custom.

"It's a crazy game, Jimmie," he mused. "Here I am sitting on top of the world—plenty of friends, plenty of money, everything I want. I've got every mob in the city under my control but Turato's, and he doesn't amount to enough to make it worth the lead. But how long will I be there?"

He slowed his pace a little as he plunged deeper into the subject that often occupied his thoughts. His broad, thick-set shoulders slumped and his swarthy, black-haired head sank lower upon his chest.

"Yes sir, boss," agreed Jimmie.

Jimmie understood very little of what Nucci was saying, but he always agreed with him. He was little more than twenty, with slick black hair and a handsome face, but he had no more intelligence than a child. Yet he did have the unquestioning faithfulness of a dog and one of the quickest and surest guns in the city.

"Yes, Jimmie," went on Nucci, "it's a crazy racket. I'm a fool to be in it! I've lasted longer than I've got a right to expect. Look at Tomasso, and Murphy, and Goldman, and Meyers—big shots all of them, and they all got bumped off. And I know I'll get bumped off some day, too."

"Not while I'm along with yuh, boss," grinned Jimmie, patting the bulge of the automatic in the trim holster beneath his arm.

"But you won't always be beside me, Jimmie. And some day you'll get it, too. Somebody'll put a shot of lead in your back. You won't even know what happened."

"If I get bumped off," said Jimmie simply, "it'll be beside yuh, boss."

Nucci shook his head slightly and continued:

"The funny thing about it all is that I don't even want to quit. I know I'll get mine some day, but I like it. I'm ready to take my dose of lead when it comes along. I'll have to, whether I want to or not. I'm in the racket too deep to get out. The mob wouldn't stand for that. They'd turn against me if I tried it."

Such was his absorption in his thoughts that he did not see the blue sedan coming down the street toward them. But Jimmie's quick eyes noticed it at once and watched apprehensively as it came closer. His hand crept up across his chest toward the automatic slung under his arm.

It came in a split second. When the car was still fifty feet away, the barrel of a sub-machine gun poked its nose out of the rear window and erupted into spitting, chattering flame.

But as quick as it came, Jimmie acted quicker. He made two lightning moves. One was to jerk his gun from its holster; the other was to swing his left arm around, smash Nucci in the chest and send him sprawling to the pavement.

The hail of bullets brushed across Jimmie's chest and sent him staggering back. It tore Nucci's hat from his head as he fell upon his back.

But even as Jimmie tottered and collapsed, his automatic roared three times. The bullets sped straight as an arrow into the machine gunner's leering face and made of it a ragged crimson mask. The pounding clatter stopped as abruptly as it had started.

Nucci twisted up upon his hands and knees and ripped an automatic from his side pocket. The driver of the car gave a frightened glance at him and sent the car leaping ahead, almost past him. But Nucci's gun roared seven times, and at least six of the slugs struck the man. He collapsed over the steering wheel, twisting it to one side in his death agony.

A huge truck was coming at a rapid speed from the other direction. So quickly had all this happened that it did not have time to slow down.

As the death car lurched across the road in front of it, it struck it head-on, wrenching it around. The heavy bumper threw the lighter car over on its side; then caught it underneath, propelling it forward. There was the crash of broken framework and the tinkle of splintering glass. A man screamed piercingly from the wreck for a moment; then was still.

The driver of the truck was paralyzed for a few seconds while his massive machine pushed the other forward, almost crushing it. It had traveled thirty feet before he stamped on the brakes and brought it to a stop.

Nucci rose to his feet. His hat lay on the sidewalk near him. He picked it up and looked at it rather foolishly. The entire crown had been torn away by the machine gun bullets.

Jimmie was lying upon his side. His hands were clutched to his chest, and red oozed from beneath his fingers.

"Are yuh awright, boss?" he begged.

Then he smiled and died.

Nucci looked about him. The street was almost clear of people. Those that had seen the battle and the accident had ducked into doorways. They had no desire to be questioned by the police nor to be held as witnesses.

One man ran up to him, a short stocky Italian. He was Pepe Ricoco, one of his gang lieutenants.

"Take the rod, Pepe," he ordered, handing him the automatic. "You get rid of it. Some cop might take a notion to frisk me. And you take care of Jimmie here."

"Sure, Al. They didn't plug yuh, did they? I saw it from the corner and come as quick as I could."

Nucci did not answer. He walked to the wrecked car and peered into it. The driver and the machine gunner had been killed before the collision. He did not recognize either of them.

In the back seat lay a third man, his head twisted back over his shoulders at a horrible angle. Nucci leaned farther over the wreck so that he could see his face.

"George Drake," he muttered to himself. "So Turato has decided to start things, has he? Well, this is going to be his finish."

• • •

The driver of the truck, who had been staring owlishly down at the wreck beneath his front wheels, suddenly came to life and leaped out into the road.

"You did it!" he shouted at Nucci. "I saw yuh! I saw the whole thing!"

Pepe Ricoco stepped up and grasped the driver's arm tightly.

"Pipe down, you!" he rasped. "D'yuh know who he is? If yuh don't, it's time yuh found out. He's Al Nucci."

The driver peered uncertainly at Nucci, then shrank away, his face paling with terror.

"Say, I didn't know—I didn't recognize— Cripes, I didn't mean any—"

Nucci stepped up to him and jabbed him in the chest with one stiffly outstretched finger.

"Listen, you punk!" he said with deadly intentness. "You never saw me! There was only one guy that did all the shooting—him over on the sidewalk. That's your story when the cops come. Get that straight and stick to it. You won't get in any trouble, but if you do, I'll get you out. Remember—you never saw me!"

His cold gray eyes bored into the other man's. His iron face was implacable.

"Sure," stammered the driver. "I gotcha, Mr. Nucci."

Nucci pressed a bill into his hand, turned away and started down the street.

The driver's eyes followed him. It was not until Nucci had turned a corner that he looked down at the bill in his hand. He gasped. It was a hundred dollar bill.

Nucci did not quicken his pace. He knew that none of the people in that district would testify that they had seen him do the shooting, though perhaps hundreds of them had looked furtively out of windows and had recognized him. Many of them were alcohol cookers for his gang and owed their livelihood to them. The others would not dare to. They knew and feared the "spot" and the "ride."

As he hailed a cruising taxi, he heard the shrill siren of a police squad car dashing to the scene of the battle. He smiled a grim, wintry smile as he stepped into the cab.

"The Nucci Restaurant," he ordered the driver.

As he settled into the seat, he discovered that he still held the torn remnants of his hat in his hand. He scowled at it and crushed it into his pocket.

When he got out in front of the restaurant, he handed the driver a hundred dollar bill.

"Do you know who I am?" he asked.

"Sure, Mr, Nucci," grinned the driver.

"Then forget that you've seen me. Your story is that you were on the south side."

The driver grinned again and touched his cap. Most of the stock of the company for which he worked, was owned by Nucci, and he had learned to obey orders.

Nucci stepped into the ornate and fashionable restaurant that bore his name and stopped before the cashier's cage.

"Nick," he addressed the fat German, "tell the boys I want to see them in the back room in fifteen minutes."

"Sure, Al," said Nick. "Some of them are around now and I think I can get hold of the rest."

Nucci went up the stairs to the second floor and entered his apartment. It was garishly, suffocatingly furnished with gaudy furniture, tapestries and paintings. He had expended a fortune on it. Though he lived simply, he demanded the last word in luxury in his home.

A woman dressed in filmy gold and red lounging pajamas was seated in a chair by the window reading a newspaper. She lowered the newspaper when he entered and looked up at him. She was his moll, Bess Collins. Her languorous, provocative eyes were mascaraed, her sensuous lips were red, and her hair fluffed about her head in golden curls. A gang leader can afford the best that comes along in flashy women.

"They got Jimmie," he announced.

Bess slowly laid the newspaper down and rose to her feet. She moved with an almost tigerish, sensuous gait.

"What—what happened, Al?" she asked.

Nucci went to a cabinet and took out a bottle of Scotch and a whiskey glass. He poured out a drink before he replied.

"Some of Turato's rods chopped him down. I just missed it."

He took the torn hat from his pocket and tossed it on a table. Bess picked it up and examined it, wide-eyed.

"We had just left Spunello's," he continued, "when some of Turato's mob in a car spotted us. They drove up and started work on us with a chopper. Jimmie knocked me down just in time, but he got it in the chest. He got the chopper before he passed out and I got the driver. Then the car ran into a truck and the other guy in it got his neck broken."

Bess threw her arms about him and pressed her golden head against his chest.

"Oh, Al!" she cried. "You—"

He put one arm about her and pressed her reassuringly. With the other he picked up the drink he had poured out and downed it.

"If it hadn't of been for Jimmie, I wouldn't be here," he said.

He felt no gratitude for Jimmie's sacrifice as he spoke. He had picked Jimmie as his special guard so that he would be certain that there would be another man to receive the bullets intended for him. Jimmie's sacrifice had been no more than he had expected of him.

"Al, some day they—they'll kill you!" Bess cried.

"Yeah," he grunted, smiling tight-lipped, "some day they'll bump me off. But they didn't get me this time! And it's not going to keep me from sticking to the racket."

He put one hand under her chin and tipped her head back so that he could kiss her. She gave her lips to him, clinging to him.

He released her and stepped back. Then he took off his coat, laid it carefully across a chair and disappeared into the back rooms to wash. He reappeared in a few minutes slipping on a shoulder holster. He took out the automatic and examined it to be certain that the clip was fully loaded; then shoved it back into the holster.

"Al, where are you going?" asked Bess.

"Down to see the boys," he answered, slipping on his coat.

"But what are you going to do?"

"Nothing except to bump off Turato and his mob."

She threw her arms around him and stopped him at the door. "Can you meet me by ten o'clock, Al?"

"Well, maybe. Yeah, I guess so. We're not going to monkey around with Turato very long. I'm going to polish him off quick."

"The Rainbow Night Club at ten, then? You know those south side joints that I've been trying to line up for you? Most of the proprietors have agreed to meet me there. And that means that they're hooked."

Nucci patted her shoulder affectionately. "Good girl. I thought you'd be able to do it easier than my gorillas. Sure, I'll be there and ready to talk business to them."

"Meet me at the little side entrance. I've got a private room on the second floor. When we get through with them we'll make whoopee."

She raised her lips for a second kiss. Nucci gave it to her; then passed down the stairs to the restaurant and stopped before the cigar counter.

"A Corona, Nick. Are all the boys here?"

Nick set out the box of cigars. "Yeah, they're all waiting for you, Al. Except Steigler. I guess he didn't get back from Chi yet. Anyway, I couldn't get hold of him."

Nucci chose a cigar and lit it. Then he went to the back of the long restaurant, nodding to various friends on the way. At the end of a corridor, he turned into a small room. Half a dozen men were seated about a round table. A waiter was serving drinks.

He sat down at the table and took a drink, though he left it untouched. His hat was pulled down low over his forehead so that his face was in shadow and his eyes gleamed like two points of fire.

He glanced about the gathering. There was Pepe Ricoco, to whom he had given his automatic, Guiseppe Garselmi, Frank Miller, Joe Grogan, Jack Peri, and Bill Macphersen. They were all there except Joe Steigler.

When the waiter had left and the door was locked against interruptions, he took the cigar from his mouth and said:

"I guess Pepe's told you what happened."

An angry growl greeted his words.

He suddenly leaned forward and tapped the table top sharply with his finger tips as his eyes swept across the men there.

"Now listen, you gorillas. I know who did this! It was Turato's mob!"

There was a chorus of incredulous exclamations.

"Turato hasn't got the guts," objected Macphersen. "He'd be afraid to try a trick like that."

"You're wrong, Mac," Nucci answered. "I recognized the guy in the back seat that had his neck broken. He was George Drake, one of Turato's men. I don't know who the other two birds were—probably imported rods."

"By God!" cried the explosive Guiseppe Garselmi. "We'll take Turato for a ride this time! He can't get away with stuff like that on us!"

There was a burst of approval. But Macphersen, more cautious and foresighted, objected.

"How're we going to do that, Al?" he asked. "We don't know where Turato and his two-bit mob hang out. When we chased them out of their joint up town, we never did learn where they holed out."

"Hell, do you think I'm a dummy?" sneered Nucci. "I don't run this mob that way. I've known Turato's hangout for three months. I've had men go through it from top to bottom. I just didn't think it was worth the lead to bother with them."

"Where are they?" demanded Jack Peri.

"They've got a place down by the river. It used to be a warehouse—the Sholsky place."

"You mean that old shack—"

"Yeah, that's where they are. And we're going to get them tonight! I'm setting it for nine o'clock. They'll be expecting us to do something, but not this quick."

"But will they be there then?" asked Macphersen.

"You're damn right they'll be there! After this boner they've pulled, they won't dare go out on the streets. Unless they take it on the lam."

"Well if they're there, we'll get them," growled Macphersen.

"I'm going to be in on this myself," went on Nucci. "Mac, you and Guiseppe can help me. You go out now and pick up about twenty good rods. Have them here at twenty minutes to nine sharp. Pepe, you get three cars ready and have them in the alley. And Frank, you get us three choppers and half a dozen small pineapples."

Macphersen, Pepe Ricoco and Frank Miller left. Nucci settled down with Guiseppe Garselmi to work out the plans of attack. He drew a plan of the Sholsky warehouse and they worked over it. A waiter served a meal to them.

At eight thirty gunmen began to drift into the back of Nucci's restaurant. Jack Peri took them into one of the back rooms and saw that they all had plenty of weapons and ammunition. The three cars drew up in the alley.

At fifteen minutes to nine they started. Nucci, Guiseppe Garselmi and Bill Macphersen each had charge of one car and six gunmen.

They sped across the city in single file, skirting the business district and penetrating far into the south side. It was a place of dark, dead factories and deserted buildings. The few men slinking through the streets stopped and stared after the three cars that whined past them.

When they neared the warehouse, they separated, each to park within a block of the building. Then they left the cars and went ahead on foot. Nucci's plans called for them to attack each of the three entrances simultaneously.

The warehouse was dark and silent. The windows set high in the wall were boarded over and showed no crack of light. The only sounds were the distant rattle of the street cars and the scuff of their feet upon the pavement as they approached.

Nucci carried a Thompson sub-machine gun under his arm. It was ready to fire with a hundred-cartridge drum in place. The six men bunched behind him had their revolvers and automatics in their hands.

Nucci looked at his watch and waited calmly while the men shuffled impatiently. He had to give Guiseppe Garselmi and Bill Macphersen time to get to their positions before the other two entrances.

The hands of his watch touched nine o'clock.

"All right," he said.

Two of his men threw themselves against a door and crashed it in. At the same time they heard a smashing splintering from around the side of the warehouse where Guiseppe Garselmi was trying to force an entrance.

Nucci found himself running down a long corridor with his men at his heels. It was pitch black, but they had no need of lights. All of the men had been acquainted minutely with the plans of the building.

The muffled sounds of gunplay came to them. Shrieks, shouts, the reverberating roar of a shotgun. Then the dancing tattoo of a machine gun . . .

Just ahead of them was the crack of light beneath a door—it was the inner council room which Turato used. The sound of the firing was louder from behind this door. Evidently Bill Macphersen had reached it before them.

Nucci threw his shoulder against the door. It flung him back.

"Break her down, boys," he commanded.

Two of his men flung themselves against it. The door creaked but did not give. They threw their shoulders against it again, and then again, grunting heavily.

"Just a minute," ordered Nucci.

He scratched a match and in the flare located the heavy lock. He raised the sub-machine gun and drummed half a dozen bullets into the mechanism.

As he drew back, the men cast their weight against the door again. With a splintering of wood it gave and swung inward. They fell upon their hands and knees just in time to escape the withering fire that sang over their heads.

Nucci saw a lighted room in which half a dozen men stood at bay on one side. They were shooting through a door on the other side. He understood at once what had happened. Bill Macphersen had not been able to reach them through the room on that side without running the risk of sacrificing all his men.

Shielding his body behind the door frame, he held the machine gun out and swung its muzzle in an arc that covered the end of the room. Death spurted from it in a licking stream and mowed down the men that stood at bay there. As they went down, they answered with a fire that zinged past his wrists.

Then their fire stopped. Nucci released the trigger of the sub-machine gun and stepped into the room. It was a shambles; the furniture was broken, the walls were sprayed with bullet punctures. On one side lay the six dead men.

"Mac! Guiseppe!" called Nucci.

Then one of the figures on the floor stirred and sat up. It was a short fat Italian. Turato! And he held an automatic in his hand.

Even as Nucci saw him, the automatic belched fire and a bullet sang past his head. He jerked aside as a second bullet scorched his cheek. Except for that jerk he would have been dead.

At this same instant his machine gun pounded into flame. Turato never had a chance to fire again. The last remaining cartridges in the sub-machine gun drummed into his body. When the fire stopped Turato was dead.

Bill Macphersen came running into the room, his men behind him.

"You all right, Al?" he asked. "We tried to get to them, but we couldn't manage it. They had a straight line of fire on us down that hall."

Nucci rubbed his cheek gingerly where Turato's bullet had caressed him. Death had been close to him this time. A few inches more and his name would have been written down as one of the big shots of history.

"Any of your boys hurt, Mac?" he asked.

"Naw. One of them got a slug through his shoulder, but it doesn't amount to much."

"Where's Guiseppe?"

"Cleaning up upstairs."

Just then Guiseppe Garselmi and his men came in.

"Everybody here?" inquired Nucci. "Then beat it. You can't tell—the cops might be around to see what the trouble is."

They filed out. Guiseppe Garselmi accompanied Nucci to Spunello's soft drink parlor, where they retired with Spunello to a back room.

"A toast," said Guiseppe, lifting his glass of Chianti, "to Turato and his mob. Long may they live—in hell!"

They drank the toast.

"And another toast," spoke up Spunello, "to the big shot, Al Nucci!"

At ten minutes to ten Nucci rose to leave.

"You want me to go with you, Al?" asked Guiseppe.

"No; don't bother. I've got an appointment just down the street."

He walked to the Rainbow Night Club, which was only a few blocks away. He passed the ornate entrance and went around to the dark side entrance that opened upon stairs leading up to the second floor.

Bess was waiting for him there in the shadows.

"Are you all right, Al?" she asked. "How was the show?"

"The show was good. Turato and his mob are done."

She brushed a kiss against his lips. "Come on upstairs, now. Most of them are here."

"Well, they better be ready to talk business."

He followed her up the steps. At the top they turned into a hall and went down it. Nucci was feeling almost jovial. He had concluded one good piece of business this night, and he was about to put across another. The addition of the south side joints would mean quite a bit of extra money. He could have forced them to buy liquor from him before, but he had preferred to go about it peacefully.

Bess opened a door and entered. He followed; then stopped, astounded. For he was staring into the muzzle of a gun. And behind the gun was—Bill Macphersen, his most trusted lieutenant!

"What the hell," he said.

"It is hellish, isn't it?" asked Macphersen.

Bess laughed harshly, almost hysterically.

"What's this—a bumping off party, Mac?" inquired Nucci.

"You're damn right it is!" jeered Macphersen. "I've decided that you've been running things just a little too long. I'm going to get some of the gravy myself. With you out of the way, it'll fall into my lap."

Nucci turned and looked at Bess. She returned the look defiantly, her golden head held erect. Her red lips were compressed into a straight line.

"Is this your scheme of getting rid of me, Bess?" he asked.

Bess laughed harshly again. "Yes, it is, you big baboon. I'm tired of you. I'm sick of your guts. And Mac and I are getting rid of you."

"I see," said Nucci, slowly.

So it had come at last! He had reached the end. He had just escaped death at the hands of Turato, to be betrayed and killed by his own moll.

"The cops are going to find your body in some ditch," jeered Macphersen. "In another moment I'm going to plug you. Then we'll cart you out in a car and dump you some place where they won't find you for a long time. If you got any prayers to say, Al, you better—"

At this instant, Nucci made a lunge for the gun in Macphersen's hand. He had not looked at his lieutenant with the purpose of throwing him off his guard. If he could once knock that gun aside, they would be on even terms.

But he was not quick enough. The gun roared twice and Nucci felt a jabbing, tearing pain in his chest. He staggered back against the wall, holding himself upright by a tremendous effort.

"Not quite quick enough, Al," sneered Macphersen.

For a few moments Nucci could not speak. The pain in his chest seemed to be tearing at his heart. He put his fingers to his chest, trying to staunch for a few seconds the flow of his blood.

He knew that he could not live with those two bullets in him. They had just missed his heart and his lungs were punctured. Even a surgeon would not be able to save him.

He regarded Macphersen steadily.

"Mac," he said, "I always trusted you, but you've got my guts now. And you'll get the mob. But you won't last long. You won't last as long as I did. You haven't got the brains. Some guy that you'll trust will get your guts, too."

He grinned heavily with lips specked with bloody foam.

Macphersen laughed ringingly. "You're just talking, Al, and you know it."

Suddenly Nucci couldn't seem to hear so well. He felt his knees crumpling beneath him and he could not stop them. The floor was tipping up toward them. He struck it heavily.

As through a muffling fog, he heard a shout.

"They're in there!" came the words.

Abruptly the laugh died on Macphersen's lips. "That's Greggson!" he cried. "Damn him, he's double-crossed us!"

"Quick! The window, Mac!" screamed Bess.

Nucci heard it all as a confused jumble. He was aware that the door was being broken down, that there was a rapid exchange of shots. Then quiet.

"What's this?" asked a voice.

He felt himself being turned over on his back. The lights hurt his eyes, though he could see nothing clearly.

"Cripes! It's Al Nucci!" exclaimed the man that had turned him over.

Nucci saw that he was a uniformed policeman. Standing about in the room were other officers.

"Hello—boys," he said.

The policeman kneeling beside him examined his wounds. "I'm afraid you're a goner, Nucci," he said. "You can't live with bullets like that in you."

Nucci nodded his head slowly. He had never been afraid of death, nor was he now.

"What about—Bess—and Macphersen?" he asked.

"They're dead. We had to plug them. Greggson gave us the tip at the last minute that they were going to pull a bumping party here. Lost his nerve, I guess. But he didn't know they were going to croak you."

Nucci gave a little crackling laugh that brought blood to his lips and choked him. The pain seemed to be disappearing; nothing was quite distinct; he felt numb.

"You're going, Nucci," warned the policeman. "If you've got anything to say, you'd better say it."

Then a little smile flicked the corners of Nucci's lips.

"It's a crazy racket," he said. "Here I am double-crossed by my own moll, and she gets hers before I pass out. You can't beat it."

"You said a mouthful," agreed the officer.

Nucci had. He was dead.

Their hands went up!

ALIBI'S HOLIDAY

*Jerry Marlin waited to keep a date with a girl—while Fate,
in the boots of a cracksman, brewed a poisonous dish from
Death's menu!*

COULD JERRY MARLIN HAVE KNOWN THE POISONOUS DISH that Fate, in the person of Hymie Borson, was brewing for him, there would have been some quick action—

But he didn't.

As it was, Jerry was sitting in his car getting angrier every minute. Helen Scott hadn't showed up yet, though it was already one o'clock in the morning and she got out of work at twelve-thirty.

"Rats!" he growled.

He peered again, impatiently, through the window of the car, hoping to see her.

There was no one in sight. The cold wet fog, thick and impenetrable, blotted out the city streets and accentuated the blackness of the night, so that the lights of passing cars and flashing signs were only vague, luminous blobs. It was an ideal setting for a crime.

Jerry looked at his watch.

"Ten minutes," he decided. "Then I blow."

He settled himself comfortably behind the steering wheel, lit a cigarette and inhaled deeply the warm, soothing smoke.

And at this very moment Hymie Borson was brewing the poisonous dish he intended for Jerry.

Less than a quarter of a mile away, the decrepit Armstrom Building was dark and silent, its rows of dirty windows on the upper floors lost in the banks of fog.

On the second floor, hidden by a turn of the dimly lit corridor, an inanimate form huddled against the wall. It was the night watchman. He was unconscious, his hands bound behind him, his face streaked with blood that flowed from a deep gash on his forehead.

And on the floor above him, a light glowed behind the ground glass of the door which was labeled:

Aaron Dubrovsky
Goldsmith and Jeweler
Walk In

Hymie Borson and two of his henchmen had "walked in" by the simple expedient of using the master keys taken from the watchman.

"Buzz" Walper had experienced little difficulty in opening the massive safe in the cubbyhole office. With an electric drill he had bored a hole beside the combination shaft, then manipulated the tumblers into the proper position through this aperture.

It had netted them a very tidy haul. There was a fine collection of precious and semi-precious stones which had been left with Dubrovsky for setting, several ingots of pure gold, a small amount of platinum, various pieces of finished jewelry and around two thousand dollars in cash.

"Pretty sweet!" Hymie Borson commented.

Buzz Walper grunted, and busied himself packing away his tools and the plunder.

"Sweet is right!" chuckled "Snowboy" Klein in his almost childish treble.

He stood in the door of the inner office, on guard, one hand hovering close to the heavy caliber automatic in his shoulder holster. His thin pallid face showed the unmistakable signs of a moker, a user of cocaine. Snowboy Klein was filled to the gills with snow, as deadly as a cobra, and as irritable and quick to strike.

"And now," said Hymie Borson, "for the finishing touch."

He grinned as he took from his pocket a flat cardboard box. With a gloved hand he removed the cover and lifted from it a large revolver.

This weapon belonged to Jerry Marlin. Until tonight, when Snowboy Klein had stolen it, it had been kept in a bureau drawer in Jerry's room. Its highly polished nickel surface bore a fine set of Jerry's fingerprints.

"One ticket," said Hymie Borson, "to the Big House for J.R. Marlin."

"He! He!" laughed Snowboy Klein.

Hymie Borson carefully placed the gun on the top of the rifled safe, just back from the edge so that it was concealed in the shadows. It gave the appearance of having been placed there by its owner to be out of the way, and yet handy, while he worked on the safe, and then forgotten.

"Perfect," the mob leader said. "If the coppers ever get to one J.R. Marlin, he won't have a leg to stand on. He won't even have an alibi, because I called his sweetie and told her not to wait for him. He won't be able to prove where he was at this time."

Snowboy Klein snickered his admiration.

"The finishin' touch!" he echoed.

In every crime engineered by Hymie Borson and his little mob there was a "finishing touch." It consisted of something left behind, some clue or object which was calculated to mislead the police, and perhaps to point in the direction of some other criminal.

This was done as a matter of safety. Hymie Borson thought it better to leave misinformation for the police than no information at all. It started the dicks off on the wrong path and after the wrong man.

Whether or not the cops caught the crook who had been framed did not matter. Occasionally, when the police seemed determined to find a victim, Hymie Borson tipped them off. With a fall guy set for the rap, they were not likely to pry deeply. It was just a matter of insurance.

"A clever guy," Hymie Borson said, "always fixes it so that when things get hot there's some sucker to take the jolt for him."

Buzz Walper was standing ready, the loot in a suitcase, his tools in a kit.

"Ready, Buzz?" the mob leader asked. "Okay. Let's pull out."

Then there was a sudden warning hiss from Snowboy Klein. The three of them froze, their ears cocked.

In the corridor outside they heard a slow, almost inaudible creaking of floorboards. It was as though feet were advancing cautiously, stealthily.

"That damn watchman!" muttered Hymie Borson.

Snowboy Klein breathed a muffled oath. His eyes began to glitter frostily and an automatic appeared, as if by magic, in his hand. Buzz Walper set his suitcase and kitbag soundlessly on the floor and drew a length of lead pipe from his pocket.

"I'm gonna smoke that—" began Snowboy Klein.

"Careful!" warned Hymie Borson.

The footsteps stopped. Then, after seconds, the door was flung open and a figure lunged into the room.

It was the night watchman. His face was streaked with blood and his eyes were dazed, as though he were not fully aware of what he was doing. He carried a large revolver.

Two guns blazed at the same instant. But the watchman fired only once, and his bullet thudded harmlessly into the wall. Then he was dead, with a bullet through his heart.

Snowboy Klein, his drug-crazed mind obsessed with the desire to kill, fired six slugs into the body before it slumped to the floor.

There was silence for a moment while the thunder of the guns still seemed to reverberate in the room.

"Jeez!" said Hymie Borson.

Buzz Walper shrugged, and slipped the lead pipe back into his pocket.

"We better take it on the lam," he advised.

Hymie Borson came to life.

"One minute," he said.

He took Jerry Marlin's gun from the top of the safe, handling it in his gloved hands very carefully so as not to obliterate any of the fingerprints. He sighted it on the dead watchman's body, pulled the trigger twice, then laid the gun on the floor.

"Let's move," he said.

The ten minutes which Jerry Marlin had promised to wait stretched into fifteen. At last, his patience exhausted, he got out of the car.

"I'm going to see what's holding her up," he told himself.

His car was parked upon a side street, where there were no parking regulations. He turned upon the main street and walked to the middle of the block, where a large electric sign announced *Antoni's Restaurant*.

Antoni himself was presiding at the cash counter.

"No, Miss Scott is gone," he replied, in answer to Jerry's question.

"How long ago?"

"Twelve thirty, like always. She got a phone call maybe fifteen minutes before that, but I don't know what about."

Mumbling his thanks, Jerry left.

He ran into a figure which loomed out of the fog, muttered an apology and hurried on. So he had been stood up! Given the air. Left to cool his heels while she probably went out with some other fellow.

Jerry was in a bitter frame of mind when he reached his room. He threw his clothes about, kicked a chair out of his way.

Then, opening a bureau drawer to get at a pint of Scotch he had hidden away, he stopped, astonished. A revolver which should have been there, in plain sight, was missing.

Hurriedly, he went through the other drawers. But the gun was gone. And he clearly remembered having seen it in its drawer only two hours before!

Evidently a thief had entered his room during his absence. He went through his other possessions, found nothing missing, and decided that the loss of the weapon was not worth bothering about.

The next morning, however, Jerry received a distinct shock which changed his mind.

He was in a lunchroom, eating breakfast and reading a newspaper account of the looting of Aaron Dubrovsky's safe and of the murder of the night watchman of the Armstrom Building.

The account related that the only clue left behind was a revolver, from which two shots had been fired, and which apparently had been dropped in the excitement. It bore a fine set of fingerprints which the police hoped to be able to identify. The make and the serial number of the gun were given, as well as the fact that the right-hand pearl butt plate bore a cross-shaped scratch.

The paper slipped from Jerry's nerveless fingers. For this gun was unquestionably the one which had been stolen from him! The make, the serial number, the scratch—everything tallied.

But how could this have happened? The theft of the gun and the murder of the watchman had occurred at almost the same time. Whoever had done it, must have gone almost directly from Jerry's room to the Armstrom Building.

And why would a man who was skilled enough to open a large safe, descend to pilfering a gun from a room?

Jerry couldn't figure it out. It didn't make sense. He had more than a vague premonition of trouble ahead.

He was glad that the gun had come to him through underworld channels. It would make it impossible for the police to trace it to him, and thus to involve him in the crime.

Hymie Borson, at almost the same time, was also reading the story in the morning papers.

But his interest was focused, not on the description of the gun found, but on a paragraph which was headed:

Jeweler's Insurance Offers $10,000 Reward

Ten thousand dollars! A neat sum. It would come in handy, particularly since he was thinking of pulling up stakes and moving his base of operations to some other city.

And why shouldn't he have it? Or at least a part of it? What was there to prevent him from tipping off the police about Jerry Marlin, on condition that he got half the reward.

Hymie Borson's eyes narrowed with thought as he tipped back in his chair and gazed at the ceiling of his tiny office. On the other side of the thin partition which separated him from the small garage he maintained as a front for his criminal activities he heard the roar of a car being tested. An El-train shrieked past the rear of the building, drowned for a moment all other noises.

He had not thought of using the frame-up in this way. It had been done as a protection, to be used as a last resort to avert police suspicion by furnishing a ready victim.

But why throw over a chance for five grand of easy money? He and his mob were in the clear. There was no chance of their being implicated, if he went about it right. He could tip off some cop, keeping his identity secret. Jerry Marlin was set for the rap, without the possibility of beating it. The five grand would drop right into his lap.

Hymie Borson nodded, satisfied that the scheme was air-tight. He was unknown to the police, except to the patrolman on the beat, who considered him a reputable business man. He could go to any detective, certain of getting enthusiastic cooperation.

And now that he thought of it, this was a good way to get on the right side of the police. Some day he might need the favors they could give.

Four o'clock that afternoon found him waiting in front of the brownstone building which housed the police department. The shifts changed at that hour; and when a certain heavy-set man came down the steps, he grasped his arm and pulled him to one side.

"Sergeant Crowley?" he asked.

"Yeah," was the reply.

"Could I talk to you for a minute, alone? I—I've got a tip for you about this Dubrovsky robbery."

The officer gave him a sharp glance, then walked with him to the courtyard at the side of the building, where they could confer together without interruption.

They talked for several minutes. Sergeant Crowley nodded a number of times.

"Okay, Mr. Borson," he said, "I'll look into this."

"And the reward? I thought—maybe—"

"You want a split? Half be all right?"

Hymie Borson shrugged, as though it did not really matter to him. But he could not keep the covetous light from his eyes.

"Sure," he said. "Of course, maybe this Marlin isn't guilty. I'm just telling you what I heard one of my customers say."

"I'll find out all right," Sergeant Crowley promised grimly. "If he is, he'll get the chair. Well, thanks for the tip."

That evening Jerry Marlin stopped at Antoni's for dinner. He had a few minutes' conversation with Helen Scott before he went back to a table. What she told him left him even more puzzled and perturbed.

"You're sure you don't know who phoned you?" he questioned.

"No."

"What'd they say?"

"Just that you were busy and wouldn't be able to see me."

Jerry frowned. First his gun was stolen and used in a murder; then Helen received a mysterious call telling her not to wait for him.

He had a vague hunch that there was something sinister behind this. Surely the two things must be linked in some way. Yet what was there in common between a stolen gun and a mysterious telephone call? He could see no logical connection between them.

Helen dropped her hand on his arm.

"Jerry! Is something wrong?"

"Don't know, kid."

He explained to her, then, what had happened. Her alarm grew as she listened to him.

But they did not have the opportunity to talk for long. Antoni bustled up to the counter. He disapproved of his employees visiting during working hours, so Jerry reluctantly went back to a table, promising to meet her after work.

He was abstractedly devouring a steak when a heavy form dropped into the chair opposite him. Startled, he glanced up to meet the cold gray eyes of Sergeant Crowley.

" 'Lo, Jerry," said the officer.

"Hello, sarge," responded Jerry. He liked the bluff, honest detective, but had little enthusiasm for a talk with him at this moment. Nor did he like the grim light in his eyes.

"Mind if I sit here?" Sergeant Crowley settled himself comfortably in his chair.

Jerry waved his knife.

"Go ahead. Have a roll and some butter."

The officer shook his head, waved away a waitress who hurried up.

"How's things been goin'?"

"About the same."

"Been pullin' any tricks?"

"Tricks?" Jerry repeated. "You know I'm on the straight and narrow."

"Hope so. What'd you do last night?"

"Nothing."

"How about one o'clock?"

Jerry stiffened. The approximate hour, according to the papers, at which Dubrovsky's safe had been robbed and the watchman killed.

"Nothing," he answered.

"Got an alibi?"

"Alibi? What do I want an alibi for?"

"It might come in handy."

The officer's eyes bored into his. Jerry stuffed a piece of steak in his mouth and chewed it with a nonchalance he did not feel.

"Nope," he replied. "I haven't got an alibi."

"Too bad."

Sergeant Crowley took a folded napkin, spread it out in front of him. Carefully placing his fingers at the very base of Jerry's water glass, which Jerry had half emptied, he moved it to the center of the napkin.

"What's that for?" Jerry asked.

The officer did not answer him. He took from his pocket a camel's hair brush and a small bottle filled with a fine black powder. The brush he dipped into the powder, so that its end was coated, then brushed it lightly across the outside surface of the glass.

The result was a series of well-defined smudges. The fine powder had adhered to the glass only where Jerry's fingers had left their oily impression.

Sergeant Crowley then compared these smudges with three small photographs which he took from his wallet. Jerry recognized them as fingerprint photographs.

When the officer finished, he looked up. His eyes were bleak, his lips grim.

"You're elected," he said.

"Elected?" asked Jerry. "What for?"

"It looks like the hot squat."

A chill ran down Jerry's spine. He put down his knife and fork slowly, leaned forward.

"Let's have it. The whole thing."

"Sure," said Sergeant Crowley. "Aaron Dubrovsky's safe was cracked last night. The watchman was shot and killed. We found a gun with fingerprints on it. Those fingerprints are yours."

"I see," said Jerry.

His head was whirling. Framed on a murder! He saw now the connection between the stolen gun and the phone call. The gun with his fingerprints on it pinned the crime on him; the phone call, which prevented Helen from meeting him, made it impossible for him to produce an alibi. It was an inescapable combination.

Sergeant Crowley put away the brush and bottle. With the napkin he polished the glass.

"Want to finish your meal?" he asked.

Jerry nodded. He had no appetite left for the food, but it would give him time to think.

He choked down the rest of his meal in silence. More and more the hopelessness of his position was forced upon him. With the evidence that the police had against him, the hot squat, or at least life imprisonment, was a certainty.

There was only one "out"—to find the man responsible for the frame-up. But how could he if he were lodged in jail? Particularly when he had no idea who it was.

Jerry finished his dessert, picked up his meal check and rose to his feet.

"I'm ready," he said.

"No tricks, now," warned Sergeant Crowley, following close behind him.

Jerry stopped at the cigar counter, pushed the check and a five dollar bill toward Helen. Her alarmed eyes flickered questioningly from him to the plainclothes officer, who wore no insignia of his profession.

"Have a cigar, sarge? Couple cigars, sister."

Helen started slightly at the word "sarge" and the informal way Jerry addressed her. Sergeant Crowley, however, was looking at the boxes in the glass case and did not notice it.

She brought out the box he indicated. While he was engaged in picking out a cigar, her eyes met Jerry's in quick interrogation. He tipped his head back with a rapid jerk, then took a second cigar from the box.

Without another look at her, Jerry scooped up his change and followed the officer from the restaurant.

"We can get a taxi down here a block and a half," he suggested.

"Suit yourself," said Sergeant Crowley, taking his arm and setting off in that direction.

They had almost reached the corner when Jerry heard the click of a woman's heels behind them. Then a woman's voice, crying.

"*Help! Help!*"

Sergeant Crowley, with an officer's instinct to preserve the peace, half loosened his grip on Jerry and swung around.

Jerry chose this moment to act. Pivoting on his toes, his fist flashed through an arc, all the power of his shoulders behind it. It met the chin of the unprepared officer with a *crack*. The cigar, bitten in two, fell to the sidewalk; and Sergeant Crowley's face assumed a foolish expression as he slipped into unconsciousness.

Instantly, Jerry shifted his grip so that he held him upright. Then Helen was at his side, helping him.

"Good kid," he complimented. "You got my signal."

Only one passerby had seen this, and he stood watching them, as though hesitating whether to interfere.

"Quick!" Jerry said. "We've got to get him into my bus. It's right down this side street, here."

Together they carried the unconscious man the few feet to the car and dropped him into the tonneau. Helen sprang into the driver's seat and sent the car rocketing off, while Jerry manacled the detective with his own handcuffs and appropriated his gun.

Two minutes later, when she had twisted the car around several blocks and was certain that there had been no pursuit, Helen brought it to a stop on a dark side street. Sergeant Crowley, sprawled on the seat beside Jerry, was still unconscious.

In as few words as possible Jerry explained to her what had happened. Helen listened in silence until he had finished.

"Then you've got to take it on the lam?" she asked.

"Looks like it. With the framed-up evidence that the police have got against me, I'd probably get the chair if I came to trial. Unless—"

"Unless what?"

Jerry shrugged hopelessly.

"Unless I could find out who framed me and get the goods on them. It'd be my only chance."

"But—haven't you any idea who did it?"

Jerry lit a cigarette while he thought desperately, wracking his brain for some answer to the dilemma. None came to him.

"I can think of three or four guys that might have done it. But what's the use? It'd take a week to check up on them. And that's just a week more than I've got. If I could only put my finger on one of them—say, you talked to the guy that did it! Maybe he said something. . . ."

"No," said Helen. "He just called up, started to say that you wouldn't be able to see me, then there was a loud rumbling noise so I couldn't hear what he was saying. When this ended—"

"Rumbling noise!" Jerry interrupted. "What kind?"

"Well—like—like an elevated train. Yes, I'm sure that's what it was."

"That's something. Anything else?"

"When I could hear him again, he said that you wouldn't be able to see me because you'd gone out on a job. Then he hung up. That's all I can— but come to think of it, there were some other noises in the background! It sounded like automobile engines running. As though he were talking from a garage." Helen's excitement mounted. "Does that help any?"

"Does it help any! A garage near an elevated . . . It gives me an idea. Say, did this fellow have a kind of low, flat voice?"

"I—I think so."

"Hymie Borson! He runs a little garage down on Archer, right in back of the elevated. I've heard that he pulls frame-ups like this, just so he'll always be in the clear. I think I'll give him a shake-up and see what comes out."

There was a sudden muttering and gasping beside him. The inanimate form of the detective stirred, then sat up groggily.

"What—happened?" Sergeant Crowley asked dazedly.

Jerry grinned.

"You got in the way of my fist," he said.

"Knocked out," said the detective. He regarded the handcuffs on his wrists for a moment, then gingerly rubbed his chin. "Knocked out and kidnaped," he commented. "That was pretty slick, Marlin."

"Uh-huh," agreed Jerry. "Sorry, but I had to do it. Now we're going to go places and do things. Helen, you hop back here and watch the sergeant while I drive."

Helen Scott climbed into the back seat and took the gun. Sergeant Crowley's eyes narrowed speculatively as he watched Jerry slide behind the wheel and leave them alone.

"Careful, Mister Detective," warned Helen. "Don't try anything. This gun might go off, you know."

Sergeant Crowley eyed the gun in her hand askance.

"How about us both being careful?" he suggested. "What is this, anyway? You taking me for a ride?"

"Nope," answered Jerry, throwing the car into gear. "This is a sightseeing expedition."

"Okay with me," said the detective. "Just so I don't see no holes blown in my hide."

Jerry drove to Archer Street and turned south on it. When he had nearly reached the towering structure of the elevated tracks, he swung the car into a dark alleyway. In the deepest shadows he stopped and switched off the lights.

"Listen here—" began Sergeant Crowley.

But Jerry wasn't listening. His hand dived into a side pocket of the car, came out with a loaded automatic.

"Keep an eye on the sergeant," he advised Helen.

Then he disappeared, slipping off into the darkness.

A hundred feet farther down the alley a patch of light fell through a garage door which had been left open a crack. Jerry crept up and peered cautiously through it.

He saw a typical small garage. On one side was a wooden partition for the office and supply room; on the other side a row of cars were parked against the wall. In the center of the room a mechanic was experimenting with a high-powered car, jerking the throttle up and down so that the engine roared like an airplane. The only other man in sight was a second mechanic, who sat in a chair tipped back against a ceiling brace, not far from the rear door.

Jerry pulled his hat low over his eyes, hunched his shoulders in a dejected attitude, and squeezed through the door. The mechanic in the chair immediately came to his feet.

"Outside, bum!" he ordered.

"Lissen," whined Jerry, approaching closer, "how about a—"

"Outside, I said!"

The mechanic's arms reached out for him. Jerry ducked under them, coming up to one side. As he rose out of his crouch his fist, starting from his knees, swung up in a sizzling arc that ended flush on the other's chin. The mechanic's head snapped back, then his knees gave way under him and he pitched to the floor.

Jerry did not waste a second glance on him. He knew that he was out. But the second mechanic had still to be reckoned with.

The man was already out of the car, a wrench in his hand. His lips moved in a shout, but the roar of the engine drowned it out.

"Stick 'em up," said Jerry.

His words could not be heard, but the gun which appeared in his hand made his meaning evident. And, after a moment's hesitation, the mechanic dropped the wrench and raised his arms.

It was only a minute's work to bind the two men with a coil of wire. Two wads of oily waste served efficiently as gags.

This finished, Jerry advanced toward the office. He listened at the flimsy door, but could hear nothing but the roar of the high-powered motor behind him.

Automatic in hand, he stepped into the office and closed the door behind him.

A pudgy man sat at an office desk, his feet propped up on its scarred surface. He was reading a newspaper, his pouched eyes glinting with avarice.

"Up with 'em, Hymie," invited Jerry.

Hymie Borson's feet came down from the desk with a crash as he stared at the bore of the automatic pointed at his head. The newspaper slipped from his fingers and fluttered to the floor.

"Marlin!" he gasped.

Then his arms jerked into the air and his face mottled with fear.

"Yeah," said Jerry. "I came to check up on this frame-up, firsthand."

"I didn't do it!" choked the gang leader. "I swear to—"

Then he broke off suddenly, aware that his very words had betrayed him. By admitting knowledge of a frame-up, he admitted his own complicity in it.

"Cough up," ordered Jerry. "Otherwise one of these slugs'll be choking your windpipe."

Hymie Borson's eyes, which were riveted on his face, abruptly focused on some object behind him. A faint flicker of relief crossed his countenance, and was instantly suppressed.

Jerry whirled around—too late.

There was a flash of dull metal streaking through the air. A short length of lead pipe struck his wrist with paralyzing force. The automatic leaped from his nerveless fingers and clattered to the floor.

Buzz Walper stood in a door which opened upon steps leading to the basement. His face was expressionless as he stepped into the room.

"Get him, Buzz!" roared Hymie Borson, heaving himself to his feet.

Jerry met Buzz Walper before he could take a second step. Feinting with his useless right arm, he crashed through his guard with a powerful left hook to the jaw.

Buzz Walper stumbled backwards. His heel caught upon the raised sill of the door. He fell back, disappeared through the doorway, and bumped down the flight of stairs.

At the same moment Jerry heard a *swish* of air. From the corner of his eye he saw the shadow of a chair swinging at him. He whirled away, in a desperate attempt to escape, but the edge of the seat caught him a terrific blow on the forehead.

There was a bursting stab of pain in his head. But it was not more intense than the bitter realization that he had failed. He heard Hymie Borson's laughter ringing in his ears as he sank to the floor.

When consciousness filtered back into his dazed brain, he was lying on his back on a cold, clammy cement surface. Overhead a powerful electric light shone into his eyes. Jerry judged that he had been carried down to the basement of the garage.

Hymie Borson towered over him.

"Come to, eh?" he grunted.

With an effort, Jerry sat up.

"Spill it!" rasped the gang leader.

"Spill what?" asked Jerry.

"How you knew I framed you."

Jerry essayed a feeble grin.

"Don't you wish you knew?" he taunted.

Hymie Borson cursed.

"Squeal, you rat! Come clean!"

Jerry shook his head. He could not speak, even to save himself from torture. If the gang leader learned that Helen Scott was but a few feet from them, it would mean her death, as well as that of Sergeant Crowley.

Hymie Borson was livid with rage.

"Get the hose," he ordered. "We'll hammer it outta him, if we have to beat his brains out."

Buzz Walper rose leisurely to his feet and took a short length of rubber garden hose from a table. He flexed it experimentally a few times, then slouched forward, his eyes gleaming.

"Give it to him!" rasped the gang leader.

As the hose was raised for the first blow, the stairs creaked warningly. Then a voice roared:

"Reach, you mugs!"

Sergeant Crowley was crouched on the steps, his revolver leveled. Helen Scott was just behind him.

Buzz Walper acted in a split second, before the others could recover from their surprise. Instead of bringing the hose down on Jerry, he straightened his elbow and released the hose. It sped from his fingers as straight as an arrow, directly toward the detective.

A gun thundered. Buzz Walper pitched to the floor, clawing at his shoulder where the sergeant's bullet had wounded him. The end of the hose struck Sergeant Crowley in the forehead. He lost his balance and fell down the stairs.

The next second Snowboy Klein had his automatic out, in a draw that was so fast it was almost a blur of motion. He aimed it at the detective's head and pulled the trigger.

Snowboy Klein, dope fiend that he was, was an unerring shot. Had the bullet struck where he intended, Sergeant Crowley would have become only an inanimate mass of flesh.

But Jerry Marlin acted just as quickly. Leaping to his feet, he caught the other's wrist and forced it upwards. The bullet passed just over the detective's head. Then Jerry twisted Snowboy Klein's wrist until the gun dropped from his fingers.

From then on it was man to man. Snowboy Klein had a drug addict's maniacal strength, but without his treasured automatic he was almost helpless against a man skilled in fighting. A minute, and he collapsed.

Buzz Walper had been out of the struggle. And meanwhile Sergeant Crowley had snapped handcuffs on Hymie Borson's wrists.

The detective surveyed the carnage.

"You were nuts to try this alone," he said.

"Yeah?" said Jerry.

"But not nuts enough," Helen put in, "to let you drag him to the electric chair."

Sergeant Crowley grinned.

Jerry looked from the detective to the girl.

"Say, how come you butted in?" he asked. "I thought I left you back in the car."

"I'll say you did," agreed Sergeant Crowley. "But after you left, we got to talking. And when I told your girl here that Hymie Borson tipped me off, and she wised me that you were going after Hymie, we both decided that it was time to forget little differences and work together for a change. Damn good thing we did, too."

"I see," said Jerry.

Sergeant Crowley took out a cigar, bit off the end.

"You know, there's ten grand reward on this case. I promised Hymie half of it. But he's got himself caught now, and won't have any use for it. You two might as well have the five grand. You've earned it. How'd that be?"

Jerry looked at Helen. She returned the look.

"I'd say that'd be okay," Jerry said.

And the only dissenting voice was a deep growl from Hymie Borson.

Analysis of "Alibi's Holiday," excerpted from "New Horizons for Mystery Stories" by August Lenniger

"ALIBI'S HOLIDAY," BY RICHARD CREDICOTT, is a detective-adventure story presented omnisciently, and objectively following Jerry Marlin, ex-con "on the straight." Jerry is waiting at 1 a.m. for his girl, Helen Scott, restaurant cashier, who gets off at 12:30. He waits until a quarter after one, goes home, and finds his revolver has been stolen.

Meanwhile Hymie Borson, clever cracksman who runs a garage to camouflage his real profession, and who believes in providing the police with a "fall guy" on all his jobs, has robbed a jewelry establishment and killed the watchman, using Jerry's gun and leaving it for the police to find. He had called up Helen Scott and told her not to meet Jerry for he had been called away on a job. The next day, seeing a $10,000 reward, Hymie decides to tip off the police and get half the reward. He gives Sergeant Crowley the "dope" and Crowley promises to split.

That night, Crowley finds Jerry in the restaurant where Helen works, asks him if he has an alibi for 1 a.m. the previous night, to which Jerry can only answer in the negative, and cleverly gets Jerry's fingerprints, which are exactly the same as the pictures Crowley has of the prints found on the gun. Jerry has no alternative except to accompany Crowley to headquarters.

They go to the desk, where Jerry pays his check and offers to "buy the Sarge a cigar." He fears Helen hasn't caught his meaning, but when they are a few feet from the store there is a woman's cry of "Help!" and Jerry uses the opportunity to knock out the Sergeant. Jerry and Helen bundle him in Jerry's car, handcuff him with his own "bracelets" and "lam." Questioning Helen about the mysterious phone call of the preceding evening, Jerry gets a clue, and follows it. Crowley has regained consciousness in the rear seat, with Helen guarding him with his own gun. They drive to Hymie's garage, where Jerry tries to clean up the gang that framed him single-handed. Helen, left outside to guard Crowley, reaches an understanding with the detective, who now sees the significance of Hymie's "tip-off," and the two of them arrive just in time to save Jerry's life. And Crowley decides to "split" the reward with Helen and Jerry.

Mr. Wyn asked me to point out particularly the human element in this story; it provides a realistic, sympathetic touch that grips the reader's emotions. Often writers are puzzled over how much love interest or woman interest they can bring into a detective story. Some years ago we seldom saw love interest in any but the novel-length detective story, but the last few years there has been a general tendency to be more lenient in this respect. To a certain extent, the popularity of the underworld story in which the gun moll often figures prominently is responsible for this; at any rate, if a love interest will help to complicate your plot, it is permissible. Just how far it can go is suggested by the several stories just synopsized; it should never get sloppily sentimental or overshadow the main issue, which is always the solution of a vital mystery. Sex is the motivation of a good many crimes. Not all men are murdered because a wastrel nephew can not wait for his millionaire uncle to pass on naturally.

THE LAST DEAL

*Chut was a wise guy—but he pulled the double-cross once
too often and talked himself into a hail of hot lead!!*

"FORTY GRAND," SAID SAM BEEMAN. "THAT'S MY OFFER."

His cigar described a circle as he gestured, then popped into his little, round mouth. He blinked owlishly through a mist of smoke.

Paul Kennedy maintained a thoughtful silence. His long, slender fingers drummed slowly on the edge of the desk, in time to the throbbing music of the orchestra outside on the dance floor.

His partner, however, did not receive the offer so calmly. Chut Segal hoisted his bulk to his feet, his arms waving wildly.

"Forty grand!" he sputtered. "*Mein Gott*, you are tryin' to rob us! You take me for a fool, huh? Forty grand! Why—why—" The words trailed off as his round, oily face became florid.

Paul Kennedy looked at Chut Segal with unutterable disgust in his eyes. A stinging retort rose to his lips, but he choked it back and turned to Sam Beeman.

"Look here, Beeman," he said, "this club is easily worth eighty grand. I figure sixty as a fair price for it. It's the most popular night club in the city. There hasn't been a week, not even the worst, when we haven't cleared over a thousand on it. And the average runs between four and five grand."

Sam Beeman seemed remote, behind his cloud of smoke. He blinked again, shrugged his shoulders and spread his hands.

"Maybe so," he conceded. "But suppose the D.A. gets it knocked off? Then it ain't worth forty cents."

"The D.A. isn't acting against night clubs."

"Can't he change his mind?"

Chut Segal brought his fist down on the desk.

"Listen you, Beeman!" he roared. "We ain't givin' this club away."

"So?" inquired Sam Beeman. "And maybe I ain't playing Santa Claus."

"Santa Claus, bah! Why—"

Paul Kennedy's voice cracked like a whiplash.

"Shut up, Segal! Can the hot air!"

Chut Segal choked and grew red. His eyes met Kennedy's in a glance of hatred. But, in obedience to the command, he became silent.

"Now," went on Kennedy, "what's your last offer?"

"Forty grand," said Beeman.

"Make it fifty."

"No."

Kennedy thought for a moment. He peered through the mist of smoke at the blinking eyes set in the round, cherubic countenance. Then he nodded.

"Cash?" he asked.

Sam Beeman tapped his breast pocket.

"Right here."

"Okay."

Kennedy rose to his feet with a lithe grace. He moved to the wall of the small office and pushed a button in the wainscoting. A panel snapped back, revealing a small wall safe. He twirled the dial.

"Wait a minute!" protested Chut Segal. "Ain't I gonna be consulted on this? I own half this club."

Kennedy paused a moment and looked up. Chut Segal fell back a step before the menacing, cold steel directness of his eyes.

"You," said Kennedy, "are going to do what I tell you to—you dirty double-crosser!"

He finished the combination, opened the safe door and drew out a sheaf of papers. Taking off the rubber band which bound them together, he tossed them on the desk.

"Leases and contracts," he said. "We'll make out a bill of sale to you for the furnishings."

The necessary papers were made out and signed by Kennedy and Segal. Sam Beeman pocketed them, then counted out forty one thousand dollar bills upon the desk.

"Right?" he asked.

Chut Segal's eyes glittered avariciously at the sight of the bills. But Kennedy anticipated him and picked up the green packet.

"We'll put these in the safe until we close tonight. And, Segal, don't waste your time trying to open it. I had the combination changed today."

He tossed the bills into the yawning door of the safe and twirled the dial. Chut Segal threw him a look of baffled hate, turned on his heel and left.

"My last night here," said Kennedy. Then he nodded to the new owner. "Well, Beeman, look it over. I'm going out on the floor, now. If you've got any questions, I'll be at my usual table."

He touched a match to a cigarette, took a deep inhalation, and sauntered through the door that opened upon the main floor of the night club. Then went directly to his own table, in a protected corner, and sat down facing the orchestra. He dismissed, with a wave of his hand, the waiter who hurried up.

The tables were crowded with a gay throng of formally clothed men and women. Naked shoulders and arms gleamed in the light. Jewels sparkled with multi-colored coruscations. Forbidden liquids bubbled in glasses.

The orchestra, in its gilded, ornamented alcove, was playing some wild, almost barbaric music. The polished dance floor, between the circles of tables, had been cleared for a special act. Kennedy leaned forward to watch it.

Six men, hardly more than boys, handsome in evening clothes, were dancing in the modern manner, with a studied awkwardness, feet slapping the floor in regular rhythm. They moved exactly in unison, with the same gestures, resembling a row of puppets moved by the same strings.

But it was not on them that Kennedy's attention was fixed. He was watching the girl who danced in front of them, her slim body clothed in a smart red and black riding costume. She bore in one hand a long black-snake whip and, as she whirled and pirouetted, it lashed out, to its full length, its end cracking like the explosion of a pistol.

Then she turned upon the men dancing behind her. The whip lashed out, striking the floor at the feet of one of them, in an imperious command. The man danced out and his arms encircled her for a few steps, only to be thrown off as she whirled away from him. When he approached her again, pleadingly, the whip cracked, and he returned to the line. This was repeated with each of the other five men.

When the act was finished, there was a patter of applause. Kennedy leaped to his feet and clapped with the others.

The girl, who was looking in his direction, nodded and smiled. After repeated bows, she walked toward him, carrying the whip folded up in one hand.

"Like it?" she asked, dropping into a chair beside him.

"It's a knockout, Marianne!"

Kennedy's eyes were hungry as they swept over Marianne Elstan. With her small hand nestling in his, her body close to his, her subtle perfume rising to his nostrils, he almost forgot the disappointment of having had to sell the club.

"Well," she asked, "is the deal over?"

He nodded moodily.

"Beeman took everything. Everything, that is, except your contract."

"How much?"

"Forty grand."

"Forty thousand!" Marianne gasped. "Why this club ought to be worth twice that."

"It is," he agreed. "But that's all Sam Beeman would put on the line. And there isn't a big market for night clubs. Damn Chut Segal!"

Marianne was silent, appreciating Kennedy's feelings. He and Segal had started the club together, and it had been a huge success, due largely to Kennedy's efforts. Then Segal had begun to dip his fingers secretly into the receipts, sometimes taking as much as half of the night's income.

Kennedy had eventually discovered this, of course. It meant a break-up of the partnership. But Chut Segal, hating Kennedy for having discovered his pilfering, refused to sell out to his partner. Nor would he buy Kennedy's share, for he knew himself incapable of operating the club alone.

As a result, they had to sell it to Sam Beeman at a sacrifice.

After a moment Kennedy looked up, a grin again on his face.

"Well, Marianne, how about it?"

"I'm ready," she answered.

"Tonight?"

"Tonight."

"Then as soon as the performance is over, we start out—together." He touched one hand to his breast, where the outlines of a billfold could be seen. "I've got thirty grand here, saved up for over a year. And I get half of the forty in the safe, making a grand total of fifty grand. With which, I think, we can start a pretty neat little club in some other city."

Marianne leaned her head against his shoulder.

"You bet," she said.

There was a sudden whirl of activity, hoarse shouts, barked commands. Feet stamped into the room. A gun roared thunderously and a man screamed. The orchestra broke off raggedly.

Kennedy leaped to his feet, made a grab for his hip pocket—only to remember that he had left his gun in the desk in the office.

"Stick 'em up! Reach high!"

A man crouched in the entryway, a submachine gun in his hands. Its muzzle waved back and forth, so that it covered everyone in the room. The man's face was covered with a black handkerchief which left only his eyes exposed.

Simultaneously two more men appeared at the swinging doors which led into the kitchens. They, too, were masked, and one of them bore a second submachine gun.

"No false moves!" warned the man who was armed only with an automatic, and was, apparently, the leader.

There was a stark silence. It was broken only by the moans of a hysterical woman who had fallen to the floor in a semi-faint.

A hundred pairs of hands were raised into the air. There was no thought of resistance. Newspaper accounts had too thoroughly familiarized the people with the machine gun's ability to spray hundreds of bullets in a minute. They had too often seen gruesome pictures of gangsters and racketeers who had been bumped off by that method.

Kennedy raised his hands with the others. He was filled with a mad, baffled rage, but he didn't dare show any resistance for fear of endangering Marianne's life.

"That's right, folks," the leader of the bandits said cheerfully. "Nobody's gonna get hurt if they act nice. Now I'm gonna take up a collection. And I'm warnin' you that you better kick through with what you've got."

He began at one side of the room and worked his way around it. Watches, rings, necklaces, billfolds—everything disappeared into a capacious grip which he carried. A few women murmured as precious jewels were roughly snatched from their persons, but the ever-present, menacing machine guns dissipated any attempt at resistance.

Kennedy saw Chut Segal surrender his billfold, and noticed, subconsciously, that the bandit leader did not touch the rings on his fingers. A sudden bitter suspicion sprang into his mind.

The bandit leader arrived at last before Kennedy and Marianne.

"You're the big shot of this outfit, ain't you?" he asked.

Kennedy tried to pierce through the man's disguise, but couldn't. He did not remember ever seeing him before. He carefully stored away in his memory the intonation of the man's voice, vowing that, if he ever met him again, he would exact revenge.

"Go to hell!" he said.

"Smart guy, ain't you?" sneered the bandit. "Got any change on you?"

His fingers went unerringly to Kennedy's breast pocket, drew out the billfold. He opened it, flipped the stack of bills through his fingers, and gasped.

"This is *some* dough!" he chuckled. "Thanks, bud, for the contribution."

Kennedy ground his teeth in helpless fury. The savings of a year gone like that. The money which he had expected to set himself up in business again.

The bandit leader ran his fingers over Marianne, found nothing, and passed on. In a few minutes he had completed his search. His grip was filled almost to the brim, and he snapped it shut. At a signal, the man who had been stationed at the kitchen door joined him and the other man in the entryway.

"We're leavin' now," the bandit leader announced. "Thanks a lot for the kind contributions, friends. And anybody that wants to follow us will get a taste of hot lead, dished up special by a Tommy-gun."

He and his men backed out of the entryway and disappeared. A moment later there was the roar of a motor speeding away.

For a few moments there was silence. Then pandemonium broke out. Men roared in protest, women shrieked their losses. But none ventured near the door through which the bandits had disappeared.

Kennedy dropped into a chair. He knew the futility, as well as the danger, of attempting to follow them.

"Cleaned!" he groaned.

He paid no attention to the bedlam about him. Nor did he think of calling the police; they did not molest the night clubs, but, on the other hand, they gave them no protection.

Sam Beeman fought his way through the crowd to Kennedy's table. His cherubic face was glum, his eyes blinking mournfully.

"I'm ruined!" he cried. "What a thing to happen! Nobody will come here any more. I'm ruined!"

"Yeah?" said Kennedy, sympathetically. "Well, they cleaned me out pretty slick."

"What'll I do?" pleaded Beeman.

"Do?" said Kennedy. "Nothing. Nothing to do."

"But can't the police—?"

"Call 'em if you want," Kennedy answered indifferently.

Sam Beeman disappeared, threatening vaguely to see the police commissioner about it. Other people were leaving as fast as they could get their wraps. Most of them would rather stand their losses than delay there and suffer the inevitable newspaper publicity.

Kennedy watched the club being emptied.

"Well, kid," he said to Marianne, "it doesn't look so hot for us now. Thirty grand out of fifty just like that."

"Leaving you twenty," she said. "And I've got four or five myself."

He patted her arm.

"You're the real goods. Oh, I guess we'll get by. Have to."

Chut Segal joined them. He was chewing viciously on a cigar.

"*Mein Gott!*" he said. "This is awful. They took me for ten grand. Damn good thing you put that forty grand in the safe, or they'd of got that, too."

Kennedy looked at his former partner sharply. He remarked again that Chut Segal wore a very valuable diamond ring which had not been touched.

"Yeah," he answered. "It *was* a good thing."

"Where's Beeman?" asked Segal.

"Gone. Said something about the cops."

"What the hell!" Segal chuckled. "If he wants to be nuts, let him. Let's divvy up now and clear out."

"Suits me," agreed Kennedy. "Be back in a few minutes, Marianne."

They went across the now deserted floor and into the office. Segal shut the door behind them and waited while Kennedy manipulated the combination of the safe.

Kennedy got the door open and took out the packet of money. He looked up to see Segal pointing a revolver at him.

"I'll take that dough," said Segal.

Kennedy cursed himself for his carelessness. He regarded Segal steadily, estimating his chances of leaping on him and wresting the gun from him.

"Don't try it," warned Segal, reading the intention in his eyes. "I said give me that money."

Kennedy's eyes were contemptuous.

"A rat to the last," he said.

He tossed the packet of bills to Segal. The latter caught them and slipped them into his inside coat pocket. There was a sneering grin on his round oily face.

"So," Kennedy said, "I guessed right."

"Yeah?" said Segal. "Guessed what?"

"That you engineered this robbery tonight. I half thought you might try some such rotten stunt. You gave yourself away when you didn't have your gorillas take that ring from your finger."

"You've got a good guesser, ain't you?" sneered Segal. "Maybe you can guess what I'm gonna do next?"

"I'll bite."

"Right now I'm takin' you for a ride. Maybe that guesser of yours can tell you how you'll feel with a couple slugs buzzin' around in your belly."

"Afraid of me, eh? Afraid my slugs might catch up with you?"

"Me, afraid?" Chut Segal laughed harshly. "Nope, just careful. I'm not takin' any chances. Now I think we'll just walk out of our private entrance and hop into my bus. Bein' as how you won't be with us much longer, I'll let you drive it."

Kennedy had his eyes on the revolver. It was held unwaveringly on him, ready to fire on an instant's notice. He had hoped that Chut Segal would relax his attention for only a fraction of a second—just enough to give him a fighting chance to knock the revolver from his hand—but Segal was watching him with the wary eyes of a fox.

"Okay," he said.

He turned toward their private door which gave upon a passageway opening directly upon the neighboring alley. Perhaps he would find some opportunity while in the car to make a break.

"Not leaving, are you?" came a clear feminine voice.

Kennedy whirled around, saw Marianne Elstan standing in the door which opened upon the dance floor. She was still dressed in the red riding costume, with the whip in her hand.

Segal licked his lips. He was standing so that he could see both Marianne and Kennedy, but could keep his gun pointed at only one of them.

"Just goin' for a—uh—ride," he said.

"I see," said Marianne, staring at the gun in his hand.

Kennedy tensed himself. For an instant the gun's muzzle had wavered. But, before he could leap, it centered again upon his heart.

"Better keep out of this, Marianne," he said hoarsely.

"It would be a good idea," commented Segal, smiling evilly. "I could just as well take the two of you for a ride, you know. Maybe I ought to at that."

"I think not," said Marianne, calmly.

Her arm raised, came down. The folds of the whip lashed out, its black length hissing through the air like a serpent. Segal gave a frightened cry and turned the revolver toward her. But, before he could pull the trigger, the end of the whip snapped like a steel wire about the fingers that held the revolver, cutting through the flesh and down to the bone.

Marianne jerked back on the whip. The revolver flew from Segal's hand, exploding in midair. The bullet buried itself harmlessly in the door-jamb beside her.

At the same instant Kennedy launched himself. He struck Segal like a battering-ram, his fists pounding him mercilessly. Segal was the larger and stronger man, but he was taken by surprise. In defense, he wrapped his arms about Kennedy and they fell to the floor together.

As they rolled over and over, locked in each other's arms, Kennedy managed to insert one hand inside the lapels of Segal's coat. A quick flip, and the packet of money slid beneath a desk, unnoticed by Segal.

They were on their feet again. Marianne had retrieved the revolver, but dared not fire for fear of hitting Kennedy. But there was no need of her aid. Kennedy was quicker and more hard-hitting, and was easily Segal's master.

A sudden plan popped into his mind. Instantly acting on it, he drove Segal back toward the door, striking through his guard with blows that jolted him to the heels.

"You dirty double-crosser!" he snarled. "I'm going to kill you!"

Segal was panting heavily and his face was beet-red from the exertion. Sweat rolled from his forehead. He gasped every time that a blow struck him, and his eyes were terror-stricken.

Abruptly he turned and bolted, running wildly through the door and across the deserted dance floor. Marianne raised the revolver to fire after him, but Kennedy struck her arm down.

"What did you let him get away for?" she demanded.

"I had a reason." He swooped down, retrieved the packet of money from under the desk, then jerked a loaded automatic from a drawer. "We're going to follow him. He framed that job tonight. We may have a chance to get the loot back from him."

They darted through the door that led to their private entrance. When they reached the end of the passageway, they opened the outer door only a crack so that they could look out into the alleyway, but could not be seen.

A moment later Chut Segal rushed down the alley from the street. He sprang into a waiting car, roared the motor into life, and sped down the alley to the street.

Kennedy wasted no time in following him. He had his car parked nearby, and it was only a second's work to get it started. When he reached the street, he saw the tail light of Segal's car bobbing a block ahead.

He set out to follow it, keeping far enough behind so that Segal would not be likely to see him amid the midnight traffic. Segal, apparently, did not suspect that he was being trailed, for he headed across the city at a moderate rate of speed.

They penetrated far into the southern part of the city, leaving behind them the lights. Segal finally drew up before an old loft building which, to judge from its exterior, had not been occupied for years, and disappeared into its dark interior.

Kennedy parked his car a block distant. From there, he and Marianne advanced on foot. The street was deserted; they met no one. The only sounds came from the railways off to the east.

There was no sign of life on the first floor of the loft building. The few windows on the second floor had been boarded over, but a sliver of light showed through a crack.

He tried the door through which Chut Segal had disappeared. It was locked, but the wood was old and rotten. He put his shoulder against it and pushed, and it opened almost without a sound.

"I'm going in, Marianne," Kennedy whispered. "You stick around outside. If you hear any gunfire, be ready to take it on the lam."

"Think again," she retorted. "I'm going in with you."

"But—" he began to protest.

She pushed past him, into the dark interior, and was swallowed up by the shadows. Kennedy shrugged; he knew the impossibility of attempting to persuade her to adopt a saner course.

Overhead, they could hear the muffled sound of voices. The ceiling shook and swayed as feet tramped on it. A chair scraped on the floor.

He found the stairs. They crept up them together, testing every tread before they put their weight on it.

Off a hallway at the top a door was open. Through it a swath of light fell. There was the rasp of an oath; the clink of a glass being dropped on a table.

Figures moved in the room. One of them was Chut Segal. He was backed up against a wall, his face contorted with fear.

"*Mein Gott!* You don't mean—?" he chattered.

A harsh laugh answered him.

"You rat, Segal! Why shouldn't we? Why should we divide up with you?"

"But I framed the job! If it hadn't of been for me, you could never of pulled it. Listen—"

Kennedy caught at Marianne's arm, pressed it. The double-cross! Chut Segal had come here expecting his share of the night's robbery, only to find that his men had turned against him.

Things were happening so fast that Kennedy had no chance to intervene, even had he wanted to. Segal clawed for his pocket and jerked out a gun. Even as he did so a gun roared and a spot of crimson appeared on the front of his shirt.

Segal swayed and went down. More shots poured into him, and his gun answered them. Then his body jerked and went still, the gun dropping from nerveless fingers.

There was a silence during which the roar of guns still seemed to echo.

"Geez! He got Mike!" husked a voice.

"So much the better! That leaves only two of us to divvy up the swag."

Kennedy chose this moment to step forward, estimating correctly that just after this double killing their vigilance would be most lax.

"Up with your paws!" he rasped.

Two men whirled to face him, jaws agape. On the floor two dead men stared at the ceiling with sightless eyes. On the table was a grip which Kennedy recognized.

One of the men went for a gun. Kennedy drilled him through the shoulder, pulled the trigger again only to hear a futile click from his automatic. It had jammed.

He threw himself upon the second man before he could reach a pistol that lay on the table, beside the grip. As he whirled him away from it, Kennedy's fists lashed out and caught him squarely on the jaw. He went down, limp and unconscious.

The wounded man had sunk to the floor, gripping his injured shoulder with his other hand and groaning softly. Kennedy snatched up the gun from the table, but the fight had gone out of both men.

He peered into the open grip upon the table. It was filled almost to the brim with jewels and billfolds. The bandits, apparently, had not as yet touched it.

He reached into it, searched until he found his own billfold. Its thirty thousand dollars were intact.

"We'll turn the rest of this junk over to Sam Beeman," he said. "He can see that it gets back to its proper owners."

Marianne knelt beside the body of Chut Segal, quickly straightened.

"He's dead," she said.

"Yeah," said Kennedy, "he tried the double-cross just once too often. Probably never occurred to him that somebody else could work the double-cross also. I think, kid, that I'll keep his share of the forty grand we got for the club. He won't be needing it—not where he's going."

TICK O' THE CLOCK

The Right Word at the Right Time Turns a Trick.

DAN NORTON, ACE OPERATIVE OF THE FARWELL DETECTIVE SERVICE, squinted at the *Evening-News* through the festoon of smoke curling up from the cigarette dangling in his lips. His attention was centered upon the column which was headed:

GRAND JURY FAILS TO INDICT SCARPIO
States That Evidence Is Insufficient and Circumstantial

He grinned as he finished the account and tossed the newspaper on the desk.

"So Scarpio beat that rap," he said. "Well, it's what we wanted."

Randall J. Mathews, attorney-at-law and candidate for election as district attorney, nodded thoughtfully. He sat behind his desk in his law office, toying with a pencil as he stared moodily out of the window at his elbow, across the panoramic scene of the lighted city beneath him. He was a middle-aged and gray-haired man, reserved and austere in manner.

"Yes, it's what we wanted," he agreed without enthusiasm. "But I still regret having had to resort to any such underhanded methods."

Dan crushed his cigarette in a tray on the desk and grinned infectiously.

"Aw, why think of that?" he protested. "District Attorney Meisbaum is just as big a crook as Al Scarpio. You should worry what you have to do to show *that* to the public. Why you're doing 'em a favor! And you've got the election in the bag. Meisbaum hasn't got a chance of reelection."

He understood the humiliation the attorney felt and did his best to divert him. Mathews was running upon the Reform Ticket, pledged to put an end to the hook-up between the underworld and crooked politics. He had hoped to conduct his candidacy upon strictly orthodox lines, appealing to the common sense of the public for support. The futility of that, however, had soon become apparent, for the mass of the voters were apathetic and those in power were too firmly entrenched to be easily unseated.

In desperation, Mathews had been forced to jettison his principles and fight fire with fire. Since the public did not realize the veniality of its officials, he had to prove it to them.

For this purpose he had chosen to concentrate upon the Shendahl murder. A month before, Barton Shendahl, gambling king, had been murdered in the office of one of his gambling establishments. That Al Scarpio, rival gambling king, was his slayer, there was little doubt, though there was no direct proof.

County politicians, in league with Scarpio, had done their best to hush it up. District Attorney Meisbaum had refused to prosecute the gambler, pointing out that the evidence against him was entirely circumstantial.

In the normal course of events, Barton Shendahl's fate would speedily have been forgotten. But Mathews seized the opportunity thus fortuitously offered to him to expose the district attorney. He saw that if Meisbaum could be forced, by continued pressure, to take Al Scarpio before the grand jury, and then were to fail to indict him, it would mean the end of his political career.

He had engaged the Farwell Detective Service to investigate the killing. Dan Norton had been assigned to the case, and he had been successful in finding two witnesses who had seen the gambler leave Barton Shendahl's office immediately after the sounds of the shots. It was far from sufficient evidence, but when published in the papers and commented upon in editorials, it left Meisbaum no choice but to act.

The outcome of the grand jury hearing had been a foregone conclusion from the first. It was almost a farce, for the district attorney did not dare indict Scarpio. He had suppressed some of the evidence and had presented the remainder in an unfavorable light. And thereby, though he had saved the gambler, he had effectually eliminated himself as a candidate for reelection.

After a pause, the lawyer brought his gaze back from the window.

"You're right, of course," he told Dan. "I got what I set out to get. And I should be satisfied, I suppose."

"That's the spirit, Mr. Mathews," applauded Dan. "This isn't any funeral—except maybe Meisbaum's."

The lawyer sighed and selected a cigar from a teakwood humidor. He was touching a match to it when they heard steps in the corridor, followed by a knock on the door. The match flickered and went out as his glance crossed the young detective's.

"I'll see who it is," said Dan.

He opened the door and peered into the semi-obscurity of the corridor. Then a gun materialized in his hand.

"Well, if it isn't Al Scorpio himself! And Spats Parker. Shall I let 'em in, Mr. Mathews?"

The lawyer hesitated, then nodded grimly.

"Come in, boys," invited Dan. He did not pocket his weapon, but held it in readiness. "And keep your hands in plain sight," he added.

A short plump man edged through the door. He was immaculately attired, and a huge diamond blossomed in his gaudy cravat. His crinkly black hair, sleek with oil, reeked with perfume. He was followed by his bodyguard, Spats Parker, only slightly less elegantly garbed and perfumed.

Dan kicked the door shut and ran his hands expertly over their bodies, ignoring their scowled protests. He removed a wicked-looking automatic from Spats Parker's shoulder holster, then said, "Okay."

Mathews did not greet his uninvited guests. He stared at them with unconcealed hostility.

"Congratulations to our next district attorney," Al Scorpio said, smirking genially.

He dropped his rotund body with a plop into the chair which Dan had vacated. Drawing off his pigskin gloves, he deposited them, with his hat, upon another chair. Spats Parker took up a position behind him and glowered at Dan, who was engaged in removing the cartridges from his automatic.

The lawyer pushed his chair back so as to increase the distance between him and the gambler.

"You didn't come here to offer me your congratulations," he stated angrily. "If you have any business with me—which I can't imagine—come to the point."

Scorpio looked pained. "Look here, Mr. Mathews," he protested, "what's the use of hard feelings? You got the election sewed up now. After what happened today, Meisbaum might as well fold up and disappear from the picture."

"Well?"

"As I said, there ain't any use of hard feelings. I beat the rap for the Shendahl killing. And you got the district attorneyship handed you on a platter. We both got what we want, and we ought to be satisfied. Why can't we get together and be friendly for a change?"

The lawyer snorted. "Friendly! You can't talk friendship to me, Scarpio. You don't know what the term means. What you *do* mean is that you want me to give you something. Are you trying to buy future immunity from me?"

"You got me wrong, Mr. Mathews," the gambler was quick to protest, his swarthy face expressive of injured innocence. "I wouldn't even try to buy future immunity from you, because I know it couldn't be done. I know you won't take grease money. And that's okay with me."

Mathews clamped his unlighted cigar between his teeth and searched his pockets for a match.

"Just *why* did you come here, then?"

Al Scarpio fidgeted in his chair and recrossed his legs. Then he blurted out:

"It's this Shendahl rap, Mr. Mathews. What I want is that you shouldn't open it up again."

"Eh!" The lawyer was frankly astonished.

"Yeah. I didn't bump off Shendahl, no matter what Norton says. Why, him and me was pals! I ain't saying that Norton framed me with those witnesses, but—"

"You better not say that," warned Dan grimly.

Scarpio shot him a scowling look of hatred, then turned back to the lawyer.

"Shendahl getting put on the spot was a bad break for me all around, any way you look at it. Just because I was there a few minutes before it happened, everybody wants to hang it on me. And I didn't do it."

"So you told the grand jury," Mathews observed ironically. "Do you expect me to believe it too?"

"Well—maybe not. But let's be reasonable, Mr. Mathews. Meisbaum had enough evidence for an indictment—you got him that—but he never could've got a conviction. Any good mouthpiece would've laughed him out of court. And you couldn't get a conviction, either. It'd just be wasting your time and my time to try it. Let's just cross that off the books and forget about it. Anything you get on me in the future is okay. I'm just asking you to lay off this."

Mathews stared at the gambler with unconcealed astonishment. Dan Norton was quite as much surprised at Scarpio's strange proposal, for he knew that the lawyer had no intention of reopening the case, in the event of his election. As things stood, and without more evidence, it would have been just as the gambler said—a waste of time.

Al Scarpio, seeing that his words had made some effect, hastened to drive the wedge in further.

"That ain't so bad, is it, Mr. Mathews? I'm not asking much; and if you'll agree to that, I'll see that there won't be any trouble at the polls. I'll even go further than that; I'll chip in with a contribution to your campaign fund. Twenty thousand dollars ought to come in handy, hadn't it?"

He took out a well-filled wallet and began to count out thousand-dollar bills. For a moment Mathews was so startled that he could say nothing. Then his chair rasped back as he came to his feet.

"Scarpio, put your dirty money back in your pocket! I won't take it under any guise. You've got some clever scheme in the back of your head, but you can't tangle me up in it. You aren't in the habit of paying out good money for nothing."

"All I want to do is save both of us a lot of trouble. I—"

"You can save yourself some trouble right now by getting out! I've listened to you long enough."

"You're turning me down?" Scarpio's plump face turned ugly.

"You've had your answer."

"See here, Mr. Mathews—"

Dan Norton tapped the gambler on the shoulder.

"You heard what Mr. Mathews said, Scarpio. Scram."

Scarpio jerked away from his hand as though it were red hot. Then he shrugged and stood up, stuffing the bills back in his wallet.

"If that's the way you feel," he addressed the lawyer, "okay. But I'm warning you that you better change your mind. And damn soon, too!"

"I never change my mind," said Mathews.

Scarpio jammed his hat on his head and stalked from the office in an ominous silence. Spats Parker followed at his heels, accepting with ill grace his cartridgeless automatic and slamming the door behind him.

Dan wrinkled his nose in disgust.

"What a smell! You'd think guys like them could afford better perfume."

"It isn't the cost of the perfume—it's the kind," explained Mathews. "Sit down, Norton; I want to put a proposition to you. That's why I asked you to drop into my office tonight. I've talked with Mr. Farwell about it, and he's agreeable. But I've delayed broaching it to you until I was fairly certain of my election."

"Shoot," grinned Dan, lighting a cigarette.

"It's this: If I'm elected district attorney, I want you to work from my office as my chief investigator."

"Eh?" Dan sat up very straight, exhaling the smoke from his lungs with a startled whosh. "D'you really mean that, Mr. Mathews?"

"I certainly do. You're exactly the kind of man I need for the job. Of course, the work will be dangerous, and—"

"Damn the danger!" cried Dan. "Gimme the job."

He was exultant, for this suited him exactly. He could not have asked for better. Criminology was his sole absorbing interest in life. He had a natural flair for detective work and an intuition which, supplemented by a keen reasoning mind and a capacity for hard work, had already enabled him to make somewhat of a name for himself, though he was still young.

He had started as a patrolman on the city police force. But he had soon learned that promotion to the detective division meant either long years pounding a beat, or playing politics, currying favor from those higher up.

He had resigned in disgust and entered the Farwell Detective Service. The work was drab and monotonous, for the most part; but Mr. Farwell, recognizing his ability and taking a liking to him, had given him a share in the investigation of all the most interesting cases brought to the agency.

Now, however, as the investigator for the district attorney, there would be no limit to his work. He would be informed of the details of every serious crime committed within the borders of the county. If the work of the city police or the sheriff did not satisfy him, he could carry on their investigations from the point at which they left off.

Mathews smiled tolerantly at his almost boyish enthusiasm.

"It's agreed then. Well, we'll have four years ahead of us to prove whether we can do anything against men of Scarpio's breed. And now I think I'll drop into my campaign headquarters for a few minutes before I go home."

"I wish you'd let me go with you," Dan said suddenly, when they reached the street where the lawyer had his car parked.

"Want to join the preelection celebration? I'm afraid you'll find it too tame for you."

"No, it isn't that. But I've been thinking over what Scarpio said. He may not have meant it, but—"

"You mean his threat?"

"Well, yes. Scarpio was pretty mad, and he's just crazy enough to try to put you on the spot."

"You think there's any danger?"

"I hope not, Mr. Mathews." Dan was very serious, almost pleading. "But I wish you'd let me go with you, just on the off chance. I could stay with you until midnight, and then get one of the agency men to finish off the night. You ought to have a guard—at least until after the election is over."

The lawyer clapped him on the shoulder. His austere face broke into a smile.

"Nonsense, Norton! You've let this get on your nerves. Scarpio wouldn't dare attack then."

"His kind would dare anything—if he thought it would mean money in his pocket," Dan said glumly. And that's exactly what your death would mean to him."

"It would more likely mean the electric chair," the lawyer said dryly. "And Scarpio won't forget that, because he's a coward at heart. No, I don't think there's anything to be feared from that quarter. Even if there were, I couldn't keep a guard with me night and day. We've got ourselves into this—"

"I suppose you're right," Dan admitted reluctantly. "And still—"

The lawyer climbed in his car.

"Forget it," he advised. "Can I drop you somewhere?"

"Thanks, but I'll go out and see Mr. Farwell now, if he's at home. I'll take the street car."

He was thoughtful as the car drew away from him. He lit a cigarette and watched it until it swung around a corner.

Mathews was right, of course. If there was any danger, it was too remote and improbable to be considered. They had gone into this with their eyes open, and now they could not show the white feather.

Yet, despite the reassurance of his logic and the ridicule of the lawyer, he felt definitely apprehensive. His intuition told him that Scarpio would not accept his defeat supinely, and would do his best to strike back. And he had never known his "hunches" to be wrong.

But there was nothing to be done. Mathews had refused his offer. And he could not very well hang on his heels in a quixotic attempt to ward off what might be only a mythical danger.

It was almost half-past nine when he left the home of his agency chief. The streets before the small apartment building were nearly deserted by the evening traffic, and the few street lights furnished only a vague illumination.

Dan lit a cigarette before he started for the near-by street car line. As he snapped the match away, he heard a soft step behind him, and then a cold, round object bored into his spine.

"Don't pull that rod," a rasping voice warned him.

Dan stopped motionless. The smoke from his cigarette curled up past his eyes and mushroomed against the brim of his hat. His hand had automatically flashed to the pistol in his shoulder holster, but he drew it away empty and held his arms out from his side.

"Easy, now."

A hand snaked over his shoulder. It slipped under the lapel of his coat and withdrew the automatic from his holster.

"All right, guy," spoke the man behind him. "Get goin' toward that bus down the street there. An' no funny stuff!"

Dan started toward the dark sedan which was parked fifty feet away. The gun continued to prod into his spine with uncomfortable pressure.

"Careful with that roscoe, Spats," he suggested. "I don't want to get shot by accident."

"Know me, do yuh?" snarled Spats Parker. "Well, you're goin' to know a lot more things pretty quick, wise guy! An' if you get yourself shot—it won't be no accident!"

Dan sighed. He took a deep drag on his cigarette, then spat it out. He did not even contemplate the thought of resistance. Spats Parker was a vicious killer, lightning-fast with a gun and a deadly shot. Unless some unforeseen circumstance presented itself, he was helpless.

The car was empty, unlighted. Dan slid behind the steering wheel and his captor seated himself beside him, shifting the gun to Dan's ribs.

"Get the bus goin'," ordered Spats Parker.

Dan switched on the lights and the ignition, and started the motor. He put the gears into mesh and turned the car out into the street.

"Just drive around for a while," went on Spats. "We got plenty of time. There ain't no hurry."

"Thanks," Dan said dryly. "Maybe you'll tell me what the idea is."

"Can't you guess?" gibed Spats. "You're on the spot—goin' for a ride! So take a last long look around you—because you ain't goin' to be seein' these things any more."

"No? What does Scarpio figure to get out of bumping me off?"

"You got lots of questions, guy."

"Sure I have. And why not? I'm the guy that's taking this ride—not you. Haven't I got the right to a little inside dope?"

Spats Parker chuckled. With his right hand he fished a cigarette from his pocket and touched a match to it. Not for an instant did he remove his eyes from Dan.

"Curiosity killed a cat," he spoke sententiously. "But as long as you're gettin' killed anyway, and it isn't curiosity that's goin' to do it, I guess it won't hurt none if I spill a little info. Scarpio's havin' you rubbed out because you saw him try to grease Mathews.

"Yeah. He figgered that if he knocked off Mathews, he'd have to rub you out, too. He couldn't leave you to make trouble for him. An' so he's goin' to rub the two of you out together."

Dan's mind reeled. His hunch had been right! Scarpio was striking back at them.

"Has—Scarpio got Mr. Mathews now?" he asked.

"Sure he's got him! We picked him up in his car half an hour ago, when he was leavin' his campaign headquarters."

"Scarpio's crazy!" Dan cried. "He can't get by with it."

"Yeah, he's crazy—like a fox," retorted Spats Parker.

"*You* think so."

"I know so, wise guy. Because it's goin' to look like an accident. Just a harmless little accident, with the two of you gettin' knocked off. At three minutes after ten your lights go out—*bang!* An' then the papers will be writin' articles about how it was too bad, an' a lot of bunk like that."

"Why three minutes after ten?" asked Dan. "And what's this accident going to be?"

"You'll find out soon enough," Spats said noncommittally. He glanced at his watch. "We got twenty minutes yet. An' Scarpio told me not to get there too soon."

"Tell me, Spats," Dan asked, "what's Scarpio doing this for?"

"Still askin' questions," chuckled the gangster. "Anybody, to hear you, would think it made some difference if you knew the answers."

"Just curiosity," responded Dan. "I've got a hunch and I'd like to know if it's right. I think Scarpio is afraid of the Shendahl case."

Spats Parker shrugged. "Oh well, why not? Where you're goin', nobody'll care what you know. Yeah, you're right. Scarpio is worried about the Shendahl case."

"Why?"

"Because there was a witness to that kill, you dumb cluck! One of the croupiers—Bonelli, his name is—saw it. He took it on the lam, and Scarpio hasn't been able to put the finger on him, or he'd been rubbed out. Scarpio figgers that he's waitin' until Mathews is D.A., and can really offer protection, then he's goin' to come forward and do his stuff."

Dan's mind clicked. If that were true, Scarpio had reason enough to be afraid. The testimony of one witness who had seen him fire the fatal shot would put him in the electric chair.

Spats looked at his watch again.

"Ten to ten," he reported. "Time we was gettin' there. Turn right at this next corner."

There was a chain drug store on the corner, its window brightly lighted. Inside the window was a Western Union clock. Its hands pointed to eleven minutes to ten.

"Your ticker's slow," Dan said abruptly. "That clock in the window there says three minutes to ten."

"Huh?" Spats Parker swore and swung around in his seat to look at the clock before they were past it. In doing so, he lowered his guard for a fraction of a second.

It was time enough for Dan to act. His left hand flashed down and seized the gangster's wrist, turning the gun away from him. It belched into flame, and a bullet scorched across Dan's ribs and ricocheted from the steering post column. Dan's other hand fastened upon Spats Parker's neck in a strangling grip, pushing him forward and off the seat.

The gangster's fist jolted against Dan's jaw with crushing force. Stars floated before his eyes as his senses reeled, but he hung on with desperate strength. He could not twist the gun from Spats' hand, and he dared not release it.

The car swept on, driverless, while the struggle raged in the front seat. The wheels bounced over the low curbing, almost overturning the engine. And then it crashed, head-on, into a telephone pole.

Dan was flung violently against the steering wheel, the breath knocked from his lungs. And after that, until he succeeded in sucking air into his tortured lungs once again, he was almost unconscious.

His first thought was of Spats Parker. The gangster was slumped forward in his seat. His head lay upon his knees, resting against the dashboard.

Dan grasped his neck and pulled him upright. His head lolled lifelessly upon his shoulders. There was an ugly bruise upon his forehead, where it had struck against the windshield. He had not been cushioned against the shock, as Dan had been by the steering wheel.

He tried desperately to rouse him, to shake him into consciousness.

It was hopeless. Dan let the body slip from his hands, and it fell into the corner of the seat.

He racked his brain, trying to think of some way to save the lawyer. Four minutes to ten, his watch said. Seven minutes before the lawyer was to die. So short a time, and yet enough, had Spats only told him where Scarpio had taken Mathews.

He raged at himself for not having questioned the gangster further. And now it was too late; Spats Parker might be unconscious for hours, might not even live.

Suddenly he sucked in his breath noisily. An accident at three minutes after ten . . .

His mind leaped to Death's Corner. It was a railroad crossing in the factory district, midway between the business section and the outlying suburb in which Attorney Mathews lived. It had been so named because of the frequency of fatal accidents which had occurred there.

He recalled that a passenger train pulled out of the Union Depot at ten o'clock. And, at almost exactly three minutes after ten, it would pass Death's Corner!

In a flash he comprehended Scarpio's entire scheme. And it was fiendishly ingenious and simple.

The lawyer's car would be placed on the middle of the tracks at Death's Corner, as though it had stalled there on the way to the lawyer's home. Attorney Mathews and Dan would be placed in the front seat, unconscious. When the engine struck the car, they would be instantly killed. And there would be no reason for anyone to suspect that it had been other than an unfortunate accident.

• • •

Six minutes yet . . . still time enough to save the lawyer, if he could get there. But no time to call for help.

His heart racing madly, Dan started the car. It had stalled at the moment of the crash, but luckily it had not been seriously damaged, beyond a broken front bumper and a leaking radiator. He backed it away from the telephone pole and headed down the street at full speed, ignoring the people who had already begun to gather there.

Death's Corner was scarcely a quarter of a mile distant. In the heart of the dimly lighted factory district, it was quite deserted this late at night. Dan passed only a single watchman as the car sped its jolting course over the pitted brick pavements, past the dark, silent buildings.

Then, in the distance, he saw a blinking red light—the automatic warning signal which hung over Death's Corner. It swung back and forth like a pendulum, in accompaniment to a jangling bell.

And beneath it, squarely upon the tracks, was the dark bulk of a car.

Dan stamped the accelerator to the floor boards. He heard the eerie shriek of the train whistle, twice repeated, as the locomotive picked up speed on leaving the station.

Death's Corner would not have reaped its grim harvest had the railroad tracks cut straight through the city. But they curved along the river bank, then turned sharply at Death's Corner. Vision of the tracks on both sides was blocked by the towering factories. A driver of a car approaching the crossing could see the warning signal, but no train.

The car shot by a figure waving its arms. Scarpio. Dan caught a glimpse of his open mouth, screaming a warning. Evidently he thought that Spats Parker was driving, arriving there too late.

Then he slammed on the brakes. The tires shrieked protest as they skidded and jolted to a standstill. The car came to a stop only a few feet from the tracks.

With a single motion, Dan leaped out, Spats' automatic in his hand. Behind him, Scarpio was running toward him, shouting; but he paid no attention to him.

The train's whistle split the night again. The roar of its approach echoed thunderously through the factories.

"Spats! You damn fool! It's too late!" Scarpio was yelling.

Dan plunged madly toward the lawyer's car. It was dark—and then suddenly it was illuminated with a blinding brilliance. Around the curve swept the great single eye of the locomotive, lighting the track before it like a flaming white sun.

A shot snarled past Dan's shoulder. Scarpio had discovered his mistake, and was shooting at him grimly. All thought of the "accident" was gone; the gambler wanted only to make certain that the both of them were dead, and then flee from the scene before his identity was discovered.

As Dan reached the car, the engineer saw the danger. The brakes set with a crash, but they were powerless to stop the onrush of the steel monster. Steel slid upon steel, and a stream of white fire danced from the track.

Dan wrenched open the car door. The lawyer was slumped lifelessly over the steering wheel. He did not move when Dan pulled him from the car, but slipped to the tracks and lay there motionless. Dan seized him under the arms and dragged him away . . . not a second too soon.

A huge shape shot past him. A blast of air struck him that all but whirled him from his feet.

Then a rending, tearing crash. The locomotive caught the car, smashed it to bits, and scattered the pieces on both sides of the track.

Another bullet fanned Dan's cheek. Scarpio was still shooting at him. His swarthy face was contorted with rage.

Dan snapped back a shot. Scarpio emptied his gun in a mad burst, then turned and began to run. Dan felt too weak from the reaction of saving the lawyer to follow. He dropped to one knee and took careful aim before he pulled the trigger.

His shot struck where he intended. Scarpio stumbled and rolled upon the pavement, his knee cap shattered.

Dan had just finished handcuffing the gambler when the lawyer staggered up to them.

"So you—got here, boy," he said. "I knew what was happening—but couldn't seem to help myself."

"They nearly got me, too," Dan admitted. "But Scarpio won't be causing any more trouble."

"No—I think not." Mathews regarded the prostrate man with grave satisfaction. "He'll be spending the next few years in prison for this night's piece of work."

"He's lucky if that's all he gets, Mr. Mathews," Dan grinned. "Because Spats Parker obligingly explained to me that there was a witness to the Shendahl killing."

"A—a witness?"

"Yeah. One of Shendahl's croupiers. And he's anxious to testify, if he can be guaranteed protection. And so I think we can schedule Scarpio for the next session of the electric chair."

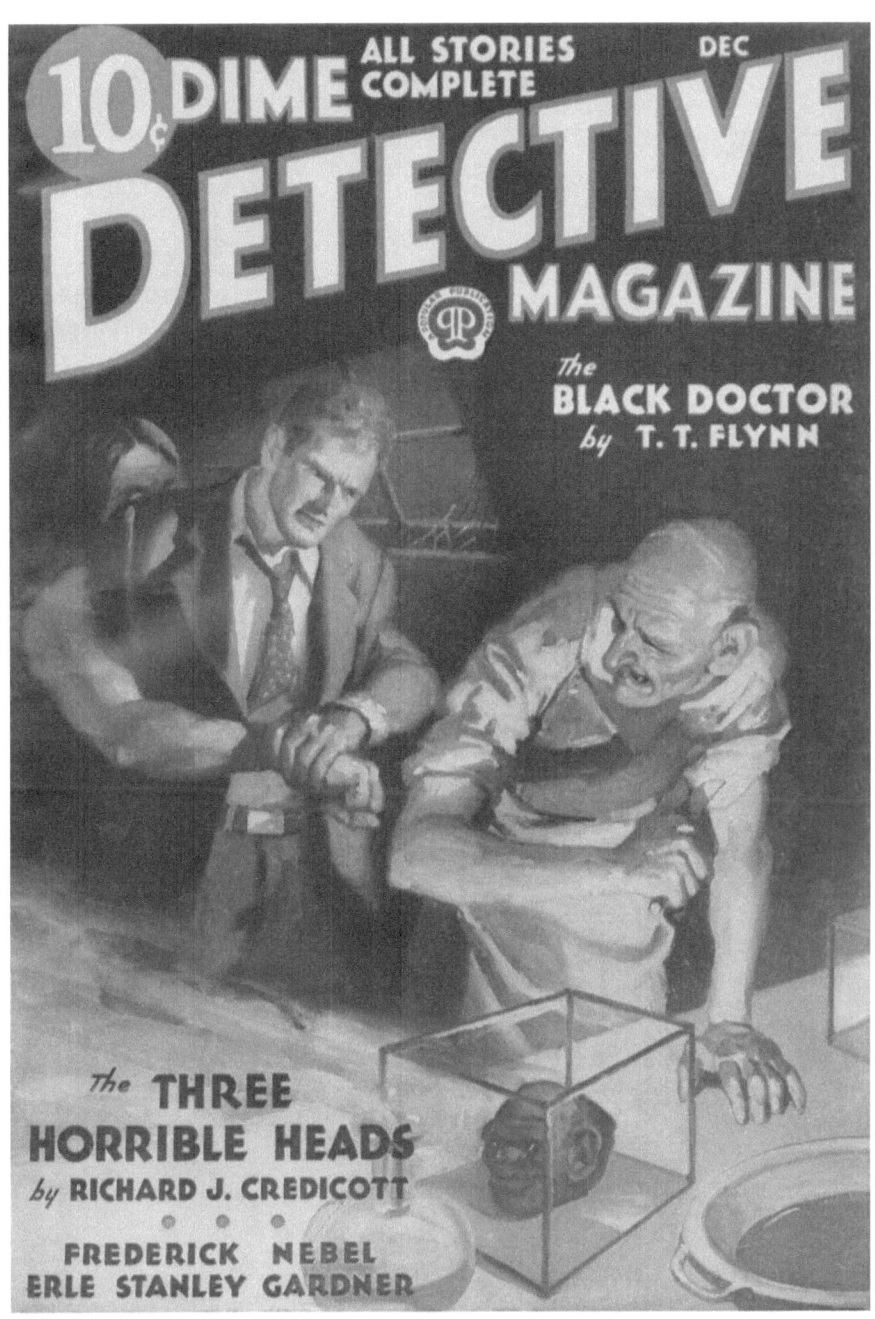

Cover painting by William Reusswig

The doctor dropped to one knee beside the dead man.

THE THREE HORRIBLE HEADS

There they lay—each in its own glass case—three horribly shriveled leering human heads. And Fletcher recognized the faces, even in their mummied state. Knew it was only a matter of moments before his own would make a fourth in the grisly collection.

I
DEATH STRIKES TWICE

IT WAS FIFTEEN MINUTES TO SEVEN in the morning when Kokura, James Van Styne's diminutive Philippino servant, discovered that the lock on the apartment door had been broken from the outside.

He gazed wide-eyed at the damage, then trotted to the door of his master's bedroom and rapped sharply. When he received no reply to repeated knocks, he opened the door and put his head inside.

The next instant he was running hysterically down the corridor, screaming so loudly that the house detective, roused by a telephone call from a tenant, lost no time in getting there.

"Dead, sair!" gasped Kokura. "All blood, sair—blood everywhere! And his head—"

The house detective hastily silenced the terrified boy and dragged him back to the apartment. He took a single look into Van Styne's bedroom and promptly notified the management, who in turn called the police.

The police investigation began slowly and rapidly gathered momentum. Two precinct detectives arrived within fifteen minutes. Ten minutes later came the usual swarm of men from detective headquarters—plainclothes officers, fingerprint experts, photographers, followed shortly by Dr. Durand, medical examiner, and Inspector Thomas Sullivan.

And at exactly seven-thirty in the morning the prolonged ringing of his bedstand telephone roused Anthony Fletcher from sleep.

"This is Sullivan," came the voice over the wire. "Sorry to get you up so early, but a murder case has just broken and we need you."

Fletcher swore under his breath. "Look here," he pleaded sleepily, "won't this keep for a few hours? I was up all night, working on the Jellico case for the commissioner. Just got to bed two hours ago—"

"This case won't keep," said Sullivan. "It's hot—red hot. James Van Styne, the big Wall Street broker and millionaire, was murdered last night. We found him in bed, his head cut clean off."

Fletcher sat up and began to pay attention.

"And," went on the police inspector, his voice rising, "the head's gone! We can't find it!"

"So," said Fletcher. He lit a cigarette and blew a cloud of smoke at the ceiling. "It sounds interesting, Sullivan. I knew Van Styne. He lives at the Lusonia, doesn't he? I'll be right over."

Anthony Fletcher was a physician by training, specializing in psychology and pathology. He was head of the department of criminology at the university and the author of a number of well-known books on the subject. He held a commission in the police department, lectured at the police academy, and was frequently called upon for help when some crime baffled the central-office detectives.

He was of medium height and built with crisply black hair. His eyes were gray and piercing. He would have been called handsome had his forehead not been so high.

It was Fletcher's contention that all crimes could be solved. He utilized all the resources of modern science. But more than that, he utilized that mysterious new science, psychology, to untangle trails not open to the test-tube and microscope. He believed that the skilled psychologist should map out the campaign for the solution of a crime, just as an architect makes the plans for a building which others will construct.

A taxi bore him to the Lusonia. It was one of the older apartment hotels, just off the Avenue, of faded magnificence, famed for its quiet exclusiveness. It was patronized by those who value spaciousness above modern cramped smartness.

A uniformed officer met him at the door, saluted, and took him up in the elevator to Van Styne's apartment on the third floor. The detectives had been shunted into the corridor in expectation of his arrival, and Sullivan and Dr. Durand had the place to themselves.

"I haven't disturbed the body," said Dr. Durand. He was a stolid and energetic little man, very competent, and delighted to work with Fletcher. "I knew you'd want to see it just as we found it."

Fletcher nodded briefly and accompanied them into the bedroom. It was large and gloomily furnished with heavy oak furniture and thick rugs. Drapes had been drawn from the high windows and the morning sunlight streamed across the bed.

It revealed a gruesome sight. A man—or what was left of a man—lay in a pool of clotted blood. He was short and fat, with round protuberant stomach, clothed in brilliant scarlet pajamas.

And the gory pillow, where his head should have been, was ghastly—for upon it lay only the short stump of a neck.

"Done while he was asleep," said Dr. Durand in his precise fashion. "The head was cut off with a single blow. No other wounds that I can find. If you look closely you can see where the knife slashed down through the pillow. The man who did it must have been abnormally strong."

"Or have used a weapon suited to such purposes," said Fletcher. "A machete, for instance; or perhaps a scimitar or bolo. Have you determined the time of death?"

"Around two o'clock in the morning, I should say."

"There's no trace of the head?"

"It's gone," answered Sullivan, shuddering as he turned his eyes from the corpse. He was a big, sandy-haired Irishman, and an excellent officer. "We've searched this apartment from top to bottom, and it isn't here. Not a trace of it! What do you make of that?"

"Nothing, just yet," said Fletcher dryly.

He completed an examination of the room and asked how the murderer had gained entrance. Sullivan showed him the broken lock on the door.

"Looks to have been done with a jimmy," he said. "How the murderer got in—unless he lives in the hotel—I don't know. But they've got a rotten system here; anybody can walk in or out, and they don't check up on 'em. We haven't been able to find anybody that saw anyone suspicious. Want to see Van Styne's servant?"

Kokura had recovered from his hysteria, though his eyes were red. Somewhat reassured by Fletcher's friendly attitude, he answered his questions willingly.

"Meestair Van Styne come home mebbe ten las' night," he said. "He had small package. Take it into libr'y and read til mebbe twelve, then go to bed. And this morning—"

"A package?" growled Sullivan. "You didn't say anything about that before."

"Your policemens shout and I did not remember, sair," replied the boy gravely.

Sullivan reddened. Fletcher, having witnessed Sullivan's men questioning suspects before this, smiled and suggested that they take a look at the library.

It proved to be more of a trophy room than library. The walls were hung with the heads of animals. On racks and in cases were primitive bows and arrows, clubs, swords, and more modern hunting rifles. Over the fireplace was a huge anaconda head, mounted with gaping jaws.

"Your master was a big-game hunter?" asked Fletcher.

"Yes, sair," said Kokura proudly. "He hunt in Africa, South America. I go with him, help him."

Fletcher's gaze swept about the room, photographing every object and storing it away in his memory. It was his theory that the psychologist, by studying the environment with which a man surrounded himself, could pierce through to the very mainsprings of his character.

His attention was suddenly arrested by a strange group of objects on the mantel. There were half a dozen of them, little doll-like heads no bigger than a large orange. Their faces were grimacing, distorted, hideous; grotesque travesties on the human features. Had it not been for their long, tangled, black hair they might have been taken for the stuffed heads of monkeys.

He balanced one of them on the palm of his hand. He knew it to be a human head, such as is preserved by the little-known Jivaro Indian tribes on the upper reaches of the Amazon.

"Meestair Van Styne buy those on river, in South America," Kokura volunteered. "They real heads, shrunk like raisin."

As Fletcher replaced it on the mantel, Sullivan gave an exclamation. His hand came out of a wastebasket with a small cardboard box and a wadding of paper. He unfolded the paper and smoothed it out on a desk. On it was pasted a small red cartouche, resembling an imperial seal in design.

"That package he had," announced Kokura.

"So," grunted Sullivan. "And now what the devil was in it? Couldn't have been very big; not more than four or five inches square. And that's a funny-looking seal."

"It's a Russian coat of arms," said Fletcher. "I've seen it before. Prince Alexis uses it. He claims to be of the Russian nobility, though the Russian royalists will have nothing to do with him. He has a sort of showroom and art gallery on Fifth Avenue and deals in modern painting and sculpture, most of it worthless. He's made himself the center of the modernistic art world in New York, and more than a few wealthy old ladies consider him the last word in such things."

"Prince Alexis!" exclaimed Kokura, with an expression of distaste.

"You know him?" queried Sullivan.

"Oh, yes, sair. He go to South America with Meestair Van Styne."

"That sounds promising, Fletcher," said Sullivan. "I think this package and what was in it will bear looking into. It might have been something valuable, something the murderer wanted—"

He broke off as the desk phone rang. It was a call for him. When he hung up his square face was flushed with excitement.

"That was the commissioner. There's been another of these murders. Man found with his head cut off, no sign of the head. And that man was a watchman in this Prince Alexis' art gallery!"

II

THE JIVARO HEAD

PRINCE ALEXIS' ESTABLISHMENT was a modernistic structure of granite, three stories in height. To the right of the show window was a tall portal of burnished metal. The thick glass of the door bore in small aluminum letters the simple inscription *alexis*.

Sullivan seized Fletcher's arm as they were about to enter. "My God, look at that!" he cried. "More of those crazy heads."

The window presented a strange exhibit for a private art gallery. Ranged in a semicircle were a dozen shrunken Jivaro heads. Concealed lighting made them stand out starkly against the black velvet background, emphasizing their weird ugliness.

In the center of the exhibit was a figure which at first glance appeared to be a Negro dwarf. It was scarcely thirty inches in height, naked except for a loin cloth. It was the shrunken body of a full-grown man, preserved with consummate art. It gave the disquieting impression of a twisted, misshapen gnome emerged from the bowels of the earth. Its little pinched face, its broad flat nostrils, its leering slit of a mouth, were like nothing human, or rather something subhuman created by the gods in a malevolent mood.

"Is—is it real?'" asked Sullivan hoarsely.

"It's real enough," said Fletcher. "It's uncommon to find the entire body shrunken, though there are several specimens in one of the museums here."

"Ugh! It gives me the creeps."

They entered and found a group of clerks and policemen. The clerk who had found the watchman's body was still white and shaken from the experience.

"Bensen, the night watchman, should have been here to open up for me this morning," he said. "I had to use my own key and, when he didn't appear, I became worried and started a search. And I found him—on the third floor, horribly mutilated—" He stopped and licked his lips.

"Is this Prince Alexis here?" demanded Sullivan.

"No, sir. But we've telephoned him and he should arrive any minute."

The clerk took them to the third floor in the elevator. It opened into a long corridor, thickly carpeted, and decorated with odd bits of sculpture.

In the center, near closed double doors, two detectives stood by a dark huddle on the floor. Dr. Durand commenced his routine examination briskly, rattling off his findings as if dictating a letter.

"This man was killed in exactly the same manner as Van Styne. His head was cut off with a single blow by some sharp instrument. Probably he was lying in this very position when it was done. At least, the slash in the rug beneath the neck tends to prove that. No other marks upon the body. I should say, purely as a guess, that he was struck on the head and knocked unconscious before the decapitation; though, since the head is gone, we can't verify that."

"And the time of death?" asked Fletcher.

"Around one o'clock. Possibly a bit later."

"That is, before Van Styne was murdered?"

"Unquestionably."

"You think the same man did it?" asked Sullivan.

"It begins to look like it," said Fletcher, and turned to the detectives. "Did you search for the head?"

"Not us," one of them answered. "We looked around a little but didn't find it. When we phoned into headquarters, we got orders to hold everything for you. But"—and he pointed dramatically at the double doors—"if you want to see something, take a look in there!"

The clerk who had brought them up coughed discreetly. "It contains the collection of Dr. Hartzell," he said. "Perhaps you noticed the specimens in the window as you entered."

"Dr. Franz Hartzell?" asked Fletcher. "The authority on head hunting?"

"The same, sir. He and Prince Alexis are close friends. When Dr. Hartzell returned from South America last week, the prince suggested that he might use this gallery for an exhibition."

"I've read Dr. Hartzell's book *Head Hunters of the Ages*," said Fletcher. "He's the one authority on that branch of anthropology. Let's take a look at this collection, Sullivan."

Followed by Dr. Durand, they entered the door at which the detective had pointed. The gallery was long and narrow, paralleling the corridor. It was without windows, roofed with skylights which tempered the brilliancy of the morning sunlight to a soft glow.

A row of tables ranged the walls. Upon them was perhaps as weird and ghastly a collection as had ever been assembled. It was composed entirely of heads and skulls, hundreds of them, gathered from every corner of the world, wherever the grizzly practice of head hunting has been known.

There were Dyak heads from Borneo, staring at them with their unnaturally distended eyes of whitened wood. Bamboo poles from Assam, topped with bleached white skulls. Heads taken in the Balkan Wars of 1912-13, with the long locks of hair by which they were carried. Skull racks from New Guinea. Heads from the Amazon, Nigeria, Fakiristan, the Philippines, Formosa, Malaya, Indo-China. And another complete shrunken figure similar to the one which had been in the window.

"Good Lord!" blurted Sullivan. "Why would any sane man want to collect these things?"

"Scientific investigation," said Fletcher. "It is impossible to understand the men of other ages, or even many of the primitive races of today, without an understanding of head hunting. It is practiced, even today, in many parts of the world, and goes back to Paleolithic times, thousands of years ago. The general theory is that the soul of man resides in the head, and that the taker of a head brings to himself, and thus to his family and tribe, the strength and virtues and fertility of the man slain—"

"Stop it," groaned Sullivan. "I don't want to hear it. It's got my head swimming."

Fletcher's gray eyes were bright with interest and he would not be stopped.

"Yes, there must be some sort of connection," he said. "Here we have three men—Van Styne, Dr. Hartzell and Prince Alexis—all interested in the same dark subject. Van Styne was murdered and his head taken. The watchman taking care of Dr. Hartzell's collection met the same fate. Surely a remarkable set of circumstances to explain away as coincidence!

"The common interest of these three men in head hunting must have some sort of bearing upon these crimes. With that as our starting point, we must find the focusing point, the nexus of this strange chain of events."

At that moment a detective announced that Prince Alexis and Dr. Hartzell were waiting for them downstairs. Sullivan, visibly relieved that the investigation was taking a concrete turn, ordered them sent up.

"You talk to 'em, though," he told Fletcher. "You know what you're talking about—and I don't. Anyway, the commissioner put you in charge of this."

Prince Alexis was a distinguished figure in impeccable morning dress, set off by a glittering gold decoration on his breast. His body was tall and powerful, though he walked with a slight limp.

Looking at his thin aristocratic features and his dark beard and mustache cut in the fashion of the last Romanoff czar, Fletcher told himself that here was a man to reckon with. The blood of Cossacks or the boyars ran through his veins. He was accustomed to command, to exact obedience, to bend people to his will—particularly women, if the stories of him were true. He wore an air of hauteur and arrogance that antagonized Fletcher.

"So," he said tonelessly, looking down at the body; and shrugged and turned away.

Dr. Franz Hartzell, however, dropped on one knee beside the dead man. He remained immobile for a moment, then rose slowly to his feet.

Once he had been tall and large-framed. But advancing age, or perhaps some tropical disease, had crooked his spine and dried the flesh from his body. The skin of his face was like wrinkled parchment stretched over a bony framework. His high domed head was bald except for a tonsure of straggling white hair.

"You found him—like this?" he asked, gesturing toward the dead man without looking up.

"We did," said Fletcher, and introduced himself, mentioning that he had read the scientist's book.

Dr. Hartzell seemed scarcely to have heard him, so deeply was he immersed in thought. "Very strange," he muttered, half to himself. And then, becoming conscious of the eyes watching him, he glanced up.

Fletcher got a shock when he saw the scientist's eyes. He had seen such eyes before, in men whose brilliant intelligences had carried them to the brink of insanity. They were set deep in cavernous sockets, their dark fire almost hidden by lowered lids. For a moment he thought he detected a strange expression in them, one of terror or fear, but it vanished instantly and he could not be sure.

"Prince Alexis phoned me of this—this terrible thing," the scientist explained. "He thought that, under the circumstances, I should know of it."

"I'm glad you came," said Fletcher. "I may have a few questions to ask you later.

Fletcher was convinced that Dr. Hartzell knew something, or had some well-founded suspicion, but that could wait. He turned upon Prince Alexis, who stood leaning upon his cane, wrapped in uncompromising silence.

"I am hopeful that you can help us," he said. "You knew this watchman and his duties. Can you suggest any motive for his murder?"

"It is utterly incomprehensible to me," replied the prince coldly.

"You have things of value here? Anything that might attract the attention of thieves?"

"That is true. Much of the statuary and paintings are priceless. But my clerks inform me that nothing has been taken. They did not, of course, check Dr. Hartzell's exhibition."

"I think it would be worth while to do so," said Fletcher. "Dr. Hartzell, would you mind checking over your specimens and telling us whether any is missing. This crime is so lacking in clues that we can't afford to pass up anything."

The scientist agreed and entered the gallery. He walked the length of it and stopped suddenly before a table. "They're gone!" he cried hollowly. "Four of my heads have disappeared."

"Heads?" queried Sullivan.

"Shrunken Jivaro heads," explained Dr. Hartzell, and he gave the description of them which Sullivan asked. "Though why they should be taken," he added, "I cannot imagine. They have no great value, save from a collector's standpoint."

"Nor from any other standpoint?" asked Fletcher, eyeing the scientist closely.

Dr. Hartzell stared at him queerly. "I don't grasp your meaning," he said.

"No matter," replied Fletcher carelessly. "You will, perhaps, a bit later. Did you know James Van Styne?"

"Slightly."

"And you, Prince Alexis?"

The Russian nodded.

"You traveled with him in South America?"

Prince Alexis stared hard at Fletcher. His eyes grew cold and his cane tapped softly on the floor. "You seem to have been investigating me," he said dryly. "Yes, Van Styne and I were in South America together. We are both members of the Tropical Explorers' Club. May I inquire why you ask?"

"I ask," said Fletcher, "because Van Styne was also found dead. He had been murdered. His head was cut from his shoulders and is gone."

The two men reacted to this startling information in different ways. Prince Alexis dropped his cane and stooped to recover it. If his face showed confusion, it was composed when he straightened to face them. Dr. Hartzell caught his breath in an audible gasp; then his mouth shut like a steel trap and his eyelids veiled his eyes.

Fletcher went on to give them the salient details.

"It is impossible to believe," he concluded, "that these two crimes are not the work of the same hand. In both, the method of murder was the same. But the link that binds them together is stronger than that."

He paused a moment. Prince Alexis, his bearded face inscrutable, lit a monogrammed cigarette and Dr. Hartzell rubbed his chin with a skinny hand.

"Van Styne's servant informs us," continued Fletcher, "that his master returned about ten o'clock last night. He carried a small package. That package bore your seal, Prince Alexis. We found the package, empty, in the wastebasket. Whatever it contained apparently has vanished."

"And I am to explain," sneered the Russian, with unaccountable hostility. "Luckily for me it is very simple. Van Styne was, as I am, interested in head hunting. At his suggestion I brought him here last night to show him Dr. Hartzell's collection. He expressed a desire to purchase one of the specimens and, as Dr. Hartzell had given me certain of them to offer for sale, I sold him one. I personally wrapped it in a package and gave it to him."

"And that specimen?"

Prince Alexis smiled icily. "It was a shrunken Jivaro head. Not an Indian's, but a Negro's."

Fletcher nodded to himself. It was as he had expected. It made the mystery more puzzling, because the shrunken heads in Van Styne's library had all been those of Indians.

The murderer had taken the heads which Van Styne had brought home with him.

III

THE THIEF THAT LIMPED

WITH THIS DISCLOSURE THE INVESTIGATION RAN UP AGAINST A BLANK WALL. They had charted the appalling course of the murderer, but had not the slightest clue to his identity.

As for the motive—

"It's insane," declared Sullivan, when they discussed it later in the day. "It's the work of a madman. This murderer is a head hunter himself. So far he's taken seven heads—two live and five dead ones. He may not stop there. And what does he want 'em for?"

Fletcher could not answer this question, nor many others which he put to himself. Bizarre conjectures presented themselves to his mind. Heads were occasionally used in magical rites. Could this be the work of followers of some new *voodoo* or *obeah*?

The explanation, while ingenious, was too fanciful to satisfy him. And it did not fit the facts.

The watchman's murder could be dismissed from consideration. The murderer had patently come to Prince Alexis' gallery for the shrunken Jivaro heads. Since no locks had been tampered with, Bensen must have admitted him. This did not mean necessarily that the watchman knew or recognized the murderer. He might have been forced to unlock the door by the menace of a weapon through the glass, which would not stop a bullet. It seemed reasonable to suppose that the watchman had been killed to prevent a later identification, and not for any personal motive. The cutting off of his head might have been incidental, or the result of a mad lust for heads.

As for Van Styne's murder, that was more difficult to explain. Had the murderer particularly wanted the shrunken Negro head? If so, how had he learned that the broker had purchased it that very evening? There was the possibility, of course, that the watchman, who had known of the transaction, had told him. But why, having once gained entrance to the apartment and found the Negro head, had he taken Van Styne's life?

Fletcher was convinced that Prince Alexis and Dr. Hartzell knew more than they had told, or had well-grounded suspicions. Several hours questioning, however, failed to glean any additional information from them. The Russian preserved his attitude of hostility and said nothing; and while the scientist was persuaded to talk at length on the theory and practice of head hunting, he also said nothing.

The utter mystery of the two crimes both baffled and challenged Fletcher. This was a type of murder so different from the ordinary run that routine police methods did not suffice to deal with it. It fascinated him, absorbed his time to the exclusion of everything else.

As was to be expected, the newspapers greeted the murders with whoops of joy. Nothing so spectacular or fraught with morbid drama had occurred in months, and they made the most of the "Head Hunter," as they quickly termed the unknown murderer.

They developed many theories, only two of which merited any attention.

The first was the theory which Fletcher had considered and discarded. That the murders and the thefts were the work of a cult of voodooists, perhaps of Haitian origin. They required the heads for their worship of Damballa, the fearsome snake god, to propitiate his fury.

The second theory was equally sensational. It supposed that Jivaro Indians had come to New York to recover the heads of relatives and friends treacherously slain from ambush. The two murders had been revenge for the possession of the heads.

The Gallery Alexis became suddenly popular, and crowds thronged it throughout the day. Prince Alexis cannily took advantage of this and charged admission. Enormous prices were offered for specimens from the collection. The publishers of Dr. Hartzell's book found it necessary to rush a new edition through the presses.

As for Dr. Hartzell, he appeared first bewildered, then pleased with the publicity he received as the one authority upon the subject of head hunting. He wrote articles for the newspapers, most of them couched in language too technical for laymen, and delivered several lectures.

The always morbid imagination of the public had gone mad.

• • •

On the third night the Head Hunter struck again.

It was not until the next noon that a stevedore discovered the headless body hidden behind the piles of an ancient wharf. The dead man was never positively identified, though he was thought to be a homeless tramp who had drifted into the city.

The police, quite unable to connect this logically with the other murders, tried to pass it off as an unrelated crime. The newspapers would not have it, and gradually came to agreement upon one theory.

These murders were the work of a high priest, a *papaloi*, of a cult of voodooists. He required the freshly killed head of a man—the "goat without horns"—for his terrible and unspeakable ceremonies. He had struck three times, and could be expected to strike again and again, until the police ran him to earth and put a halt to his satanic activities.

Their prophesy seemed to be justified, for the headless death struck twice the following night.

The first victim was found in an alleyway in the early hours of the morning. The man was a clerk in a drugstore, and had evidently been on his way home, after working late, when the killer leaped upon him and dragged him into the alleyway.

The second victim was discovered, several hours later, by a policeman making his first morning round through Central Park. The body was almost hidden under a clump of bushes, and it was not until he had dragged it out that he saw it was headless.

Papers in the pockets identified the man as Charles L. Greenwald, senior partner of the law firm of Greenwald, Roberts and Harrison. He had left his home at eleven the preceding night for a short walk through the park, as was often his custom. From the state of *rigor mortis* which had set in, it was established that he had been slain at about midnight, perhaps a half hour before the clerk had been attacked.

Greenwald's murder brought a development which at first promised to bear fruit. It was rumored that the lawyer had been associated with Van Styne in certain financial transactions, not strictly within the letter of the law. But so secret had these been that not even Greenwald's partners knew their nature, nor were there any papers bearing upon them remaining.

"It's becoming more and more hopeless," Sullivan told Fletcher wearily. "I'm almost ready to believe this voodoo theory, crazy as it is. At least it offers something to work on."

"It's not entirely beyond the realm of reason," admitted Fletcher. "There are powerful voodoo cults in Harlem, even in the heart of New York. It's rather the fashion now, though I think few would go to such lengths."

His face was thinner and his eyes bespoke lack of sleep. For more than a week he had been driving himself relentlessly. The call of mystery and adventure and danger was in his blood, and until he had solved these crimes and seen the murderers taken into custody he could not rest.

Sullivan suddenly leaned forward and pointed his cigar at Fletcher. "Look here," he said, "why don't you have another try at this Prince Alexis and Dr. Hartzell? You've admitted you think they're hiding something, or at least know more than they've told. And I'm convinced of it, though I can't get anything out of 'em. Damn it, when I talk to 'em, they just sneer at me in their superior way!"

His square face crimsoned and his eyes glittered.

"You know what I think?" he continued. "They've guessed who this—this Head Hunter is, because he's somebody they know and who is interested in head hunting. And they're afraid—afraid that if they talk he'll get them!"

"It's possible." Fletcher glanced at the wall clock then reached for his hat and gloves. "I've got an appointment with Dr. Hartzell at eight o'clock, and it's nearly that now. Prince Alexis is out of town, but I hope to reach him in the morning. If anything develops, let me know."

He gave himself over to serious thought as a taxicab bore him up the crowded, noisy lane of Fifth Avenue. During the afternoon several theories had begun to crystallize out of his subconscious mind. He had a hunch that one of them would prove the right one.

Dr. Hartzell's home was in the Fifties, not far off the Avenue. It was a narrow stone structure with a bleak, gloomy exterior. Its heavily curtained windows showed no lights.

He had scarcely touched his finger to the bell when the door swung open. A voice with a foreign accent roughly bade him enter. Fletcher glanced sharply at the man, saw a short stocky figure, straight black hair, a reddish complexion. He judged him to be an Indian, probably of South American extraction.

Without another word he was shown into a long narrow room, illuminated by a single desk lamp at one end. It had a musty, ancient odor. The walls were lined with bookshelves and glass cases. In the deep shadows he caught sight of tom-toms, barbaric costumes, unfamiliar weapons, savage idols.

Dr. Hartzell was hunched behind the desk. The light from the lamp streamed upon his high domed head, his pointed nose, his bony chin. He pushed away the books in front of him and greeted Fletcher without rising, motioning him to a chair.

Fletcher lit a cigarette and inquired whether the scientist had heard of the two murders discovered that morning. Upon learning that he had not, he outlined them.

"Incredible!" murmured Dr. Hartzell. "It is unbelievable that such things can happen in a modern city. If this were one of the outposts of civilization, one might— But you have not told me your errand."

Fletcher crushed out his cigarette and drew his chair closer to the desk. "I want your help, Dr. Hartzell," he said.

"My help! How could I help you?"

"By being frank with me. Whenever I have talked with you, you have had an air of holding something back. Prince Alexis has had somewhat the same attitude. What you know or suspect may not seem of any importance to you, but these murders have become so serious that we can't afford to pass up any clue, however unpromising it may appear."

Dr. Hartzell cupped his chin in his long fingers. For seconds before he spoke he stared into the shadows.

"Of course I cannot speak for Prince Alexis," he said at length. "Of late he has been distant toward me and we have scarcely exchanged two words, so I don't know what theory he holds. But I did notice something peculiar, something that puzzled me. Yet it seemed so silly, so utterly preposterous that it could have any bearing upon these murders, that I did not mention it.

"Briefly, it is this: I brought back with me from Ecuador six shrunken heads which I had secured from a certain tribe of Jivaros. I had reason to believe that those heads had been taken in a raid but a week before I got there, but that did not concern me.

"Four of those heads I put on exhibition at the Gallery Alexis. It was those four which were stolen. A fifth was among those I gave to Prince Alexis for sale. It was the Negro's head which he sold to Van Styne. Interpret that as you wish. I think it only a coincidence—though a rather remarkable one."

Fletcher was disappointed, though interested. He remembered the newspaper theory of vengeful Jivaro Indians coming to New York to recover the heads of slaughtered relatives. He mentioned it to Dr. Hartzell.

"Sensational nonsense!" snapped the scientist. "Jivaros try to retaliate against their enemies, but it is impossible to imagine such ignorant, poverty-stricken savages finding their way to New York—"

"That accounts for five of the heads," said Fletcher. "What became of the sixth?"

"I have it here. Care to see it?"

Fletcher nodded and Dr. Hartzell disappeared into the hall. He was gone for some minutes and Fletcher fell into a reverie. This development was unexpected, but it did not conflict with the theories he had formed. Rather, it lent additional color to one of them.

He was roused suddenly by a loud shriek. It was the despairing cry of a man in mortal terror.

It took Fletcher but an instant to slip out his automatic, gain the hall. There he paused, uncertain from which direction the cry had come. The darkness of the hall, his unfamiliarity with the house, confused him.

Then the cry was repeated and he saw that it came from a door at the rear which showed a ribbon of light at its base. He heard the crash of bodies and muffled oaths.

Shouting, he ran the length of the hall and flung open the door. It gave into a small room, brightly lighted. Against the wall was a stack of small cases, some of them open.

Dr. Hartzell lay on the floor, twitching convulsively. A thin ribbon of red ran from a gash in his forehead.

And close by his head was a heavy, broad-bladed knife, of the type known as machetes in tropical America. Its point was embedded deeply in the flooring, so that it stood out at an angle from the floor.

"He went—out the window!" gasped the scientist.

Fletcher saw at a glance that Dr. Hartzell was not severely injured. It was more important now to capture his assailant than to stanch his wound. He leaped to the open window at the rear and scrambled through it, fell cat-footed to brick pavement below. It took a moment for his eyes to accommodate themselves to the darkness; then he saw that he was in an alleyway.

At the same instant he heard feet and saw a shadowy figure shuffling away. It broke into a hobbling run, as though one leg were crippled. He caught sight of a face turned toward him, the features almost hidden behind a thick black beard and the downturned brim of a hat.

He shouted a warning to the man and ran toward him. But when he reached the spot at which he had seen him he was gone, swallowed up in the darkness. There were a dozen hiding places and, without a flashlight, he was almost helpless.

After five minutes' futile search Fletcher returned to Dr. Hartzell's home. The scientist was sitting up on the floor, wincing a little as his Indian servant wound a bandage about his head.

"He got away from me," Fletcher said briefly. "What happened?"

"I—I scarcely know," answered the scientist. "I heard the window go up and started to turn around. Then something hit me on the head and I fell down. I saw a man standing over me. He swung a machete at my neck, but I squirmed aside and it struck the floor. I got to my feet again and tried to fight, but he knocked me down again. Then I heard you shouting and the man disappeared through the window."

"Did you recognize him?"

"No. But he must have been this fiend the papers call the—the Head Hunter! He had a black beard. And I think—he walked with a limp."

A picture of Prince Alexis flashed across Fletcher's mind. The Russian was black-bearded and had a limp. But it was hard to reconcile the impeccable proprietor of the art gallery with the skulking figure he had lost in the alley.

And yet Dr. Hartzell had hinted at strained relations with Alexis—

Fletcher examined the machete, hoping to find a trace of fingerprints. The wooden handle bore none and the blade was brightly polished.

"By the way," he asked, "did you find the sixth head you were going to show me?"

"I had it in my hand when I was attacked," said Dr. Hartzell. "I must have dropped it." He looked about the floor and his eyes slowly widened with horror. "Why—why it's gone!"

IV

THE SHRUNKEN MAN

IT WAS AN HOUR PAST MIDNIGHT. There was no moon, no stars, and a thick fog upon Fifth Avenue set each street light apart from its fellows, leaving a pool of darkness between them.

A man detached himself from the shadows, moving stealthily across the face of the buildings. He was clothed in black and had a hat pulled down over his eyes so that his face was invisible.

When he reached the show window of the Gallery Alexis, he paused a moment to peer through the glass. The lights had been turned off several hours before and its grisly exhibit was only a shadowy blur.

The man raised his arm. Clasped in his fist was an object the size of a paving brick. He brought it down once, twice, three times against the plate glass, and it broke with a loud report, sprinkling fragments of glass about him.

At the same instant, touched off by hidden wires, an alarm bell overhead set up a raucous clamor. The man glanced up, startled; then quickly thrust his arm through the large aperture he had made. He brought it out with a bulky object and began to run down the street with a hobbling gait.

Before he reached the corner a whistle shrilled. Above the clangor of the alarm echoed the pounding feet of a patrolman. The man tried to increase his speed, but stumbled and fell. The object he had taken from the window whirled from his hands and rolled into the gutter.

There was no time to recover it, for the patrolman had burst out of the fog and was swooping down on him. The man scrambled to his feet and ran, dodging down a side street, where the mist curled about his figure and hid him from pursuit.

When the squad cars arrived, the patrolman was relieved of his duty and sent to detective headquarters. Inspector Sullivan and Anthony Fletcher had only that minute returned from Dr. Hartzell's home. Their investigation had been thorough but without profit. The bearded man seen by Fletcher had left no fingerprints, no clues, nothing by which he might be identified.

They listened to the story of the policeman, then inspected the object which the window breaker had dropped.

It was the shrunken figure of the human body which had been the central exhibit in the window of the Gallery Alexis. Beneath the glaring droplight in Sullivan's office it seemed even more hideous and repulsive. Its broad lips leered at them with gnomish mockery, as though daring them to probe its secret.

"Good Lord!" Sullivan cried in awe. "Won't there be any end to this? It's the devil himself that's doing these things. Look here, O'Connor," he addressed the patrolman, "can't you give us any sort of description of this man?"

"No more than I did, sir," replied the officer. "It was that dark and foggy I never got a good look at him. He had on dark clothes and ran with a limp. And I think he had a beard."

"It's the same man who attacked Dr. Hartzell," said Sullivan. "The one you saw, Fletcher. The Head Hunter. At last we're getting close to him."

Fletcher wondered. After his own encounter with the bearded limper he had played with the idea that Prince Alexis might conceivably be the marauder. But this new development seemed to preclude any such possibility. Why in the world would the proprietor of the gallery break his own window for the purpose of robbing something to which he had easy access every day? There didn't seem to be any answer to that.

Fletcher was subjecting the shrunken figure to a minute examination. He prodded its face, scratched the skin with his fingernail, broke off a strand of hair and held it to the light. An exclamation broke from him.

"Found something?" inquired Sullivan.

"I don't know. . . . I believe I'll ask Dr. Durand to look this over. It's just possible—"

"He may be here now," said Sullivan eagerly. "He was going to drop in as soon as he finished a case on Pell Street." He lifted a desk phone and barked a question, then hung up with a grunt. "He's downstairs and is coming right up."

The medical examiner entered and nodded to them. He gave only an indifferent glance at the tiny body on the desk. "The Head Hunter again," he guessed.

"It may be," said Fletcher. "I'd like you to do a personal favor for me, doctor. Take this little mummy to your laboratory and give it a thorough examination."

"What do you want to know?"

"Everything. How long the man has been dead. His race, his age, his probable description."

Dr. Durand agreed and departed with the shrunken figure tucked carelessly under one arm. Sullivan eyed Fletcher curiously.

"You've got something on your mind," he declared. "I don't suppose there's any use in asking what it is."

Fletcher smiled as he rose to leave. "Not just yet. We'll wait and see what Dr. Durand has to report."

He returned wearily to his apartment and tumbled into bed. A night's rest was what he needed to clear his brain. To-morrow he intended to attack the problem from a fresh angle, and his hunch that the case was near to conclusion was stronger than ever.

How long he had been asleep he did not know. A soft, rasping noise reached his consciousness and galvanized him to immediate wakefulness.

He did not move, but lay rigid, his eyes sweeping the darkness. If anyone were there, he was invisible. Then he saw that one of the windows, which he had opened but a few inches, was all the way up. He remembered the narrow stone coping which ran about the building just beneath his windows. It was wide enough for a man to stand on, to inch his way from the fire escape to his bedroom windows.

He heard a soft, scuffling sound. Feet moving stealthily over the carpet toward him.

Fletcher's pulse raced. The Head Hunter? Was he to be murdered as Van Styne had been, his head cut from his body, carried away? . . .

His hand slid under his pillow, felt the cold hard outlines of his automatic. Its flat bulk nestled reassuringly in the hollow of his hand. One finger found the safety catch, snapped it off.

The click it made was distinctly audible in the dead silence. Perhaps it was that which saved Fletcher's life. The intruder waited no longer, but made a leap to the bed and brought a huge knife down on the pillow in a swishing arc. But his aim had been hasty and Fletcher was able to scramble out of the way, slipping from the bed and falling to the floor.

His automatic barked at the vague shadow which pursued him around the foot of the bed. In the almost total darkness he missed. The next instant the weapon leapt from his fingers as the leg of a chair struck his wrist with paralyzing force.

He gritted his teeth and made a lunging spring from the floor. His fist sank deep into a stomach and air whistled through set lips. But that did not stop the full-armed swing of the chair crashing down upon his head.

Fletcher tottered and slumped to the floor. He was still conscious, but his muscles and vocal cords would not respond to the messages sent to them.

He had no doubt that his assailant was the Head Hunter. And he expected nothing but the swish of a knife through the air, the feel of its blade biting into his neck . . .

Then he heard a door slam. It was the outer door of his apartment. Dazedly he realized that the Head Hunter, unaware of his helplessness, or fearing that the occupants of neighboring apartments had been aroused by the shot, had fled.

It seemed to take minutes for him to crawl to his feet and snap on the light. He recovered his automatic and staggered through his apartment into the hall. Doors were opening, heads were peering out, and he heard a woman shrieking for the police.

But the Head Hunter had vanished. An open fire-escape door showed the direction of his flight. It was too late to pursue him.

Fletcher returned to his bedroom. Upon his bed was a machete, similar in design to the one he had found sticking in the floor of Dr. Hartzell's store room. As had been the case with the other, it bore no fingerprints.

It was late the next morning when Fletcher entered Dr. Durand's private laboratory. He found the little medical examiner, wrapped like a mummy in the habiliments of his profession, fussing over a microscope. He removed his mask and rubber gown and showed Fletcher into his tiny office.

"I found something," he said, when he had a cigar going. "Don't know whether it's what you expected, Fletcher. That mummy is the body of a white man."

"You're certain?"

"No doubt about it. I examined the skin, the hair, the nails, the wax in the ears. I wanted no mistakes and made every possible microscopical and chemical test. The hair is that of a Caucasian, not an Indian's or Negro's. The skin is white, though it has been dyed black. The wax in the ears still bore a trace of the dust and smoke of cities."

"How long has he been dead?"

"Less than a year, probably not as long as six months. Do you want to check my tests? I have everything in readiness."

"No need of that," said Fletcher. "Can you give me a description of the man?"

"Very little. Without a skeleton to take measurements from it's nearly impossible. I should say he was a German or Pole, of medium height, probably between fifty and sixty years of age. He had black hair. A plastic surgeon might be able to do something about reconstructing the face; I don't know. Tell me—what does it mean?"

"That remains to be seen," said Fletcher thoughtfully. "I've an idea it may prove important—in a roundabout fashion. You've informed Inspector Sullivan of your findings? . . . No matter; I'm going to see him in a few minutes."

Sullivan, however, was not expected in his office for several hours. While

Fletcher was chatting with the lieutenant in charge a call came for him from Prince Alexis.

"I would like to see you as soon as possible," the Russian said. "You could come to my gallery, perhaps? I am ready to tell you who—who the Head Hunter is."

When Fletcher arrived at the gallery, Prince Alexis was limping impatiently about his office. His bearded face was haggard and he was puffing nervously at a long cigarette.

"Mr. Fletcher," he began, "I suppose you have resented my attitude of indifference and—well, call it hostility. But if you know of my unfortunate experiences with your New York police, I think you understand. I come to you because you are—a gentleman."

Fletcher nodded. He knew that the Russian had been unjustly suspected of being connected with diamond smugglers, and had been subjected to a year's surveillance which must have been galling to him—enough to embitter him against the police.

"James Van Styne was a very dear friend," continued Prince Alexis. "When he was murdered I swore to myself that he would be avenged. Just how, I did not know. I suppose that even then I had a suspicion of the truth. But it was so vague, so uncertain, so utterly lacking in proof, that I did not care to mention it.

"Now I have that proof, though I did not come upon it until a few hours ago. When I returned to the city early this morning and learned what had happened—the attack upon Dr. Hartzell and the robbery of my show window—my terrible suspicions became a certainty and I made a quiet investigation."

Prince Alexis paused to light a fresh cigarette. His hands trembled a little as he held a match to it.

"I think I can make you understand more easily," he went on, "if I preface my theory with an explanation. Dr. Hartzell is a strange man, a genius in his field. I consider him mentally unbalanced—but then, isn't it said that all geniuses are touched with insanity? I have known him for years and do not pretend to understand him. He has an overwhelming passion for scientific investigation that has carried him into places no other man has dared to go, that has impelled him to do things normal men would not do.

"But that, as I said, is the preface to my theory. You have heard of Emil and Paul Jorgens?"

"The famous explorers?" said Fletcher. "The two men who are reputed to know South America better than anyone else?"

"The same. But perhaps you do not know that they and Dr. Hartzell are implacable enemies. How it started I do not know—nor would they tell. At any rate the two brothers headed an expedition into the jungles of Ecuador about a year ago. They never came out nor was any word heard from them.

"It may have been a coincidence that Dr. Hartzell entered that territory at the same time. I do know that Dr. Hartzell came out—and Emil and Paul Jorgens did not. There was a rumor at the Tropical Explorers' Club—not generally credited—that the Jorgens did not come out because they were dead. And that they were dead because Dr. Hartzell, in his mad hatred of them, had natives ambush and slaughter them.

"It sounds mad—but then, as I have explained, I think Dr. Hartzell a little mad. I myself did not believe the rumor until I learned this morning that the shrunken figure had been taken from my window. And then a ghastly thought leaped into my mind. It was incredible, unthinkable, unbelievable. Nevertheless I found a picture of the Jorgens brothers and compared it with my mental picture of the shrunken figure which was taken.

"And, Mr. Fletcher," concluded Prince Alexis, "that figure was, I am convinced, the shrunken body of Paul Jorgens!"

Fletcher nodded, not greatly surprised. He had been prepared for just such a revelation. "You have that picture?" he asked.

The Russian gave it to him. It showed two men standing on the prow of a boat, jungle in the background. They were of a stocky Polish type. The hair on Fletcher's neck rose as he looked at the shorter man on the left.

There was an unmistakable resemblance between him and the gnomish figure Dr. Durand had proclaimed to be a white man.

"They are the same," he said, and went on to tell of Dr. Durand's examination.

"It's the last proof we need!" cried Prince Alexis. "And I will tell you something else. Dr. Hartzell, in his zeal for scientific knowledge, has actually participated in head hunts with the natives and helped them prepare the heads. Perhaps it was he who prepared Paul Jorgens' body."

Fletcher winced. He'd seen many forms of murder, but nothing to match this. Certainly it was gruesomely unique not only to kill one's enemy, but also to shrink his hide to the size of a large doll, to make it into a grotesque and hideous travesty of the living man. . . . He asked a question, anticipating the answer.

"And Emil Jorgens?"

"Emil Jorgens escaped! Somehow he made his way through the jungle to the coast. He is now in New York. One of the members of the Tropical Explorers' Club saw him, though he disappeared into a crowd before he could speak to him. He said the man was wasted away to a shadow, bearded, and apparently crippled, for he walked with a limp."

Fletcher thought once more of the figure he had seen shuffling away from Dr. Hartzell's home. And the policeman's meager description of the man who had broken the window of the Gallery Alexis.

He looked at the picture again. Yes, he was certain now that he could recognize in Emil Jorgens the man he had seen in the alleyway.

"Emil Jorgens is the Head Hunter," continued Prince Alexis. "His experiences have snapped his mind. He has reverted to the savagery of the people he studied. He is aping their methods in dealing with enemies. He has a purpose, but has wandered far from it, killing almost indiscriminately. Last night seems to have been the first time he kept to it, and he almost succeeded both in murdering Dr. Hartzell and recovering the body of his brother."

"If Jorgens is in New York," said Fletcher, "depend upon it that the police can find him."

Prince Alexis suddenly scowled and stroked his beard. "I suppose this seems like disloyalty to a friend," he added. "But I know you can never prove that Dr. Hartzell brought about Paul Jorgens' death. I tell this to you only so that you can safeguard Dr. Hartzell's life. He is in danger as long as Jorgens remains uncaptured."

Fletcher smiled grimly. "And so the police must protect a murderer from revenge," he said. "It will be done, Prince Alexis."

V

THE DEVIL'S LABORATORY

THE INTERVIEW CONCLUDED, Fletcher called detective headquarters and learned that Sullivan had not yet returned. Not wanting to wait for him, he proceeded at once to Dr. Hartzell's home.

It seemed deserted and it was only after he had rung the bell some half-dozen times that the door opened. The scientist confronted him sourly; then permitted himself a smile as he recognized his visitor and invited him into his study.

"I thought it must be the reporters again," he explained. "They've been making my life miserable this morning. Have there been any fresh developments?"

Fletcher looked narrowly at Dr. Hartzell as he spoke. The man was extremely nervous. His deep-set eyes jerked constantly from one side to the other, as though he dreaded some horror which might be lurking in the shadows.

"You've heard of the attempted robbery at the Gallery Alexis?" asked Fletcher.

Dr. Hartzell nodded.

"That robbery," continued Fletcher, "brought to light a rather astonishing fact. The shrunken figure with which the thief tried to make off was the body of a white man."

The scientist's fingers clenched upon the edge of his desk like bony claws. "Impossible!" he burst out.

"Dr. Durand has proved it in his laboratory. And we have identified the body, so we know its race. The man was Paul Jorgens."

Dr. Hartzell whispered the name after him. His eyes blazed with hatred. He opened his lips to speak, then closed them tightly.

"I have learned the entire story," went on Fletcher, "though much of it is guesswork. It is said that you instigated Paul Jorgens' murder. That you yourself prepared his body—"

"You're insane!" rasped the scientist, coming to his feet. "I secured that body from a tribe of natives in Ecuador. I did not inquire where it came from—nor did I care. If it should be Jorgens' body, as you say, I was ignorant of that."

"That may be. But did you know that Emil Jorgens is now in New York?"

"Emil Jorgens—in—New York?" Dr. Hartzell fell back into his chair. His domed forehead beaded with sweat. He wiped his lips with the back of his hand.

"No doubt about it," said Fletcher. "He has been seen and recognized by a man who knew him well. His description tallies with that of the man who attempted to carry off the shrunken figure—the body of his brother."

The scientist abruptly leaped to his feet and strode the length of the room. "I can't believe it," he muttered. "When he crawled away and escaped into the jungle, he was badly wounded—" He broke off, becoming conscious that he was speaking aloud.

Fletcher was watching him like a hawk, missing nothing of the other's agitation. He had a purpose behind this interrogation other than merely warning him of the danger. He wanted to drive the man beyond the limits of his mental endurance.

"It was Emil Jorgens whom I saw last night, fleeing from this house," he pursued relentlessly.

"Come back to kill me," said Dr. Hartzell. "Come back for revenge."

He continued to pace about the room, muttering to himself. He seemed to have become oblivious to Fletcher's presence. Fletcher made no comment and waited patiently for the breakdown he was sure would come.

There was a small glass case standing on the table against the wall which he had not noticed before, and he let his eyes rove over it. It contained a shrunken head, which instantly arrested his attention. It was dyed a darker hue, he thought, than the others he had seen, and did not seem to have the same facial contours, which he recalled in those at the Gallery Alexis.

But it was not that which riveted his gaze upon it. It was its remarkable resemblance, distorted and shrunken as it was, to some face filed away in his memory.

• • •

He stared at it, forgetting for the moment the striding figure behind him. Forgetting everything in his intense concentration. Every lineament of that hideous little face was familiar to him; yet he could not place it, rack his memory as he might.

At last, convinced that his imagination was tricking him, he began to turn away. And as his eyes swung obliquely from it; as he saw it from the corner of his eye, his memory clicked.

It was the head of James Van Styne!

It had, in miniature, the same bulbous nose, the same sagging jowls, the same squinting eyes and bushy eyebrows. Though less than five inches in diameter, the craftsman who had shaped it had preserved the human character of it with diabolical art.

As he gazed at it with dawning horror, a step sounded behind him. Under the hypnosis of his discovery, he was slow to act. Hands came about his chest and locked, pinning his arms to his sides. The hot, fetid breath of Dr. Hartzell's Indian servant fell upon his neck as he was held helpless.

Dr. Hartzell was laughing when his captor swung him around.

"So! You have caught on at last, my friend! Then you know that I am the Head Hunter!"

After the first attempt to struggle from the encircling arms, Fletcher stood quiet. He was in the power of a madman and he would need all his wits if he were to stand any chance of escape. He regarded the scientist with level eyes.

"I have suspected it since yesterday—perhaps even before that," he said. "I knew that only a brain such as yours could conceive and execute such monstrous things. Tonight I had hoped to goad you to the point of admitting it, or giving me some proof. But, until I found Van Styne's head, I could not prove it."

Dr. Hartzell threw back his head and laughed. His voice had taken on a fiendish rasping quality. The light striking up against his face made it look a death's head, parchment skin stretched tightly over its bony frame.

"You guessed too late," he mocked. "Yes I—I am he whom the papers call the Head Hunter."

A change had come over him. Gone was the reserved scientist, gone was the terror-stricken man, to be replaced by the homicidal maniac, mad with the lust for blood.

"You are the first to learn my secret—I should have kept that head upstairs with the others—but it doesn't matter. You will be the last. The secret dies with you. And your head, with Van Styne's and all the rest, will go to swell my collection."

He got a rope and with the aid of his servant bound Fletcher's wrists behind him. They took him to an upstairs room almost bare of furniture.

Against the wall was a gas range and several kettles. Beside it was a small table, on which was an outlay of knives, bottles, several buckets of what appeared to be sand—and three more horrible heads, each in its own glass case.

Fletcher guessed that they were the heads of Dr. Hartzell's latest victims. One of them he thought he recognized from a picture he had seen of Greenwald, the unfortunate lawyer, who had been found in the park, and now his own head was to be added to the three in view— He riveted his gaze on the monstrous group and a cold sweat broke out on his forehead.

"My equipment," Dr. Hartzell was explaining. "I am the greatest head preserver in the world. Greater even than the Jivaro masters of the art—under whom I studied until I surpassed them. My servant was a Jivaro sub-chief; but he preferred to follow me, the greatest exponent of their sacred art."

He slipped off his coat and donned a rubber apron which enveloped him from chin to feet. Meanwhile his Jivaro servant had lighted the gas stove and was putting kettles and pots on the flames, filling them with sand and water.

Behind his back, Fletcher tensed his wrists against his bonds. They gave ever so slightly, enough so he could twist two fingers up and begin working on the knots. The scientist had not thought to remove his automatic from its holster; and if he could get his hands free long enough to get at it, he might be able to turn the tables.

"Van Styne's head was a masterpiece, a work of art," he said, sparring for time. "Will you tell me what your technique is?"

"If you read my book, you should know," answered Dr. Hartzell proudly. "Of course I employ certain refinements which are my own secret. Be assured that your head will be shrunken very carefully. I will prize it highly. You saw Van Styne's head; it is perfect, without a blemish."

"Why did you kill him?"

Dr. Hartzell was testing the blade of a knife on the edge of his thumb. The question touched off his murderous rage and he swung around with a snarl.

"I killed him because I hated him! When I left for South America, I entrusted my fortune to Van Styne and Greenwald for investment. And they stole it, lost it, robbed me of almost every penny!"

The mysterious connection between Van Styne and Greenwald!

"And the others?" asked Fletcher.

"I killed the others because I wanted heads. Except the night watchman at the Gallery Alexis. I knew the stupid police might suspect me, so I robbed my own collection to turn suspicion from me. The watchman had admitted me and knew me, so he had to be silenced."

Fletcher thought he understood everything now. Dr. Hartzell, already partially unbalanced, had become completely insane when he learned that his fortune was gone. Rightly or wrongly blaming Van Styne and Greenwald for the loss of his wealth, he had avenged himself upon them. Then, carried off by his mania, or perhaps by the fame he had attained as the one authority upon the subject which was engaging everybody's attention, he had been unable to stop.

The ropes about Fletcher's wrist gave a little more. He had one of the knots untied, and he thought that with a few seconds' more time he could slip his hands out.

He froze as he saw Dr. Hartzell looking at him piercingly. But the scientist was thinking of something else, and his lips curled in an insane leer.

"Perhaps I shall not take your head after all," he said. "No, I believe that I shall consign you to a better fate. I will preserve your entire body, make it into a beautiful little doll, as I did with Paul Jorgens. Your head, your body, your limbs will be shrunken together until you are like a little monkey. Would you like that?"

Fletcher shrugged. And he took advantage of the shrug to give his wrists a powerful wrench, putting all the power of his shoulders into it. The knots, partially untied, slipped enough so that his hands were almost free.

The scientist muttered to himself and turned away. On the very instant his back was turned, Fletcher hunched his shoulders again and jerked his wrists free from the ropes. His hand snaked toward his shoulder holster.

But he had miscalculated in one important respect. His fingers, numb and half paralyzed from the constriction of the bonds, were awkward and he almost dropped his gun as he drew it out.

And Dr. Hartzell must have been expecting just some such move. With a shriek he leaped across the room, caught the gun's muzzle in his left hand and twisted it away from him.

The Jivaro Indian struck him with a crash and he fell on his back to the floor, almost carrying Dr. Hartzell down with him. The automatic whirled from his fingers and dropped into a corner. The scientist cursed gutturally and brought the knife he still carried down in an arc for Fletcher's heart. Fletcher caught his wrist in the nick of time, held it so that the point of the knife was suspended several inches over his chest.

But he could not hold it there for long. The Indian was choking him and his vision blurred. The scientist's mad face hung over him like some monster's, jaws slathering as he tried to push the knife downward.

Fletcher was fast losing strength. He felt the point of the knife prick his ribs, but he could not push it back, try as he might. A moment more . . .

Then a shriek rang through the room. Dr. Hartzell cried out in alarm and leaped away, taking the knife with him. For an instant the Indian loosened his strangling hold upon Fletcher's throat. Fletcher gasped air into his tortured lungs, then put everything into a single effort. He kicked upward with his legs, turning a backward somersault. His toes caught the Indian in the chest, drove him away like a battering-ram.

Fletcher came to his feet like a cat. He sprang upon the Indian just rising from the floor and met him with short-armed jabs that battered his face, his stomach, and ended with a knockout blow to the jaw.

As he straightened up, something rolled gently against his ankle. He looked down, then jerked his foot away. It was a human head, eyes open wide, blood still spurting from the neck.

Dr. Hartzell's head!

The scientist's body lay close to the door. Crouched over it was an emaciated, bearded figure dressed in ragged black clothes. From one hand dangled a machete, its long polished blade crimson.

The man was laughing insanely, his head thrown back, his long beard sticking straight out. His body shook as peal upon peal of merriment poured from his wrinkled throat.

"Jorgens! Emil Jorgens!" said Fletcher.

The man's laughter broke off short. His gaze swung toward Fletcher. The blade slipped from his hand and clanged upon the floor. He took a few steps backward and stopped with his back against the wall.

"What . . . where am I?" he faltered.

His face slowly relaxed. He put his hands to his head and clenched it.

"My head . . . it hurts. Something hit it." Then the light of madness faded from his eyes, leaving them dazed and frightened.

Fletcher retrieved his automatic and snapped handcuffs on the Jivaro Indian. He was not anxious to stay in this den of murder. He took Emil Jorgens' arm and guided him down to the study, where he put in a call to the police.

"But I don't understand!" cried Jorgens. "I was in the jungle with my brother—then I find myself here."

"Don't excite yourself," said Fletcher. "You've had a bad shock, but you'll come out of it all right. It'll all come back to you after a bit."

He found a bottle of liquor in the desk and poured out a drink. Jorgens gulped it eagerly.

"I remember it—like a dream," he said. "Dr. Hartzell killed my brother and wounded me, but I managed to crawl off into the jungle. Then there were months and years of starving. The rest isn't clear. . . . Did I come to New York? Was it I who was hunting for Dr. Hartzell to kill him? Last night I looked through a window and saw him. It was in the back of this house. He drove a knife into the floor and screamed—"

"A false attack upon himself," murmured Fletcher. "To divert my suspicion from him."

"And then I found my brother's body in a window. It was hideous! Shrunken up—like the Indians do. I tried to take it, but a policeman chased me. I knew Dr. Hartzell did that, so today I came to kill him. I got in through a back window and found a machete. And then I saw him attacking you— and I went mad. I killed him. And I'm a murderer."

Fletcher gripped his shoulder.

"Not a murderer," he said. "You have rid the city of a monster. You were an instrument of justice."

Cover painting by William Reusswig

THE GHOUL OF MURDER MANOR

I

MOTHER OF DEATH

THE MOON, OBSCURED by leaden clouds, gave only a pale gray light to the lonely road. Allen Jennings had to use a match before he could decipher the brass plate, set in the moldy stone of the massive gateposts.

"Stormward Manor," he muttered. "Now if the place lives up to its reputation—"

He pressed the call button, and heard the remote tinkling of a bell in the caretaker's lodge, to the right of the gate. Its windows were dark and, if anyone were there, he gave no sign of his presence.

Jennings peered through the metal grille. The private road swung past the lodge and disappeared into a gloomy wilderness of trees. This was a bleak corner of Long Island, given over to large estates and clubs. Stormward Manor comprised several hundred acres of woods, including a rocky, storm-driven stretch of coast and a small bay on which a fishing village had once been located.

He tried the bell again, and finally resorted to a bronze knocker which made the night echo with its harsh clangor. Five minutes passed, and at last he heard scuffling feet hurrying toward him. A slouching figure emerged from the woods, panting heavily.

"What d'you want?" a surly voice demanded.

Over that open coffin he hovered, like a giant vulture gorging himself upon the dead. What horror-errand could have brought him there? Why—knife in hand—should this hawk-nosed ghoul chuckle in glee above a moldering corpse?

*Jennings pulled back the sleeve—
the hand was gone!*

Allen Jennings gave his name. "Miss Mona Carrington is expecting me," he added.

"You're that New York detective, huh?"

"Criminologist—yes," corrected Jennings, smiling at the thought of being called a detective. His Manhattan office bore the simple inscription "Consulting Attorney" and he specialized in criminal law. True, he dabbled in the solution of crime and had rather a reputation as a sleuth; enough so, that the police department had several times enlisted his aid. But his few cases were handpicked. Jennings accepted them only if they seemed to offer some problem out of the ordinary.

This one, for instance.

A year ago Captain Avery Carrington, master of Stormward Manor, wealthy retired ship owner and traveler, had committed suicide by throwing himself into the sea. He died without revealing the hiding place of his famous gem collection. Since then, his Long Island home had been ransacked time and again without turning up a trace of it. And now the dead man's niece, Mona Carrington, had solicited the criminologist's aid in locating the jewels.

The gate keeper was still breathing heavily. He made no move to admit Jennings. "Maybe you are him," he growled, "but maybe you ain't. This detective was supposed to get here two hours ago. Anyway, he was coming in his car."

Jennings explained patiently: "I had trouble with my car. I was held up several hours having it fixed, and then it broke down again a quarter of a mile back."

He had the sudden impression that the gate keeper was pretending to doubt him in order to delay his entering. But why? The man had not been in the lodge, as he should have been, but had come out of the woods. Jennings wondered if he had been engaged in doing something which he did not want discovered.

"Look here," he said sharply. "Here's my card. If you still doubt my identity, telephone Miss Carrington. But I don't intend to be kept here waiting."

Jennings' gray eyes had taken on a cold gleam, colder than the moonlight breaking through the clouds. The light striking down upon his face accentuated its thinness and brought out the deep lines between his eyes and at the corners of his mouth.

The gate keeper's gaze faltered and fell away. Sullenly he produced a key and opened a side gate.

"Guess it's all right," he grumbled. "But I got to be careful, mister. You can wait in there. I'll phone the house and have the chauffeur come down and get you."

Jennings saw a path cutting straight into the woods. It was along this that the gate keeper had come. The road swung off to the side.

"Will it take long?" he asked.

"Not unless he's gone to bed."

"Then I'll walk. What's the shortest way?"

"The path but—but—" The man's voice became shrill with alarm. "You can't do that! You got to wait here!"

"Why?"

"Because—you'd be sure to get lost and—"

Jennings cut off the stammering man. This confirmed his suspicion and determined him to take the path, if only on the off chance that he might encounter something interesting.

"I'll chance it," he said. "You can phone ahead to the house. Have the chauffeur get the luggage from my car and see that it's towed to a garage for repairs. He won't have any trouble finding it; its a maroon roadster parked just off the road under a big pine about a quarter of a mile back."

The gate keeper followed Jennings for a few steps, mingling pleas with imprecations. Then, seeing that his words were having no effect, he stopped and stared after the retreating figure, cursing under his breath.

The walk had, at one time, evidently been a bridle path, and it was easy to follow. The moonlight fell in a patchwork through the laced branches overhead. The undergrowth at either side was thick and almost impenetrable, but it thinned out as the path ascended to higher ground.

Presently Jennings distinguished a light. It was not in the direction in which the path led, but off to the right, upon still higher ground. Close by was the black silhouette of a roof. Then he saw that the roof belonged to an ancient stone church, set in a gloomy copse of pine. The light came from the side, from a small graveyard.

A strange place for a light, at this time of night!

Jennings thought of the *ignis fatuus*, the will-o'-the-wisp, that weird glow which hovers over old cemeteries and swamps, leading unwary travelers to destruction. But that could not be the explanation. This light was too steady to be the product of burning gasses filtering up from decaying bodies or vegetation.

His jaw set as he started toward it. Was this where the gate keeper had been? It was at about the right distance to account for the time he had taken to reach the gate, after hearing the first clatter of the knocker.

Jennings stumbled through matted bushes and brambles. A stiff breeze, laden with the salty tang of the sea, struck his face. At the base of the hill upon which was the church, he saw the glimmer of water. This was the little bay where the fishing village had been located. Now there was only a single small cruiser anchored in it. Probably the church had served the village as a place of worship and burial ground, but now evidently both were absorbed into the estate of the manor. He could see the house itself, a sprawled pattern of lights, off to the right of the bay, perched upon the very edge of a cliff overhanging the sea.

As he neared the church, Jennings saw that the light came from the sunken entrance of a burial vault. It was at the rear of the small graveyard, in the deep shadow of the church. He climbed a rotten picket fence and crept through isles of toppling tombstones. Time had eroded their carven surfaces, chiseled away their grotesque representations of skeletons and flowers and celestial faces.

The iron-grilled door of the mortuary was open. A tangle of vines fell over a frieze of skulls, almost obscuring a graven name. It read—"Carrington."

Jennings came in from the side, until he could grasp a handful of vines and lean far enough over to peer through the entrance. Balanced there, he was witness to a weird, unforgettable scene.

A smoky lantern set on a block of stone gave flickering illumination to the interior of the tomb. On the floor, pulled from one of the niches in the wall of the crypt, was a coffin. Its top was turned back, revealing the head and shoulders of a dead man, cushioned on white silk.

A tall dark figure bent over it, working with a knife. His back was turned so that nothing could be seen of his face. His shadow wavered on the wall, looking like a giant vulture spreading its wings in flight, after having gorged itself on the dead.

Amazed, determined to be prepared for whatever might transpire, Jennings drew his revolver, leaned farther over the sunken entrance, trying to get a look at the man's face. The vines in his hand gave a few inches with a jerk. He almost lost his balance. One foot slipped, brushing against loose gravel. A few pebbles dropped upon the stone flagging with a sharp crackle.

The ghoul whirled with a scream of alarm. For an instant he poised. His low-pulled hat gave only a momentary glimpse of a hawklike nose, a jutting chin and thin snarling lips. Then he launched himself toward the entrance of the tomb, flourishing the knife.

Jennings tried to scramble back out of the way, bring his weapon to bear on the advancing figure. His foot caught in a trailing vine and he sprawled flat on his back. His head smashed against a flagstone, knocking him out for a minute.

When he came to, he knew that the ghoul was hovering over him with raised knife, but his body would not obey the commands of his brain. He expected only the searing stab of a blade. . . .

A chuckle sounded, and then running feet. When Jennings was able to stagger to his feet, the grave robber had vanished in the murky tangle of trees surrounding the little graveyard. Pursuit was hopeless, so he turned his attention to the burial vault.

The lantern still flickered upon its stone block, casting a feeble glow over the damp interior. Jennings saw his gun lying where he had dropped it, picked it up. The moldy odor of decay caught at his nostrils. He glanced about and caught his breath when he saw the face of the dead man.

It was the face of the ghoul! There were the same features—the hawklike nose, the jutting chin and the thin cruel lips.

Jennings looked to the nameplate on the door of the enclosure from which the coffin had been taken. It bore the name of Captain Avery Carrington, a death date of the preceding year. This, then, was the earthly remains of the man who had so well hidden his gem collection that a year's search had failed to disclose it.

The ghoul, during Jennings' brief period of unconsciousness, had returned to the corpse, entirely ripped away the clothes from Captain Carrington's chest. The unblemished skin of his torso was untouched, save for a spot over the sternum where the point of the knife had scratched through the skin, apparently accidentally.

But what did it mean? A corpse snatched from its grave, the clothes torn from its body. A gate keeper who had evidently conspired with the ghoul to disinter the body of his former master. And a ghoul who strongly resembled the body he had violated.

Jennings' blood quickened. He sensed a problem which would tax all his ingenuity and skill.

Then a flash of red caught his eye. Something that nestled in a fold of the white silk cushions of the coffin, burning with crimson fire.

It was a ruby, larger than a pigeon's egg, and of the same exquisite redness as a pigeon's blood. A majestic jewel fit to crown the scepter of a monarch.

"The Bohojor Ruby!" he whispered.

It had another and more ominous name. The Mother of Death, it was called. Its history stretched back hundreds of years, and was marked by a score of murders and thefts. It had literally been bathed in blood, time without number. Legend said that no man had ever retained it for more than five years—and retained his life.

Jennings picked it from its white cushioning and held it toward the lantern. Even in that feeble yellow light its brilliance was dazzling.

Then a girl's voice said: "I have you covered. Put up your hands."

II

MURDER AMBUSH

ALLEN JENNINGS CLOSED HIS HAND UPON THE GEM and raised his arms. He turned his head slowly. The slim figure of a girl stood in the door of the vault. Her hand, holding a small automatic trained on him, was trembling.

He smiled and said: "You're Miss Mona Carrington?"

She gasped. "You're Mr. Allen Jennings. But I thought—when I saw—"

Jennings lowered his arms and faced her. She was, he saw, a remarkably pretty girl, scarcely more than twenty. She wore a dark gown, and the hair which framed her youthful oval face had the bright blackness of a raven's plumage. Her eyes, staring at him so, seemed unnaturally large and black.

Hesitantly, her eyes dropped to the coffin. Her hands went to her breast as she recoiled. "It's Uncle Avery!" she breathed.

"Captain Carrington?" asked Jennings.

The girl nodded, her eyes wide with horror. Jennings shut the lid of the casket to keep the gruesome sight from her.

"What—what happened?" she demanded. "Andrews, the gate keeper, phoned me at the house that you were on the way up. I started down to meet you, and then heard a scream here—"

Jennings recounted his experience, but of the gate keeper said only: "You trust Andrews?"

"Of course," she replied. "He was Uncle Avery's—Captain Carrington's—most faithful servant."

Jennings did not pursue the question. He would talk with Andrews tomorrow, though he expected to get little out of him. It would be too simple for the man to invent a plausible excuse for his absence from the lodge and to deny that he knew anything of the rifling of the tomb.

The girl asked: "This man you found here—you saw his face?"

"Only indistinctly," said Jennings. "I got the impression of a hooked nose, a pointed chin, thin lips."

He looked sharply at the girl. She was biting her lower lip with small white teeth. He guessed that she was tortured by some inner uncertainty which she feared to voice.

"You suspect who it might have been?" he asked.

"No. No, I don't," she answered. And then she added quickly: "But—yes—those are family characteristics. I suppose that the man might have been either my uncle, Peter Carrington, or my cousin, Lester Gregory."

"You know of any reason why either of them should do this?"

"N-no."

"Perhaps," suggested Jennings, "the jewel collection is hidden here in the vault."

"You mean—but that's impossible!" she cried. "Captain Carrington kept his collection at the house. He showed it to a friend the very afternoon of the evening he died. And he didn't leave the house after that. It couldn't be here!"

It was with an effort that the dark, wide-eyed girl controlled herself. Jennings was tempted to postpone his questions until they had more cheerful surroundings. But he wanted all the facts at his disposal before he entered Stormward Manor, and so he went on.

"Your uncle's collection was large?"

"It contained hundreds of precious stones. How much they are worth, I don't know—probably almost a half million dollars. He spent much of his life in India and China, and had made a hobby of Oriental gems, as well as rare vases and statuary."

"He kept the gems in a safe?"

"So we supposed. When Captain Carrington retired from business and settled here, he had a special wing added to the house to contain his curios and relics. In one room is an enormous safe, set in concrete, guaranteed to be burglar proof. But when it was opened, after his death, the gems were not there."

"Someone may have removed them."

"Only one other man knew the combination. He was the man who installed it."

Jennings said dryly: "Safe combinations have been known to fall into the wrong hands. Particularly, if the figures were recorded where they might be found."

"That is possible," admitted Mona Carrington. "But, in this case, I doubt whether Uncle Avery had the gems in his safe at the time of his death. In fact, I doubt whether he ever used the safe for his collection. I think he had it only as a blind, while he had some other more secure hiding place for his jewels."

"A typically Oriental stratagem," commented Jennings, "used principally by the Chinese. Captain Carrington traveled extensively in China, didn't he?"

"He lived there for years and spoke the language like a native. Sometimes he even seemed to think more like a Chinese than a white man. But I have other reasons for believing that the safe was only a blind. It was not empty, Mr. Jennings. It contained six lead pennies and a short note."

"Eh!" said Jennings, startled.

The girl smiled weakly. "I know it sounds crazy. Luckily the newspapers never learned of that. Six lead pennies and a note—when we thought to find a fortune in gems! Wouldn't that have made a story? But it was just the kind of jest that Uncle Avery delighted in."

"What was the note?"

"I can quote it, word for word. It said—'The strongest lock is but a toy in the hands of the thief. Here are the keys to my stronghold and fortune—but beware to use them!' It was signed with his name."

"In his handwriting?"

"Apparently."

"Six lead pennies," mused the criminologist. "Six lead pennies and a cryptic, ironic note! The keys to his stronghold and fortune! And you want me, Miss Carrington, to use those keys, to find these hidden gems?"

The girl nodded.

The lines about Jennings' eyes and mouth deepened as he thought. This girl had not brought him here solely to deal with such an academic problem. She was actuated by more than a desire to recover a half million in jewels. He had only to look into her eyes to read the fear and dread mirrored there.

Fear and dread of what? Of the ghoul who had broken into Captain Carrington's tomb and disinterred his body? Perhaps—but she had not known of it when she had asked Jennings to come to Stormward Manor. Yet when she had talked to him over the long-distance telephone this morning, she had not been able to keep the terror from creeping into her voice.

What did she want? To find the jewels, no doubt. But behind that was some hidden and stronger thing—a fear of the unknown—or was it the known?

This was exactly the sort of problem which most interested and challenged Jennings. A lost fortune in gems, a strange suicide, a despoiler of the dead— here was mystery, indeed.

A year before, the man in this casket at his feet had committed suicide under peculiar circumstances. But had he? The criminologist put the question.

The girl's eyes flashed. "He did not!" she denied emphatically.

"The coroner's report—"

"Oh, I know what they said! I know they found his body in the water, on the rocks, beneath his library windows. They said he had jumped out—killed himself. But he didn't do it!"

"The explanation given was poor health."

"He was in poor health. But Uncle Avery wasn't the—the type. He wasn't a coward. I can't believe it of him!"

"Then," said Jennings, "excluding an accident, if he didn't take his own life, there is only one other explanation."

Her lips whispered the question.

"Murder," he said.

Mona Carrington shuddered as though she had been struck with a whip lash. She looked at the coffin, and then quickly away.

"I know. I know." Her voice repeated, almost whispering. "And I haven't—the right to say that. To accuse anybody of such a terrible thing."

"If you have any concrete evidence—"

"But I haven't." She looked into the distance. "No, I haven't what you would call clues. I was on a trip around the world at the time, and didn't return until four months after his burial. It's just that I feel—I know—that he didn't do it."

Jennings decided to let the matter drop, at least until he had more information. A year had passed since Captain Carrington's death, and a year might do much to obliterate clues, if there had been any.

He still had the ruby in his hand, and he opened his fingers so that the pale lantern light played on its glittering facets.

"Why—that's the Bohojor Ruby!" the girl gasped.

Her eyes dilated as she stared at it. She took a step toward the gem. There was fascination written on her face, horrible in its intensity.

"Want to look at it?" invited the criminologist.

Her hand went out; then jerked back. She recoiled as though he had offered her a serpent.

"No! No! I don't want to touch it!"

Her voice was shrill, almost hysterical. Jennings showed his surprise, but pocketed the ruby without comment.

"I hate that stone!" she cried passionately. "It is beautiful—like nothing on earth. But it is surrounded with an aura of envy and hate and greed. It's steeped in blood—"

Her voice choked with the intensity of her emotion. Finally she went on.

"You won't understand, Mr. Jennings. Both my father, Jacob Carrington, and his brother, Captain Avery Carrington, loved and collected jewels. Then, when I was ten years old, Uncle Avery sent my father to India to buy a famous ruby. It had been stolen from its rightful owner. My father bought it from the thief, but others learned of the sale and stabbed and killed my father when he was leaving the country. He had hidden the gem well, it was sewed into his clothing, and they didn't have time to find it. But when it reached Uncle Avery, it was still soaked in my father's blood."

"And that was this Bohojor Ruby?" asked Jennings.

"Yes. The Bohojor Ruby." She whispered the words. "And since then I've disliked all precious stones—and hated this one. Perhaps you've noticed that I wear no jewelry. I can't even wear glass beads because they remind me too much of what caused my father's death."

The girl stared at him. "Don't you understand? That's why I want the collection found. So they can be disposed of, taken away. I can't stand the thought of the jewels being so close to me. Nor can I endure longer the search which has been going on for them continuously."

"Who has been searching?"

"Both my cousin and my uncle. And, the last few days, Captain Bergstrom."

"Who is he?"

"An old friend of Lester Gregory. They are all avid, greedy in their search. For I've told them they can have a share in the gems, if they find them, help me dispose of them to advantage."

"They're yours to give?"

"Captain Carrington left everything to me."

"And what will you do with the gems if I find them?"

"Sell them for what I can get," she said simply. "I don't want them, couldn't ever wear them. I only want them taken away, where I won't be reminded of them continually. You'll find them, won't you?"

"I'll try," promised the criminologist.

He regarded the girl dubiously. But her seriousness was so evident that he had to believe her. He had not the slightest doubt that her attitude toward the gems was exactly as she had described it. Yet did she have some other motive? Jennings guessed that she did, and accused her of it.

She hesitated. "Well—yes," she admitted. "Yes, I'm afraid. Last night Stormward very nearly became Murder Manor. Someone tried to kill me. And almost succeeded."

"How did it happen?"

"I was pushed off the cliff. I have a habit of taking a dip in the ocean every night before going to bed. Stormward Manor is built on a cliff, so I have to walk to the beach at the bay. At one point the path runs only a few feet from the edge of the cliff. When I was passing this point, a man sprang suddenly from behind the trees and pushed me over the edge. I saw I couldn't stop myself from going over, and so I jumped out as far as I could. Luckily, I missed the rocks and struck deeper water. I was able to swim to the beach and return to the house by a roundabout path. Since then I've been carrying a gun."

"You saw your assailant?"

"Only as a shadow. But I heard him laughing horribly as I fell to the water."

"You recognized his voice?"

"No."

The criminologist said sharply: "Nevertheless, you suspect that the man may have been your cousin or your uncle."

The girl shuddered. "Yes, I've been afraid of that," she whispered.

Jennings remembered that she had suspected that one of them might be the ghoul who had opened the tomb. Evidently, there was little love lost between the members of the Carrington family. And it began to look as though her willingness to divide the gems was somewhat in the nature of a bribe.

He asked: "Have you told anyone of this attack?"

"Not yet."

"Then don't," he advised her. "I'm not a private detective but I believe I can protect you until this mystery is cleared up. We'll close the vault and say nothing about it. Tomorrow I can examine it. And now we'll take a look at this spot where you were thrown from the cliff."

He took the lantern and shut the doors of the burial vault. Mona Carrington led him down the rock-strewn hill, to the edge of a cliff overhanging the sea. To the right, still higher, was Stormward Manor, and to the left the little bay, a single small cruiser moored there. At the base of the cliff, waves snarled and sucked angrily over jagged, pointed rocks.

The girl indicated the exact spot where she had been attacked. A dozen feet back from the edge of the cliff were scrubby trees and bushes. Jennings circled among them, scrutinizing the scanty soil carefully, though he had little hope of finding anything.

Suddenly he whipped out his handkerchief and picked something from the ground.

"Careful, don't touch it," he warned the girl in a loud voice. "It may have fingerprints. And, if it does, it'll be enough to put whoever dropped it in prison for attempted murder."

Then a gun roared and Jennings felt the heat of a bullet as it grazed his cheek. With a single motion he dropped the lantern and threw the girl to the ground. Crouching low, he jerked out his gun and dodged through the underbrush.

But the darkness and his unfamiliarity with the terrain defeated him. He thought he heard feet in one direction, only to learn that it was the crackle of leaves in the wind. After a few minutes he abandoned the search.

"Whoever it was, got away," he told the girl. "But my ruse was successful. I thought I heard someone creeping up on us, and I tried the trick of pretending to find something, hoping to entice him closer." He rubbed his cheek ruefully. "But I hardly thought he would try to force things so quickly. However, we know where he fired from. Let's take a look at the spot."

Behind a clump of bushes Jennings found the faint prints of two feet. Between them was a small circular depression. Neither were definite enough to be of any service in identification, but Jennings appeared to be satisfied.

"We'll be getting to the house now," he said. "And perhaps it would be best to leave the lantern. We don't want to provide targets for any more bullets."

III

THE RUBY DISAPPEARS

STORMWARD MANOR WAS A REPLICA OF A MEDIEVAL CASTLE, crenelated and turreted, its ancient stone worn by the wind and storm of years. A brick wing had been added to the rear, projecting to the very edge of the cliff which dropped sheer to boiling, snarling waters.

A gloomy-faced, middle-aged butler admitted them to the foyer. His weak blue eyes were evasive.

"Gifford," Mona Carrington demanded, "did someone just come in?"

"Only Captain Bergstrom, miss," he replied. "I believe he had been to the bay, to look after his cruiser. He returned perhaps five minutes ago."

"No one else was out?"

"That I couldn't say, miss." The butler stood respectfully rigid, but his face showed surprise as well as uneasiness. "Shall I show Mr. Jennings to his room?"

"I'll go later, when my luggage arrives," said Jennings, and watched Gifford's narrow shoulders as they disappeared through a door. He thought there was something vaguely familiar about the man, but he could not be sure. The name Gifford didn't seem to mean anything; it was the fellow's face—

"So Captain Bergstrom was out," mused the girl. "I don't see how we could have missed him, unless he didn't use the path."

"You think he might have taken the pot shot at us?"

"Not him! He wouldn't have missed." They heard the tap of a cane approaching them and the girl added, her lip curling scornfully: "Here comes my uncle, Peter Carrington. Prepare yourself for a display of temper, Mr. Jennings. But pay no attention to it."

A man of sixty, dressed in somber, old-fashioned clothes, appeared in a doorway. He stopped short when he saw them and his head sank between his shoulders as he leaned heavily on a cane. Black slits of eyes glared out at them. His nose was high-bridged and arrogant, his lips thin and cruel, his jaw protruding.

He rasped: "Mona! Who's this man?"

"Mr. Allen Jennings. He—"

His snarl cut her off. His cane beat a nervous tattoo on the marquetry as he advanced toward them.

"What! Mona, I forbid you to bring him here! I told you, this morning, that I would not allow it!"

"But Uncle—"

Peter Carrington shook his cane in the criminologist's face as he came a few steps closer. His lips, drawn back from his teeth, emphasized his resemblance to a raging hawk, beak open to strike.

"Bah! I've heard of you, Mr. Jennings! I know of your cheap, sensational methods. A specialist in blackmail and extortion, eh? But you won't get a penny here. Not a red cent! You might as well take your grips and get out now, if you're hoping to bleed us."

Jennings' only response to this vitriolic attack was a slow smile. This was one of the two men whom Mona Carrington had suspected of having broken into the burial vault. Was he the ghoul? Jennings could not be certain. In build and appearance the two men seemed to be the same, yet he realized that the fragmentary glimpse he had had of the grave robber was no basis for definite identification.

The girl's face whitened until her lips were a red scar in an oval of chalk. Nevertheless, her eyes lost none of their black fire. She faced her uncle defiantly, reminding the criminologist of a beautiful child braving the anger of an ogre.

"Mr. Jennings is my guest, here at my personal invitation," she said evenly. "I must ask you to treat him as such. You and Lester have spent over a year trying to find Captain Avery's jewel collection. You've talked of it night and day, ransacked the house, made measurements and diagrams, until I thought I'd go mad watching and listening to you. Now I've brought an expert to find the jewels."

The old man laughed. "You little fool! An expert indeed! The jewels are at the bottom of the ocean!" Peter Carrington leered at the criminologist. "If you want to find them, Mr. Jennings, put on a diving suit. You might pick up a few gems—before the waves and current smash you to bits on the rocks!"

Jennings asked: "What makes you think they're in the ocean?"

"Because, if they were in the house, I'd have found them. No—when my brother threw himself into the sea, he threw the gems with him. And there they'll be till Doomsday. No sneaking detective will ever lay his hands on them."

Peter Carrington stumped toward the door. Then he turned and flung back: "Remember, Jennings, I won't authorize a cent of payment to you. I'm still the executor of my brother's will. Take my advice and get out!"

His sardonic chuckle still seemed to echo in the foyer after the tap of his cane had ceased. The girl put her hand on the criminologist's arm. "Please don't mind him," she pleaded. "It's true that he can refuse to authorize payment to you from certain funds which he disperses, but I have ready money in my own right, with which he has nothing to do."

Jennings was more interested in the interlocking mysteries which were unfolding before his eyes than he was in his fee. Though it was already late, he asked to be taken to Captain Carrington's quarters. He preferred to put himself in full possession of the facts before he went to bed. Thus he could mull over them before going to sleep.

The girl led him to the rear of the hall opening from the foyer. There was a massive door, bound in iron. On the center panel, carved in high relief, was a dragon rampant, its claws unsheathed and its jaws gaping. Its eyes were tiny green jewels, and its talons and teeth were pointed slivers of ivory.

It was Jennings' first taste of the exotic quarters he was to find beyond this door.

Mona Carrington produced a key to the lock and they entered a room, suffocatingly hot and musty with the atmosphere of being long tightly closed. She clicked on a light switch and the criminologist saw that they were in a second foyer, with a door on each side and at the end. The walls were paneled with rich carvings of Chinese rustic scenes. The rug was an Oriental, soft and deep. On pedestals were grotesque statues of Asiatic gods and goddesses.

The door on the right opened into an office, without windows and with a skylight in the ceiling. It was carpeted and paneled in the same sumptuous fashion. There was a mahogany desk and high-backed chair, a glass case with an exhibit of nautical instruments, ancient and modern, and a red lacquer screen, concealing a typewriter and dictaphone.

On the wall were a number of photographs, most of them of Captain Avery Carrington. One showed him on the bridge of an ocean liner, officer's cap as rigidly straight as his beak of a nose. In another he was posed on a diving board, dressed only in swimming trunks which revealed the dragon tattooed on his chest. A third had evidently been taken in a Chinese temple. He wore the robes of a Taoist monk, of the cult of black magic and demonology.

The room on the opposite side was also without windows. It was evidently used principally for records and storage, for there were banks of filing cases and piles of boxes. But the chief object in the room was an enormous safe. It was set in one corner and encased in a foot-thick layer of concrete.

The girl manipulated the dials and swung open the ponderous circular door. From the interior she took a sheet of paper and a small enameled box. The paper was the note which she had quoted. Jennings read its ironic message, and then inspected the contents of the box.

It contained six Lincoln pennies. They scratched easily with the thumb nail and their weight told Jennings that they were indeed lead counterfeits. They had evidently been cast from the same mold, for they were dated alike.

Jennings said, thoughtfully: "The keys to his stronghold and fortune, eh? Mind if I keep one?"

Mona Carrington nodded assent, then returned the box and note to the safe. They went to the third door of the suite. Crossing the threshold Jennings was first aware of the uncomfortable stuffiness and musty odor of antiquity of this dark room; then the girl located the switch which controlled the ceiling light.

It was a large room, running the full width of the wing. There were windows only on the side facing the sea. One wall had bookshelves extending to the beamed ceiling, jammed with titles in many languages. Several cabinets contained swords, jeweled daggers, various forms of hand weapons. Other cases exhibited small statuary and vases. On the walls were big-game trophies, priestly vestments rich in gold-and-silver design, suits of Japanese armor. On the mantel of a fireplace was an exquisitely wrought jade figure of Buddha.

The note of China and the Orient permeated everything. This was the library and museum of a world traveler and scholar. Jennings walked slowly about the room, eyeing the different items with silent appreciation.

Mona Carrington said: "It was here that Uncle Avery spent almost all his time."

She pushed open one of the tall casement windows. The salty breeze that flung back the heavy drapes was welcome in the hot stuffiness. The crash of waves was an unceasing diapason of sound.

She added: "And it was from this window that Uncle Avery was supposed to have thrown himself."

Jennings leaned out and looked down. The cliff fell straight for forty feet. The boiling, foaming water at its base was a luminous green and white in the darkness. Lifting from it were black gleaming points of rock.

As the criminologist turned back from the window, two men entered the room. The younger, a man of about thirty-five, Jennings guessed to be Lester Gregory, for he had the hooked nose, thin lips and jutting chin of the Carringtons. His eyes were black and passionate, triangulated with dissipation. A cigarette hung from his lips, and he sucked on it nervously.

"Ah, Mona!" he exclaimed. "Gifford told me that you were here with a Mr. Jennings, the famous detective."

His voice was insolent, with an undercurrent of hostility. He plainly resented Jennings' presence and did not much care whether he showed it. Yet he smiled blandly as he shook hands.

A flicker of annoyance crossed Mona Carrington's face as she introduced her cousin. Then she glanced at Jennings obliquely, questioningly. He understood her silent inquiry.

Was Lester Gregory the man he had glimpsed in the burial vault? He had almost made up his mind that it had been Peter Carrington, but now, seeing the other, he was not sure. Both had the same facial appearance, despite their difference in age. It might have been either of them.

The second man, Captain Bergstrom, was below average height, but stocky and compact, with the promise of tremendous strength not belied by his crushing grip. His head, with its huge jaw, seemed almost square. His stiff sandy hair was clipped so close to his scalp that it gave him the impression of being bald. On his upper lip was a bristle of mustache. His complexion was sallow, as though he seldom ventured into the sunshine.

He murmured: "I've heard of you, Mr. Jennings. It's a pleasure to meet you."

The criminologist felt the impact of his personality. Lester Gregory was the type who would always act in a roundabout, treacherous fashion to gain his ends; but here was a man who would go at things directly, striking through all obstacles. And who would be ruthless, too, caring little for what happened to those whom he brushed aside.

Yet at the same time Jennings felt that Captain Bergstrom welcomed his presence. Mona Carrington had told him that the two men were friends, working together to find the hidden treasure. Why, then, should the one welcome and the other resent him?

Lester Gregory flipped his half-smoked cigarette into the fireplace and immediately lighted another. "I suppose," he sneered, "that Mona brought you here to find the Captain's gem collection."

"And what if I did!" flashed the girl. "I couldn't stand any longer your eternal futile searching. And you're not to interfere with him, Lester! I've told him my feeling toward the jewels. You've had your chance at finding them and you've failed—miserably. I want this whole damnable business cleaned up—settled—and quickly!"

Lester Gregory laughed unpleasantly, then sneered. "Oh, I don't doubt that he'll find them! But you have a nice job cut out for you, Mr. Jennings. It'll try even your reputed skill."

"Now, now," rumbled Captain Bergstrom placatingly. "There's no need to quarrel, Lester. You've looked for a year, without success. Let's step aside and give Mr. Jennings a chance."

He laid his hand heavily on the younger man's shoulder, but the latter shrugged it off. "All right," he said. "I'll enjoy watching an expert at work."

Mona Carrington's lustrous black eyes appealed to Jennings. He was sorry for her, caught helplessly as she was in this maelstrom of hate and dissension and greed. He wanted to be able to reassure her, but what he had learned thus far had only served to aggravate the mystery.

"Don't expect too much," he warned them. "Just from a cursory examination of these rooms I can see that there are thousands of possible hiding places. . . . And Mr. Peter Carrington has told me that he thinks the jewels were flung into the ocean."

A harsh laugh greeted his statement. Peter Carrington tapped his way into the room, followed by the gloomy-faced Gifford.

"Don't expect too much!" he gibed. "Don't expect anything! I tell you, the jewels aren't here! No, when Avery committed suicide, he flung his pretty baubles into the ocean along with himself."

He glared about him, as though expecting disagreement. Lester Gregory exhaled a cloud of smoke and smiled sneeringly, but said nothing. There seemed to be a twinkle of amusement in Captain Bergstrom's cold eyes.

Jennings chose this moment to play one of his trump cards. If it were to be worth anything, now was the time to use it, when he might surprise an admission from one of them.

He said: "At least one of the gems was not flung into the sea."

"Eh?" inquired Peter Carrington.

Jennings took out the Bohojor Ruby and let it tilt on the palm of his hand.

"Recognize it?" he asked.

There was a sound of hushed silence. All eyes were caught and held by that globe of living red fire. Mona Carrington broke the spell first, grimaced and turned away to the door.

"The Bohojor Ruby!" whispered Lester Gregory.

His fingers trembled as he snatched up the gem and held it to the light. His black eyes kindled with a lustful, possessive glow. He was whispering, as though entranced: "The Mother of Death! It's the Mother of Death!"

Reluctantly, he allowed his uncle to take it. The latter glanced at it casually, nodded, and passed it to Captain Bergstrom, who turned it in huge fingers while the butler looked over his shoulder.

Lester Gregory demanded, savagely: "Where did you get it?"

"I found it," said Jennings.

"Where?"

"That I don't intend to reveal—just yet."

The criminologist's trump card had failed to bring in a trick. If any of these men had guilty knowledge of the gem, he had concealed it admirably. All had seemed equally amazed to see it. But he could still hold in reserve the secret of where he had found it. Not even Mona Carrington knew that.

Lester Gregory's fists clenched and he took a step forward. His eyes burned madly, recklessly.

"You've found the Captain's jewel collection!" he shouted. "You took this from it. But you're going to tell us where it is! You're going—"

Captain Bergstrom deposited the ruby on the top of a horizontal glass case and grasped the infuriated man's arm as he seemed about to spring on the criminologist.

"Easy, Lester," he cautioned. "Go easy, boy."

Lester Gregory snarled and tried to tear out of his grasp. He might as well have tried to escape a gorilla. Captain Bergstrom caught his eye, gave him a warning glance, and he subsided sullenly.

Peter Carrington's thin face was tight-lipped and grim. His cane tapped slowly on the rug.

"Jennings," he said, "this calls for an explanation—which it seems you don't propose to give. You've been in this house for less than a half hour, to my positive knowledge, and yet you casually produce one of my brother's most valuable gems."

Jennings smiled mockingly. He had no hope of cooperation from any of these men, unless it might be Captain Bergstrom. It was just possible that, by antagonizing them, he might learn more than if he acted in a conciliatory fashion.

He admitted: "Probably it does seem strange."

"Well?" snarled Peter Carrington. "Are you going to explain—or are you going to let us think you mean to appropriate this fortune for yourself as soon as our backs are turned?"

Jennings glanced toward the ruby which glimmered on the show case. But he gave no answer because at that instant there was an explosion and the room went dark.

For a moment, thereafter, the silence was as intense as the blackness. Then Mona Carrington screamed, and it broke the spell which held them. Lester Gregory cursed, Peter Carrington barked alarmed questions, and feet tramped.

Jennings tried to keep his sense of direction. There had been, he remembered, a floor lamp somewhere behind him, and he backed toward it. But somehow it eluded his questing fingers.

A chair crashed and he heard a cry of pain. In the jumble of voices he could not identify it, but he did identify the sodden thud of a body striking the floor.

Then he found the lamp and jerked the pull chain. The room flooded with light.

Five of them stood in various attitudes of defense. The sixth, Gifford the butler, lay on the floor, his face with the pallor of death on it. A tracery of red ran across his high forehead, from a wound just under his sparse hair.

"He's dead!" chattered Peter Carrington, lowering his uplifted cane.

Jennings knelt beside him. "I don't think so," he said. "The wound isn't deep enough—"

A cry interrupted him. Mona Carrington was pointing a trembling finger.

"The Bohojor Ruby! It's gone!"

IV

WHAT DREAD HAND?

ALLEN JENNINGS HAD ALREADY NOTED THIS FACT, having expected as much when the light was extinguished. He snapped at the distraught girl: "Some water, please! And a medicine kit, if you have one."

He felt the prostrate man's pulse. It was regular and increasing in strength. Jennings used a clean handkerchief and wiped the trickle of blood from his forehead.

"A shallow wound," he commented. "Made by a heavy, blunt instrument."

Peter Carrington glared at him. "Think I did it?" he snarled. "Want to look at my cane, eh?"

The criminologist saw no trace of blood on the polished cylinder of wood. But this was not conclusive, for the bleeding could not have started until after the weapon had rebounded from the skull.

Captain Bergstrom still held the poker taken from the fireplace. His broad face cracked into a smile.

"I'm another suspect, I imagine," he said amiably.

He held out the poker, but Jennings waved it away. It was, he observed, smeared with soot, and Gifford's wound was quite clean.

The girl returned with the water and a small medicine cabinet. The criminologist washed out the wound, applied antiseptic, and taped a bandage in place. Gifford had recovered consciousness, and now he climbed groggily to his feet,

"A spot of brandy would do him good," said Captain Bergstrom.

He took a carafe and tray of glasses from a cabinet. After the butler had gulped a glass of the sparkling liqueur, both he and Lester Gregory sampled it.

"Gifford, who did it?" demanded Mona Carrington.

"I don't know, miss," he replied. "The lights went out and everything was confused until something struck me on the head. . . ."

Captain Bergstrom growled: "The first question is, who put out the light?"

The rug was sprinkled with fragile bits of glass from the electric bulb. Under an exhibition case Jennings found a rock the size of a hen's egg.

But all disclaimed having seen it thrown. Jennings had been looking at the jewel at the time, and he questioned the girl, who had been facing the others.

She shook her head. "I wasn't expecting anything like that," she said. "But I should say that whoever put out the light also took the ruby. And whoever took it still has it. I was in the door all the time and no one passed me."

Lester Gregory suggested: "The stone might be on the floor."

When they found no trace of it, after a thorough search, Jennings said: "This puts it up to you pretty squarely. I suggest that you allow me to search you."

"We will not!" blustered Lester Gregory.

Peter Carrington sneered: "And how about yourself, Mr. Jennings? This strikes me as a rather clever scheme upon your part to possess yourself of the Bohojor Ruby and turn suspicion on us. Mona evidently knew that you had found it, and so you could not pocket it and say nothing."

"I will also submit to search," said the criminologist. "Gifford is beyond suspicion and can conduct it."

Captain Bergstrom said sharply: "Mr. Jennings is right. I insist that his suggestion be carried out." His eyes glinted strangely and a menacing tone crept into his voice. "There is something very peculiar going on here, and I mean to get to the bottom of it."

Lester Gregory grumbled a surly consent. Peter Carrington began to protest, but a warning glance from Captain Bergstrom silenced him. The girl retired to the foyer and shut the door while the butler conducted the search. It was without result, so far as the Bohojor Ruby was concerned; but pistols were found in the pockets of both Captain Bergstrom and Lester Gregory.

"Satisfied?" snarled Peter Carrington.

"Perfectly," answered Jennings. "But I want to point out that the stone may have been concealed in this room. It's too late now to make a thorough search, and so I propose to lock these quarters and go over them more carefully tomorrow."

They locked the heavy door with the carved dragon and Jennings put the key in his pocket. The chauffeur had returned with his luggage some time before, and Jennings asked Gifford to precede him to his room to help unpack. Then he accompanied Mona Carrington to her room and made an inspection of it.

"You may be in danger tonight," he told her, "though I hope not. Keep your door locked and open it for no one but me. And have your automatic handy."

"You know who took the Bohojor Ruby?" she asked eagerly.

"I have an idea, but it needs confirmation. And now I want information. You trust Gifford?"

"Why—of course. He was my father's personal servant, and since his death has been like a father to me."

"What do you know about Captain Bergstrom?"

"Very little. I first met him, four or five years ago, when Lester brought him home. He had a yacht and I understood he was quite wealthy, a Wall Street broker. I don't know where he got his title; perhaps from the fact that he commanded his own boat. I believe that now he has lost most of his fortune."

"He seems to exercise considerable influence over your cousin."

"He's a forceful, powerful man," she said, and added, "and—a dangerous man. I wouldn't want to cross him. I think he and Lester used to operate together in the market, and I've had an idea that their methods were not always what they should be."

Jennings gave her a few more words of caution, made sure she had locked the door behind him, and went to his room. Gifford had his luggage unpacked and pajamas laid out. He was respectful, reserved, and his undue nervousness might have been the result of the blow he had received.

The criminologist dropped into a chair, lit a cigarette, and regarded the butler with speculative eyes.

"Gifford," he said, "I've seen your face—or certainly at least a picture of you—before. Your name has not always been the same?"

"What—what do you mean, sir?" the man cried agitatedly.

"Some years ago a middle-aged clerk in a Wall Street bond house got into trouble and killed a man. Before the police could lay hands on him, he had skipped out. He was never found. That man's name was Gillham."

The little butler seemed to wilt and fade away. His eyes were sick and his lips trembled as he tried to speak.

"You are Gillham," continued Jennings. "I am sure of that now. I remember the case well, for I once had occasion to go into it."

The butler grasped the back of a chair for support. "It's true, sir," he cried desperately. "But I swear to you that I killed the man in self-defense! The police would never have believed it, however, and I had to hide away. Mr. Jacob Carrington, Miss Mona's father, knew all the circumstances, and he hid me here until the hunt died down, and then employed me as butler. Tell me, sir," he begged, "you aren't going to turn me over to the police now, after so many years of faithful service—"

Jennings said: "The past is past—Gifford. I've told you this merely to prove that you can trust me. I need your help. Ostensibly I'm here to find Captain Carrington's gem collection, but actually it is to protect the life of your mistress."

"To protect—her life?"

The criminologist related the circumstances of her first attack. "What I want from you," he finished, "is information. You know this house, the people in it, the cross currents of emotion. Who would have a motive to kill her?"

"Who doesn't, sir?" demanded the butler. "Both Mr. Gregory and Mr. Peter Carrington! Mr. Gregory has always hated her because she was their uncle's favorite and was to inherit his fortune! And Mr. Peter hated her father and he hates her. Were she to die, Captain Carrington's fortune would be divided between the two of them. Isn't that motive enough, sir?"

"How about Captain Bergstrom?"

"He scarcely knows her, sir."

"Anyone else?"

"I don't think so, sir." Gifford was silent for a moment, then blurted out: "But there's something else I should tell you about, sir. Something about Captain Carrington's suicide—"

"You don't think it was suicide?"

"No, sir. It was murder!"

"Eh?" said Jennings. "You can prove that?"

The little butler said: "I believe so, sir. The coroner put it down as suicide, when he looked at the body after Mr. Gregory had recovered it from the rocks outside the windows, and consequently the police were never called it. Even if they had been, you can understand that I would have kept as far out of their way as possible because of—of my own identity. I was not sure, then, though I suspected. You see, sir, several days before he died, Captain Carrington told me he thought he might be murdered."

"By whom?"

"He didn't say, sir. Only that he didn't much care, because his health was so bad."

"But what makes you sure it was murder?"

"This, sir. After the funeral when Captain Carrington's body had been placed in the family vault, I went to his rooms to tidy up. And, in his museum, I found a terrible thing. I'll get it, sir, if you'll wait a minute."

Gifford disappeared and presently returned bearing an object wrapped with a towel. When the wrapping was removed, it disclosed a quart fruit jar, sealed with an air-tight top. It was filled with a colorless liquid. And in it was a human hand! It had been cleanly severed at the wrist, and was bleached to a horrible, doughy whiteness.

"I found this in one of the cabinets, sir," explained the butler. "It was wrapped in a handkerchief and covered with dried blood. I was afraid to show it to the coroner because he might start an investigation and discover who I was. But at the same time I had a hunch not to throw it away, and so I put it in this bottle of preservative formaldehyde and hid it."

Jennings examined this grizzly exhibit and asked: "What connection has this with Captain Carrington's death? It might have been in the cabinet for months before you found it."

"It had not been placed there until at least after dinner that night, sir. When Captain Carrington retired to his museum after dinner, he asked me for a fresh handkerchief. I brought him one and it was that handkerchief in which this hand was wrapped. And it was soaked with blood."

"You know whose hand it is?"

"Unfortunately no, sir. But I have always believed that Captain Carrington was thrown from the window, and that this hand came from one of the men who did it."

"Was there any blood in the room?"

"No, sir."

The criminologist knit his forehead as he stared at this ghastly exhibit. It seemed well nigh impossible to explain. The butler's reasoning proved beyond doubt that it had been cut from a living body within a few hours of Captain Carrington's suicide—or murder. But, if there had been no blood—and such a wound would have bled copiously—where, then, had the amputation been performed? And why? And for what reason had the hand been secreted in the cabinet?

He asked: "Who was here the night he died?"

"Mr. Gregory and Mr. Peter Carrington, sir. And I have reason to believe that Captain Bergstrom was also here. At that time he smoked a gold-tipped cigarette with his monogram, and I found the stub of one on a tray in the museum. I did not see Captain Bergstrom himself, but it would have been easy enough for him to have moored his yacht in the bay and slipped into the house. I was with the other servants in our quarters."

The criminologist nodded thoughtfully. He seemed to be learning a little about everything except the riddle of where Captain Carrington had hidden his jewel collection.

He asked the butler about that.

"I don't know, sir," Gifford admitted, "and I saw as much of Captain Carrington as anybody. He was a strange, peculiar man. But I'm sure he kept the jewels somewhere in his quarters, because, when he wanted to show them to anybody, he'd lock the door and in five minutes he'd be ready. I always supposed he used the safe."

He paused, then went on. "But if you want my opinion, sir, whoever killed him took his jewels. Though," and he looked puzzled, "I can't imagine where you found the Bohojor Ruby."

Jennings did not enlighten him. He had learned everything the butler had to communicate, and he dismissed him for the night.

Mystery was piling on mystery, but some of the pieces were beginning to fit together. He thought he saw a picture emerging slowly from this tangled skein of events.

V

COLD STEEL

IT WAS AFTER MIDNIGHT when Allen Jennings descended the stairs. The grandfather's clock in the foyer was booming the half hour softly, hollowly. The beam of his flash stabbed through darkness until it rested on the raised head of a dragon, carved upon a door panel. Its green-jeweled eyes stared out at him balefully, menacingly.

He used the key which Mona Carrington had given him and locked the door after him. He went directly into the library-museum and moved a floor lamp close to the teakwood table on which the carafe of brandy and tray of glasses still stood. Choosing one of the glasses, he used a small brush and dusted fine black powder on it. The result was a series of well-defined fingerprints.

Jennings studied these carefully, jotting down a row of figures on a pad of paper. When he finished he had the mathematical formula for the fingerprints of a right hand.

Then he used a telephone in the office and put in a long-distance call. Within a few minutes he was talking with Ramsey, deputy chief of the Federal Secret Service in New York. He read off the classification he had made and asked: "Check those prints for me, will you? I'll hold the wire."

The answer came, after some delay. "They belong to Al Barlow. Where in the world did you get them?"

Al Barlow! Once that had been a name to conjure with in the underworld of New York. He had been the ruler of the huge drug ring which had supplied New York with its narcotics. Rich, powerful, able to gratify his every whim, he had spent lavishly, maintained a luxurious yacht, and posed as a patron of the arts. It was even rumored that he had had as silent partner a wealthy society man.

But crime monarchs rise and fall, and Al Barlow was no exception. It had begun with a change in administration at the city hall which had cost him valuable protection and political connections. Then smaller competitors had combined into larger gangs and nibbled at his territories. Hijackers, in one swift raid, had captured a store of drugs worth millions. Finally Federal narcotic agents, seeing the king slipping, had completed the debacle by using Uncle Sam's mailed fist.

Al Barlow had, of course, escaped prison, but discreet bribes had cost him the better part of his fortune. And then, his power broken, his gangs scattered, his wealth lost, he had faded into obscurity and been forgotten.

Jennings asked: "What's Barlow's recent history?"

Ramsey chuckled. "Don't you know? Last spring his yacht was wrecked on the Jersey coast. The Coast Guard picked him up and turned him over to the New Jersey authorities. They had some sort of charge against him and he got a one-to-ten sentence. I've heard that he was released a week or so ago."

"Anything against him now?"

"Not us! There's plenty of big fish in the ocean without bothering about has-beens. And these days it takes big money to stage a come-back."

The criminologist gave another fingerprint classification. He had obtained it laboriously from the severed hand the butler had given him. After another delay, the reply came back.

"That checks with the prints of Luigi Borelli, one of Barlow's men. He dropped out of sight some time ago. Look here, Jennings, what's up?"

"I'm not sure yet," answered the criminologist, and hung up.

A voice said: "Aren't you, Jennings?"

Captain Bergstrom, alias Al Barlow, stood in the door. His huge hands were thrust in his coat pockets, and there was a suggestive bulge under one pocketed hand. His stocky, compact body, topped by his square scowling face, was a pillar of strength and menace.

"I saw you slipping down, Jennings," he continued, "and I guessed something interesting was up. Luckily I had a key and was able to listen in on your conversation. Well, now that you've discovered that I'm Al Barlow, what are you going to do about it?"

His flat voice dwindled off. Jennings smiled disarmingly and waved him to a chair.

"There's nothing to do," he answered. "My errand here is to find Captain Carrington's jewel collection, but I am interested in how you fit here."

Captain Bergstrom relaxed a little. He brought his hands from his pockets, with them a cigarette case, which he offered to Jennings. The criminologist took one of the gold-tipped cigarettes, initialed with an ornately monogrammed letter "B."

"How do I fit?" Captain Bergstrom smiled quizzically. "I'm here for the same reason you are, Jennings—to find the gems. You know that if we find them, the girl has promised to give a share of what they bring to Gregory and Carrington. And Gregory and I need one of those shares to finance a certain business venture. . . ."

Jennings remembered that Ramsey had said Barlow was broke, that he was a has-been and would remain such unless he obtained new working capital. Lester Gregory was, of course, Al Barlow's silent partner—the society man of rumor. Evidently both had been ruined by the cleanup which had swept Barlow from his underworld throne, and they were seizing upon this desperate expedient to amass enough ready cash to carry them back into the racket.

Captain Bergstrom suddenly leaned forward. "Look here, Jennings," he clipped, "there's no need for us to quarrel. You know who I am—or was. O.K. You know I'm clean with the law. We might just as well get along together, because I'll be here as long as you are."

Jennings said: "I'm agreeable."

"And," went on Captain Bergstrom, "I want to offer my help in finding the jewels. I don't suppose you'll want to cooperate with me, and I don't expect it; but there's no reason why I can't cooperate with you. Though I must admit," he added, gloomily, "that about all I can tell you is several hundred places where the gems aren't hidden."

"You think they're still here?"

Captain Bergstrom regarded him narrowly. "Don't you? That fool of a Carrington couldn't be right, could he? D'you think the Captain could have thrown them in the sea when he committed suicide?"

Jennings shrugged. "I'm still acquiring facts," he said. "Theories will come later."

"Oh, the jewels are here," said Captain Bergstrom, confidently. "They've got to be here. Yet neither Gregory nor I could find them, and we went through these rooms with a fine-tooth comb. We removed every one of those Chinese panels from the walls, took apart most of the furniture, and tore up things in general. . . . The search has been thorough enough."

"You found nothing?"

Captain Bergstrom laughed. "We found plenty . . . secret drawers and panels, filled to their brims with jewels. But the jewels were slum—worthless paste and glass. Each time we thought we had the real thing, but when we got the stuff in a good light we saw our mistake."

"What about the note and lead pennies in the safe?"

"Oh, that? Another of the captain's jokes, just like the secret drawers. How could a lead penny be a key?"

Jennings did not attempt to answer, though a wild hunch had occurred to him. But so many other things were clamoring for explanation that he gave it little thought for the moment.

"I don't suppose," hazarded Captain Bergstrom, "that you'd explain where you found the Bohojor Ruby? . . . Well, never mind. But I would like to know what happened to it. You didn't conduct that disappearing act yourself, did you?"

Jennings said: "I was as surprised as you!"

Captain Bergstrom scowled blackly. "It was one of us in that room," he rasped. "If I'd only had my eyes open—" He glanced obliquely at the criminologist. "Have you thought that the girl might have done it herself?"

"Eh? Mona Carrington?"

The other shrugged. "Just an idea, that's all. Take it for what it's worth. But she doesn't have an exactly natural or normal attitude about the jewels."

"I think the explanation she gave me of her feeling toward them is extremely plausible. They have brought nothing but tragedy into her life—particularly the Bohojor Ruby," Jennings said.

Barlow shrugged again.

The criminologist found it difficult to suspect Mona Carrington, though he had to admit to himself that it was not an impossible theory. Of them all, the girl had had the best opportunity to have tossed the stone which had put out the light. And she alone had not been searched. Even had she been, however, there had been the chance to dispose of the gem when she left to get the medical kit.

Yet he doubted that her intense dislike for the ruby could have carried her that far. Jennings recalled her reaction to his offer to let her examine the Mother of Death in the burial vault. Certainly her behavior at that time was genuine, completely unfeigned. Captain Bergstrom, he was now sure, had had nothing to do with the ruby's disappearance. The man was obviously sincere in his desire to aid in finding the jewels—indeed, he had everything to gain and nothing to lose by their being found.

He was still deeply absorbed in the problem when they left Captain Carrington's quarters and parted at the head of the stairs. He had opened the door of his room and advanced a step into it before he realized that something was wrong. When he had left, a desk lamp had been lighted. Now the room was in total darkness.

He sensed rather than heard the swish of the blow directed toward him. In the fraction of time left to him, measured in the split second it took a knife to travel a few inches, he could not fend off the thrust. Before he could raise a hand, its point would slip home in his heart.

Jennings swayed quickly to the left. A cold length of steel hissed between his chest and right arm, slitting through the material of his coat. He clamped his arm tightly to his side, twisted away and fell forward. Only thus could he prevent the knife from being jerked back for a second blow. Any attempt to grasp at the hand which held it would be fatal.

The hand retained its grip upon the hilt for a part of the fall, and then its fingers were torn away. Jennings came down on his knees and threw himself into a forward somersault. A blow lashed against his head, almost stunning him.

As he came up on his hands and knees, he saw a shadow flitting through the door. For only an instant it silhouetted against the dimly lit corridor—scarcely long enough for him to distinguish, before it vanished, the vague outlines of a man.

When Jennings reached the corridor, his head still ringing from the effects of the blow, he found it empty. He rapped on Mona Carrington's door and received her sleepy assurance that she was all right before he returned to his room.

The knife lay on the floor where it had been dropped. He picked it up carefully. It was a Japanese dagger, with a bronze filigreed guard. Its greenish-yellow blade was without trace of fingerprints.

Then he caught sight of something on the bed. A note pinned to the counterpane, over the pillow.

> Mr. Allen Jennings—
> And now you try your hand at the mystery of where Captain Carrington concealed his jewels. It will be interesting to watch your deductive skill pitted against his carefully guarded secret.
> You have the key, the lead penny. Beware that you use it, if you find the lock!

A challenge—and an ironic warning! And it was unsigned.

Jennings studied it carefully, but found no clue to the identity of the writer. It had been composed on a typewriter with badly worn type, printed with an uneven pressure.

"Easy enough to identify the machine," the criminologist told himself, "if I can find it. Certainly, the man who tried to slip a knife between my ribs didn't leave this note. It's evident that I have at least one well-wisher at Stormward Manor—as well as one would-be assassin. Or perhaps two would-be assassins, if the fellow who took a shot at us was aiming at me."

And then he added, smiling wryly: "My well-wisher hints at knowing a great deal. Or was he bluffing? Too bad that he didn't tell me what this secret is and how to use the key!"

VI

CAPTAIN CARRINGTON'S SECRET

LEADEN CLOUDS HUNG LOW IN THE SKY, rolling slowly under the drive of a sultry wind. A dull morning sun etched their edges with silver and glimmered on the furrows of whitecaps. At the base of the cliff on which perched Stormward Manor, breakers ate at the rock, smashed at it with ageless mad fury, flinging fingers of spray and foam high into the air.

Allen Jennings leaned from one of the windows of the library-museum. The outside of the brick wall was flush with the cliff, separated from it by a narrow stone coping. He shuddered as he thought of a body hurtling down, down, to that seething cauldron of rocks and boiling waters.

He said: "I want you to point out, Gifford, exactly where Captain Carrington's body was found."

The little butler pointed with a tremulous finger. A half-dozen feet to the left, twin points of rock, fallen in some past age from the cliff, lifted like spires. Scarcely a foot of space separated their black slimy peaks, almost inundated as the waves flung themselves up against them.

"Right there it was, sir. His body had fallen between them. He was wedged in tight, otherwise the waves would have carried him away."

"He was badly injured?"

"Frightfully, sir. His back was broken and his face—it was so terrible I didn't look at him. The water was unusually quiet that morning, and Mr. Gregory got him off with the help of the chauffeur, before the coroner arrived."

Gifford drew back from the window, looking a little nauseated at the memory. Mona Carrington's eyes were liquid black pools of horror.

Jennings asked: "In which cabinet did you find the object you showed me?"

The butler indicated a teakwood cabinet, to the right of the window and against the wall. On its doors, in jeweled mosaic, was the design of a dragon rampant. Inside, was a collection of Chinese pottery and jade. The criminologist had Gifford point out the exact shelf on which he had found the severed hand, and then dismissed him.

"Perhaps you had best go, too," he told the girl. "I've worked out a theory of where the gems are hidden, and it might not be pleasant to watch me test it."

Mona Carrington shook her head. "I'll stay," she said. "I'm not hysterical and won't bother you."

Jennings had expected as much, for the girl had proved that she had courage. He seated himself on the edge of the window embrasure and lit a cigarette.

"In that case," he said, "I'll explain my theory before I start. I don't propose to search blindly—too much wasted time. And I'd likely have no more success than your cousin and Captain Bergstrom. The better method is to reason out the kind of hiding place a man like Captain Carrington would choose, and then look for it."

The girl nodded, without comment.

"You, yourself," went on the criminologist, "sketched the solution when we talked in the burial vault last night. You said that Captain Carrington used the safe only as a blind, while he had some other more secure hiding place for his gems. Evidently he realized that any safe man can make, man can break open, using modern scientific tools. Carrying your reasoning a little further, we can understand that a man who would use such an elaborate precaution to throw robbers off the track, would not trust a valuable jewel collection to such prosaic hiding places as secret drawers and panels."

"But there are secret panels," she reminded him.

"Yes, but only for the purpose of further safe-guarding his collection. The safe was his protection, his first pretense. If that were broken open and discovered empty, there were still the secret drawers and fake jewels which must all be investigated."

Mona Carrington asked, bewildered: "But if not a secret drawer or panel, then where? You seem to rule out everything. And the jewels are certainly here, someplace."

"I agreed that they are here," said the criminologist. "And I am not ruling out all hiding places, but merely pointing out that we must look for one more ingenious than drawers and panels. We must look for one such as a man like your uncle, versed in all the lore and guile of the Orient, would choose. And that practically eliminates the interior of these rooms."

She stared at him, uncomprehending.

Jennings went on: "Having reasoned this far, we'll look for a clue in another direction. The position in which Captain Carrington's body was found leads to interesting speculation. The assumption was that he committed suicide by throwing himself from the window. You believe that he was thrown from it. But neither theory fits the facts. The two rocks between which he was found are more than six feet to the left of the window. Even had he jumped in that direction, he could not possibly have fallen between them."

The girl grasped his logic quickly. "Then he must have fallen from the roof," she said.

"Or the coping outside the window," he added. "You will notice that it is wide enough for a man to stand on. And the wall, though apparently perpendicular, actually slants slightly inward."

Mona Carrington leaned out the window and looked at the narrow shoulder of stone. The sheer drop to the raging waters made her heart beat faster and she paled.

"You mean—he was walking on that little ledge!" she cried. "But that's impossible! And why would—"

"Suppose that his hiding place was accessible only in that manner. It would be perfect protection, for no one would ever dare venture on that little ledge—or suspect him of doing so."

Jennings flipped his cigarette from the window and watched it turn over and over in its fall, until a splash of foam sucked it into the green depths. He felt a little sick at the thought of venturing out on that narrow coping, where the slightest misstep meant horrible death, but he swiveled his legs through the embrasure until they hung outside.

"It's not nearly as dangerous as it looks," he assured the girl. "But you'd better keep back from the window, where you can't see me."

He grasped the window sill and lowered himself until his feet touched the ledge. It was broader than it looked, wide enough to take the full length of his shoes. And, with the slight inward slant of the wall and the pressure of the breeze, he found it not at all difficult to maintain his balance.

He inched his way slowly to the left, not daring to look down. His nerves tingled with the thrill of danger, though he knew that Captain Carrington must often have traveled this way—if his reasoning were correct.

Then he found what he sought. An iron ring, set in a shallow depression of the brick wall.

He pulled the ring experimentally. It gave easily, with a rattling and grating of chains. A section of the coping slid outward, then tipped downward as though pivoted on hinges. It disclosed a hole in the face of the cliff, at the base of the brick wall, with steps running into the hewn rock.

Jennings crept down the steps into darkness. He arrived at a small room, with roof so low that his head almost scraped against the ceiling. Probably the ceiling was the floor of the library-museum, or the rock on which it rested.

He lit a match and found an electric wall bracket, supplied by a hidden conduit from the house. It spattered a harsh white light on the rough stone walls and floor. There was only the single entrance into the room. It was sparsely furnished with a desk, a cabinet and a few chairs.

Close to his feet a fiber rug was thrown over something. It did not conceal the humanness of its outlines. Jennings drew back the rug, and his pulse leaped at his not unexpected discovery.

He had uncovered a corpse, or rather the skeleton of a man. It had evidently been there for some time, for only a trace of dried flesh adhered to the bones, seen through rotting, mildewed clothing. The empty eye sockets pooled dark shadows which stared at him mockingly. An old-fashioned watch attached to a chain lay across his chest.

Jennings pulled back the right sleeve. There were the ulna and radius bones of the forearm, but the hand was gone!

"Luigi Borelli," he muttered. "Evidently he died just where he lost his hand."

He heard a choked cry behind him. Mona Carrington was crouched on the steps, staring down at the corpse. The wind flung wisps of hair about her face, its raven blackness contrasting vividly with the red slash of her lips and the chalk of her cheeks.

"You shouldn't have come," Jennings said sternly. "It was too dangerous—"

"I wanted to," she replied simply. She was still staring at the draped form. "What—who was that?"

"Luigi Borelli."

The name meant nothing to her. She averted her eyes from it and surveyed the room.

"Uncle Avery's secret room," she whispered. "And he never gave me a hint of its existence. But look! It's the dragon design again!"

She pointed to a Chinese console cabinet in the corner. On the upper panel, over the hinged doors, was carved in almost full relief the dragon rampant. Its jaws, fanged with slivers of ivory, gaped wide. Chinese in spirit, superb in the delicacy and feeling of its execution, Jennings judged it to be the work of the same artisan who had designed the other dragon panels.

Mona Carrington opened the doors of the cabinet. Behind them was a recess some ten inches in depth. At the rear of this was a series of jewelers' trays, arranged in shelf fashion. One of the trays had been pulled out a half inch, and in it, upon a bed of black velvet was the gleam of myriad gems, living flames of white and yellow and crimson and sapphire.

The girl's eyes dilated. She stared at the jewels much as a bird might stare at the hypnotizing eyes of a serpent. Slowly, jerkily, her hand went toward the trays. . . .

"Don't!" snapped Jennings dropping the rug back over the hideous thing on the floor.

She did not heed him, if she heard. Her breathing was spasmodic and rasping. Her hand trembled as it continued toward the cabinet.

The criminologist grasped her shoulders and pulled her away. She shuddered as the spell was broken, and gave a piteous little bleat.

"I—I can't help it!" she cried. "I hate them! But they fascinate me—"

"I know," Jennings said soberly.

The rampant dragon stared malevolently at them with its green-jeweled eyes. It seemed more than carven wood, more than a harmless representation of a mythological monster. It was a sentient, living creature, guarding a fabulous fortune in gems. It seemed to be able to leap and strike, to rend and tear with its talons and fangs. . . .

Jennings took his handkerchief and folded it diagonally, rolling it to the thickness of his finger. In the end he made a small slip noose and dropped it over the knob of one of the trays. He drew it tight, carefully to keep his hands entirely outside the cabinet.

Then he tugged upon the end of the handkerchief, so that the tray was drawn out a half inch. Instantly, there was a click and whirr. He caught a blurred glimpse of a polished blade swinging down from a recess in the top of the cabinet. Down it swept in a straight line, sheering through the material of the handkerchief as though it were tissue. And then it sprang back into its hidden sheath.

"So that's how that poor devil lost his hand," muttered Jennings. "He found the cabinet, tried to seize the gems—and death struck without warning. Probably he died from loss of blood."

He had read of such devices before. They were characteristic of the Satanic guile and cunning of which the Oriental mind was capable.

As he was studying the cabinet, a voice rasped behind him: "Turn around, Mr. Jennings! And take care that you don't reach for a gun!"

Peter Carrington was crouched on the steps, the tails of his long cloak flapping about him. The harsh light striking up against his hawk nose and pointed chin made him look more than ever like a bird of prey. His cane was in his left hand and a large-bore revolver in his right, aimed unwaveringly at the criminologist.

"Uncle Peter!" gasped the girl.

"Uncle Avery's secret room and he never gave a hint of its existence," the old man parroted and started to laugh.

His mirth held all the raucousness of a vulture's scream. His eyes blazed hatred at the girl, so that she stumbled back until her back was against the rough stone wall.

"Surprised to see me, eh?" he sneered. "Well, I've been watching you for several minutes. Allow me to congratulate you, Mr. Jennings, on your cleverness in finding this place. Your reputation scarcely does you justice."

Jennings inclined his head in response to the tribute. Peter Carrington's eyes flickered about the room without for an instant letting down his guard.

"Ingenious of my poor dead brother to have constructed a secret room like this," he said unctuously. "But then, I might have expected something like this from him. His taste ran to the extravagant and bizarre. Except for you, Mr. Jennings, his jewel collection might have remained here, unsuspected, until the end of time." Then he added, with mock mournfulness: "As you, too, will remain here."

The girl pleaded: "Uncle Peter, you—"

He cut her off. "And I regret that you must also be included, my dear. Though it's a pity that all that fresh young beauty must molder away, giving delight only to blind worms."

"But—why—"

"You can guess, my dear. Because I do not care to taste prison. And that's just where Jennings would put me. Oh, don't think that I don't know that the real reason you brought him here was to trap me! He knows I wanted your fortune, that I pushed you off the cliff, that I shot at both of you there again, and that later I failed to knife him in his room."

The girl's horror mounted. The old man chuckled, gloatingly, with sadistic pleasure.

"No, Mona, I'm too canny to put my head into the noose. Thanks to your detective discovering this room, I can now dispose of you so your bodies will never be found, never rise to confront me, as they might if I had been successful the first time. The two of you will rot here, disappeared without trace. A bullet in each of you will never be heard outside this room And then I can enjoy my brother's fortune—and jewels!"

Jennings jeered: "Think so? You're sure of that, Mr Carrington? Then take a look at this?"

With his toe, he kicked the rug from the skeleton. The old man's eyes turned toward the gruesome relic and for a moment were held by its horror.

At that instant, Jennings leaped. The revolver roared but the bullet only grazed his shoulder harmlessly. He reached the old man before he could fire a second time and tore the gun from his grasp. Peter Carrington screamed as he stumbled and went down. He did not rise.

"Struck his head against the wall," panted the criminologist. "He'll come out of it, after a while."

"Mr. Jennings!" gasped the girl. "Do you think that—he really meant to—"

"I'm afraid so."

"But did you know that he—"

"I guessed it. You saw the footprints in the bushes, after the shot fired at us. There was a circular mark between them, the print of a cane. But there'll be no more danger from him."

A flat voice cut in: "And so drop that gun, Mr. Jennings! You won't need it!"

VII

The Lead Penny

Captain bergstrom, alias al barlow, was standing on the steps. Lester Gregory crouched behind him. Both held large automatics.

Allen Jennings dropped the revolver and, at Captain Bergstrom's order, kicked it over to the steps.

Captain Bergstrom said: "We came just behind Mr. Carrington, without his knowing it. We were in time to hear his dramatic pronouncement concerning your deaths. It seems," he added, ironically, "that we've been nursing a viper at our breasts! I never imagined Peter was the blood-thirsty sort."

He chuckled as he stepped down into the room, but his square face was grim. He held his automatic trained on the criminologist as steadily as though it were gripped in a vise. He radiated solid power and confidence— and menace.

Lester Gregory crept after him, resembling a vulture even more than his uncle had. His cheeks were flushed and his eyes burned with a mad fever. "Where are the gems?" he demanded, hoarsely.

"Captain Carrington was clever," pursued Bergstrom, ignoring the interruption. "Who but you, Mr. Jennings, could have guessed that he had a snug retreat like this—or found it?"

Lester Gregory pushed impatiently past him, but recoiled as his foot crunched against the skeleton. "What's this?" he demanded tremulously.

"Luigi Borelli," said Captain Bergstrom, almost betraying surprise. "I'd recognize that old turnip of a watch he carried, anywhere. Even though what's left of his face doesn't tell much. Hm-m-m. This explains a few things which have always puzzled me. So Luigi got this far, eh?"

Lester Gregory stepped over the skeleton and past his uncle, who had recovered consciousness and was crawling feebly across the floor. He shifted his gun to his left hand and went to the desk, began wildly rummaging through its drawers.

Captain Bergstrom looked musingly at Jennings. "I wonder how much you know," he said. "I suspect that you have a very good idea of what happened here, a year ago."

"Probably," said the criminologist, "a better idea than you."

"Yes. Yes, I can believe that. You are clever, Mr. Jennings—but perhaps you have been too clever."

"You mean—"

"I haven't entirely decided. But I fear that, much as I respect you and great as your service has been to us, I must repeat Mr. Carrington's dramatic pronouncement concerning your abrupt demise."

"And the girl?"

Captain Bergstrom's cold eyes swung to Mona Carrington. She put up her head and met his gaze contemptuously, without flinching.

"The pronouncement includes her," he said, flatly.

Lester Gregory turned from the desk with an oath. "I can't find the jewels!" he growled.

Then he caught sight of the cabinet, in front of which the girl had been standing. "Get back!" he snarled. "Get out of my way!" He pushed her brutally aside. His eyes glittered madly as he saw the rows of trays and he shouted; "They're here! A fortune in stones!"

His hand went toward the trays as Mona Carrington remembered.

"Don't! Don't, Lester! There's a—"

She grasped his left arm, but with an oath he dealt her a blow which sent her staggering back against the criminologist. Then, before Jennings could interfere, it had happened.

As his fingers closed on a tray and jerked it out, there was a click and whirr. Again that razor-sharp blade of steel clove through the air. Faster than the eye could follow, the knife swept down, and was instantly withdrawn to its sheath.

Then silence.

The girl forgot to breathe. Captain Bergstrom forgot to watch Jennings, but the latter was gripped by sheer, sickening horror.

Lester Gregory stood frozen. Dumbly, incredulously, he looked at his severed wrist, spouting blood with each beat of his heart. He looked at his hand, laying against one shoe, staining the black leather with bright crimson.

And then he shrieked, insanely and shudderingly. His automatic clattered to the floor. He seized the bleeding stump with his left hand, trying to staunch the flow of blood.

"God! My hand! I'm bleeding to death!"

Jennings might have gotten the drop on Captain Bergstrom then, but sheer horror of the deadly effectiveness of the device held him rooted. The stricken man's screams rasped his eardrums as he staggered toward the stairs.

"A doctor!" he blubbered. "I've got to get a doctor! I've got—"

None thought to stop him as he stumbled up the steps. He disappeared and they still heard his screams, high-pitched and terrible. They rose higher and higher, blood-curdling in their shrillness . . . and then were abruptly silenced.

A picture rose in Jennings' mind, a picture of needle-sharp rocks lifting from raging, boiling waters, of a body hurtling down upon them. . . .

Conquering his paralysis, he swayed to one side and sprang toward Captain Bergstrom. During all this, the other's gun had not wavered by a fraction of an inch from the line it had held, and so the bullet missed the criminologist and ricocheted from the stone walls. Then Jennings caught the muzzle of the gun and tipped it up in a leverage which could neither be broken nor endured.

Captain Bergstrom released his hold upon the weapon, but dealt the criminologist a sledge-hammer blow on the shoulder which drove him reeling across the room and numbed his arm so that the gun dropped from his fingers. Then they faced each other on even terms.

Mona Carrington crouched in the corner by the jewel cabinet, sobbing with terror. Her uncle was on his hands and knees, shaking his head slowly from side to side.

Jennings paused only long enough to suck in a lungful of air before he returned to the battle. Captain Bergstrom was heavier and more powerful, but he was clumsier than Jennings and did not have the criminologist's scientific knowledge.

They crashed with a thud of fists. Captain Bergstrom fought silently, unemotionally, dealing blows which would have felled the slighter man had they landed squarely. Jennings always managed to take them on arms or shoulders, but his own blows seemed to have no more effect upon the other than they might have had upon a bag of sand.

He was weakening fast and he knew that he could not long stand this terrific punishment and drain upon his strength. Captain Bergstrom reached vulnerable spots oftener and oftener.

Then Jennings slipped and went down to his hands and knees.

Captain Bergstrom could have finished him with a fair blow, but he chose to use foul. His toe lashed toward the criminologist's chin. By a superhuman effort, Jennings ducked out of its way, then came out of his crouch like a coiled spring released. His fist crashed home on Captain Bergstrom's chin with every ounce of his body behind it. An agonizing pain shot up his arm and he knew that his knuckles were broken. He staggered on his feet, realizing that if this blow did not end the fight, he was done for.

For seconds, Captain Bergstrom stood upright. But his eyes had gone blank, and he swayed forward and crashed headlong on his face.

Then a voice spoke: "That was good work, Jennings!"

A man stood on the steps. His face was that of a hawk, with hooked nose, thin lips and jutting chin. But his lips had a genial twist at the corners, and his black eyes were sparkling.

To Jennings' swimming gaze, it at first seemed that Peter Carrington was standing there. Then he took a grip on himself and said: "Welcome, Captain Carrington!"

"Ah! You know me?"

"We have met before. . . . It was in your family vault, Captain Carrington. You were examining the coffin in which you had been buried."

"In which I was supposed to have been buried," corrected Captain Carrington. Then he turned to the girl, who was staring at him with a frozen, incredulous face. "Mona! Don't you recognize me?"

She gave a little hysterical cry, ran and threw her arms about his neck. Sobbing, laughing, she said: "Oh, Uncle Avery, I—I thought—they told me—"

"There, there, Mona." He embraced her trembling body tenderly. "I'm a long way from being dead. Very much alive, in fact, and prepared to live for quite a few more years."

Still holding the sobbing girl in his arms, he looked about the room. Peter Carrington had recovered enough to sit up against the wall, but his eyes were still dazed. Captain Bergstrom lay on the floor where he had dropped.

"Quite a battle you had here, Jennings. I had Andrews, the gate keeper, stationed where he could see whether you were successful in finding this little cubby-hole of mine. I was hiding in his lodge, and when he reported that you had succeeded, I hurried here as fast as I could, and arrived just in time to see you finish Captain Bergstrom." He nodded toward his brother and asked: "What's he doing here?"

Jennings told him as gently as possible. The old man's eyes hardened. "I'm not surprised," he said, bitterly. "Well, I think I can handle him. He's always—but what's that hand on the floor?"

The criminologist explained.

"I am sorry, of course," said Captain Carrington, "because he was my nephew. But I can't say that I greatly regret it. He had an evil mind and a criminal character." He gestured toward Captain Bergstrom. "You know who he is?"

Jennings answered, "Al Barlow, former leader of the largest dope ring in New York."

"And utterly depraved, if ever any man was! My nephew was associated with him. That, Mr. Jennings, is why I am not sorry that he is dead. He was headed straight for prison—or the electric chair. Some letters of his once fell into my hands and I learned of the whole thing. Lester had furnished the money and together they had organized one of the most vicious gangs in the state. I faced Lester with the fact, but he only laughed at me and boasted of it, thinking I would not be willing to drag the name of Carrington through the mud of an investigation by exposing him. Then, when they had lost their gang and fortune—but perhaps you can guess that part of it?"

"I believe so," said Jennings. "They faced you, the night you disappeared, and demanded that you turn over to them your gem collection. They meant to dispose of it and get sufficient capital to set themselves up in the dope racket again."

Captain Carrington peered at him sharply. "You seem to know a great deal," he commented, dryly. "Perhaps you can go on with the story?"

Jennings continued: "You refused, of course. And then they very likely tortured you for the combination of your safe. Since the safe was found unopened, you did not give them the combination—or gave it incorrectly. While they were in the storage room, trying to open the safe, you were left in the library with Luigi Borelli and one other man. You somehow bought their betrayal, perhaps by promising to turn the gems over to them if they allowed you to escape. At any rate, you led them to this secret room, by way of the window and coping. One of them either fell or was pushed from the ledge into the sea. The other, Luigi Borelli, when you showed him your jewel cabinet, reached in to seize the gems—and lost his hand. He died here. Then you took his severed hand, wrapped it in your handkerchief, returned to the library and hid it in a cabinet.

"Why you did this last, I don't know. Nor do I know why Al Barlow left without extracting your secret and taking your collection. But he did take you with him. Then a storm came up and his yacht, the only thing left to him, was wrecked on the New Jersey coast. You escaped in some manner, but he was captured and put in prison for a year. In the meantime, Lester Gregory had recovered the body of the man who had fallen into the sea and buried it as yours.

"A year passed. Lester Gregory was not able to find the gems and, when Al Barlow was released from prison, he returned here to aid his former partner in the search. And you, too, returned at the same time. With the help of Andrews, the gate keeper, you opened the family vault, no doubt curious whose body had been buried for yours. You had already visited this room and taken from your collection the Bohojor Ruby, your most precious stone. This somehow dropped from your pocket into the open coffin. Then I interrupted you and you fled. I found the gem and exhibited it in the library. You were watching from outside the window, perched on the coping. You threw the rock which put out the light, slipped through the window and took the stone, but were forced to hit Gifford over the head in order to get away in time. And later you visited my room, or sent Andrews, and left a note of warning."

"Correct in every detail!" exclaimed Captain Carrington. "But did you know, last night, that I was still alive?"

"I guessed it," said Jennings, "though I wasn't sure. It seemed the only way to explain the facts. I did know that the man in the coffin wasn't you. One of your pictures in your office shows you with a coiling dragon tattooed on your chest. You had ripped away the clothes from the chest of the corpse, and there was nothing tattooed there."

"I had wondered about that myself," admitted Captain Carrington. "Andrews had seen the body which was passed off as me, and even he thought it was I. I understand that the face of the corpse was badly mutilated, and evidently my nephew got some crooked undertaker to do a clever job of reconstructing it. He probably supposed that I had died in the storm which wrecked Al Barlow's yacht.

"But do you want the rest of the story? When this fellow's hand was cut off"—he gestured toward the skeleton—"he attacked me with a blackjack and struck me several times over the head. I remained conscious but dazed. Later, I learned that I had received concussion of the brain.

"Why I returned to the library and put the hand in the cabinet, I don't know. Barlow and my nephew found me there, my head bloody, my sanity gone. They gave up their attempt to find the jewels and carried me to the bay and put me on board the yacht. There Al Barlow stripped me of all identifying marks and put out to sea, intending to throw me overboard when they were well out. But the storm came up and wrecked him. In some miraculous way, I managed to get off on a raft and remain afloat. It drifted for days before I was picked up by a tramp steamer. My mind was gone and, without identification, I was placed in a hospital at the first port they touched. There I remained for almost a year before I recovered my strength and sanity. Then I returned here.

"Andrews was the first man I met, and he acquainted me with everything that had happened. I realized that my life wouldn't be worth a cent if either Al Barlow or my nephew found me. It would have been easy enough to have gone to the authorities and had the two of them jailed, but that would not have been recompense for the suffering they had caused me. I wanted revenge, and I wanted to take it in my own way, and at my leisure.

"And so I hid in the lodge with Andrews. When I learned, the next day, that my niece had called upon you for help, it made it more interesting. You almost upset my plans when you discovered me in the burial vault, but I got away without your recognizing me. When I discovered, later, that I had dropped the Bohojor Ruby in the coffin, I knew that if you had found it, it would give you one more mystery to solve. And yes, it was I who took the Bohojor Ruby from the library. I was watching the proceedings from the coping, outside the window, and I couldn't resist the temptation to inject still another element of mystery.

"I thought that I had the perfect hiding place for my gems, and yet, thinking it over that night, I was not sure that it could long escape a man like you. And so I had Andrews put the note in your room, knowing that the hint would be enough to save you from injury."

Captain Carrington paused, then asked, pointedly: "By the way, Jennings, have you solved the secret of my jewel cabinet? It was given to me, years ago, by a Chinese mandarin, and you have seen how deadly its operation can be."

Jennings took the lead penny from his pocket and pushed it through the gaping jaws of the rampant dragon carved on the upper panel of the cabinet. It slipped into the throat of the monster and slid from sight.

Then he reached casually into the recess.

Mona Carrington's hand leaped to her lips as she stifled a scream of warning.

But the trays slid out easily, without click or whirr, without a flash of the terrible knife.

"An ingenious device, eh?" said Captain Carrington. "The coin falls upon a balance which disconnects the huge spring which operates the knife. It was designed to be used with a popular Chinese coin of the last century. There were none of exactly the same weight in this country, and so I had a penny cast in lead to the correct weight."

He scooped up a pile of jewels and poured them in a glittering cascade from one hand to the other. His eyes brightened and took on the fanatical gleam of a gem enthusiast, to whom these expensive baubles were more precious and beautiful than life itself.

"Look at them, Jennings! The colors of the rainbow, the sheen of the stars, imprisoned in imperishable ice! Beauty eternal as the sun. And Mona, some day these will be yours. Yours!"

He thrust his hands, loaded with shimmering gems, toward her.

The girl shuddered, as though a blast of icy wind had struck her, and turned away.

RICHARD J. CREDICOTT HAS STORY IN CURRENT ISSUE, DETECTIVE MAGAZINE

The current issue of the Dime Detective magazine contains a 30-page story by Richard J. Credicott. of Freeport, entitled "The Ghoul of the Murder Manor." The story is the closing one in the publication and is illustrated. Mr. Credicott has had a wide variety of stories accepted by several publications and is quite versatile in his writings.

Freeport Journal-Standard,
June 16, 1933

1922 *Polaris*

OFF-TRAIL PUBLICATIONS
Specializing in the era of American pulp fiction

THE WEIRD DETECTIVE ADVENTURES OF WADE HAMMOND
By Paul Chadwick
Volume 1: 10 stories, 180 pages, $18
Volume 2: 10 stories, 172 pages, $18
Volume 3: 10 stories, 202 pages, $18
Volume 4: 9 stories, 232 pages, $18

> *The Wade Hammond stories complete in four volumes. In these chilling adventures, all from the classic 1930's pulps,* Detective-Dragnet *and* Ten Detective Aces, *freelance investigator Wade Hammond battles a series of weird enemies. Some of the best of '30s pulp fiction.*

DOCTOR COFFIN: The Living Dead Man
By Perley Poore Sheehan • Introduction by John Wooley
8 novelettes, 178 pages, $16

> *Weird stories from* Thrilling Detective, *1932-33. A former character actor who faked his own death, Doctor Coffin runs a string of mortuaries by night and fights crime at night. One of the strangest detective series.*

SUPER-DETECTIVE FLIP BOOK: Two Complete Novels
From the pulp *Super-Detective*:
"Legion of Robots" (November 1940) by Victor Rousseau • Introduction by John McMahan •• "Murder's Migrants" (March 1943) by Robert Leslie Bellem and W.T. Ballard • Introduction by John Wooley
2 short novels, 174 pages, $18

> Super-Detective *started as a Doc Savage-like adventure pulp, then changed format to hardboiled detective. The* Flip Book *features a novel from each of the two phases with intros exploring the historical background. Exciting!*

PULPWOOD DAYS: Volume 1: Editors You Want To Know
Edited by John Locke • 180 pages, $16

*Numerous articles from the writers' magazines by and about pulp editors, with ample biographical profiles. Editors include: Frank E. Blackwell (*Detective Story, Western Story*), Ray Palmer (*Amazing Stories, Fantastic Adventures*), Edwin Baird (*Weird Tales, Detective Tales*), and many more.*

GANG PULP
Edited by John Locke • 19 stories, 294 pages, $24

Hardboiled stories of the criminal underworld from the first year (1929-30) of the gang pulps: Gangster Stories, Racketeer Stories, *etc. These violent tales came under immediate censorship pressure; the history is explored in an in-depth essay. "A remarkable work of popular-culture scholarship"*—MYSTERY SCENE, *Fall 2008.*

THE GANGLAND SAGAS OF BIG NOSE SERRANO
Volume 1: Dames, Dice and the Devil
Volume 2: Horses, Hoboes and Heroes
Volume 3: Hell's Gangster
By Anatole Feldman • Introductions by Will Murray
Each: 4 novels • **Volumes 1-2**: 266 pages, $20 • **Volume 3**: 224 pages, $18

The complete Big Nose Serrano novels from Gangster Stories, Greater Gangster Stories, *and* The Gang Magazine, *1930-35. Feldman was the best of the gang pulp authors, and Big Nose was his most inspired creation, the berserking king of Chicago gangsters.*

CITY OF NUMBERED MEN: The Best of Prison Stories
Introduction by John Locke
12 stories, 278 pages, $20

> *During Prohibition, famed publisher Harold Hersey turned America's disintegrating prison system into the hardboiled* Prison Stories *(1930-31). Included are stories from all six issues of this ultra-rare pulp, the startling history of* Prison Stories, *complete cover gallery, and "Harold Hersey: Tales of an Ink-Stained Wretch," the first comprehensive biography of pulp publishing's most colorful character.*

THE MAGICIAN DETECTIVE: And Other Weird Mysteries
By Fulton Oursler
Introduction by John Locke
7 stories, 210 pages, $18

> *Fulton Oursler was one of the great editors of his time, ruling over the Macfadden publishing empire for two decades. But stage magic was his first love, and, in his heart, he remained a conjurer in a black cape and top hat. In this collection of early fiction, Oursler's bewitching imagination takes flight in tales of magic, murder and mesmerizing mystery. Also featured is an in-depth exploration of the astonishing career of Fulton Oursler.*

GHOST STORIES: The Magazine and Its Makers
Edited by John Locke
Vol 1: 19 stories, 256 pages, $24 • **Vol 2**: 15 stories, 272 pages, $24

> *Macfadden's* Ghost Stories *(1926-31) presented haunted tales in every exciting arena: the Western Front, gangland, aviation, the Klondike, the circus, etc. The personnel behind* Ghost Stories *were a fascinating group: poets and scholars, war heroes and war correspondents, adventurers and Bohemians; a few became prolific pulpsters; a few became bestselling authors. And a few led haunted lives. Vol 1 includes the history of* Ghost Stories, *bios of every editor, and every Vol 1 author. Vol 2 includes bios of every Vol 2 author, every cover artist, and a gallery of all 64* Ghost Stories *covers.*

HOBO STORIES
By Patrick & Terence Casey • Introduction by John Locke
6 stories, 332 pages, $20

> *The Caseys were two brothers from San Francisco who broke into the pulps while still teenagers. Within a few years, they had conned their way into the prestigious pages of* Adventure. Hobo Stories *reprints their series of exploits of a teenage hobo and his dog from* The Saturday Evening Post *(1914) and* Adventure *(1916-21). Included is their story of a teenage pulp writer from* Romance *(1920); and a lengthy introduction which explores the lives of the Caseys and the origins of their hobo stories.*

OUTDOOR STORIES
By J. Allan Dunn • Introduction by John Locke
3 stories, 190 pages, $16

> *Presented are all three of Dunn's long-forgotten tales from the ultra-rare* Outdoor Stories *(1927-28). These gripping adventures, set in the exotic places of another day, rank with his best work. The featured story is the novelette, "New Guinea Gold," an epic tale of friendship, survival and revenge. Also included is a history of* Outdoor Stories, *a biography of editor Edmund C. Richards, and an examination of Dunn's role in the magazine.*

THE PERIL OF THE PACIFIC: The Complete PEOPLE'S Serial
By J. Allan Dunn • Introduction by John Locke
168 pages, $14

> *Dunn's Japanese invasion epic is future history, published as a five-part serial in* People's *in 1916, but set in 1920.* Peril *pits a force of American irregulars armed with futuristic technology against a relentless naval empire bent on conquest. Dunn uses San Francisco and California's Central Coast as his main settings, drawing upon his well-traveled past more than in any other story he ever published.*